Morisco

Morisco

Hilary Mason

NEW YORK
ATHENEUM
1979

Copyright © 1979 by Hilary Mason
All rights reserved
Library of Congress catalog card number 78-73071
ISBN *0-689-10960-1*
Manufactured by Halliday Lithograph Corporation,
West Hanover and Plympton, Massachusetts
First American Edition

To Jennifer, Alan and Mac

"Faits sur mesure pour le romanesque ils sont
prêts à entrer en de merveilleuses fictions,
et nous ne croyons pas, pour notre propre compte,
que ce soit un mal. Il y a des sujets, des temps,
des lieux, où le romanesque est inséparable de
l'Histoire . . ."
    Henri Bosco

Preface to "Les Corsaires de Salé"
        by Roger Coindreau

"'What care I for the king of England's ships,
or all the Christian kings in the world; am not
I king of Sallee?' But we made him sing another
song in a short time after, for we went to work
with him another way that he dreamed not of."

         John Dunton
   "A True Journal of the Sallee Fleet," 1637

Morisco

I

Sir Anthony Van Dyck, standing, brush poised, before his easel, observed his latest fashionable subject with professional interest. Since he was patronized by King Charles I and Queen Henrietta Maria all the élite of London society flocked to his studio. Most of his work these days consisted of routine prestige portraits, all highly competent, uninspired and exquisitely flattering. If the results were not the best of which he was capable yet his clients got what they expected and deserved.

The woman who was sitting for him now resembled numerous other wealthy ladies whose lushly opulent charms he had recorded on canvas. Lady Celia Lovell's face was oval, pink and white and dimpled. Her eyes were large, dark and long-lashed. Her rich brown hair was arranged in elaborate ringlets, an array of kiss curls, termed "heart-breakers", fringing her forehead. She wore a short necklace and drop earrings of lustrous pearls. Sir Anthony had perfected a technique of contrasting the texture of these particular jewels with the soft peaches-and-cream complexions of his sitters.

"Charming! Delightful!" he murmured.

The courtly little painter's compliments failed to bring a smile to the pouting rosebud mouth of Lady Celia Lovell. Aloof, cool and haughty, she played with the deep lace on her full blue satin sleeve, a picture of petulant discontent.

"A pity," he thought, preparing to execute a quick likeness. He had painted scores of such women and slept with a good many of them. Their disdainful airs, extravagant clothes and arrogant manners could not conceal from him their frustrated sensuality.

More to indulge himself than because he needed to, he looked Lady Celia over with his shrewd, penetrating, licensed painter's eye. He usually spent no more than about an hour on a portrait nowadays, doing only the face and hands himself. Most of the work was completed by apprentices who painted the sitter's garments draped on a lay figure and filled in the background according to his directions. But women had always been Sir Anthony's weakness so he took advantage of his opportunity. Keeping his distance and holding his brush at arm's length, the painter let his blandly veiled, apparently objective stare rove over Lady Celia, stripping her to the skin.

The low neckline of her gown, decorated with a titillating bow at the cleavage, revealed not only her plump shoulders but all the upper half of a generous bosom with more than a hint of rose pink nipples. Beneath her breasts her waist was remarkably well defined, giving her figure more lightness and grace than was common. The painter's interest quickened. Below the waist he guessed that the voluminous blue satin skirts and heavy petticoats concealed splendid hips and thighs whose lines he made out in his mind's eye.

He sighed a little wistfully. If time and his debts had allowed he would have liked to desert the fashionable portraiture by which he earned his living to paint a classical piece in the grand manner. Lady Celia, nude, would make a superb central figure for a composition similar to his rival Jacob Jordaans' "Allegory of Fertility" which showed the back view of an unclad nymph, stooping to display magnificent haunches while an admiring satyr crouching in the foreground gazed longingly at her.

"Allegory? Nymph?" Van Dyck smiled to himself, shaking his head. Jordaans' female was a fine strapping wench of flesh and blood whom old Jacob had painted so brilliantly, balancing subtle skin tones with contrasting shadow, that a man's hand itched to slap her behind.

Aware that Lady Celia was fidgeting under his scrutiny, irritably impatient for her hour's sitting to be over, Sir Anthony made a courteously deprecating gesture and sketched a few preliminary strokes on the canvas. He noted her peevish, sulky expression and his mouth tightened. "Spoilt bitch!" he thought. She needed stripping down and mastering to be made into a real woman. Rubens would have been the one to do it, both as a man and as a painter. Van Dyck hated to admit it, but Lady Celia was a Rubens subject really. How her rosy flesh would have glowed under the old master's hand! But Rubens was retired now, he himself was past his best and there was this uncouth miller's son from Leyden living in the Jewish quarter of Amsterdam who painted more like a god than a man and made them both look journeymen by comparison. As his brush flicked expertly, touching in glossy ringlets, he wondered what things were coming to.

Lady Celia was not interested in the painter's opinion of her. In fact, she was not interested in him at all. She thought him an unattractive, slightly vulgar little man, with his foxy colouring, obsequious foreign manner and ridiculous pride in his knighthood. She had come to his studio in Blackfriars because having her portrait painted provided an acceptable excuse for leaving home to meet an admirer. Many ladies and gentlemen used the Flemish portrait-painter's house as a place of assignation and Lady Celia, responding to the advances of an amorous acquaintance, had arranged to encounter him there.

The man was one of her husband's friends whom she herself hardly knew and she had consented to begin an intrigue with him not because he had any particular attraction for her but because she was bored, lonely and desperately unhappy.

Most people, like Sir Anthony Van Dyck, would have considered that she had much to be thankful for and would have had little sympathy for Celia Lovell. Many, knowing her to be young, a reputed beauty and the wife of a rich man, would have thought her situation enviable.

It was a year since her wedding to Sir Edward Lovell and she had entered into marriage full of excitement and high hopes. In the twelve months which had just passed she had seen those hopes dashed one by one until none was left.

Celia's appearance of fashionable sophistication was barely skin deep. Until her marriage she had lived almost entirely in the country at her parents' home of Combe Hall in Devonshire. The Craces were an old family with more real wealth than social pretensions who lived in a comfortable and homely, rather than a grand, style. If it had not been for the ambitious intriguings of Celia's elder brother, Roger, she might have married the son of a neighbouring squire and never left the Devonshire countryside in which she had been brought up.

Roger Crace, far more intelligent and unscrupulous than his easy-going, good-natured father, was not content with country life and the family's rustic style of living. He wanted advancement, a place at Court and wealth on a scale such as the Craces had never dreamed of. Under his influence, Celia also began to be discontented and to hanker for life in London. Seeing this, the astute Roger set about promoting a match between his sister and his acquaintance, Sir Edward Lovell.

Roger Crace had formed a friendship with Lovell when they were both undergraduates at Oxford and it had continued, off and on, ever since. Sir Edward Lovell was in the direct line of succession to a barony and Roger had convinced both Celia and his parents that it would be a splendid thing for the family to be allied with one of title.

Lovell, for his part, was in the habit of spending more than he could afford and was beginning to be distressed for money, especially as he had lately commissioned an imposing new town house designed by no less a person than Inigo Jones and similar in style to the Queen's House at Greenwich. Just at the time when he found himself in acute financial difficulties, Celia Crace was put in his way by her brother, his friend. Celia's personal attractions were obvious and she was cultivated and amusing without being clever, but, most important of all to Lovell, her father was willing to settle a very substantial property on her which would solve his pecuniary problems for a long time to come. In return he willingly promised Roger Crace help of all kinds in obtaining the social and political advancement the other craved.

Celia herself was delighted with the proposal. Sir Edward Lovell was personable, good mannered with a most aristocratic family and an appearance of fashionable distinction. That he was twelve years older did not seem a drawback. That he was immeasurably better educated and had tastes and habits of life quite alien to Celia's were not considered by her parents to be disadvantages. In fact, once they got used to the idea of Celia's marrying Sir Edward Lovell, her parents were more eager for the union than even Celia herself, who was willing enough.

True, she did not love her prospective husband, but she had been taught that this was not a prerequisite for marriage. It was enough that she should like him and be ready to learn to love him. This Celia was eminently prepared to do.

Surely, she had thought when she left her Devonshire home for London, a happy life awaited her there. Everyone agreed that she had made a splendid match. For the daughter of an undistinguished country squire to be marrying into an ancient titled family was a notable achievement. The future must certainly be bright.

Now, seated in Van Dyck's studio with its windows overlooking the Thames, Celia reflected bitterly how wrong she and everyone else had been. Before their marriage she and Edward had not had much opportunity to get to know one another. Once they began to do so it became increasingly evident that they were incompatible. Celia was warm-hearted, eager and passionate. Edward, by contrast, was cool, reserved and intellectual. Her enthusiasms irritated him. His coldness exasperated her. Physically they did not suit one another and neither possessed the patience and expertise that might have solved their problems. Each blamed the other. Neither made allowances. Celia, really fond of Edward and naturally ardent, was more hurt by his obvious lack of any kind of affection for her than by anything else.

Once settled in London, things went from bad to worse. Edward's family snubbed Celia and Edward himself had numerous acquaintances whose company he much preferred to his wife's. He divided his time mainly between the solemn formality of King Charles' Court at Whitehall, where his grave demeanour and aesthetic tastes made him welcome, and the gaming tables of Piccadilly where he gambled away Celia's money.

Celia was left alone a great deal. Day after day she spent idly and monotonously in their grand and beautiful but curiously empty house, growing more and more bored with the trifling pleasures with which she tried to amuse herself and more and more resentful of her husband's neglect.

For a woman of Celia's temperament in such a situation the outcome was almost inevitable.

A fortnight ago one of Edward's friends, returning to the house with him and meeting Celia, was struck by her beauty. Admiring glances passed between them. If Ralph Verney was not handsome at least he was tall, young, manly and, above all, appreciative. Celia felt herself glow and blossom under his gaze. Small attentions followed. Handing Celia into her coach, Ralph Verney squeezed Celia's arm with a slight but meaningful pressure and thrust a crumpled fragment of paper into her hand. In the privacy of her coach she read it.

> "Small is the worth
> Of beauty from the light retired:
> Bid her come forth,
> Suffer herself to be desired,
> And not blush so to be admired."

The verse was not new, not brilliant and not even Verney's own but to the neglected and frustrated Celia it seemed wonderful indeed. If Edward did not want her, did not even notice her, at least someone did!

And so, when Verney asked her to meet him at Van Dyck's she had agreed. As far as she was concerned it was a gesture of desperation designed to attract Edward's attention. If her name was linked with that of another man he could not continue to ignore her. Above all, it would be a diversion.

She fidgeted with the bronze satin stole she wore loosely draped about her and glanced at Van Dyck. She seemed to have been sitting still a very long time, longer than an hour. She could hear voices in the room below and the sound of horses' hooves clopping the cobbles in the street outside. Sunlight brought the lifting ripples on the Thames to life.

Van Dyck, absorbed in his work now, painted on, rapidly and skilfully. Although he had divined Celia's secrets he would not betray them. Like the discreet courtier he was he would reveal nothing of her inner dissatisfaction with life in the portrait he was creating. It would be merely a feast for the eye. All milky flesh, gleaming jewels and shining curls. Within the limitations he imposed upon himself he revelled in the mastery of his craft. His soul sang in the use of colour.

Celia, whose soul had ceased to sing ever since she married Edward Lovell, frowned and tapped with her foot. "Sir Anthony," she said querulously, "I really must go."

Van Dyck looked up with an apologetic smile.

"Of course, Lady Lovell. No doubt you have many things requiring your attention. Have you any instructions regarding the colour of draperies? The background? Minor figures? A boy dressed as Cupid with a tribute of roses?" He met Celia's eye. "Er, perhaps *not* Cupid, then. A Moorish slave with an umbrella? That adds a pleasingly exotic note."

"Certainly. Whatever you like."

She was impatient to escape. Verney, she knew, would be waiting for her in the anteroom downstairs which was an acknowledged place of rendezvous for fashionable lovers. Van Dyck smiled at her, wry and knowing, his paint-stained smock hiding his elegant clothes. She was rather like himself, he thought, sensual, arrogant, undisciplined, demanding. What would become of her?

"My servant will show you out, Lady Lovell," he said aloud, watching her under his foxy eyebrows as she walked to the door.

The staircase was narrow and Celia had to lift her flowing skirts carefully to avoid tripping as she went down. The words of a ribald song echoed from the anteroom:

> "Your most beautiful bride who with garlands is crown'd
> And kills with a glance as she treads on the ground,
> Whose lightness and brightness doth shine in such splendour
> That none but the stars
> Are thought fit to attend her,
> Though now she be pleasant and sweet to the sense,
> Will be damnable mouldy a hundred years hence."

There was laughter and the last line was repeated.

> "... damnable mouldy a hundred years hence."

Tears filled her eyes. She lifted her head high, walking proudly past the servant who bowed her into the room. There was silence as she entered. The men gathered round the table stood up. A glass overturned. Verney advanced to meet her, swaggering, triumphant, as though he had already made his conquest.

Seeing him, Celia experienced a sudden revulsion. His face had a mean, narrow look, she thought, petty and shallow and his hand was softer than a man's ought to be when he took hers. The handsome clothes did little for him. One of Van Dyck's lay figures would have looked as well in them.

What had she stooped to?

Stifling a sigh, she let him lead her to her waiting coach and hand her into it.

Behind them the knowing nudges and winks gave way to song again:

> "Dame Venus, love's lady, was born of the sea;
> With her and with Bacchus we'll tickle the sense,
> For we shall be past it a hundred years hence."

Van Dyck stepped back from his canvas and watched from the window with an indulgent, worldly-wise eye, then he looked again at the uncompleted picture. Massing dark thunderclouds in the background, he thought, for contrast and dramatic effect. They might also be slightly symbolic. He would give her, as he had suggested, a Moorish attendant carrying a red umbrella. He had used such an attendant very successfully in one of his most accomplished portraits.

Van Dyck did not know it, but both the thunderclouds and the Moorish figure in Celia's portrait were to prove prophetic.

So, too, were the words of the song they were singing downstairs:

> "Dame Venus, love's lady,
> Was born of the sea . . ."

2

Graceful, buoyant and streamlined as a swan, the proud galleasse breasted the tidal river, a fleet of smaller ships following, like cygnets, in her wake.

Her captain was at the helm for he would trust no one else with the crucial task of piloting her through the treacherous shoals of the river mouth with its hidden reefs. The river bed was shifting sand, varying in depth with changing winds and tides, and no map could chart a permanently safe channel clear along the course of the Bou Regreb to the open sea.

The galleasse was the biggest ship ever to sail from the corsairs' harbour of New Sallee. If she got stuck on a sandbank the captain knew that the accompanying caravels and fly-boats would tow her off but it would be a bad omen for a voyage on whose success he had staked his professional reputation and private ambitions.

So he stood to the wheel of his ship, aware that the telltale fringe of ragged white ripples marked a line of concealed rocks but eyeing more keenly still a patch of deceptively smooth water whose light colour warned him of a shallow stretch where the channel had silted up in the winter gales.

Feeling the swing and swell of the tide in the palms of his hard, seaman's hands, and knowing the way of his ship, the corsair called Jaffar Rais guided her towards the harbour bar which mariners everywhere acknowledged to be the most perilous in the world. He concentrated entirely on his task, a dangerously single-minded man.

The harbour bar of the Bou Regreb was a natural bastion of sand and rocks thrown up by the Atlantic breakers in their centuries of thundering against the coast of Africa. Because of this barrier it was hard to get in and out of the corsairs' lair during the summer months. In winter it was impossible.

Menacing as a shark's jaws, the river mouth gaped into the sea, a wedge of sharp-toothed white water between the two towns that stood upon its banks, Old Sallee to the north, New Sallee to the south. They were deadly rivals different in everything - appearance, faith, traditions, aims and destiny.

The ancient Moroccan settlement on the north bank was a sober white and grey town, low-lying, with high, austere walls looking down over silvery sands and harsh salt flats to the river.

Its ruler was a formidable autocrat, one of a class of hereditary holy men, who combined the functions of feudal lord and spiritual leader of his people. Sidi Mohammed el Ayachi was a fanatical Muslim, ascetic, devout and fiercely ambitious. To friend and foe alike he was known by his hereditary title of the Saint.

Across the river from the Saint's domain, facing it as though in brash defiance, impudence confronting dignity, the corsairs' stronghold of New Sallee stood out boldly on the great rocks at the entrance to the estuary, the red walls of its impregnable citadel towering above the sea and tinged by the fiery sun of Africa to a fierce, coppery glow.

The new city housed a cosmopolitan and lawless community of pirates and adventurers. Thirty years ago it had been nothing more than a sleepy suburb of the old town where a handful of herdsmen lived among the crumbling remains of a ruined Roman outpost, abandoned centuries before and neglected since. Then came the Moriscos.

Moors settled in Spain for generations, they had been driven from their homes into exile beyond the seas. A proud people, warlike, energetic, predatory, they found refuge in New Sallee, rebuilding and fortifying it, making it into a secure base from which pirate expeditions could sail out to plunder merchant ships of all nations and to which they could return to sell their loot. Renegades from many European countries joined the corsair community and they formed a lawless, independent republic, owing a nominal allegiance only to the Sultan of Morocco and openly defying his local representative, the Saint of Old Sallee, who regarded the Moriscos' lack of religion with fervent disapproval and their ill-gotten wealth with eager rapacity.

Like almost everyone else in the two towns, Sidi Mohammed el Ayachi had watched the launching of the new galleasse and knew something of its captain's plans which were relayed to him by various spies who hung about the dockyards and markets of New Sallee, picking up bits of information which they were prepared to pass on, at a price. Now, reclining on a low couch, a select company of friends grouped about him in one of the cool courtyards of his palace, Sidi Mohammed reflected on what he had heard.

The courtyard was a place conducive to calm consideration and clear thinking, for, like the rest of the palace, whose grim outward appearance was deceptive, it was designed in exquisite taste. A colonnade enclosed it like a cloister garth, the symmetrical horseshoe arches carved with flowing abstract designs of much beauty, and it was paved with tiles carefully cut and laid by skilled craftsmen of Fez. The water of a fountain, fed by a hidden cistern, bubbled up into a wide, shallow bowl of veined marble with a bubbling sound, soothing and delightful.

A raising of the Saint's finger brought a discreet slave, moving soundlessly on bare feet, with a tray of mint tea for his guests who sat or lay on rich cushions or carpets spread on the mosaic floor with its soft, earth colours.

"Jaffar Rais goes a-hunting," said the youngest of the guests, greatly daring, for the rest of the exclusive company were greybeards almost as venerable as the Saint himself. He knew he would be thought presumptuous, but he was aware that dark eyes watched him from behind the lattice where Sidi Mohammed's womenfolk listened, limp and listless in the heat of their enclosed quarters. "There will be wailing amongst the Christians when he brings home his prey."

A shocked silence greeted this remark. Then the Saint himself spoke.

"Jaffar Rais, as he calls himself," said Sidi Mohammed in tones of frigid reproof, "is an infidel renegade, as likely to attack true believers as Christians if there is plunder to be had. Like all the corsairs of the new town he is a follower of the Prophet in name only, using our faith as a cover for his crimes. May Allah destroy him and all his kind!"

The other older men, lacking the Saint's fire, murmured a nervously subdued assent, resting supine in their loose robes of white and grey, listening to the sound of the fountain, lulled by the scent of jasmine blossom, warmly potent, borne on the breeze from nearby unseen gardens.

Although disconcerted by the Saint's rebuke, the young man was nevertheless still conscious of the dark eyes behind the lattice resting on him and ventured to say, "Yet, my lord Saint, there are those in the new town who are faithful to Islam. My father-in-law you will acknowledge to be a devout follower of the Prophet."

"Ahmed ben Yussuf," answered Sidi Mohammed, "you are a stranger here." He paused, turning his head slightly, so slightly that the movement might hardly be observed, yet the owner of the dark eyes lowered them and moved silently away from the lattice screen. "Your father-in-law, Abd el Qader Ceron," he continued calmly, "is indeed a true believer and among the élite of the casbah, to which he belongs, there are many such. But the casbah is not the town. When we speak of the new town we mean the straggle of squalid streets that run from the foot of the casbah along the river almost to the tower of Hassan. There you will find the poor Moriscos, Andalusians, 'Castile Christians', call them what you like. They are more Spanish than Moorish, more Christian than Muslim, and they give aid and comfort to the off-scouring of Europe and all the scum of the seven seas. This Jaffar Rais you talk of is among the worst of the scoundrels they harbour. But the time is coming when we shall chase these rats from their holes. I have fought them before and am ready to fight them again and, when I do, by Allah I will drive them into the sea!"

As the Saint thundered curses against Jaffar Rais and the rest of the infidel corsairs a holy man of New Sallee called upon heaven to bless them. Standing amid the milling crowd on the quayside, the white-robed priest invoked the aid of the river spirit to help Jaffar Rais cross the bar in safety.

A sacrifice was prepared. Slaves bound a black goat, hobbled and bleating, upon a slab. It lay at the priest's feet, mouth open, eyes already glazing. The priest raised both arms above his head. His hands clasped a gleaming knife. Flashing, the blade descended and the crowd gave a gasp of primitive, atavistic satisfaction as they saw the warm blood bubble from the wound and run in red streams on to the spray-splashed stones.

The crowd looked as though they were drawn from every nation under heaven for every skin-colour known to humanity was to be seen among them, from the deep blue-black of the true Negro, through the varying shades of deep brown of desert and Mediterranean people, to the olive-touched pallor of central Europeans and the rosy colouring and fair hair of dwellers by the North Sea. They were seamen, merchants, idlers, labourers, dealers, whores, slaves and craftsmen, all in their different ways and for their different purposes drawn to participate in the booming economy of New Sallee. And all with an interest, great or small, friendly or hostile, in the success of Jaffar Rais' voyage. It would bring money to the town. They hoped some of it would come their way.

"In the name of Allah the most merciful..." intoned a fat Moorish merchant with shares in the galleasse that was nosing its way so cautiously down the river.

"Never mind your black goats and your prayers, Sliman," muttered a matter-of-fact Dutchman at his elbow. "It's only good seamanship will help Jaffar Rais now."

Jaffar Rais, had he been asked, would have agreed. Heedless of cursings and blessings alike, oblivious of everything but the task in hand, he steered his ship towards the harbour bar.

The galleasse was long and low and narrow, built on trim fighting lines and gaudily painted in blue and gold. At first glance the banked oars splaying from her sides gave her the look of a traditional Mediterranean galley, yet she was decked, masted and square-rigged like the most modern galleon afloat. In fact, she was a cross between the two, neither wholly oar-driven like the galley nor wholly dependent on wind like the galleon. This made her ideally suited to the corsairs' purpose for she combined the shallow draught and rapid manoeuvrability of the first with the sustained speed and strength of the second. She was designed for lightning raids on coastal villages where she could drop anchor in shallow inlets, her crew swarming ashore to ransack houses and carry off inhabitants. Then, if pursuit threatened, her oars could carry her far off out to sea while would-be pursuers were obliged to wait for a favourable wind before they could follow. Yet she could range further than any galley, for she could use the wind, when it served, and rest her oarsmen.

Ironically, the oarsmen of the galleasse were slaves who had been captured in raids such as these themselves. Captives were the corsairs' most profitable plunder. They could be sold, held to ransom or compelled, under duress, to throw in their lot with their captors by becoming pirates themselves.

There was very little wind, the sails of the galleasse were furled and it was the slow, steady, rhythmic swing of her oars, regulated by the beat of a reverberating drum, which now kept the ship under way.

"By the mark, four," chanted the leadsman, calling in English.

Jaffar Rais smiled, easing the wheel fractionally to port. Four fathoms. His ship drew three. Avoiding the fanged, half-submerged reef that lay ahead, he steered her skilfully towards the perilously narrow stretch of deepish water. The oars lifted, swung, dipped and lifted again. The wheel was like a live thing in his hands, making the ship respond to his will. There was so little safe room on either side and less still beneath. As they drew near the bar the ship was strangely silent except for the beat of the drum and the rattling of the slaves' chains as they threw their weight into the loom of the oars, driving the lean pirate ship forward.

Jaffar Rais held the wheel steady. Those standing round him on the poop deck and the watchers from the two towns held their breath. Would the keel clear the harbour bar in safety or would it strike, shudder and run aground, breaking the ship's back?

There was a rush of water under the prow and the watchers saw Jaffar Rais lift his arm in a triumphant wave and heard his crew's echoing shout of exultation.

"He's done it!"

The crowd which had gathered on the wharves and along the southern banks of the Bou Regreb howled enthusiastic congratulations in a babel of voices which included most European languages, several African and some Asian ones.

"Christians will be cheap in the market when he returns," said Abd el Qader Ceron, one of the proud Hornacheros who ruled over New Sallee, with satisfaction.

"Maybe they'll sell at an onion a head as they did after Barbarossa took Tunis." The Flemish renegade grinned a wide, white, wolfish grin. "I could do with some good oar-flesh at a price I can afford."

"An onion a head! By Allah, we shan't let it come to that, I promise you!" An Arab slave dealer in burnous and head rope, a lean, hard, hawkish desert man from the eastern Sahara, blenched at the thought of choice merchandise being auctioned directly to buyers at a give-away price. "Slaves are fetching good money in Algiers, especially women with light hair and young boys. That's where we'll take them to sell if fair profits are not to be had in Sallee."

"What are you going to do with the English boy Jaffar left with you, Lord Ali Zuni?"

William Trevor of Plymouth, thirty years a slave in Sallee, old now, considered a "character" by his owners and allowed certain liberties because of it, offered the slave dealer a calabash of water. He ladled it carefully from a large earthenware jar roped to the side of a thin, patient donkey, its backbone showing sharp through its hide, strings of melons and bunches of onions strung about its neck like garlands.

Ali Zuni rinsed his mouth and spat, rinsed and spat again before he finally drank deeply of the cool draught the old slave held out to him.

"I shall keep the boy until Jaffar Rais returns. He is a hostage, as you know."

"I know, God pity him," muttered the slave, bowing obsequiously as Ali Zuni flung the empty calabash carelessly back to him, catching it deftly in gnarled, cupped hands.

In the house with a carving of the hand of Fatima above the doorway, the house near the stairway of the corsairs, leading from the quayside to the casbah of Oudaia, the girl called Areefa heard the cheering as Jaffar Rais sailed out of harbour. When the man above her reached his climax at last with a grunt of satisfaction, Areefa impatiently pushed his heavy body aside, swung her long, bare brown legs out of bed and thrust her feet into the bright yellow, heel-less slippers that lay where she had kicked them off on the rucked carpet. She was fuming with rage and frustration that this drunken, boorish customer should have forced himself on her just at the very moment when she had wanted to be in the forefront of the crowd, dressed in all her best finery, waving a fond goodbye to Jaffar. The clamorous noise warned her that she would hardly be in time even for a glimpse of the galleasse before it took to the open sea and was lost to sight.

Areefa's slim, golden-hued body was naked from head to foot except for her swinging necklaces of silver, coral and limpid moonstones, her jangling bangles and the red henna dye that coloured her fingernails, toenails and pert, upturned nipples, but there was no time to adorn herself properly, so she snatched up a cloak at random and, clutching it round her, ran out into the street.

She thrust her way between the dockside loafers, necklaces and bangles jingling as she fought for a place in the front rank of spectators.

"Let me through!" Daringly she elbowed the Flemish pirate aside in her anxiety to get a sight of Jaffar Rais, pushing through to the edge of the quay where she finally caught sight of the proud shape of the galleasse cleaving its way out to sea. She thought she could even make out the figure of the man himself on the poop deck. She brought out a shapely, braceleted arm from under her cloak, waving and calling wildly in the desperate hope that he would see, would hear, would not forget her.

Then she gave a sharp cry and whirled round as she felt the cloak deftly twitched from her shoulders and whirled away, leaving her standing uncovered on the quayside, the wind whipping her black hair about her body in long tendrils.

"Give me that!" She made a dive for the cloak which the Fleming held tantalizingly at arm's length, laughing and looking her over, his comrades applauding him.

Shrieking, Areefa grabbed at the cloak, but he swung it away, seized her, flung her across his shoulder and held her fast, gripping her round the knees. She hung head downwards, helpless, her hair almost sweeping the ground, blowing round his heavy sea-boots as he bore her along.

"Let me go!"

She drummed with her fists on his back, but the Fleming only laughed, trailing her cloak with one hand, gripping her with the other, carrying her bare rump uppermost through the crowded street, ignoring her strugglings and pleadings. When he reached the house he strode in, stooping, and tossed her down on to the bed.

Immediately she crawled into a corner of it and hugged her knees. The man she had just left had rolled off the bed and was snoring on the floor.

"Come now. Don't sulk, Areefa. We're old friends, aren't we? I'll bring you an ivory necklace next time I come back from sea."

The Fleming put his arms round her, coaxing. Areefa relented, seeing it was her trade. He was not as bad as some.

"You wait, Dirk Janssen," she said, "till Jaffar Rais comes home. You wait."

And she raked his body from shoulder to buttocks scoring his flesh with her henna-red nails when he took her, because he was not Jaffar Rais and she had never wanted any man but him.

Jaffar Rais, who had forgotten, for the moment, that Areefa had ever existed, turned to one of the men who stood with him on the poop deck of the galleasse.

"You can take over the wheel now, Master Dunton. You're supposed to be one of the best navigators afloat. You might as well earn your keep."

John Dunton raised his head. By a little he was both the elder and the taller of the two, a gaunt man in his middle thirties with a worn face and troubled eyes.

He and Jaffar Rais contrasted strongly with one another.

This contrast was implicit in everything observable about them and was as obvious as the antipathy which lay like an unspoken challenge between them.

Jaffar Rais, feet astride, arms akimbo, belligerent as a fighting cock, exuded confidence. He dressed flamboyantly, arrogantly flaunting his jewelled turban and heavy, gold-hilted scimitar. Yet the Moorish clothes consorted oddly with his blue eyes, fair beard and the red-brick brown of a skin burned rather than tanned by the sun. He looked the corsair that he was; but Viking more than Morisco. The winged helmet of the ancient Nordic sea rovers would have suited him better than the turban, and an acute observer might have noted that he looked like a man who played a part, his display of restless energy designed to mask an inner conflict.

John Dunton, on the other hand, seemed to hide nothing. Patched and faded clothes proclaimed poverty, his dejected expression a settled anxiety and his manner to Jaffar Rais a certain well-controlled, reserved, but distinctly overt defiance.

"I said," repeated Jaffar Rais, when Dunton did not answer immediately, "that you might as well earn your keep, Master Dunton."

"You trust me, then, Captain Chandler?" said Dunton, approaching to take the wheel.

The captain scowled, a dark flush of anger flooding his face. He glared at Dunton.

"My name," he said, "is Jaffar Rais. If I ever had any other I have forgotten it long ago. You would be wise to forget it also. As to trusting you, Master Dunton, I think we both have good reason to know why I can do so."

Dunton shrugged slightly. He was not a demonstrative man.

"Jaffar Rais, then. It's all one to me whether you call yourself that or Thomas Chandler or Ali Baba, or what you like.

What's in a name? A man's nothing but himself when all's said and done."

"For a man with as much to lose as you have, Master Dunton," said Jaffar Rais with mounting wrath, "you speak very freely. Very freely indeed."

"Now, let's get this straight, captain," said Dunton, stepping up close to the corsair and speaking quietly but with much energy. "You've got my son held hostage in Sallee or I wouldn't be here. When I was captured you gave me an ultimatum - I must undertake to guide you safely into Mount's Bay and out again or young Dick would be sold into slavery in Algiers. That's no kind of choice for a father to be asked to make, especially about a boy hardly ten years old, but you hold all the cards, so I've had to agree to do what you want. I'm under your orders and I'll obey them as best I can, but you've not bought me body and soul, Jaffar Rais. We've made a bargain, such as it is, and I'll keep my side of it, but don't be taunting me with it every time we meet, for I'll not bear it, and so I tell you."

"All right, Dunton." The corsair returned the other's stare levelly, a grudging respect in his tone. "As long as we understand each other." He jerked his head up suddenly, scanning sky and sea. "The breeze is freshening," he said abruptly. "We'll take advantage of it while we can. I'll have all sail set. Keep her as close to the wind as you can. She's a sweet ship," he added with a swift rush of enthusiasm, momentarily softened by a glow of pride, "as sweet to handle as a woman."

"Aye," said Dunton morosely, taking over the wheel. He was a highly competent sailing master, experienced with most types of vessel currently in use at sea. Anything Jaffar Rais required of him he could do. Almost anything. He looked straight ahead, bleakly, unable to forget the look in his boy's eyes when he'd told him he was leaving him behind in Sallee. He'd tried to reassure him. Telling him he'd be back. Telling him he'd have to try to be a man. But he was only ten years old, for God's sake!

He continued to stare bleakly ahead as a salvo of orders called up the seamen, sending them running across decks, horny bare feet padding the boards then scaling the rigging as they raced to man the yards.

Released, the blue and white sails of the galleasse filled with the Atlantic wind. The ship glided forward, faster than before, very beautiful and free of motion, like a predatory bird, and clean still, not as she would be after a few days at sea. Soon the human cattle permanently shackled to her rowing benches, compelled to labour, eat and sleep in their own filth, would make her stink to high heaven.

Under a crimson banner with three silver crescents streaming proudly from her forepeak, the pride of the corsairs' fleet sped northward on her course for England.

3

By a whimsical decree of fate, Lady Celia Lovell's coach was carrying its resentful and rebellious occupant towards exactly the same place on the coast of Devonshire as where the corsair expected to make landfall.

Lady Celia had never heard of Sallee. She was vaguely aware of a remote region in North Africa called "Barbary" which was inhabited by "Turks" and "Moors" who enslaved Christians and inflicted horrible tortures on them, but she had no interest whatever in it or, indeed, in anything beyond her own private concerns, which at present wholly engrossed her.

She was feeling wronged, humiliated and furious. Who would have thought that her relatively innocent flirtation with Ralph Verney could have had such disastrous results?

Clutching at her wide-brimmed hat with its festoons of shining cream satin ribbons as she was jolted unmercifully up and down in the unsprung carriage, she glared at her two maids. The poor girls, more uncomfortable than their mistress, sat as far back as they could in opposite corners of the seat facing her and tried desperately to avoid her eye.

Even Lady Celia's spoilt lap-dog, Tray, was keeping quiet, white-fringed ears drooping, cowering under cover of his mistress's spreading bronze silk skirts and hoping she would not notice that he'd been sick on the floor of the carriage and stained the lace edging of her flounced petticoat.

The wheel hit a pothole in the track. The coach lurched so

that Lady Celia hit her head against the ceiling. Muttering words of which ladies ought to be ignorant, she rapped sharply on the window with her knuckles and told the startled outrider to warn the driver that if such a thing happened again he would be dismissed.

The man touched his hat and, out of her ladyship's range of vision, exchanged grimaces with the coachman.

"Bitch!" mouthed the driver. "As if I could help it!"

His shouted words of apology, muffled by the steady drumming of the horses' hooves, were borne away on the wind.

"It's all so unfair!" Celia clenched her hands so tight the nails bit into her palms. Immersed in her own troubles, she was quite unaware of her unfairness to other people. The two maids, noting with trepidation her mounting ill temper, stared steadfastly and nervously out of the windows, hoping she would not vent her anger on them.

Celia, her eyes misted with indignant tears, gazed unseeing at the endless miles of whitethorn hedges unravelling along the winding road, oblivious of their beauty and that of the green fields beyond them, re-living for the hundredth time since she left London the painful scenes which had preceded her departure.

Celia, returning from Van Dyck's studio with Verney in discreet attendance on her, had found the house empty except for servants. Edward was, as usual, out and not expected back until late. This was in accord with his usual habits and Celia therefore thought that she and her admirer would be safe from interruption if they spent a little time together. So far Ralph Verney had done no more than touch her hand . . .

It came as a horrible shock, therefore, when, in the midst of their first tentative embrace, when Verney's lips were just lightly brushing Celia's cheek, the door opened and Edward walked in.

It was almost, Celia thought, as though he had been

apprised of their meeting beforehand, so unexpected and inopportune was his return, so out of keeping with his normal behaviour. A painful suspicion of subtle intriguing beyond her own naïve imagining assailed Celia. Had Edward known all along? Had his friend's attentions been connived at or even initiated by him as a means to be rid of her? Surely she had done nothing to make him hate her so much? She put the idea from her.

After he came in there had been a hideously embarrassing silence which had seemed to go on for a long time but which, she now realized, could only have lasted about a minute. Edward had gone very white. His friend very red. She herself stood between them staring at each in turn with her mouth open but unable to say a word.

As might have been expected, Edward, always so well in control of himself, recovered first. He directed at Celia a look of such inhuman coldness as she had never thought to receive even from him. Then he motioned her to the door, opened it and bowed her stiffly out, murmuring in a frigid undertone that she was to go to her room and he would speak to her later. It was humiliating to be dismissed upstairs like a disobedient child to await punishment, but Edward's expression precluded argument and Celia was forced to obey.

She did linger in the hall for a few minutes, mounting the curving classical staircase slowly, leaning over the elegant balustrade in the hope of hearing what passed between her husband and his friend. But the door was tightly shut and they must have spoken very low for she heard nothing. Eventually she went to her room and waited there for a long time until Edward came.

She thought she would have been prepared for almost anything except what had actually happened. If he had lost his temper and stormed at her, even beaten her, Celia reflected desolately, it would have come as a relief, but when Edward finally confronted her it was with his usual unbearable composure.

Entering and closing the door behind him, he stood with his hand on it, speaking to Celia across the wide expanse of the room. She thought then, seeing him stand so, that the distance between them was immeasurably great.

"You will leave in the morning for your father's house in Devonshire," Edward said, fixing his gaze on the wall above her head. "I have given directions for all the preparations necessary for the journey. See that you're ready to travel as soon as it's light."

Breathlessly she said, "Don't you want to hear what I have to say?"

"There is nothing," he rejoined, "to be said. There will be no scandal. The ostensible reason for your departure is the alarmingly rapid spread of the plague. There are two cases in the next street."

He turned away and she saw that he was actually about to go without saying any more at all, as though everything were cut and dried, her future decided finally and without appeal.

She stood up. "And Ralph?"

The mention of his friend's name halted Edward. He answered, still looking away from her: "There will be a duel. Honour requires it. But Verney and I understand each other. We shall meet but retire unwounded. No one will die in defence of your supposed virtue."

That, except for a short encounter of the utmost formality when he appeared to take an arctic leave of her, was the last Celia had seen of Edward. Now, only a few miles from her Devonshire home after four days' travelling, she felt she didn't care if she never saw him again.

"It's not as if," she thought petulantly, "I'd *done* anything to deserve being sent away. All this for one peck on the cheek from Ralph Verney! Edward couldn't have been more cruel if he'd found me in bed with the wretched man. And yet he didn't really care. It's just an excuse to be rid of me. But no one will believe my side of the story. Mother will guess what's happened straight away and what on earth am I to tell her? Oh, why can men always do what they want and women never?"

A turn in the road brought them within sight of the sea and a gust of fresh salty breeze blew into the stuffy carriage. Celia, acting on impulse as she almost always did, banged on the window, shouting orders to stop. They were only a short way from their journey's end but she wanted a few minutes to collect her thoughts and prepare for meeting her family. She was dreading their well-meant enquiries.

"I want to stretch my legs," she said almost defiantly in answer to her maids' surprised looks. She had not yet reached that pitch of sophistication which enables a person to act unselfconsciously when doing as they choose, even in small things.

She pulled off her hat and stepped down into the road just as a rider, travelling in the opposite direction, appeared round the bend of it. She knew who he was almost before he raised his hand to wave to her and certainly before his delighted shout of greeting rang out.

"Leah," he said, leaning down from the saddle and beaming at her as he dismounted. "It's good to see you."

"Hallo, Sim."

She smiled more happily than she'd done for some time, standing in the dusty road, the breeze lifting her skirts like a lover. No one called her Leah now except one or two people who had known her all her life. It was the way she'd said her name as a small child, when pronouncing "Celia" had been beyond her. When she'd reached her teens she hadn't liked the babyish nickname and had been annoyed when it was used, but it made her feel warm inside to hear Sim say it as he did now, with genuine affection. He was just like a brother to her. Well, almost.

He took her arm, easily and naturally.

"I heard you were coming and rode out this way in the hope of meeting you. How are you?"

Almost without thinking they had turned into a gateway and were following a farm path that bordered the cliff edge. Far below a sea the colour of turquoise broke in white lather on buff-yellow sands. The sails of fishing boats, red and brown, rocked on the water. The breeze was fresh and tangy with the smell of deep-sea weed flung up on the beach.

Celia, who had noticed hardly anything on her journey down from London, suddenly saw that the wild rose bushes, their foliage ragged from the ravages of caterpillars, were starred with delicate pink blossoms.

"How are you?" said Sim, taking both her hands in his and asking as if he really cared and wanted to know. His face was brown, his mouth was wide and his eyes made a fan of wrinkles at the outer edges whenever he smiled, which was often, for Sim liked life and took his pleasures with a wholesome good appetite.

"You haven't changed much, Sim," said Celia fondly.

"Nor you, I hope," he said softly.

They stood together, hand in hand for a moment. Remembering.

It was ten years ago but she still recalled the smell of the apple loft. Whenever a man touched her in the way of love she felt the scent of russets and cider apples linger on her palate and in her nostrils, a clean, comforting, mouth-watering country smell.

Words she had heard read in church reminded her.

"As the apple tree among the trees of the wood, so is my beloved among the sons. I sat down under his shadow and his fruit was sweet to my taste."

The apple loft was the place where the children of the two families went when they were in any kind of trouble: Celia's family, the Craces; Simon's family, the Greenfields. It was a refuge, a place of safety, a kind of sanctuary to which you could retire when the tyrannies and injustices inflicted by the adults were temporarily too much to bear.

Celia, in tears after a scolding, found Sim there one mild

moist September afternoon, very sore from a beating he thought he hadn't deserved and making noises that sounded suspiciously like sobs.

"Sim!"

She dropped on her knees beside him in the straw of the apple loft, where the rosy pippins were stacked against the winter, and put her hand on his shaking shoulder.

"You're crying."

She was shocked. After all, he was two years older than she was, fifteen last birthday, and she thought of him as a man.

Boy-like he reacted with furious indignation, starting up at once, the tell-tale traces on his face.

"I'm not." And then, lamely, "Don't you ever tell anyone, Leah. Promise?"

Solemnly she put her finger in her mouth and drew the moistened tip across her throat.

"That's wet. That's dry ... Oh, Sim, I am *so* sorry."

And suddenly they had their arms round each other and he'd buried his face between her small breasts and rubbed it against them, childishly, for comfort, opening her dress so he could touch her nipples. Celia nursed his head and shoulders trembling with tenderness as she felt his mouth on her breast. A warm, sweet glow spread over her body.

She lay back in the straw. The boy touched her, wonderingly.

"Go on, Sim. It's nice."

"They'd make an awful fuss if they knew," he said, looking wistfully at her. "Does anyone know you're here?"

"No one. No one in the whole world."

She was a little frightened when she felt his hands on her thighs but she let him lift up her clothes and look at her and when he took her hand and pressed it awkwardly against his body she did what he wanted, feeling again that deep melting tenderness she had sensed at first.

"Leah," he said. "Leah, Leah, *Leah*."

And then his body was beating on hers and she was moving

with him, as one with him, wanting what he wanted. And it was like riding, like running through fields of buttercups, like swimming in very deep water, like burning. It was like ice and fire and the sudden swift hurt was sharp and . . . soft, soft, like a snowstorm of feathers, like sunshine on a bank of white violets. Like an apple loft in Devonshire.

That was ten years ago. She let go of his hand and turned back to the road.

"I must be going home," she said, almost pleadingly.

"You're not happy, are you?" He spoke accusingly, striding along beside her, taking only one step for every two of hers.

"Please, Sim. I don't want to talk about it now."

"You ought to have married me."

He picked up a stick and slashed at the nettles in the ditch. "Why didn't we do as we wanted? Why did we listen to our parents?"

"It's too late now," Celia said hastily, uncomfortably aware of her servants' curious stares as they waited in the road.

Sim dropped his voice. "I went to the cave the other day," he said casually. Celia looked down. The cave was another favourite place of theirs. At least, it had been until the time when they'd stopped meeting. The cave was more secret, safer from discovery.

They were nearly at the road. Sim asked urgently, in a whisper, "Celia, will you . . . ?"

"I can't talk about it now, Sim."

He helped her into the carriage, grinning his wide, cheerful grin. After all, he knew her well, very well.

"I'll ride ahead of you to Combe," he said. "My people are dining with yours tonight. It's a sort of welcome-home supper. I'll see you there."

She watched him wave as he rode away and the tired horses started to draw her carriage over the last stage of the long journey home.

4

Celia's mother, coming out to meet her when the carriage at last drew up outside the door of Combe Hall, saw the petulant droop of her daughter's mouth, the defiant lift of her chin, and realized at once that she was going to have trouble with her. Elizabeth Crace found all three of her children hard to understand. They were each in their different ways more passionate, more individualistic and more secretive than she had ever been or would ever have wished to be. She often thought that her life would be happier if her children could only be content to be conventional, like herself. Conformity made for so much more pleasantness all round. She smiled nervously, twisting her thin hands and implanting a tentative kiss on Celia's cheek.

"You must be tired after your long journey, my darling," she said.

Celia's brother, Roger, as heavy and dark as his mother was thin and fair, looked at Celia over Elizabeth Crace's shoulder and raised a quizzical black eyebrow.

"What have you been up to?" his expression seemed to say. Celia made a face at him. Probably he had guessed what had happened. He might even have the facts already. As Edward's friend, Roger would have no sympathy for her. Roger was ambitious and had hoped his sister's advantageous marriage would help his business interests, for Edward had influence at Court. So far, he had not benefited much by the alliance. Celia guessed that Roger would take the opportunity of catechizing and lecturing her about her behaviour as soon as he found her alone. She made up her mind to avoid him as much as possible.

Her father, less perceptive, more spontaneous and infinitely more warm-hearted than the other two, gave her a great bear-hug that left Celia breathless. Laughing, she hung round his neck. He was solid and strong and comfortable, smelling of tobacco and leather and, faintly, of the bracken through which he had recently been riding. The dogs yelped excitedly at his heels, barking their welcome, jumping up to greet Celia in their pleasure at seeing her again.

"Oh, my dear, your dress!"

Celia's mother exclaimed, dabbing ineffectually at the muddy animals while Celia went on laughing, her father bellowed, "Down, you rascals!" and Tray the lap-dog regarded the behaviour of the rustic hounds with city-bred contempt.

Her father kept his arm round Celia's waist as they went up the steps to the doorway where her younger sister Anne was standing beside a slim young man with a pale alert face.

"You're looking well. Remarkable pretty, my love." Celia's father gave her an affectionate squeeze and his delight in having his favourite daughter home again found expression in an exuberant flow of words. He was a handsome old man, ruddy-faced, white-haired and with a rich, deep voice.

"We were surprised to get your husband's message to say you were coming, but pleased, very pleased. Combe isn't the same without you and we're glad that Edward can spare you to us for a bit. I can understand him being worried about the plague. Wretched thing! I've known whole families die of it. It's never so bad in the country. You'll be better off here with us till it dies down in the autumn. Not but what we haven't got our troubles here. There's nothing but bad news, as I said to your brother this morning. Prices rising, wages falling and the political situation going from bad to worse. You don't know where you are these days..."

"Now, don't be bothering Celia with all your talk about politics before she's even got a foot inside the house, Father," put in Roger diplomatically. "And here's Master Hillard waiting to be introduced."

Celia kissed her sister Anne, thinking for the hundredth time that she would never understand why someone so exceedingly pretty could be so indifferent to her appearance. Anne's features were far better than Celia's own and her complexion was almost perfect, but the smooth fair hair was tucked away under a plain cap and Anne's dark blue dress was positively dowdy. Celia knew her sister's intended husband was a clergyman and a moral man but surely - dreadful thought! - he was not one of these tiresome Puritans who disapproved of everything, especially women making themselves attractive.

She found herself being introduced to him, aware that Anne was watching anxiously. Stephen Hillard was decidedly presentable, if a little stiff and serious, lacking only height to make him handsome, and Celia, who had an eye for any well-looking man, smiled a bright pert smile as she curtsied to him.

He responded with grave courtesy, somewhat embarrassed and slightly disapproving. Probably he *was* a Puritan, she thought, noting his reaction. She didn't envy Anne the prospect of living with someone so obviously strait-laced. Then she remembered her own situation and bit her lip, dreading all the explanations that were to come.

She was glad to find that they could be deferred for the time being since, as Simon had already told her, the Greenfield family were dining with the Craces. Simon's mother, plump and cheerful, kissed Celia affectionately and his sisters, horsy Ruth and gawky Patience, followed suit.

"We're longing to hear all about London," whispered

Patience in Celia's ear. "Is it as wicked as they say?"

"Worse," Celia whispered back, not knowing what they said. "Much worse."

"Oo!" Patience's mouth made a round "O" of horrified delight at the fascinating idea of so much wickedness. Simon's father, too far away to hear what passed, beamed from a distance and Celia was aware of Sim's strongly masculine presence demanding her attention in the background.

"We waited dinner for you, Celia."

Her mother's tone conveyed an anxious hint that the gentlemen were hungry and the beef would be spoiled if it were not served directly and Celia, knowing the ways of the household, responded by saying that she would be ready in a few minutes.

Neither Combe nor the people in it seemed to change much, she thought, with mingled relief and exasperation as she washed her hands and a tired maidservant put her hair to rights. Used, during her year's absence in London, to the new, handsome, classical buildings that Inigo Jones had recently made fashionable, she found Combe Hall dark, cluttered and poky.

Originally a farmhouse, added to by succeeding generations and only recently dignified with the name of Hall, Combe was a rambling place full of small panelled rooms leading into one another, rooms with ill-fitting windows and boards that creaked underfoot and strange-shaped closets where lavender-scented linen and cheeses and cordials were stored.

Tripping down the staircase with its heavy carved balustrades darkened by smoke and the fingermarks of innumerable children, Celia wrinkled her nose a little disdainfully at the mingled smells of humanity, animal life and country cooking which permeated the old house.

Her own house - Edward's house, she remembered with

faint misgiving – was so tasteful by comparison, so white, so serene, so dignified. But perhaps, she thought, her foot on the lowest stair of all, that was why she was not happy there. Perhaps here, where the earthy reek of the cow-byres and the strong tang of woodsmoke lingered and the harsh salt smell of the sea breeze blew in at every casement was where she really belonged. Perhaps she would never be a lady.

The idea was irrational, sudden, disquieting and unwelcome. Celia frowned and, pausing outside the door of the big, old-fashioned dining-room, once the original farmhouse kitchen and the only large room in the house, arranged the flowing stole she had draped round her shoulders.

"Well, how is His Majesty to get money to build ships and pay the men to sail them, then?" her father was saying belligerently as she entered. "It's a perfectly legitimate way of raising the funds that are needed. God knows we need the navy's protection here in Devon and Cornwall. Often enough our fishermen are afraid to put to sea for fear of being taken by pirates. Why, there are Salleemen in the channel every day . . ."

"What," said Celia smiling round charmingly on her assembled family and friends, "is a Salleeman?"

Sim Greenfield leapt up to place her chair for her, accidentally touching her shoulder in the process, and sat down again opposite her, his foot touching hers under the table while the grave young parson, Stephen Hillard, answered.

"It is the name given to a pirate ship sailing from the port of Sallee in Morocco, Lady Lovell. The Sallee rovers have made some daring raids on our coasts lately."

Celia, feeling the pressure of Sim's foot, hardly heard and only smiled in reply.

Mistress Greenfield, sitting beside her, murmured, "The men are arguing about Ship Money again, my dear. I declare we never hear about anything else once they get started."

"I know," said Celia sympathetically. "It's just the same in London."

She settled down in her chair. The dining-room at Combe might be dark, old-fashioned and redolent of mellow cheese and bacon boilings, but it glowed with modest, homely comfort. The long table top was beeswaxed till Celia could see her own reflection in it and the best glassware and pewter set out on it in her honour shone each with its own appropriate brightness in the light of the thick white wax candles. Her father liked to see a fire in his hearth even in summer so there was one crackling in the open grate now, the firelight playing on the family portraits of a century ago which flanked it and on the deep-set, diamond bright panes of the windows above.

Celia smiled as her eyes took in each well-remembered feature. The very apples on the sideboard, early red pippins just gathered, winked as if they had been specially polished. Even the arrival of an excellent joint of beef and particularly delicious game pie did not, however, divert the men's attention from politics for long Except for Sim, they rapidly became involved in an argument once more.

"I can't agree with you, George," Simon's father was saying sententiously, "but if the King wants money he ought to call a parliament and ask them to grant him a subsidy in the approved manner. The King's ruled without a parliament for seven years now and that's seven years too long to my way of thinking."

Mistress Greenfield fidgeted and looked at her husband imploringly, but he ignored her. Squire Crace spluttered angrily over his wine.

"I've never thought I'd see the day, William, when I'd hear you talk such treasonable nonsense! What's the good of a parliament full of Puritan scoundrels that want to turn church and state topsy-turvey and have no respect for the laws of the land? It would be a good thing if the whole lot of them went across the sea to Virginia or wherever it is they talk about these days. We want none of them here!"

Celia saw Stephen Hillard sit up very straight and look directly at her father. Anne put her hand timidly on the young man's arm as though to restrain him, but he only laid his own hand firmly over it and spoke to Squire Crace without looking at her at all.

"You will perhaps not be sorry then to hear that I am planning to leave England for the New World myself, sir."

There was an astonished silence. Everyone stared at Stephen Hillard except Anne, who looked down, colouring deeply.

Celia's brother Roger, who had hitherto had little to say, was the first to recover himself.

"Come now, Hillard, you're not serious. You can't think of leaving England."

"I am and I do," replied the parson of Combe with the utmost gravity. Celia thought it ridiculous of Roger to suggest that he was not serious. She thought she had never met anyone as serious as Stephen Hillard seemed to be.

"But it's impossible!" Celia's mother gave a soft but fervent exclamation of dismay. "You're to marry Anne. Surely you won't go away and leave her."

"No, madam. Indeed I shall not. As my wife it will be not only her duty but her wish to go with me."

He looked gently first at Mistress Crace and then, with tenderness, at Anne, who kept her eyes down and was obviously much distressed.

"You knew of this, Anne?"

Squire Crace was incredulous, but also angry. Everyone was embarrassed. Even Roger was lost for words. Celia could see that Anne was on the verge of tears. Well, she couldn't save her sister's feelings very much but she might spare her the pain of having to account for herself so publicly and unexpectedly. She answered the pressure of Sim's foot

45

on hers with an affectionate tap and deliberately knocked over her wine-glass.

"Oh dear!" she said in a loud, clear voice. "How silly of me. I've spilt this wine all over my gown."

Once in the privacy of her bedroom with Anne, whose assistance she had immediately claimed, Celia put aside all pretence.

"What did that tactless parson of yours mean by saying you were going to Virginia with him right in the middle of dinner like that?" she asked, hastily dimissing a sleepy maid who came to see if she wanted anything.

Anne, worried as she was, smiled faintly.

"Don't talk about Stephen in that way, Leah. He said what he felt he had to say. Are you all right?"

"Of course. I was just creating a diversion." Celia stepped out of her gown. "So you're going to Virginia with your parson?"

"Not Virginia. Massachusetts". Anne hesitated, stumbling over the unfamiliar name. Stephen had told her of his plans two days before and she hadn't had a moment's peace of mind since. Anticipating what her parents' reaction would be and hating the whole idea, she still couldn't bear to think of parting from him and felt painfully torn between conflicting desires and loyalties.

Celia gave her an impatient, indulgent, affectionate look.

"You always worry far too much, Nan. I should try and persuade your little parson to have second thoughts about going overseas. After all . . ."

She heard voices below in the courtyard and the clop of hooves on cobbles. Evidently some of the guests were leaving.

Celia ran to the window and looked out, peering round the curtain.

Sim Greenfield glanced up before he turned his horse's head towards the gates of Combe Hall. He was whistling a tune which Celia remembered. A tune they had learned as children.

"Come unto these yellow sands . . ." Sim whistled.

Celia waved to him from the window.

"You know, Anne," she said, "I don't think I shall be able to go to church tomorrow. Something tells me that I am going to have a headache."

5

Celia woke to find warm golden sunlight pouring in at her window and streaming across the bed. Little motes danced in it and an inquisitive humble bee blundered into the room and alighted on the looking-glass. She heard blackbird and thrush singing their full-throated defiant songs in the orchard on the south side of the house and the sea beating on the cliffs beyond. She was at home and it was good to be alive.

The sunlight was inviting. Celia pulled down the coverlet and let it play on her body, luxuriating in the warmth, stretching herself as a cat does.

A knock on her door reminded her that she was supposed to have a headache. Illness was the only excuse accepted for non-attendance at church so she would have to pretend she was unwell.

"Come in," she spoke as faintly as she could and covered her eyes with her hand as though the light hurt them. Through her fingers she saw her mother standing in the doorway, tidily dressed in her good quality, rather old-fashioned country clothes, russet velvet gown with an exquisite froth of Honiton lace at collar and cuffs, wide-brimmed hat and doeskin gloves. She held a large prayer-book in one hand and a bottle of lavender drops in the other. She was frowning slightly and looked as if she had not slept.

Celia, who had slept extremely well, felt a twinge of conscience. She guessed that, after she herself had gone to bed last night, there had been a full-scale family row. Obviously the idea that Anne was planning to leave Combe and go to America with her future husband had struck her parents like a thunderbolt. Probably they would forbid Anne to marry him and there would be much reproaching, acrimony and recrimination before it was all settled.

Her mother approached the bedside.

"I hear you have a headache," she said wearily, scarcely glancing at Celia. "I've brought you these lavender drops."

As she set the bottle down on the bedside table the church bells began to ring and she put a slim gloved hand to her temple.

"They go right through my head. Well, I must leave you. I mustn't be late." She paused a moment, looking into Celia's eyes as her daughter mumbled her thanks. "I hope you soon feel much better. I hope we all do." She turned away, pausing at the door to say bitterly, "Roger never tells me anything. You only tell me what you want me to know. I did think that Anne, at least . . ."

She gave a mournful sniff and went out.

Celia was vaguely sorry for her but conscious that there was nothing she could do to help for the moment. Lying in bed, enjoying the sunlight, waiting for the house to empty as everyone left for church, she thought with pleasure of her forthcoming meeting with Simon Greenfield.

"Come unto these yellow sands," she trilled happily, stepping out of bed on to the polished boards. The invitation had been clear enough. She knew just what he meant and where she would find him. She flipped open the lid of the chest in which most of her gowns had been placed after the journey, rummaging about for something suitable to wear. Nothing too fine or made of a fabric which would show telltale marks and give away secrets to the sharp eyes of inquisitive servants. She fished out something she hadn't worn in years, a brown cloth dress with a bodice criss-cross laced like a milkmaid's and sprigged with yellow daisies embroidered in clusters. That would do.

She pulled it on, put on a straw bonnet, listened for a minute or two at the door to make sure the house was really empty and then ran swiftly downstairs and out into the garden.

The garden at Combe was old-fashioned, not at all like the close-clipped, carefully ordered formal garden of the London home she had just left. Here everything grew riotously together, great burgeoning clumps of flowers and herbs filling the spaces on each side of the winding, mossy path. There were all sorts of pinks, from striped, strawberry-coloured "sops-in-wine" to the full-flowered, snow-white ones with silvery stems and delicious scent that were her sister Anne's favourites. There were spotted orange lilies, Canterbury bells, larkspur and columbines and some of Celia's own favourites, openhearted, blowsy pink peonies spreading their rumpled feathery petals to the sun.

Celia pulled a random handful of fragrant pinks which, brittle-stemmed, straggled over the border of the path, and pushed them down into her bodice, feeling the smooth stems cool between her breasts. They moved freely, for she had nothing on under her brown cloth gown, having left off her restrictive stays, heavy petticoats and even her smock, seeing she was going to meet Sim.

She pushed open the garden gate and hurried out on to the cliff-top path at the end of the steep-banked green lane, running along, light-hearted as a child in the sunshine.

The red cliffs were broken and scarred with bushes and small plateaux of greenery. At their feet the sands were gradually being uncovered by the receding tide. Combe's few fishing boats rocked idly at their moorings, the nets spread out on the beach to dry near the handful of white-walled cottages with lobster-pots stacked at the doors. The fisher-folk had gone to church, like everyone else in Combe village, and only the herring gulls dived and wheeled and screamed as Celia followed the narrow path that led down to the cave on the far side of the bay.

To the south-west, hull down on the horizon, the sails of a large ship had just appeared. Celia hardly noticed it, ships of all sorts were so commonly to be seen passing along the channel, and she had just caught sight of Sim Greenfield's roan mare tethered in a thicket of birches at the edge of the path, placidly cropping the grass. Seeing it there, she was not really surprised when Sim himself stepped out of the bushes, caught her round the waist, pulled her against him and kissed her heartily.

"I've wanted to do that ever since I saw you yesterday," he said with frank satisfaction when want of breath obliged him to stop for a moment. "It's been a long time, Leah."

"Too long, Sim," she said, more deeply moved by the warm ardour of his embrace that had so much of friendship and affection in it, lusty as it was, than she had thought she could be. He made a move to draw her down into the grass beside the path.

"Not here," she said, "at the cave," and ran from him, her shoes slipping on the rocks, darting in and out among the weed-strewn tidal pools, leaving a trail of footmarks in the moist sand that gradually filled with water. She laughed, hearing Sim coming after her, faster on his feet but not so nimble, swearing when he stumbled on the slimy stones at the cave entrance as he followed her in.

The cave was as it had always been, cool and dark and inviting, haunted by echoes of the sea which filled it every high tide, pungent with the deep sea smell of brown and green weed, littered with limpet shells, conical and subtly coloured, each one different. There were double dark blue mussel shells, too, mother-of-pearl-coloured inside, and flat pebbles smoothed to a soft sheen by the endless caressing of the water. Celia scooped up a handful and held them out, turning to face him.

"Look," she said breathless, laughing, "do you remember how we came here looking for them when we were children?"

For answer he dropped to his knees in the sand, taking off his coat and spreading it out with an imploring and engagingly hospitable gesture.

"What's that for, Sim?"

Celia held back, watching him with bright mocking eyes. Then she saw his face and hadn't the heart to tease him any more but lay down beside him, letting him undress her while they kissed, feeling his broad blunt fingers fumbling clumsily with the lacings of her bodice, sighing with satisfaction when his hand finally cupped her breast. They clung together. Then he bared the rest of her body, kissing and stroking her with his warm strong hands and Celia basked in his loving as she had in the sunlight. Edward had always taken her coldly and peremptorily, in haste and in the dark, as though making a casual meal for which he had not much relish, concerned only with satisfying his own needs.

Celia stroked Sim's face, feeling for him the remembered tenderness she had felt as a child. She liked to be made love to in this way, herself naked and the man clothed. At least at the beginning. Later it would be his turn.

"Leah," said Sim's voice in her ear, "if you don't help me with these damned breeches you're going to find you came here for nothing!"

He filled her as the tide had filled the cave and, in the intimate, replete silence which followed, there was a time for that complete truthfulness that is only possible when all barriers of reserve, mental and physical, are down.

"Why have you left Edward?"

Sim traced a circle round her nipple with his finger.

"I haven't. He found me kissing another man and sent me away."

Sim sat up, looking down at her in astonishment.

"Found you kissing . . . ! You mean he didn't *do* anything?"

Celia shook her head wearily. "No. He just told me that he'd made arrangements for me to come back here and sent me away with hardly a word."

"Then he's either nothing of a man or he's a damned fool. If you'd been my wife I'd have taken a whip to you."

"If I'd been your wife it wouldn't have happened at all, Sim."

"What fools we were," he said. "What fools!"

And he put his hands under her haunches, his thumbs in the hollows of her hips, feeling her hands on him also with much desire and love and longing, and the second coming together was better than the first.

When Celia finally opened her eyes she was not immediately aware of her surroundings. Sim still lay over her, his body between her parted thighs, face turned sideways and resting on her breast, dark lashes casting a shadow on his cheek, just as he had long ago in the apple loft.

Then she saw the foot. Hardly a yard from her face. A naked brown foot. Her eyes travelled upwards and she saw the complete man. A stranger. A terrifying stranger. There were others with him. The cave was full of them.

She screamed as they pulled Sim off her and when he fought and was hit on the head and bound and when they passed her roughly from hand to hand, laughing and shouting, and one of them pushed her up against the cave wall and –

"To hell with you all! Do you think we've got time for that now?"

Jaffar Rais stood in the cave, drawn sword in hand, black angry and shouting orders, gesturing his men out on to the beach. Everyone looked at him except Celia who lay where she had fallen, her hands covering her face, sobbing weakly.

Aware of him standing over her, she felt more shocked and frightened than she had ever done in her life, but she managed to get up somehow and said, with tremulous defiance, "Well, you might at least let me put my clothes on."

She hardly caught a glimpse of his face then, he was already turning away. Two of his men were dragging Sim between them. Blood streamed from a wound over Sim's temple. His shirt fluttered dismally about his bare thighs. Celia had no idea what was happening except that it was already the worst experience she had ever had and she was utterly alone and unprotected, but she grabbed at the arm of Jaffar Rais.

"Where are you taking him? Who are you? What are you going to do with us?"

He scarcely glanced at her and his cursory look did not trouble to include her face, but he shouted something to a black-bearded sailor in ragged canvas trousers who was slinking out of the cave with a bundle under his arm. Jaffar Rais strode out after the rest and the man came back reluctantly. He eyed Celia's nakedness with a lascivious expression, muttered something in a language which she fortunately could not understand and flung down a garment at her feet.

The garment proved to be poor Sim's breeches and, since her brown cloth gown was nowhere to be seen, Celia had no alternative but to put them on. The sailor was impatiently preparing to bind her hands with a length of rope and she did not care for the prospect of being handled by him while she was stark naked. Fortunately the breeches had a belt with them or she would not have been able to keep them up at all. She fastened the buckle thankfully round her waist and shook her hair forward to hide her breasts. The man grabbed her wrists and tied them together. Keeping hold of the long rope, he swung round, pulling her after him out of the cave and moving so suddenly and rapidly that Celia was almost jerked off her feet and was obliged to run to avoid losing her balance and being dragged along the ground.

Outside, an array of boats was drawn up on the sand. Besides those already beached she saw others, which looked like local fishing boats, being hauled up on to the shingle by groups of men wading in from the sea. Never before had she witnessed so much activity in quiet Combe Bay. The little half-circle of sand, usually deserted, was thronged by scores of fierce, foreign-looking intruders, many of them dark-skinned, some of them wearing outlandish clothes and all of them armed.

Celia's captor led her towards a ship's longboat almost at the water's edge. Looking back, she saw Jaffar Rais beginning to lead his men up the cliff path. Most of them were already preparing to follow him, leaving only a handful of men to guard the boats. A ship of a type she had never seen before, a big ship with great banks of oars like wings, was at anchor in the bay. The wind blowing in off the sea brought a stench with it like the reek of cess-pits.

Pirates, that's what they were, making a raid on Combe for plunder and slaves. She had heard that such things happened but, of course, she had never thought that anything so outrageous would happen in her own home, to her own family and friends.

Her captor was speaking to her, jerking his thumb towards the boat, motioning her to climb in. When she didn't obey at once he clouted her across the rump with the rope's end and she tumbled over the gunwale with a squeal, floundering on top of Sim who was lying in the bottom of the boat. Still only in his shirt, blood congealing on the side of his face, he was trussed up like a fowl and almost blue with cold, for the breeze was fresh at the edge of the sea and there were several inches of water in the boat.

"Oh, Sim!" Celia was more sorry for him than for herself. "Are you all right?"

Considering the state he was in it was a ridiculous question. Sim blinked. They'd hit him unnecessarily hard with a pistol butt and he was still partially stunned from the effects of the blow.

"Leah." He made an ineffectual effort to sit up and groaned. "My head's splitting. What have they done to you?"

"Nothing yet." She grimaced. "Sim, what on earth are we going to do?"

"What are *they* doing? I can't see a thing down here. With any luck they may have only landed for water."

She shook her head. "They've all gone up the cliff towards the village except for a few. Oh, Sim, all our people will still be in church. They won't have a chance!"

6

Stephen Hillard, Master of Arts and rector of Combe, mounted slowly to the pulpit. His feet were heavy with fatigue. After leaving Squire Crace's house the evening before he had returned to the rectory to spend the whole night in fervent prayer, or, as he would have put it, "wrestling with the Lord".

After hours of heart-searching that left him red-eyed and exhausted Stephen Hillard had decided what he must do. Vigorous self-examination revealed to him that he had been putting off making his decision and openly declaring it for fear of the consequences and he was deeply ashamed. He had been unfaithful to the Lord. For more than a year now he had been considering leaving England to go to the New World. He had friends there, godly men and women who thought as he did about purity of worship and freedom of religion, and they had been pressing him to join them and persuade others to do so. He had hesitated, doubting whether he was "called" by God to go overseas.

He thought now, after his night of ruthless self-examination, that he had indeed been so called and had ignored the call for fear of what he might lose, or rather whom he might lose. Gripping each side of the shelf on which the precious bible lay open, he surveyed his congregation, trying to avoid looking at the place where Anne Crace sat with her family in the Squire's pew. Her father had been very angry with him the evening before and had threatened all kinds of things. Roger Crace, more cool-headed, had made it plain that the family would never be reconciled to Stephen's Puritanism and that if he persisted in his intention of leaving England they would stop Anne from marrying him. Their attitude reflected that of the late King James to those of Stephen's persuasion – he must conform or else.

But Stephen could not conform. The fact that the thought of losing Anne was so terrible to him was another source of shame and guilt. He was young and he was healthy and his sexual feelings had been given him, along with his other faculties, by his all-controlling God, but Stephen believed he had been led away by "lust" and "carnal desires" and thought himself unworthy to be a minister of God.

The church was, if anything, fuller than usual. The two maids and two menservants who had travelled down from London with Anne's sister, Celia, were seated alongside the Hall servants, their pale faces, fashionable clothes and bored, superior expressions setting them apart from the rosy-faced, homespun-clad locals. Lady Lovell herself was missing, Stephen noted, and that blackguard, Simon Greenfield, too. "Marriage is honourable in all and the bed undefiled, but a whoremonger and an adulterer God will judge."

He felt that Anne was looking at him with reproach and painful perplexity, longing for some sign of comfort, but he dared not acknowledge her presence by the slightest hint. He had betrayed his Master, but from henceforward he would be faithful.

He felt the sweat break out on his forehead, conscious that even now, in the very house of God where he had come to preach the Word, to deliver a special message to God's people, he could not entirely centre his thoughts on heavenly things.

Clearing his throat with great solemnity, he announced, "My text this morning is taken from the book of Genesis, chapter twelve, verses one and two: 'Get thee out of thy country, and from thy kindred, and from thy father's house, unto a land that I will show thee: and I will make of thee a great nation.' "

He paused, as all good preachers do, for effect, and a faint sigh went up from his congregation of a hundred and twenty souls. It came from those few in it who were neither too tired, too stupid or too preoccupied to listen. Every congregation contains its quota of these categories and the one assembled in the ancient church of Saint Mabyn at Combe that June morning in 1636 was no exception. For most of the labourers and fishermen and their wives who spent all their daylight hours, from dawn to dusk, six days a week, in unremitting, exhausting and often boring toil, the church service provided their one excuse to sit idle and quiet for a short time. They did not waste their precious leisure in listening to a sermon they could not understand. The sprinkling of yeomen and tradesmen were another matter, though. Stephen knew them to be amongst his most enthusiastic supporters. So his gaze passed over the Barratts, all half asleep still after toiling till the small hours to net a pitifully small catch, and the Sanderses, who hadn't a shoe or an unpatched garment between them, and lighted on those "who had ears to hear".

Sampson Derrey, the smith, his clean, dark broadcloth Sunday coat shiny from wear and bursting at the seams when his great shoulders came into play, listened attentively to the parson's words. So did his plump, sensible wife, Susanna, and their growing family, ranged in order of age beside them. So did Josiah Martin, the sharp-faced, loquacious tailor who ran the village school, a man bursting with ideas, unconventional and full of initiative. Squire Crace did not approve of Josiah Martin, considering that he exercised a disturbing influence over his pupils.

Henry Lamb, the cobbler, was another of Stephen's adherents. He and his wife, who was as thin and trim and brisk as himself, sat with their row of tow-headed children, who were all looking preternaturally well-behaved and solemn. Every now and then Henry Lamb would look along the line and if he saw a foot swinging or a hand fidgeting he would reach out with his stick and tap it smartly. A zealous man, Henry Lamb.

Stephen Hillard did not look at Charity Lidd. He did not dare to. But he knew she was there. Only certain stories in the gospels which his assiduous reading and literal acceptance forbade him to ignore, made him tolerate her presence in church at all, for Charity Lidd was the scarlet woman of the village. She was rosy and smiling with a bosom like a pouter pigeon and plump, tight buttocks that swayed provocatively under her thin old dress when she walked. She was a farmer's daughter, a fisherman's widow and every man's wife who felt the need.

Stephen disapproved of her fiercely. He knew most of his fellow Puritans would think him wrong not to see Charity was subjected to all the savage punishments allowed by the law to fall on those who broke the seventh commandment. But he couldn't forget those other words, "Let him that is without sin among you first cast a stone at her."

"It's time you married again, Charity," he'd say whenever he met her, assiduously turning his eyes either up or down so as to avoid looking at the way her bodice and skirt fitted so tightly.

"Ah, but who'd have me, parson," she'd answer softly in her rich warm voice that was like curds and cream, "a poor widow and not so young as I used to be?"

"Charity suffers long and is kind . . ."

The text could not be appropriate, Stephen told himself sternly. Yet it was the one which came readiest to mind.

Looking down on the array of heads ranged in rows below him, some raised, some bowed, some nodding, a few turning restlessly, all dappled with light in rainbow colours from sunlight filtering through the stained-glass windows, Stephen murmured a brief, desperate prayer and began.

"My dear friends, I want to talk to you today about the

way in which God calls us to serve him. You will remember how clearly the call of God came to Abraham, to Moses, to Joshua . . ."

Tippett Collecock, agent for a rather seedy enterprise known as the New World Company, whose business was to recruit sturdy young men and women, to become indentured servants in the West Indies on the mainland of North America, yawned covertly behind his hand. This was all very fine, but he wished the parson would get down to the real business of urging his flock to go to America as soon as possible. Once they were interested, Tippett knew from experience, he would have little trouble in persuading some of the more adventurous young people to go with him to London. Once there, he would hand them over to his employers, collect his percentage and be off on his travels again.

He was a slick, sly, keen little whippet of a man, always watching his opportunity to make money out of those less worldly and calculating than himself. He glanced round the church, marking down likely-looking lads and girls who, for a flagon of ale or a bunch of ribbons, would run away from home after he'd told them about the wonderful new life in the wonderful new land.

Unlike the graceless Tippett, Anne Crace listened to every word Stephen said and never took her eyes from his face. She was very much in love with him and unhappy because everything had seemed to be so right between them and now it was all going horribly wrong and she didn't know what to do. Anne had thought that marriage with Stephen would mean a quiet and ordered existence in the rectory where she would bear his children and run his household. Of going to a new land peopled by savages, completely unknown, and living in a strange place among strangers, she had never even thought before and the prospect terrified her. He was so ardent and demanding that she had finally agreed to do as he asked, hardly knowing what she promised. Then when he quarrelled with her family about his schemes and they insisted that she was not to marry him after all, Anne felt that her whole world had collapsed about her ears.

Stephen was urging his hearers to listen to the call of God who was summoning them, as He had the Israelites, to go to a new land where they could serve Him better than they had in the old. His deep-toned, mellow voice wooed them all in general and Anne in particular, delivering the incomparable language of the King James' bible with a moving resonance.

" 'Now, therefore, arise, go over this Jordan, thou and all this people, unto the land that I shall give thee.' "

"Listen to the call of God. It may be He is speaking to you today. In the quietness let us each look into his own heart."

He paused. Anne looked into her heart and saw only Stephen. Her father, beside whom she sat, stirred restlessly. Once the sermon was over he would tell this impudent young parson exactly what he thought of him, his bristling, hostile movements indicated. Anne's eyes filled with tears.

Feeling suddenly drained of energy now that he had finished what he had to say, Stephen raised his arms for the benediction.

" 'The Lord bless you and keep you. The Lord make His face to shine upon you and be gracious unto you. The Lord lift up the light of His countenance upon you and give you peace.' "

Above the subdued murmur which greeted the concluding words a deep, clear, powerful voice rang out.

"Amen!"

Shouted in ribald tones from the back of the church it echoed, startling in its bold irreverence, from nave to chancel. Every head but Stephen's turned, the hundred and twenty necks of his parishioners swinging round in one instant as though they were all operated by a single piece of unseen but highly efficient machinery.

Stephen, abruptly brought down from the pinnacle of his

inspired eloquence, gaped.

A tall bearded man stood in the church doorway, curiously dressed in a red-striped turban, sleeveless jacket and Moorish trousers. As the population of Combe stared at him in stunned silence he advanced to the end of the broad central aisle, a pistol which he had calmly cocked and now supported over his left arm, pointed directly at Stephen's head.

"One move, parson," said Jaffar Rais coolly, "and you're a dead man."

7

The heavy pulpit Bible slammed shut and came hurtling through the air. Jaffar Rais had time to duck and it only struck him a glancing blow on the shoulder but the bullet he had meant for Stephen Hillard missed its mark and smashed into the stained-glass window above the altar, bringing down a tinkling rain of flying, coloured splinters. As the corsair's men poured into the church behind him, the congregation rose to its feet in bewildered dismay and the little parson of Combe rushed at his enemy with as much valour as Gideon smiting the Midianites.

Grappling with him at the foot of the pulpit steps, Jaffar Rais shouted above the reverberating din, "Tell your people to give in and come quietly."

Stephen, who was no match for the corsair and who was, moreover, hampered by his cassock, felt his arm cracking as Jaffar Rais twisted it across his back, but he went on struggling.

"I'm damned if I will."

"You're damned if you won't."

Jaffar Rais gave Stephen's arm such an agonizing wrench that the little parson's eyes grew hazy with pain and he felt the thick, sour taste of vomit rising in his throat. The corsair propelled him forward and pressed the point of a knife into the hollow between Stephen's jawbone and the lobe of his ear.

"Tell them to give in," he ordered. "You fool. I don't want

them killed any more than you do, but I can't hold these men of mine once they get the blood lust on them. Can't you see what's happening?"

For a devastating moment Stephen saw. His church was in chaos. The peace and order of centuries had been wrecked in an instant. Pews were overturned and books scattered. Women and children screamed, trying to escape from the encircling band of corsairs which had ringed them round and was advancing inwards. Bodies struggled together on the floor. Some of the villagers tried to crawl under the pews whilst others, panic-stricken, trampled on them in their efforts to get away.

Such men as showed fight were being brutally dealt with. Horrified, Stephen saw Sampson Derrey, the smith, hurled to the floor by several attackers who began kicking him into submission. Fists thudded. Knives flashed.

Stephen found his voice. Heedless of Jaffar Rais' dagger at his throat, he yelled, "Stop it. Stop it, all of you!"

They had to, anyway. Hardly a third of the congregation were grown men and scarcely any of them had any kind of weapon. Only the Craces and Sim's father, old William Greenfield, wearing swords as an indication of their rank as gentlemen, were in a position to offer any effective resistance and they were soon disarmed.

From the vantage point of the font, Charity Lidd, imitating the parson, hurled prayer-books and shouts of defiance at the corsairs which they ignored until one of them, laughing, grabbed her round the knees and bore her off, slung across his back.

Jaffar Rais put his foot on an overturned pew, cupped his hands round his mouth and bellowed, "Sort 'em out."

His men, who were old hands and knew their business, were already doing so. They treated the people like cattle, dealing with them as drovers do with a herd, cutting out the big males and rendering them harmless, then rounding up the others. The fifty or so fishermen, farmers and able-bodied craftsmen were bound and thrust out of the church at sword point. Even so, they had to knock Sampson Derrey down and stamp on his chest to get him to submit and Jaffar Rais bellowed furiously at them, "Don't spoil him, you fools. He'll fetch six hundred ducats in Algiers."

Roger Crace, dazed from a succession of blows and obliged to watch his father seized and bound without being able to do anything to prevent it, looked up at the sound of Jaffar Rais' voice. He'd thought he'd recognized it. Now he was sure. The corsairs, secure in their triumph, had left him unguarded for a moment and his hands were still free. He vaulted an overturned pew and sprang at Jaffar Rais' throat.

"I'll kill you, Tom Chandler," he said, "if it's the last thing I do."

"If you weren't worth more to me alive than dead it would be."

Jaffar Rais grinned down at Roger, felled and roped at his feet. His men had acted so quickly Roger had not so much as had the opportunity to fasten his hands round the other's neck.

"I'm glad you remember me, Crace," he said with a grim smile. "You'll find that I, too, have not forgotten."

He swung his foot back and slammed it brutally and deliberately between Roger's ribs. Stephen Hillard, standing dazed and momentarily forgotten, flew at the corsair, like a terrier at a wolfhound.

"Haven't you done enough without that, for God's sake!"

Jaffar Rais rounded on him savagely.

"I've been very patient with you, parson. You can thank your God you're not an old man or I tell you plainly I'd kill you out of hand. It's only the fact that your age and condition make you prime goods for my trade prompts me to spare you and him."

He kicked the groaning Roger again and Stephen, now pinioned himself, was forced to stand helplessly by as the corsairs ruthlessly emptied the church of all but a dozen or so really old people whom they pushed aside, compelling them to huddle together in a corner out of the way while they drove their sons, daughters and grandchildren before them at the sword point with oaths and threats and blows.

Roger and one or two others who had been beaten up for offering too sturdy a resistance were carried by their shoulders and knees between two of the raiders, one in front, facing forwards, his mate following, in the manner of sedan chair bearers. Toddlers who clung to their mothers' skirts and other children too small to move at the fast pace the corsairs required were hauled along roughly by arms or legs or flung across their captors' shoulders, howling dismally. Their mothers, some clutching babies at the breast, ran at the raiders' heels, breathless and terrified for their children and for their husbands who had already been herded through the grassy churchyard and out under the lych-gate.

Charity Lidd, her bodice gaping to the waist, round bare breasts bouncing up and down, was being bundled along by a lean Spaniard who had his hand twisted into her hair and carried a squalling four-year-old on his shoulder.

Harry Martin, the shoemaker's active twelve-year-old son, trying to make a break for freedom as the men and boys were driven out into the lane and towards the cliff path, was knocked down and dragged the rest of the way to the beach by one foot, being mercilessly bumped over the stony ground, his face and hands torn by brambles. The raiders ignored his cries for mercy. The boy's mother, rushing to his aid, they drove off with blows, for they would brook neither resistance nor delay.

Those of their captives who lagged behind were beaten to make them keep up, the hindmost getting the flat of a sword blade across his or her back to encourage the others.

The path was rough and broken and the pace they were being compelled to travel at too fast for all but the most active. Anne Crace, helping her mother along, was horrified when the older woman fell. The danger of being trodden underfoot by the terrified villagers was at least as great as from the boots and fists of their captors.

"Get up, dear."

Anne pulled on her mother's arms. They were amongst the last and people were rushing past them. "Please get up. You must."

Somehow she got the older woman on her feet, fixing an arm firmly round her waist so that they could stumble on together in the midst of the gasping, panic-stricken people who were being urged on past endurance by the shouts and flailing swords of the corsairs.

Mistress Crace's breath was coming painfully. She pressed her hand to her side.

"I can't go on. Leave me."

"No, no. You must. You must."

Anne had an agonizing stitch in her own side but she had just heard the high-pitched scream of the luckless last in line as the harsh sword blade landed and knew she could not abandon her mother. However exhausted she was she must go on.

Hardly seeing anything but the next step along the way, blinded by the sweat that ran down into her eyes, staggering under the weight of her fainting burden, Anne Crace struggled on. Life had suddenly become very simple for her. To keep going and not to be last was all that mattered . . .

When the church door had slammed behind the last of the corsairs the old people were left alone. Old Henry Derrey looked to have had a heart attack by the sound of his breathing and the colour of his face. Alice Whiddon just sat with her hands in front of her staring and not saying a word.

"Isn't anybody going to do anything?" shrilled Biddy Harris, wanting to know, as she had all her life, why other people didn't put things right.

"Where are they taking them?"

Susan Barratt hobbled across to the door to see what was going on and her husband, shaky on his feet too, but just as stout-hearted as he had ever been, pulled his hat down firmly over his ears and announced that he would walk to the next village for help.

Alice Whiddon kept staring at the desecrated altar, pillaged of its cloth, cross and candlesticks, and the broken window beyond.

"O God," a voice kept saying inside her, as she looked up at the place where she had always thought He could be found. "O God."

From under a bench at the back of the church a scared seven-year-old crept out, sobbing brokenly and ran to her.

"Gran," he wept, clinging to Alice's hand in the wrecked and ruined church. "Where's my mother? I want my mother."

He climbed up into her lap, tears making grimy runnels down his round, grubby cheeks, pulling and tugging at her, demanding attention and response from the hitherto all-powerful grown-up world.

"Gran, I want my mother."

But his grandmother, who had never failed him before, only stroked his hair in an absent, automatic way and, still staring straight ahead of her, said bemusedly, to no one in particular,

"Tom Chandler. My own sister's son. That's who it was. I'd know his voice anywhere. What Devil brought him back from the dead to plague us?"

8

"They're bringing them now!"

The raiders were hustling their string of frightened prisoners down the steep cliff path and Celia sprang forward instinctively, trying to make out the figures of family and friends. The guard swung round, mouthing threats, and shoved her back.

She crouched, kneeling in the boat, still craning her neck in an effort to see. Down here at the water's edge there was a fresh breeze blowing off the sea that made her teeth chatter, turning her white arms red and blue with goose pimples, making the delicate skin of her nipples sore. She clutched her breasts with her bound hands, trying to protect them.

"Can you see my mother and sisters?"

Poor Sim, lying on his back, unable to get up, was worse off than Celia. He'd been brutally bound, elbows lashed behind his back only a few inches apart, his head bleeding and his shirt hardly covering him at all.

"I can see your mother." Celia answered his agonized question whilst looking anxiously for the members of her own family. "And Ruth. They're together."

Sim struggled to get up but fell back again with a grunt of pain.

"Who else, for God's sake?"

The corsairs were wasting no time, hurrying their luckless captives along as fast as they could. Their leader, the man she had seen in the cave, was already on the beach, giving directions, marshalling the people into groups as soon as they got down on to the sand.

"There's the parson. I can see his black cassock. And that awful woman from the village with the ridiculous name. What is it? Charity Lidd? And," she paused, "they're carrying someone down. Someone in a blue coat like Roger's. I hope they haven't hurt him. Oh, what a shame!"

Disregarding Sim's frantic demands for an explanation, Celia watched indignantly as a young fisherman who had tried to run away was brought down and kicked back to where the rest of the captives were. There were more than a dozen rowing boats of various sizes drawn up around the rim of the little bay, Celia noted. The corsairs, she realized, must have commandeered all the local fishing craft.

With the same frightening efficiency with which they had acted all along they were now systematically loading their captives into the boats. Some of these had already been launched, whilst others had their noses in the water, their crews standing up to their thighs in the sea alongside, hauling the prisoners on board as they were driven to them through the shallows by the corsairs on the shore.

As soon as a boat had its full complement it was rowed out to the big ship that was anchored so surprisingly close in. The bay echoed with the shouts of the pirates and the terrified screaming of children. Celia saw her mother and sister being hauled along to the boat where she and Sim were and cried out herself.

Half a dozen pirates gripped the boat's sides, shoving its keel through the shingle. The prisoners stumbled into the sea after it, urged on by the armed men behind them, and were pushed over the gunwale to lie pell-mell in the bottom of the boat.

"Get up! Sit up! Do you want to capsize us?"

Jaffar Rais, wading through the water, the last to board a boat, shouted to the prisoners as his men gave him a hand into the rocking craft and started rowing out to the ship.

"Oh Celia! What has happened?"

Celia's relief at finding that neither Anne nor her mother had actually been harmed had made her forget her own wild disarray. Now, encountering her sister's horrified and compassionate gaze, Celia came as near to blushing as she had ever done in her life. Good, innocent Anne evidently believed that she must have been raped and dragged from her bed at Combe Hall.

"You'll catch your death, ma'am," muttered Tippett Collecock, who, sitting close by Celia in the crowded boat and already feeling the qualms of sea sickness, yet glanced admiringly at her. "If my hands weren't tied I'd lend you my coat."

As in all horrible situations there was an element of the ridiculous and Celia lingered for a moment on the brink of laughter and tears until a shout from one of the other captives distracted all attention away from her.

"My God, they've fired the Hall! The Hall's burning!" The boat rocked perilously as the prisoners turned to follow the line of the pointed finger. A gasp of dismay went up from all but the young children among them. Forgetting their individual peril, they watched the cloud of smoke rising from the big house on the headland and orange flames beginning to appear, flickering at the windows.

"Oh my house! My house!"

Celia's mother, temporarily roused from the torpor of shock and exhaustion, moaned and wrung her hands.

"Keep still," ordered Jaffar Rais, tugging at an oar. "Do you want to be drowned? Never mind your house, Mistress Crace, be glad you and yours have all got whole skins."

"Why did you do it?" Celia, feeling more outraged by the sight of her home burning than at anything else she had seen happen on this incredible day, stared at him in anger and amazement. A shower of spray sent up by the oars drenched the prisoners to the skin as she spoke and they began shivering with cold as well as with fear. She felt

Anne's hand on her arm, warning her to keep silent, but she had to ask the questions that came bubbling up out of her.

"How do you know about us? Who are you? What are you going to do with us?"

"Give way there! Bend your backs! Do you think we've got all day?"

He was urging his men to row faster and ignored her. They were almost under the lee of the large foreign ship when Celia repeated her last question, more for the sake of the others, cowering and trembling round her than because she was in any doubt herself.

"Ship your oars!"

Jaffar Rais leaned forward as they came alongside.

"I'm going to sell you, one way or another, all of you. I'm in business for slaves and ransom. Do as you're told and you'll come to no harm. The better you are the more I'll get for you. But I warn you - don't give any trouble."

The boat was bumping up against the ship's side and Jaffar Rais leapt for it, scaling the bulwarks hand over hand with an arrogant agility that made Tippett Collecock, who was feeling distinctly queasy, catch his breath in reluctant admiration. They heard the corsair captain's voice above them.

"Deck there! Look alive! Loading net!"

The large, coarse-meshed rope loading net landed among them and the seamen, endeavouring to keep the heaving boat steady, prepared to disembark their human cargo. The net was roughly spread out and one of the corsairs motioned to Celia impatiently, showing three fingers. She looked at Anne.

"You and I and mother. There's no help for it. If we hesitate they'll make us. It's better if we go together."

It was the most frightening as well as the most undignified way of being transported and, bundled together, hoisted in mid-air and finally dumped down on the deck, they were tumbled out dizzy and confused.

Anne and Mistress Crace were hustled away below but Celia, hampered by having her hands bound, couldn't get up and found herself sprawled at the feet of Jaffar Rais, lying across his boots. He looked down into her eyes with a dominant, triumphant look. The ultimate male stare.

"If you were a gentleman," said Celia, "you'd help me up."

"If you were a lady," he said, "I might."

But he grinned, stooped, twisted two fingers into the rope that fastened her hands and jerked her on to her feet, keeping hold of her bonds because the motion of the ship threatened to take her off balance again.

"Little Leah Crace," he said. "Always a bold one, weren't you?"

The suspicion, the odd sense of something familiar about him, came back to her strongly.

"How do you know who I am? Who are you?"

He laughed. "All of us village boys fancied you, little Leah, but you never noticed any of us, just wiggled your hips and kept your nose in the air when you went past. Do you remember Tom Chandler?"

Tom Chandler. With the name vague memories came flooding back. Celia recollected a lanky boy with a runny nose.

"Tom Chandler from Combe Hollow? But you ran away to sea. We thought you were dead."

"Very much alive. No thanks to the Craces. But perhaps," he looked keenly at her, "you don't know about that?"

"Tom Chandler. Why, you're one of us. You ought to be ashamed."

The words came unbidden, spontaneously. She was past being afraid. He yanked her up close to him, his fingers still twisted into her bonds.

"Ashamed, is it? And what about you? It seems to me you don't know what shame is. I know how my men found you in the cave. I saw you myself."

With his free hand he drew her hair back over her shoulders

and looked at her body.

"Little Leah Crace," he said. "Squire's wanton daughter. My father used to say you were that hot under the tail you could boil a kettle on it."

She flew at him.

"Oh, if my hands were free."

She heard his men laughing. A knife whisked under her nose, so sharp it severed the ropes round her wrists as easily as slicing an apple.

"Do what you like," said Jaffar Rais. "But afterwards I swear I'll take those breeches down and tan your backside for you."

If they'd been alone she'd have risked it, but the other men were watching. She stood rubbing her wrists resentfully.

"I've wasted too much time on you," he said, pushing by her and she fell back against the bulwarks, wet hair lifted by the wind, cold and alone and, now that her anger had evaporated, very much afraid.

There were no other prisoners in sight, only the crew of the galleasse. She expected to be ordered down into the hold where she had seen the others disappear, but a man approached her. She looked at him in alarm, but he only held out a coat to her and, averting his eyes, said gruffly, "You'd better put that on and come with me."

She put the coat on thankfully. He reached out an arm to steady her as the ship lurched. The banked oars had come into play. The drum beat. Whips cracked. Fetters rattled as the galley slaves sent the oars forward. The galleasse was alive with noise and activity, bucking as she clove the waves.

Startled, Celia clutched the coat round her.

"What's happening?"

"We're getting under way, that's all," the man said grimly, steering her along the deck. "Mind your step and keep hold of me. She rolls a bit. It's the shallow draught."

Celia didn't understand what he said but his manner was

reassuring. He was not like the others, she saw. He was a quiet man with a drawn face and sad eyes.

"Where are you taking me?"

"Captain's cabin," he answered, his lip twisting with distaste. "I'm sorry. Orders," he added, as if that explained everything.

"Help me," she said desperately. He was guiding her to the cabin on the poop deck. Above them the blue and white striped sails began to belly out.

"I wish I could," he said briefly, guiding her up the short companionway and pausing at the cabin door. "Can't, though. I'm by way of being a prisoner myself."

Celia hesitated at the door, but he opened it and pushed her gently inside.

"Don't go!" He represented sanity, normality and a comforting reminder of the secure world from which she had been so suddenly and brutally snatched.

"I must." He paused. "Try not to anger him. When he's pleased he's generous. My advice to you is to do what he wants with a good grace. Since you've no choice you'd be well advised to do as you're told and make the best of it."

"Is that what you do?" asked Celia bitterly as he closed the door on her. "Is that what you do?"

9

John Dunton forgot about Celia the moment he left her, partly because he loved his wife, left forlorn in Rotherhithe with their three little daughters, and worried about her all the time he was not worrying about his young son, held hostage in Sallee, but mostly because Jaffar Rais hailed him.

"Look here, Dunton, we're in luck!"

The corsair captain was in high good humour and Dunton was quick to see the reason. The fast-moving galleasse had almost run down a small cargo ship, which was lying, more or less becalmed, directly in their path. Dunton ran his eye over her. Nice little craft. A three-masted caravelle, lateen sailed, something under a hundred tons burthen. With those lines she'd have a fair turn of speed.

"She's as good as ours."

Jaffar Rais rubbed his hands. The ship was just the size and tonnage to fetch a good price in Sallee. To say nothing of the cargo and the crew.

"She's as good as ours," he repeated as the galleasse's guns delivered an admonitory shot across the smaller vessel's bows, warning her to heave to.

"You haven't taken her yet," grunted Dunton. A puff of smoke from the caravelle's gun ports signalled her captain's defiance.

"Fool!" Jaffar Rais' brow darkened. "I don't want to damage her with gunfire. She'll have to be boarded. They won't put up much resistance."

Dunton grunted again. When his own ship, the *Mary*, much about the size of the one now in danger, had been attacked by Jaffar Rais, he'd fought till overpowered by sheer weight of numbers. He'd thought then as he thought now, that he'd rather have been killed than taken prisoner. Only, he was a God-fearing man and perhaps it was wrong to think that way. Worse still, perhaps it was cowardly!

He watched moodily as the galleasse's longboats were launched overside, crammed with corsairs, fresh from the triumphs of their successful raid on Combe and eager to make another quick and easy killing. What chance did the caravelle's crew of a score or so seamen have against the corsair's couple of hundred cut-throats?

As a fight it was hardly worth watching. There were a few more ineffectual shots from the caravelle's small, light cannon, a brief hand to hand struggle on her deck as the captain made a gallant but hopeless stand and the watchers on the galleasse saw the St George's cross being hauled down from the caravelle's masthead.

The crew of the galleasse cheered wildly. The capture of this prize meant a substantial rise in the share each man would get from the proceeds of the voyage. Only Dunton looked glum. The episode was too like what had happened only a few months ago when his ship had been captured along with himself and his son. He wondered how the boy was. He didn't sleep much when he was off watch and when he did the boy's face came always to mind.

Jaffar Rais clapped Dunton on the shoulder.

"Taken without the loss of a man!" he crowed, his face flushed with triumph. "This voyage'll make all our fortunes. Yours, too, Dunton, if you'll only throw in your lot with us. What do you say, man? Come on now. I'll make you prize-master of this caravelle. I can't say fairer than that."

Dunton turned to face Jaffar Rais. The corsair must feel very sure of him to be prepared to trust him so far whilst they were still within sight of the English coast.

"What makes you think I'll accept your offer?" he asked guardedly. "I'm a prisoner and not a renegade like yourself."

Jaffar Rais laughed. "Oh, we all say that at first. Some are a bit more obstinate and take longer to make their minds up, that's all. Murat Rais, the old devil, made mine up for me with a rope's end. Well, once my back healed, I was grateful to him. Who wouldn't rather be what I am than a wretched slave on the oar benches or in the fields?"

Dunton thought that, rather than be a traitor to his religion and his country, he would, for one, but he said nothing.

"I said I'd make you prize-master."

Jaffar Rais spoke peremptorily, not liking Dunton's silence. He liked talking himself. Laconic people bothered him. "What do you say?"

"What I've always said," replied Dunton. "I'll obey your orders."

"Cold, sour-faced bastard, aren't you?" Jaffar Rais frowned. "You can thank your stars you're a first-class seaman, Dunton, or I'd have no truck with you."

"I've said I'll obey your orders," muttered the other. He knew that Jaffar Rais was in something of a quandary, being short of prime seamen capable of laying and steering a course. He doubted if anyone else aboard the galleasse was familiar with the dangerous Channel waters. If Jaffar Rais wanted to get his prize back safely to Sallee he would have to rely on Dunton to sail it there for him.

"Very well, then. I'll put you on board with a prize crew as soon as we've inspected the cargo. Oh, and Dunton," the renegade added, as the seaman turned away after acknowledging the order, "I've left strict instructions about your son. As long as you sail with me, he's safe. But if you break our bargain, Ali Zuni will sell him in Algiers. He's a nice-looking boy, isn't he? Fair hair and blue eyes. White skin. Takes after his mother, I shouldn't wonder. There's always a good market for boys like that. Just remember."

John Dunton was not a swearing man, preferring thought and action to words, but his face and his knuckles went very white. Jaffar Rais glanced at the clenched fists and, seeing the other had reached the limit of endurance, said in a flat, authoritative voice, "I'll have Mustapha allocate you a prize crew of reliable men. I'll have all but six of the seamen on the caravelle taken off her. I don't want you to have any trouble with attempted mutiny. We're a bit overcrowded here so some of the less troublesome prisoners had better be transferred to the prize. All right, Dunton, you can go now."

By "less troublesome prisoners" the corsair captain meant those incapable of fighting, docile women and young children. The prisoners, crowded together in the dark, stinking after-hold, looked up, blinking, as the hatch cover was removed, daylight streamed in and the grinning face of a Corsican renegade, one ear missing, a great gold ring in the other, peered in. There were cries as he leapt down among them, followed by two comrades as villainous-looking as himself, and began dragging some of the women out.

Anne Crace, seeing the Corsican lay hands on her mother, rushed to defend her. All the village men were now not only bound but had irons on their legs as well and so could do nothing. The Corsican grabbed Anne. When he tore at her dress she screamed and there was pandemonium in the hold as all the captives gave tongue together, thinking they were going to be murdered.

"Belay that!"

The face of John Dunton, grey with disgust at the sight he saw and the task assigned him, appeared at the hatch.

"Don't be afraid. Nothing's going to happen to any of you. I've orders to take twenty women and children aboard a ship that's just been captured. Those who come with me will be safer than those that stay here. You have my word on it."

"And why," said Stephen Hillard, who had just experienced

the worst moment of his life when he saw Anne seized by the Corsican, "should we believe you?"

"Because," answered Dunton wearily, "I'm speaking the truth. It seems to me, parson," he said, looking at the tattered remnants of Stephen's cassock, "that someone in your calling ought to know when a man's doing that. Now then, you!"

His last words were to the Corsican who had climbed back on to the deck, dragging Anne.

"Just stand aside, ma'am," Dunton said quietly, putting her behind him. She jumped as the Corsican landed at her feet, his head thumping so hard on the deck after Dunton hit him that the earring he wore broke free, leaving the torn lobe of his only ear bleeding.

Dunton blew on his knuckles, glancing quickly at Anne's torn gown and then away again.

"Has the man done you any harm, ma'am?"

She shook her head. "No harm. No harm at all."

"Good. Get the other women to come, will you? None of them will be hurt or insulted. I can't promise much but I can promise that."

"Yes," she said. "Yes," feeling the first stir of hope since she had found herself a prisoner. Most of the other women followed her without protest to the waiting boat. Some were too apathetic and others too terrified to register any protest. A few of the younger ones, including Charity Lidd, were prevented from coming and one or two who clung to their husbands were not forced to go with the group destined for the captured ship. Once they had gone the hatch was closed again and darkness descended once more on those who were left behind in the hold.

Stifled sobs broke out.

"Oh come on now," said the irrepressible Tippett Collecock, looking round him impudently at the drawn and shadowy faces of his fellow prisoners. "While there's life there's hope. Anyone for a game o' cards?"

There was silence for a moment, then Stephen Hillard chuckled.

"Not with your pack, Tip."

Tippett Collecock leaned forward, meeting the other's eyes in the murky twilight of their prison.

"Good for you, parson," he said with surprised respect. "You put up the best fight of any of us. I didn't know you had it in you."

"I didn't either." Stephen smiled. Collecock was a rascal, but an engaging and plucky one. "It didn't do much good, though," the parson added ruefully, looking at his bound hands and then back at Tippett Collecock. "Do you think that between us we can do something for Greenfield? He's in a bad way."

"Well, there's a bit of water in a bucket here." Once he got over his surprise at being appealed to, Collecock rallied round, crawling over to join Stephen beside the groaning Sim.

"I think one of my ribs is broken," said the voice of Roger Crace from a corner.

"I hope someone thinks to feed my stock."

"Will anyone come to help us?"

"I'm hungry. I want to go home."

The voices of men, women and children, faceless in the dark prison, came from every side. Above them all Charity Lidd could be heard to say, in tones of positive conviction, "We must get out of here. We must."

At least they had the consolation of each other's company. Celia, locked in the captain's cabin, had no one to talk to. However, she was fortunate in being neither imaginative nor sensitive and so was not tempted to think her situation worse than it was.

She looked round the cabin. It was small, smaller than she had expected, for the galleasse was a fighting ship and the corsairs were a relatively democratic community whose leaders lived under much the same conditions as their men while at sea. Nevertheless, Jaffar Rais was a successful captain and his profitable voyages had earned him a certain prestige, a right to creature comforts not enjoyed by the rest.

The cabin was panelled in a pleasant, light-coloured wood, rather like oak. A carpet was spread out over the floor and there were cushions scattered over it. Celia was puzzled to find it so bare of furniture. There was not even a bed. True, there was a small table, bolted to the floor, in one corner, but it was covered with maps and charts and curious instruments, whose purpose she could hardly guess at. Apart from the table, the only other piece of furniture was a large chest.

Celia was as curious as Pandora and the chest was irresistible to her. It was not locked and opened easily. The contents were very interesting to her for Celia liked clothes almost as much as she liked men and the chest was packed with garments. She would have to have felt herself in far more danger than she actually did not to have been diverted by what she found.

On top was an assortment of men's clothes, some ordinary European-style coats and breeches for every-day wear, but flamboyant garments of Eastern design underneath. Most of them were long, simply cut robes in rich fabrics, such as silk or taffeta. There were some splendid colours, purple, gold, crimson and vivid striped effects. There were shoes, too, made of an unusual yellow leather, the toes turned up quaintly at the ends.

At the bottom of the chest there was something even more intriguing, a collection of women's clothes which Celia guessed had been looted from the wardrobe of some great lady or other, for there was a peacock-blue satin gown sewn with brilliants which Celia thought were probably real sapphires. She held it up against her and was disappointed to find it not only much too short for her but evidently made for someone altogether less generously endowed than herself. She put it aside and drew out the nightgown.

At least, she presumed it to be a nightgown, though it was like no garment designed for wear in bed that she had ever seen before.

It was long, it was full and made of a material so diaphanous as to be completely transparent. Putting her hand under its mistily light folds, Celia gasped. Every tiny line, every mark, was wholly visible. When she held it to her shoulders and looked down she could still see clear through the doubled fabric.

The door opened.

"Put it on," said the voice of Jaffar Rais.

10

"You give a lot of orders."

He was alone. With her hands free and John Dunton's coat round her, Celia faced him confidently. He'd taken off his rakish turban and some of the dare-devil bravado of the Barbary corsair seemed to have been shed with it. He looked a little weary, less sure of himself and younger than he appeared when in command. Celia no longer felt afraid of him. When all was said and done, he was only Tom Chandler from Combe Hollow.

Her air of defiance made him smile.

"Please yourself," he said carelessly, sprawling out on the cushions with his hands behind his head.

"A well-made man," Celia thought instinctively, and then was angry with herself for thinking so.

The door opened again and a delicious smell titillated her nostrils as two Moorish servants entered the cabin, one holding the door carefully for the other who bore a large brass tray laden with covered dishes, wine in a carafe and fruit. They placed the tray beside their master, arranging it so that the contents were not spilt by the rolling of the ship, removed his boots, bowed and withdrew.

"Hungry?" Jaffar Rais lifted a quizzical eyebrow and the lid of a dish at the same time. Sniffing the appetizing aroma in the breath of warm steam, Celia realized that she was indeed very hungry, having eaten nothing since a light breakfast early in the morning. The smell of the food was so tempting it made her mouth water. Seeing her expression, he laughed.

"You're welcome to share my meal. Put on what you're holding and come and join me."

She fully intended to say she would do no such thing but she suddenly felt so extremely empty that the sight of him taking a mouthful of food with obvious relish was too much for her. After all, she thought recklessly, dropping Sim's breeches and shedding Dunton's coat, he wouldn't see more than he had already. She drew the transparent gown over her head, almost afraid to handle it for fear it should come apart in her hands. It was as fine as a cobweb and floated round her like a cloud. Her nipples, standing up under it, held the filmy folds out from her body.

Jaffar Rais, his eye kindling, made room for her beside him on the cushions.

"You look well in it," he said with frank pleasure. "Not all women have the figure for it."

Celia was too intent on the food to care what he thought. It was a dish of rice, coloured golden with saffron over which a richly flavoured sauce, full of luscious-looking pieces of meat and choice vegetables, had been generously poured. She longed to begin on it, but there was no cutlery, not so much as a single knife or spoon.

"Do as I do."

Jaffar Rais demonstrated the technique of eating with the fingers by dipping his own into the dish, deftly rolling the morsels he picked up into a ball and popping it into his mouth. It looked easy, but when Celia tried to follow his example the greasy handful slipped between her fingers, splattering the flimsy finery he had compelled her to wear.

Jaffar Rais sprawled back on the cushions, shouting with laughter.

Celia was furious.

"Ignorant clod," she thought angrily. "He's deliberately

making a mockery of me. Indecent dress. Impossible meal. I'll show him!"

She was determined to satisfy her hunger first, however, being convinced that whatever she had to face she could face it better on a full stomach, and persevered with scooping up handfuls of the rice and meat she found to be both tasty and filling.

Although there was no cutlery, square table napkins of soft linen were provided.

Wiping her hands clean and glancing at Jaffar Rais, who was lying back and watching her with evident satisfaction, Celia said coldly, "I suppose you find pleasure in trying to humiliate me."

"Humiliate!" He fastened angrily on the word. "If I'd wanted to do that I'd have thrown you to the crew. I could do it now if I chose."

She did not doubt it, but, as always with Celia, other instincts were stronger than those of anger and fear. This time it was curiosity that triumphed. She met his fiercely threatening look with one of candid enquiry.

"You're Tom Chandler from Combe Hollow," she said wonderingly. "Whatever happened to make you like this?"

He took her wrist and drew her close to him. His skin was very clear and brown above his fair beard, she saw. His muscles rippled hard under his sleeve and against her body when he took hold of her. The filmy robe afforded no protection at all and the touch of his hand on her breast was as though it had been directly on her bare flesh.

"Why don't you ask your brother?" he demanded, suddenly and surprisingly.

Celia, who had not anticipated further conversation, was startled.

"Roger! What has he to do with it?"

"Everything! He owns the farm, doesn't he? The land that should have been mine. The land I was born on. Combe

Hollow. How did he get it?"

His grip hurt her and the anger that possessed him was genuine and frightening.

"How should I know?" Celia was confused. "Roger bought Combe Hollow when it came up for sale after your father died. He paid a fair price for it, as far as I know. Everyone thought you were dead."

"Everyone but your brother." He was shouting at her, though her face was only inches from his own. "Roger Crace knew I was alive and a prisoner in Sallee. My father went for help to him about selling the farm to raise the ransom money. It was sold but Roger Crace kept both money and farm. My father wrote to me before he died. Your brother condemned me to a life of slavery and that's what I would have had but I had the sense to turn Turk, as you say, and join the corsairs. That's how I came to be what I am, Leah. I'm what your own brother made me."

"I don't believe you." It sounded pure fantasy to Celia. "You must be mad."

Then she looked at his face. There was more hurt in it than rage. Whether what he said was true or not it was clear he believed it. She frowned. Roger had wanted Combe Hollow Farm and Roger had it. Roger usually got what he wanted. He never was too scrupulous. She loved her brother but she was not blind to his faults. A sudden fear assailed her.

"What are you going to do to him?"

"Well, now," Jaffar Rais spoke calmly, his feelings temporarily relieved by the outburst which had given vent to them. "He's in for a hard time. Harder than the rest. But exactly how hard rather depends on you, little Leah."

After all it was only what she had expected. When he kissed her she had to respond, partly because he kissed very well and partly because she'd never had much talent for resisting a man whom she found attractive and who really wanted her. Anne and her mother would have been deeply shocked, but then, they were virtuous whereas Celia had never cherished any such illusions about herself.

They drank wine from the same cup and kissed again, his hands wandering about her body. They were hard, but firm and gentle and she experienced relief as well as pleasure.

"Do you love Sim Greenfield?" he said suddenly. Celia, already drowsy with wine and the physical longing he was awakening in her, was troubled by the unexpected question. Then she felt the need to be on her guard. Jaffar Rais was leaning over her, his hands on either side of her shoulders as she lay back on the cushions, the filmy robe drifted into a wisp above her thighs. His face was in shadow.

"Sim?" She smiled mistily. "Why talk about him? I've got a husband, you know. A rich husband in London."

Jaffar Rais laughed. "Why, of course, you would have. That's my little Leah, thinking of the main chance, as always."

Leah sighed, thinking briefly of Sim and hoping he would not have to pay an even higher price for their illicit meeting in the cave. Was it possible it had happened on the morning of this very same day?

"What are you thinking of?"

Jaffar Rais spoke roughly, seeing that all her attention was not on him. The provocative garment she wore did not hinder him at all, but he tore it off.

Celia put her hands on his chest. His body was warm and strong.

"Of you," she said, "only of you."

And for the moment it was true. It was not in Celia's nature merely to lie back and endure and, besides, she still needed to compensate for a year of frustrating and loveless marriage. Her encounter with Sim had, if anything, only sharpened an appetite already keen. So it was not hard to please Jaffar Rais. She had only to follow her own natural desires. Physically they suited one another and their pleasure was mutual.

Jaffar Rais gave a deep, gusty sigh of satisfaction, stretched himself and lay back.

"Good enough for any man," he said, and went straight to sleep.

That, of course, *was* disappointing. After a moment or two, Celia raised herself carefully on her elbow, looking down at him and wondering what to do. He lay on his back beside her, snoring a little, with his mouth open. Seen so, he did not appear very formidable, yet he had everyone she loved in his power. She was thinking about what he might do to them.

It was dark in the cabin, but not quiet. All around were the sounds, strange to Celia, of a sailing ship in motion. The creaking of timbers. The slapping of the waves against the ship's sides. The soughing of the wind in the sail and, everywhere, voices, voices. They would not be left alone together much longer, Celia was sure of that. If she was to act at all she must do so quickly. A vague but desperate idea was forming in her mind. If only she had a weapon!

There was one ready to hand. Two, in fact, for when he'd first lain down beside her, Jaffar Rais had put aside his sword and dagger and they lay where he had left them, close by him on the carpet. Celia was tempted. With a dagger held to his throat what might he not be compelled to do?

She felt behind her for John Dunton's coat and huddled it round her, taking care not to disturb the sleeping man. She looked at him once more and once more at the dagger. Then very gingerly, and without touching him, she leaned over his body, cautiously reaching for the dagger hilt.

As her fingertips touched it both Jaffar Rais' hands came down hard, one on her wrist, the other on her rump. The first stayed where it was, grasping Celia's hand, in an iron grip. The second rose and fell several times, thwacking her behind as she lay helplessly face downward across his loins, John Dunton's coat half-way up her back.

Celia, who had not been subjected to such treatment since

she was a small child, protested loudly, but he went on till she relinquished her hold on the dagger. Then he pulled her astride him and, finding her already stimulated by his brisk handling, thrust directly into her. It was a manner of lovemaking she did not know, but it gave her more excitement and more satisfaction than she had experienced before. The release of feeling left her wholly relaxed, completely sated and totally exhausted.

"Not quite such a fool as you thought, am I?"

There was real triumph in his voice when he saw how entirely she had surrendered to him, how submissive she was, how docile.

She closed her eyes, no longer capable of any action, wanting only rest.

He laughed softly.

"I think I'm safe to go to sleep in earnest now. Funny, I always fancied you, little Leah."

II

"Master Dunton, I must speak to you!"

The little caravelle was being tossed up and down on the waves like a cork and Anne Crace had a struggle to keep her footing on the wet decks, moving painfully from one handhold to the next, impeded by the long skirts which clung clammily round her legs.

John Dunton, pilot and prize-master of the *Jacob*, standing at the helm in the steerage with the quartermaster, a Dutch renegade named van der Velde, saw her coming and cursed inwardly. Her words were borne away from him on the wind but he guessed she was coming to plead with him on behalf of the twenty women and children lodged aboard the *Jacob*. On Jaffar Rais' orders they had been placed amidships, below decks in the orlop. It was dark there, he knew, and there were rats and cockroaches, but no bedding. It was barbarous, but what could he do? There was no end to his problems.

The wind had veered and was contrary, he was sailing as close to it as he could, but they had already lost sight of the galleasse which was far away to the south-west, heading for the Scillies and Ushant.

Jaffar Rais had allocated Dunton a score of corsairs as a prize crew in addition to six of the *Jacob*'s own men whom he had been obliged to leave on board, but he had deliberately selected Dutchmen and Spaniards, not trusting Dunton with a crew of English renegades lest the temptation to make common cause and seize the ship for themselves should prove too much for his compatriots. The half-dozen Dutchmen spoke good English, like most of their nation, and were used to Channel conditions, but the Spaniards, mainly from the south and accustomed to galley work in the Mediterranean, hardly pulled their weight.

Anne Crace, a determined girl, Dunton noted, had reached the steerage and was repeating what she had called to him when she was struggling along the deck.

"Master Dunton, I must speak to you."

He sighed. It was useless to tell the girl she had no business to be there and that there was a rule of silence in the steerage. He handed over the helm to the Dutchman.

"Full and by," he ordered.

"Full and by it is," said van der Velde, glancing up dubiously at the reefed topsails.

"I can't speak to you now, ma'am," said Dunton to Anne, trying to speak firmly and not to look at her white face with its pleading expression. "I have the working of the ship to see to. We're in for some rough weather. Get below or I can't be responsible for your safety."

"*Safety!* Do you know what conditions are like down there?"

Anne Crace was not only determined, she was spirited and, moreover, she was a lady and not accustomed to having her requests brushed aside by those she regarded as belonging to the lower orders. She looked accusingly at Dunton. "One of the women is in labour."

"Good God, ma'am!" He was astonished that she should even mention such a thing. "What do you think I can do? I'm a shipmaster, not a midwife. Get some woman to help you."

The wind was freshening and would soon be blowing a full gale. He could not hold his course.

"Get below," he ordered her again, turning back to the helmsman.

"But we need mattresses and sheets and candles and water and fresh . . ."

"Get below!" He shouted at her, feeling at the end of his tether. "I'll have the things sent to you when I can. If we've got them."

She was only young, he thought, as she went, having to be content with his promise of help. She couldn't be much older than his eldest girl, Jenny, who was rising fifteen. He wondered if he'd ever see Jenny or her two sisters again. And there was his wife, Rachel. They'd been married sixteen years but each time he parted from her to go on a voyage was as bad as the first. She'd been three months pregnant when he'd last seen her. The little one would be six months old by now and he didn't even know if it was a boy or a girl.

"Blowing a gale," said the Dutchman, eyeing him curiously. "Should we drop anchor and ride it out or change course and run before it?"

Dunton grunted, wondering what the renegade was up to, suggesting the very thing he was tempted to do.

"I've a wife in Volendam." The Dutchman was solid, square, sensible, his eyes a clear, light blue, frank and candid like a child's. "I want to see her again." He sighed wistfully. "I like my own country, my own woman, the good, plain food I'm used to. Jan and Hendrik and the rest, they think the same."

"So." Dunton faced the man, still not sure he could trust him. The Dutchman stood steady at the wheel, returning his look without flinching.

"I've a son held captive in Sallee. *I* want to see *him* again," Dunton said.

"I know." Van der Velde nodded slowly. "But there are English merchants there. Won't they keep an eye on him?"

"Well, there's two I know, Willoughby and Woodruff. They said they'd do what they could . . . What the hell are you getting at?" Dunton broke off angrily.

The Dutchman shrugged. "Only that perhaps . . . you worry too much about him and not enough about the rest of your family. The wind's east by north-east. If we change direction and run before it we can make one of the Channel ports by morning. We can always claim we were blown off course. No one will be any the wiser. No one can blame you."

"What about the rest of the corsairs?" Dunton wavered. He hated the whole business. Deep within himself he knew, too, that even if he kept his side of the bargain to the letter Jaffar Rais and his confederates in Sallee might not keep theirs. Perhaps Richard was beyond help even now and there was Rachel and his other children to think of.

"I can vouch for all the Dutchmen," said van der Velde. "We all got together as soon as we knew we were to sail with you and the others chose me as spokesman. That's six. Then there's the six English sailors who were taken prisoner with the ship. They'll join us. No question of that."

"No," said Dunton. The six crewmen of the *Jacob* were all young and active. Their looks showed clearly enough how much they hated being under the corsairs' orders.

"With yourself," said van der Velde, pausing significantly, "that's thirteen. There's only a dozen or so Spaniards and Moriscos. If we take over during the night we can catch them unawares and batten them down under hatches till we reach port when we can hand them over to the authorities as pirates."

"You seem to have got it all worked out," said Dunton grudgingly, trying to hide his excitement. It provided a way out of the trap in which he had seemed so inextricably caught. He suddenly felt comradely towards the Dutchman, realizing that he himself had been so deeply sunk in his own personal anxieties he had forgotten that others might share the same fears and longings. He smiled at van der Velde, who grinned back. For a moment they were like two boys planning to play truant, cheerfully conspiratorial.

"You'll not regret it." Van der Velde's pale blue eyes had brightened with enthusiasm. "It's three years since they forced me to join them – it was that or row in the galleys – and there hasn't been a day since but I longed to be home. I..."

"It's getting dark," said Dunton, cutting him short. "If we're going to do anything we must act quickly."

It was characteristic of him that, once he had made up his mind on a course of action, he followed it through rapidly and decisively.

"Once we get the Spaniards out of the way, disarmed and under lock and key, we can do as we like with the ship. But we mustn't let them suspect anything. There's some tough customers amongst them and we've women and children aboard. You say you can vouch for the rest of the Dutchmen?"

"Absolutely."

"Well then," said Dunton heartened by the prospect of positive action, "I'll speak to the *Jacob*'s bo'sun, what's his name? Bolitho!"

Bolitho was a lean Cornishman, dark and spare and keen-looking, like a knife on edge. You didn't notice how strong he was until you saw his big hands with the powerful, sinewy wrists. He had a black eye to show for the fight he'd put up against the corsairs and his coarse shirt was in ribbons.

Summoned to Dunton's cabin, Bolitho faced him with surly defiance, not trying to conceal the hostility he felt for the man who had taken over his ship from her rightful master.

"You wanted me?" he said contemptuously to Dunton. "Renegade! Pirate!" he was thinking. "I'd like to get my hands round his throat."

Dunton, who guessed his thoughts, looked Bolitho straight in the eye.

"I'm not what you think me," he said. "I don't like this business any more than you do. I was forced into it. Couldn't help myself. Look, the Dutchmen and I want to take over the ship and run her into one of the south coast ports, Portsmouth, maybe, or one of the harbours on the Isle of Wight. Are you with us?"

"Is this some kind of trick?" Bolitho was all tense, hard-eyed suspicion. "What are you up to? First you seize the ship, then you want to give her up again. What's your game, Master Dunton?"

He leaned on the table in the small cabin, facing Dunton in angry perplexity.

"There's no trick." Dunton sighed impatiently. "I was taken prisoner by the Moriscos, just as you've been, and you'll find yourself coerced into doing what I've been made to do, the Dutchmen as well, if you don't listen to reason. It's surprising what they can make you do when they start being persuasive," he added grimly.

"I know. I've heard. I met a lad once that had been a prisoner in Barbary." The tough Cornishman straightened up, remembering. "He hadn't an inch of flesh on his back that wasn't scarred and he wasn't right in the head, either."

He looked at Dunton, sizing him up.

"All right then. I reckon all of us that's left on the *Jacob* will do our best to get her into an English harbour. I'd sooner trust you and the Dutchmen than those bloody Spaniards, Master Dunton. When it comes down to it, I don't think me and the rest of the lads has got much choice. What do you want us to do?"

It worked out easier than Dunton expected. As with all such ventures, the planning, the timing, the waiting were all important. And he was lucky for once, for the wind continued to blow from the east. Had it been south-west, the plan could hardly have succeeded. It seemed to him a sign of Divine favour, as it had to the Englishmen facing the Armada fifty years before, that the wind should be in the right quarter.

The prize crew of the *Jacob* had been divided into two watches, mainly on language lines. English and Dutch in one, Spaniards in the other. Jaffar Rais had miscalculated badly when it came to judging the Dutchmen's feelings, thought Dunton grimly. He must have thought that, because they made no parade of them, they had none.

There were whispered conferences below decks as the twelve desperate men planned their takeover. Dunton had given the key of the arms store to Bolitho and firearms had been issued to the Englishmen who knew how to use them. When the Spaniards came off watch they were to be taken by surprise and barricaded in the fo'c'stle where they were to be kept under guard until they made landfall.

After hesitating a few minutes, Dunton decided to tell Anne Crace what was going on. Not to know what was happening, to be uncertain, was, in his opinion, the worst part of any ordeal. He felt she had the right to be informed. Besides, she would be able to keep the other prisoners under control and prevent them panicking when things got rough.

Entering the orlop, he narrowly missed being hit on the head by an indignant matron armed with a piece of wood who was standing guard.

"For God's sake, mistress!" he expostulated, fending her off. The low-beamed space between decks was dark, crowded and smelled strongly of vomit and crowded humanity. Two or three of the half-dozen small children were keeping up a thin, insistent wailing.

"Mistress Crace."

Dunton stooped, speaking quietly. The women nearest him edged away, drawing their children protectively into their arms, but Anne Crace came to him, appearing out of the dark with her sleeves rolled up and her lilac silk dress of the morning horribly dirtied.

They faced each other in the gloomy orlop.

"We can't go on like this," she said. "The children..."

"I know." He took her arm. "Listen. There may be a noise later on. Some shooting perhaps. There's nothing to be afraid of. Keep everyone down here as quiet as you can.

Above all, stay where you are until I tell you it's safe to come out."

Her face lit up with returning hope.

"You mean you're going to . . . ?"

He motioned her to silence.

"With God's help you should all be safe ashore within twenty-four hours."

He was turning away as she said, "Good luck."

"I'll need it."

In the steerage he took over the helm from van der Velde.

"Everything's ready," said the Dutchman reassuringly, seeing Dunton's set face. "Jan and Bolitho are standing by with the rest. None of the Spaniards suspects anything. We'll set on them as soon as they come off watch."

It was very dark and the thin Channel rain was slanting cold across the decks.

"Go and see it done," said Dunton to van der Velde, and the Dutchman spat in his hand, looked to the priming of his pistol and made his way forward purposefully to where the other conspirators waited for him in the waist.

It seemed a long time to Dunton before anything happened, yet the tall hour-glass beside him released very few of its dark red grains from its upper globe into its lower before he heard the sound of startled shouts and scuffling from the fo'c'stle. There was a thud of running feet on the deck, a cry, a splash, a pistol shot. A door slammed and all was silent.

Dunton felt the sweat run down his wrists as he held the wheel of the *Jacob* fast. Then van der Velde was beside him and Bolitho, grinning from ear to ear in his moment of triumph.

"Never knew what hit 'em," he said. "They're all lodged safe in the fo'c'stle with the doors wedged and two of our men standing guard with calivers ready primed if one of them makes a move. So far all they've done, barring the one that went over the side, is bang on the doors begging to be let out." He laughed. "They'll soon get tired of that."

Van der Velde beamed at Dunton.

"Well, mynheer," he said, clapping him on the shoulder. "We're safe now to set all sail and steer our course for England."

"Yes," said Dunton. But it wouldn't be all plain sailing, he knew that. There would be many problems still to face and he felt a sharp stab of remorse as he thought of Richard and Jaffar Rais' threat.

"My God," he thought. "What on earth am I going to tell his mother?"

12

After the galleasse and the *Jacob* parted company the galleasse bore away swiftly to the south-west, the overseers' whips cracking across the straining backs of the slaves, chained eight to an oar, who rowed till lashing brought no response from their exhausted bodies and they had to be revived with morsels of bread soaked in wine thrust into their mouths.

Then light came and the wind changed, filling the sails. The merciless drum-beat ceased, the overseers' whistles sounded an end to labour for the time being and the slaves sank into instant oblivion, slumped in their chains, still seated at the oar bench because there was not space enough to lie down.

Rounding Ushant the galleasse met hell and high water in Biscay. Her shallow draught made her roll and wallow in the heavy grey seas, waves breaking against her sides and sending showers of drenching spray across her decks.

Four days and five nights she ran before the wind, buffeted by the Biscay storms. They were four days and five nights of extreme peril, stultifying hardship and constant fear for everyone on board. For the corsair crew there was herculean labour. For their captives there was unspeakable miserable confinement in the dark, stinking, overcrowded hold.

Jaffar Rais forgot triumph and vengeance and everything but the need to keep his ship afloat. The emergency absorbed him utterly and he was as near being at peace as he ever was.

He knew that if the galleasse lost her mainmast or suffered any other major damage he was lost, for he dared not put into any port on the French coast for repairs. As a Sallee pirate, an Ishmael of the seas, at war with the navy of every Christian king, he ran the risk of having his ship impounded and his crew made prisoner once he came under the guns of the French harbour authorities. So he drove himself harder than his overseers drove the galley slaves, leaving the helm only for brief intervals when he could no longer keep his eyes open, sleeping lightly for an hour or two before going back to take over the wheel again. He never took off his clothes, though they were soaked again and again, like those of the seamen, going aloft in imminent hazard of their lives, and he ate as they did, when and where he could, not knowing what it was he put in his mouth.

To all intents and purposes, Celia did not exist for him but lay discarded and unregarded in the cabin. On the first day of the storm, before she succumbed to overwhelming sea sickness, she ventured out on to the deck two or three times, only to be driven back by the force of the wind or the brusque oaths of the corsairs when she got in their way.

When the violence of the ship's motion prostrated her she vomited constantly. At first she had strength enough to make some effort at cleaning herself but afterwards, when paroxysms of retching had reduced her to a flaccid and trembling wreck, she lay apathetically in her own dirt, robbed of all vigour of mind and body.

On the morning of the fifth day she woke from a broken, dream-haunted sleep, aware of a great change but not comprehending, in her twilight of semi-consciousness, what it was. Then she realized. The fearful heaving, ploughing and plunging had ceased. The ship, that had seemed to buck like an unbroken colt, now moved no more than a steady old grey mare tethered in a stall. The storm was over.

Suddenly the door of the cabin swung open and Jaffar Rais appeared, his figure looming dark with the light behind him. Celia wondered wearily, in her weakness, why it was that his shape towered so above her, for he was not taller than other men.

He took a step forward and the door closed behind him. Then he fell. He did not lie down, but fell, keeling over from the ankles like a tree axed at the base of the trunk and lying where he fell in a heavy stupor of unconsciousness deeper than sleep, his breathing stertorous, intermittent, laboured.

Celia sat up and looked down at him, thinking for a moment that he had had some kind of seizure. Then, as his breathing became more settled and regular, she realized that he was worn out and had collapsed from sheer fatigue. From time to time during the last few days she had been aware of his presence as he occasionally snatched a little rest, lying down in the cabin for a short while before forcing himself to return to his unremitting labour. Now that the storm had ceased physical exhaustion had pole-axed him. His cheeks were sunken and grey and he slept like the dead.

Leaning on her elbow, she watched him for some time. It was a new experience for her to see him weak and helpless. She thought what a strange chance had thrown them together at a crisis in her life and remembered with incredulity the night in which they had made love which now seemed so distant and unreal that she began to wonder if it had been a dream.

A shivering took him. He stirred and murmured. Hardly knowing what she did, Celia reached for a heavy boat cloak that lay among their scattered garments on the floor of the foetid, airless cabin and covered him with it. Stray wisps of hair clung to his forehead, damp with sweat. She smoothed them aside. He was in her power at this moment. If she drew his dagger she could kill him. And herself.

Even in her extreme wretchedness Celia smiled at the essential incongruity and ridiculousness of the idea.

"Who am I to be thinking such high-minded, classical thoughts?" she said mockingly to herself. "Am I to play

Lucretia to his Tarquin? I am Celia Lovell who was Leah Crace and, God forgive me, I was never virtuous. Even with far greater reason than I have I could never thrust a dagger into anyone, much less into myself. As for Tom Chandler, here, if I killed him, what possible good could it do me or the others? His crew are not better than he is and may well be worse. I'll bide my time."

In a few moments she too was asleep.

A splattering handful of water thrown in her face awoke her.

Celia gave a faint shriek and sat up spluttering. Jaffar Rais stood over her, his hands on his hips. She did not know how long he had slept but he was obviously revived, looking vigorous and refreshed. She herself felt neither.

"Get up," he said.

Celia put a hand to her head. She was dizzy. Her limbs were like jelly. The inside of her mouth was furred and foul.

"I can't," she said and fell back with a groan.

"You'd rather lie there like a pig in the straw, would you?" He laughed. "Come on out of that."

He picked up a blanket and, ignoring her feeble protests, rolled her in it, swinging her up into his arms and carrying her out on to the deck as easily as though she had been a small child.

A canvas sling had been rigged, hammock-wise, near the taffrail, and Jaffar Rais dumped her in it.

"Fresh air," he said. "Fresh air and food, that's what you need," and left her.

Celia was too weak to argue. Few things are so completely demoralizing as a really bad bout of sea sickness and, though the thought of food revolted her, the fresh air did indeed make her feel a good deal less wretched. She dozed most of the day, still not strong enough to take any interest in her surroundings, but she managed, much to her surprise, to eat a little kus-kus and to keep it down before she returned to the cabin at dusk. It smelt cleaner than it had done and she lay down to the deepest, sweetest sleep she could ever remember.

Her awakening the next morning was even ruder than that of the day before. The splash of water was followed by a shaking as Jaffar Rais hauled her to her feet.

"Wash yourself," he said, indicating a leather bucket on the cabin floor, swilling to the brim with cold sea water. "And don't be all day about it," he added, seeing her hesitate. "We're going ashore."

Celia looked dubiously at the leather bucket and then down at her filthy garments. She'd never been so dirty in her life, but the cold sea water looked singularly uninviting.

Jaffar Rais leaned against the bulkhead, arms folded. Celia glanced at him, wishing he would go away.

"Are you going to watch me?"

He grinned. "Yes, I am. Get on with it."

She shrugged, turning her back on him, and stripped and washed in the sea water that felt icy and sticky to her body. Her hair was a problem. Long and thick, it had become unpleasantly matted. She drew strands of it between her fingers, grimacing.

"Another bucket?" Jaffar Rais was impatient. "Come, I'll help you."

He bawled for more water and Celia held a hastily snatched robe before her as a seaman slapped a second bucket down inside the cabin, slopping the contents over her feet.

"Kneel down," Jaffar Rais urged her, "and put your head in."

There seemed no help for it, so she went down on her knees, pulling her hair forward and rinsing it in the water. After a moment Jaffar Rais knelt behind her, scooped up a handful from the bucket and poured it over Celia's head, chuckling when she squealed. He was in a very good humour, for the time, she thought, feeling him press close up against her, the firm contours of his body hard against her own yielding flesh. She had to suppress a desire to wriggle her hips in response.

"Come on," he said again, drawing her to her feet, his hands under her armpits. She wrung the water from her hair, combing through the wet locks with her fingers and preparing to put on the long red robe which he held out to her.

It was very loose and full and made of some kind of heavy silk with a pattern of flowers woven into the fabric. She tied her hair back with a sash, twisting it into one long, corkscrew curl which she brought forward over her shoulder, noting with distaste how drips from the end of it marked the shining silk of the robe.

"I must look awful," she said.

"No." Jaffar Rais' tone was curiously tender. "You look good enough to me, little Leah."

Seeing her surprised expression he frowned, saying with determined coarseness, "You've got good haunches and you don't hold back from a man, that's all I ask of any woman."

He took her by the arm and led her out on to the deck. The sky was cloudless and after the dark closeness of the cabin the sunlight dazzled her. She shielded her eyes with her hand and looked around.

The galleasse was moored in a narrow inlet, hardly a hundred yards wide. Its sides were steep and wooded with tall trees growing down almost to the water's edge. Ahead was a narrow strip of shingly beach and more trees beyond, forming a green wall. Boats laden with barrels were plying back and forth between the ship and the shore.

Celia rubbed her eyes and stared.

"Where are we?"

He laughed at her bewilderment.

"Come, I'll show you."

He guided her back into the cabin where he spread out a map on the table, weighting the top corners with a boxed loadstone and a heavy book.

"Ever see a mariner's chart before?"

Celia shook her head, momentarily forgetting her fatigue as she looked at the intricate drawing he had unfolded before her, fascinated by its patterns of capes and bays which resembled ragged lace. The land was painted mostly brown and yellow, speckled here and there with tiny pictures of forts, houses, mountains, farms and trees in bright colours like the illustrations in an old book of hours.

But the yellow land was only a deep border at the top and two thirds of the map were taken up by a bright blue expanse marked "Western Sea" with the more imposing title, "Maris Occidentalis Pars" beneath. A huge whale with cavernous, fanged mouth, tridentine tail and gushing spout appeared to be about to gobble up a three-masted ship whose crew had apparently abandoned her to her fate since none were to be seen on her decks or rigging. On the other side of the doomed vessel, beyond an elaborate rosette displaying the points of the compass, was a carefully drawn oval frame containing a sun flanked by two gaudily plumed, surprised-looking parrots and the legend:

"A description of the Sea Coastes of Galicia beginning from Cap de Finisterre unto Cammo, done according to the true situation and appearing thereof."

The inscription ended with a flourish and the date 1588.

Jaffar Rais planted his finger squarely on the chart, to the left of a brilliant parrot, where two serrated oblongs with a dusting of smaller ones round them were shown afloat in the midst of the blue ocean surrounded by drawings of anchors and numbers indicating the depths of surrounding.

Celia spelt out the name, "Isles of Bayonna", but she was no wiser as to where they were. Jaffar Rais took pity on her perplexity.

"We're off the coast of north-western Spain. This anchorage that we're in is in one of these islands marked here in Vigo Bay. We'll stay here a day or two to take on fresh water and make good the storm damage. There's time, too, for a little pleasure."

"Pleasure?" Celia looked questioningly at him as they walked out into the sunlight again.

He nodded. "I've driven my men hard. They need some drink and a few other diversions to keep them in good heart. The cargo also requires some attention," he added grimly but his last words were lost on Celia. She was watching with growing dismay what was happening below them in the waist of the ship. There, the hatches had been unbattened and the captives were being brought up from the hold.

Men, women and children, covered in filth and weak from the effects of their close confinement, emerged from the darkness into the sunshine, some of them too feeble even to stand upright. Seeing their condition, Celia cried out involuntarily, darting a quick look of anger at Jaffar Rais. He took no notice of her but stood with folded arms, surveying the state of his human cargo with a coolly professional eye.

An elderly man detatched himself from the group of prisoners, staggered a few steps and then fell heavily to the deck. Celia, who immediately left Jaffar Rais' side and ran to help, was within six feet of the prone figure before she realized who it was.

"Father!"

Squire Crace was so dishevelled and besmeared with dirt that his daughter had not at first recognized him. Kneeling down, Celia took his head on her lap.

"Celia?" He looked up at her with a vague, puzzled air so unlike his usual cheerful, confident one that she wept for the first time since her capture.

Around her on the deck the rest of the prisoners collected. Supporting her father in her arms, Celia examined each face anxiously, searching for her loved ones and shocked by what she saw.

Family groups clung together, some individuals crying, some staring about as though in a frightened daze, others, seemingly rendered too apathetic by sickness to take any interest in what was going on, merely lay on the deck.

Roger Crace, haggard and filthy like the rest, shouldered his way forward.

"Leah! You're all right then?"

She exclaimed with relief at the sight of him but he frowned, looking at her red Moorish robe.

"Where have you been, Leah? What has he done to you?"

"Never mind that," she answered impatiently. "Where are Mother and Anne? And Sim Greenfield and . . ."

Stephen Hillard replied to her questions, kneeling down by her on the deck with a howling child in his arms.

"Sim's here," he said. "He's a bit feverish, but better than he was. Anne and your mother . . ." He paused and then went on gently, "Well, we don't know for sure. They were taken into the other ship. Perhaps our gallant captor knows." He stood up to confront Jaffar Rais who had come down among them, a dozen or so of his men following.

Celia was aware of Sim in the background but before their eyes could meet Jaffar Rais came between them, standing face to face with the little parson of Combe.

"Master John Dunton has his orders," said the renegade to Stephen Hillard, "and he knows better than to disobey them. We may have lost sight of the *Jacob* for the time being but Dunton will bring her and the other prisoners safely to Sallee as soon as he can. In the meantime, parson, what's the count? There should be a hundred and two of you."

Jaffar Rais looked round on the cringing captives with a dull, business-like eye that calculated but registered no emotion. They might have been so many bales of cloth for all the feeling he showed, Celia thought resentfully. Yet she knew him to be capable of warmth and even of tenderness.

"We're a hundred and one now," Stephen Hillard answered, indicating a woman who stood clasping a very quiet, limp child. She was oblivious of everything about her and was crooning to it in a low, monotonous sing-song. "God forgive you, Jaffar Rais."

"I have lost a good oar slave, drowned in the storm," replied the corsair, without so much as glancing at the bereaved mother. "I need an able-bodied man for a replacement. How about you, Roger Crace?"

Celia was obliged to watch while two of the corsairs seized her brother. Helpless to intervene, she and Sim exchanged despairing glances. Sim's head was bound up in a dirty cloth. He was hollow-eyed, dressed in some disgusting rags, and had several days' rough growth of beard on his face and throat, but at least he was on his feet and in no immediate peril. It was Celia's brother who faced the corsair captain in his wrath.

Jaffar Rais beckoned his overseer forward, a huge man with a drooping black moustache and a shaven head who carried a heavy whip. The renegade jerked his head at Roger who, with one arm twisted across his back, had ceased struggling.

"Take a look at him, Bastiano."

Jaffar Rais added some words in a foreign tongue which made the watching corsairs laugh. The overseer tore Roger's shirt off his back and began feeling his muscles with finger and thumb. Then he pinched in his cheeks, forcing his mouth open to examine his teeth. He handled Celia's brother much as farmer might look over a work horse he was considering buying.

"For God's sake!" Celia, crouching on the deck, her father's head in her lap, appealed to Jaffar Rais. "What are you going to do with him?"

"Make him work for his living," the renegade answered vindictively. "That's something he's never done in his life before."

"Have pity," she said.

"As he did on me?" Jaffar Rais rounded on her furiously. "Ask him what became of the ransom money my father entrusted to him to redeem me from slavery. Because of him I suffered three years of hell. Then I found out the truth and learned to plan revenge." He glared at his cowering captives. "You know me, all of you. Tom Chandler from Combe Hollow. Roger Crace brought this on you. I'd never have raided Combe but for what he did to me. Now he's brought to book for it. Why don't you tell them the truth, Crace?"

"I'm not guilty," said Roger Crace desperately as the resentful murmuring of his fellow prisoners died away. He saw how they recoiled from him, preparing to reject and make him their scapegoat. "It's true the ransom was raised but I thought you were dead, Chandler. Everyone thought you were dead. I swear to God I'm not guilty."

"Swear all you like." Jaffar Rais cut him short. "You're as guilty as hell and you know it. Well, there'll be times when you'll *wish* that *you* were dead, especially if Bastiano finds you don't pull your weight." He turned to the overseer with a brusque order. "Strip him down and shave his head and chain him to the oar bench."

Seeing her brother being dragged below, Celia pleaded with Jaffar Rais.

"Won't anything persuade you to be merciful?"

Jaffar Rais looked at her coldly. "A good ransom, Lady Lovell." She saw, with despair, that he would brook no interference as he said in the same unfeeling tone, "Hard cash is what weighs with me. You had better get in touch with your rich friends and relatives in England as soon as you can and prevail on them to send the money for your ransom as soon as possible. If it is delayed the conditions of slavery in which you will be kept are likely to deteriorate. The same applies to all of you," he went on, with a warning glance at the people of Combe, most of whom trembled before him. "As for Roger Crace, the life of a galley slave is not usually very long, so his case is particularly urgent."

"But you promised . . ." Celia cried out angrily to him, but Jaffar Rais only laughed, pulling her to her feet, compelling her to leave her father lying on the deck.

"I could get all I wanted from you without promises,

little Leah, and you know it," he said.

"Harlot!" Sampson Derrey's wife, who had stood silent with the rest until now, suddenly awakened out of passivity and flew at Celia, scratching her face and tearing at her hair.

"No!" Stephen Hillard pulled the frantic woman back by the arms before the corsairs could get to her. "Mistress Derrey, control yourself. We are all at this man's mercy, Lady Lovell as much as any. 'Judge not that ye be not judged.' "

"You're a peacemaker, little parson," sneered Jaffar Rais, taking Celia's arm, as, shaken and frightened by the unexpected attack, she stood panting, with one hand pressed to her injured cheek. "Yet you threw the good book at me in Combe church."

Stephen Hillard looked at him levelly.

"I wish my aim had been better," he said.

"You're a bold man," said the corsair with a hint of approval in his voice. "You should have been a soldier not a priest."

"I want water and food and medicine for my people." Stephen Hillard spoke with angry compassion. "And the children at least must be allowed more fresh air and sunlight. They'll die in that black hole of a hold."

The corsair nodded. "I know. All that will be attended to. It's in my interest to see that the cargo reaches Sallee in good condition. I'm particularly anxious that those unlikely to be ransomed remain fit. It will affect their market price materially. Now, Lady Lovell, if you are ready."

With a parade of mock politeness he handed her to the ship's side. Celia looked down and saw a boat bobbing below. Between her and it stretched a long and fragile-looking rope ladder.

"Well," said Jaffar Rais, smiling contemptuously, "you're not afraid, are you?"

She was, extremely, but there was nothing for it but to climb down. The flowing red gown would get in the way, so she reached between her legs and pulled the back hem up, tucking it into the front of her sash and climbing down the rope, hand over hand as she had seen the seamen do.

"Well done."

Jaffar Rais, beside her in the boat, grunted approvingly, but she turned away from him, looking back at the ship where she had been compelled to leave her father and brother and Sim and the rest, feeling miserable and ashamed. For the first time she wished she could share their captivity, appalling as it was, rather than enjoy the doubtful privilege of being Jaffar Rais' mistress. She was an outcast now. Mistress Derrey's action had been symbolic of what the rest felt.

"It's terrible," she said, hiding her face in her hands. "Those poor children."

"Was their life so much better at home?" he asked harshly, pulling her hands away, as the seamen in the boat laid to their oars and rowed for the shore, the still blue water sparkling in the sunshine and curving away in ripples from their blades. "The labourers' children live in squalor from the moment they're born. Have you been inside a poor man's cottage, Lady Lovell? You'd think you were in a dog kennel if you went into one. Poverty and hardship and disease is all they know. The likes of you batten on their misery. You and yours brought me to this and you and yours are no better than I. But cheer up," he added mockingly, "you and yours are having the privilege of being allowed to make some amends."

"You're very cruel," she said.

He shrugged. "Not more so than other men when they have the power. Many who seem to be kind are only weak."

The boat was almost at the beach and he swung his legs over the side. Standing thigh-deep in the water he held out his arms to her.

"Well, do you want to swim?" he said when she hesitated.

Reluctantly, feeling the boat heaving perilously under her feet, she stood up, leaning towards him and he immediately took hold of her, carrying her in his arms up the sloping ridge of sand till they reached the shelter of the trees where he set her on her feet.

The sand was whitish-grey, gritty between her toes. She saw, without interest, how the fleshy stems of a creeping plant with heart-shaped leaves spread its long tendrils out almost to the brink of a shallow rock pool. She looked back towards the ship, full of regrets and belated concern for those of her family and friends still aboard.

Jaffar Rais, standing beside her, gave a cursory glance at the men who were filling water barrels from a stream that trickled down between boulders into the rock pool, and took her arm.

"Don't brood or worry," he said briefly, guiding her along a narrow, twisting path that led through the closely growing trees. Their branches met overhead shutting out the sun.

"How can you say that?" she demanded reproachfully. The cold ruthlessness with which he had treated the other prisoners made her feel a distinct dread of him. She suspected, too, that his seduction of herself was only a part of his revenge, a calculated and public humiliation of a woman whose family had wronged him.

"The worst is over for your friends," he said matter of factly as they walked together along the winding track. "You heard me tell the parson they were to be well treated. In two weeks, at most, the voyage will be over and we'll land them safe at Sallee."

"And then?"

They had emerged from the shelter of the trees and come out on to another stretch of sandy beach, much smaller than the one they had left. It was bathed in sunlight, grateful after the oppressive darkness of the wood and it was quite deserted except for the figure of an old man, stooping over a fire, who straightened up and waved to Jaffar Rais when he saw them coming.

The man was frail and bent and his mahogany-brown face

was wrinkled as a wizened apple. He was dressed in a curious patchwork of cast-off clothes, awkwardly held together by a broad leather belt that fastened round his waist with a large brass buckle. He grinned a gap-toothed grin as they approached, saying something in a strange language as he pointed to food which was cooking on a makeshift grid over the glowing ashes of the charcoal fire he had been tending.

Jaffar Rais dismissed him with a word and a touch on the shoulder and the old man shambled off, limping away into the shade of the trees along the path they had just travelled, leaving them alone together.

Celia saw that two rough woollen blankets of peasant weave, striped in red and yellow, were spread out on each side of the fire. Jaffar Rais waved her to one of them while he crouched over the embers, examining two fair-sized fish, wrapped in smouldering leaves, which lay on the grid, and poking about in the ashes with a stick.

Celia looked at the food and the blankets. She was tired and weak and hungry and the full danger of her situation as the corsair's prisoner was now overwhelmingly clear to her. She sat down reluctantly on the blanket with her chin on her knees, arms clasping her legs and staring out to sea. The tiny bay was sheltered and very blue and calm. A few feet away the gentle waves slid into ripples touched with swiftly vanishing foamy froth as they died out in the sand.

Jaffar Rais stood up.

"It's not quite done," he said cheerfully, indicating the food, unbuckling his heavy swordbelt and letting it fall to the ground, peeling off his breeches and kicking them aside, standing there in his shirt.

"You don't swim, of course, being a lady. Even you wouldn't dare be so unconventional. A woman has to be very poor and a nobody in England to enjoy such pleasures as that."

He stripped off his shirt and she watched him run down

naked into the water, broad-shouldered, narrow-hipped, small-buttocked, a lean, muscular, physically desirable man. When he had done splashing and swimming, he came back to the fire and stretched out on the blanket, letting the sun dry him.

"Fish is done," he said suddenly, sitting up and whisking them off the grid, exclaiming over his burnt fingers with such a typically masculine reaction that Celia had to smile.

"Let me do it."

There were no plates and the burned crust of leaves and clay in which the fish had been wrapped was charred black. Celia removed it gingerly with a sharp-ended stick, taking care not to let the steaming fish, so well-cooked that it threatened to fall off its bones, drop into the sand. There were fruits, covered from the flies, piled in the corner of her blanket, and she took some of the leaves laid over them to serve the fish in. Jaffar Rais took his in both hands, biting into it with appetite, white flakes falling from his mouth into the dark mat of hair on his chest.

Celia attacked her own portion more cautiously, but she found that, despite the primitive preparation, the fish was perfectly cooked and delicately favoured. She felt much better after she had eaten it. Jaffar Rais, lying naked on the other side of the fire, poured wine from a stone jar with a wicker covering into two earthenware cups. He leaned across, handing one to her and, as she bent forward to take it, she saw how ridged white scars, like skaters' tracks, criss-crossed his back down to the thighs.

"You must have been terribly beaten to be marked like that," she said involuntarily as her hands closed round the cup.

"No worse than they treat vagrants in England," he answered with a shrug, "and men of education and quality now, or so I hear, if they happen to speak or write things that King Charles doesn't like. It's not only the vile Turks," he grimaced sarcastically, "that use torture, you know, little Leah. Try some of this pineapple. It's good for your inside when you've been sea sick, or so they say. It seems good to me at any time."

He sliced into the hard rind of the fruit, cutting generous rings of it with his dagger, trimming off the scaly skin and picking out the brown parts with the point.

"What are you going to do to Roger?"

Jaffar Rais paused and frowned as she asked the question, but he did not answer Celia until he had eaten several bites of the succulent fruit and wiped the juice off his mouth with the back of his hand.

"I told you," he said shortly. "Make him work. Oh, I'm not going to torture him for the pleasure of it, if that's what you think. I might have wanted to once, when I learned it was he that had embezzled my ransom. In fact, I used to lie awake thinking of things I'd do to him, if once he came into my hands. But thinking and doing are two different things. Besides," he turned over and smiled at her, an intimate smile that made her tremble, "I haven't done so badly after all."

"Then why not have mercy?" She felt she must intercede for the others now that he seemed in this gentle, approachable mood.

"Why not take off that robe and let the sun get to your body?" he countered smoothly. "You'll feel better for it."

He saw her apprehensive look and laughed. "Oh, don't worry. I won't touch you. At least, not in that way, and not yet. Not till you want me to. It's always better that way."

"Yes," she said doubtingly. The sun was invitingly warm and relaxation and good food and wine made her feel a little light-headed. The red silk robe was easy to slip out of. She lay on her side, her head turned away from him and drifted into a pleasant doze.

She woke to feel his hand on her left buttock, gently kneading the flesh with his fingers. She sighed and wriggled and stretched as they strayed into the sensitive hidden parts of her body, creating a pleasant fluidity. He was lying so close to her that when she turned to him her nipples hardened instantly as they rubbed against his chest, responding to the random touch.

He took her wrists, drawing her hands down to his loins and she stroked him delightedly, enjoying the warm, happy twilight of the senses that sun and wine and good food can sometimes blessedly bring.

His questing finger, expertly sensitive, brought her to a pitch of exquisite pleasure that amounted almost to pain until their ardent coupling relieved it.

"Was it true what you said?" she asked, when there was time and breath and need, at last, for words.

"Was what true?"

Everything was an anti-climax now, but it did not matter, as they lay together, naked and unashamed with nothing to cover them but the broad bright heaven.

"That all you ask of a woman is that she should have good haunches and not hold back from a man?"

He laughed. The laughter welling up from within him out of sheer joy and content.

"No," he said, kissing Celia lightly on the brow. "It was a lie, though I didn't know it then. But I shan't tell you the truth. It would make you unbearable."

"Ah," she said, resting her head on his shoulder. "Just as long as I know."

They had lost count of time, but the echoing hail brought Jaffar Rais to his feet, clutching a sword as naked as himself which he drew instantly and instinctively the moment he realized they were not alone, turning in the direction from which the noise came.

Celia also got up, forgetting to cover herself in the haste and surprise of the moment, and saw the old man they had first seen at the fire standing among the trees with a seaman whom she recognized as one of those from the galleasse.

"Ships in the bay."

"How many?" Jaffar Rais went running up the beach

without so much as waiting to pick up his clothes.

"Three," shouted the sailor. "Spanish ships of war."

They vanished together into the trees, leaving Celia forlorn among the ruins of the love-feast with only the old scavenger for company. As he came towards her she snatched up her crumpled red silk robe and pulled it on.

Taking little notice of her, but mumbling to himself, the old man stuffed into his mouth scraps of cold food that he found amongst the now grey ashes and gathered up Jaffar Rais' scattered clothes. He signed to her to follow him, pointing towards the trees.

When she hesitated he said impatiently, "Rais. Jaffar Rais," as though the name and the man himself were all that mattered.

Celia followed him, realizing with a sense of helplessness and dismay that this was true of her. She was in love with Jaffar Rais and from now on would not know where her loyalties lay.

She overtook her guide and ran along the woodland path towards the sound of shouting.

13

John Dunton stood at the door of his house and waited. It was late, it was dark and he was very tired after his long journey from Southampton. He had been obliged to walk most of the way, begging lifts from passing carts wherever he could, for his pockets were almost empty and he needed the few coins he had to buy bread and pay the price of a night's lodging in the villages he passed through on his way home to London.

He was a proud man who had never been in debt to anyone in his whole life and he felt the humiliation of his near destitution keenly. Even now, at the end of his journey, and though he had gone hungry all day, he still had a few groats left.

The meagre amount of money had been enough to convince the suspicious beadle at Dartford, whom he encountered in the last stages of his painful pilgrimage home, that he was not a vagrant.

"Prisoner escaped from captivity on the Barbary Coast and on his way home to . . . Rotherhithe."

The beadle had spelled out the words hesitantly, narrowly scrutinizing the letter written for Dunton by the justices of the peace at Southampton who had acquitted him of the formal charge of piracy brought against him after he sailed the *Jacob* into harbour on the Isle of Wight.

Dunton had tried to look nonchalant in the face of petty officialdom whilst chafing at the endless frustrating delays which hindered his reunion with his family. He jingled the coins in his pocket ostentatiously.

The beadle's eyes gleamed.

"We get a lot of forgeries, Master Dunton." The beadle scratched his nose apologetically, handing Dunton back the letter. "There are all sorts of scoundrels on the roads these days, up to all sorts of tricks, pretending to be wounded soldiers and shipwrecked sailors, just so as to claim relief from the parish or as an excuse for sponging on kind-hearted citizens. You wouldn't believe."

"I think I would," Dunton had said wryly, folding his letter and putting it away again. As a man of simple probity he was finding the mistrust that greeted him everywhere hard to bear.

Things had looked bad for him at first. When he had admitted to the Southampton justices that he had been aboard the corsair vessel that attacked and took the *Jacob* they seemed to fasten on to that one fact and not be interested in any extenuating circumstances. A pirate, their accusing eyes said plainly, is a pirate.

Luckily, Bolitho had spoken up for him and also Mistress Anne Crace. Since she was a lady of good birth and breeding they had been more prepared to listen to her than anyone else. Learning from van der Velde about Dunton's son Richard, held hostage in Sallee, she had been able to convince the hostile magistrates that he was indeed a prisoner who had acted under duress. It was mainly on her recommendation that they were prevailed upon to release him.

The moment he knew himself to be free to leave, Dunton had gone to thank Anne Crace. She was in the house a hospitable merchant of the town had made available to the prisoners rescued from the *Jacob* until they could return to their own homes. Since they were first brought ashore she had been tireless in her care of them.

"You're going home," she said, getting up from the bedside of a sick woman and coming towards him as he stood, hat in hand, just inside the doorway of the crowded house.

"I can't wait to be there," he replied, anxious to be gone. "I've sent letters but there's been no answer."

"There'll hardly have been time for any reply to reach you," she said with quick understanding, instinctively seeking to soothe him. "Your wife will have her hands full getting ready for your homecoming without wasting time writing letters."

"Yes." He smiled suddenly. "Yes. And Rachel's not much of a hand at writing. Wonderful housewife, though," he added quickly, fearful lest he should have slipped into the least appearance of a disloyal criticism. "Wonderful mother, too."

"I'm sure she is," said Anne Crace gently. "Have you seen the baby that started on his way into the world just as you and the others locked those Spanish pirates in the fo'c'stle?"

She held up an infant, wrapped in a blanket and laughed. "We're going to call him Jacob."

"What else?" Dunton smiled, glancing at the child. His own youngest would be more than six months old now. "I must go. Goodbye and thank you, Mistress Crace."

"Farewell, Master Dunton." Anne Crace gave the formal words an informal and feeling emphasis.

Now, five days later, he waited, fretting impatiently on the doorstep of his house in Rotherhithe, footsore and weary and finding these last minutes spent listening for the sound of his wife's footsteps harder to endure than all the months before.

They were a long time coming, those footsteps, and when at last he heard them, he knew they were not Rachel's but some other woman's.

"Now, who's there?" asked a firm female voice from the other side of the solid oak door.

Dunton was ready to laugh outright with relief as he recognized the familiar tones of his wife's elder sister.

"It's me, John. Open up, Judith. It's not like you to keep a man waiting outside his own house when he's just new come home from sea."

"John!"

Chains and bolts were swiftly loosed and the door swung open. Judith Rainsborough, plump, neat and plain, grey-curled, pink-cheeked and smelling faintly of lavender, stood in the doorway holding a candle and staring open-mouthed.

"Oh, John."

She put the candlestick down and hugged him, sobbing.

"Well, let me in," he said laughing. "Where's Rachel and the girls?"

He looked over her shoulder to see his eldest daughter, Jenny, looking round the edge of the kitchen door, long fair hair streaming down over her white nightgown.

Next minute she was in his arms and he was sitting in his own chair at his own fireside with Dorcas and Deborah, his younger daughters, both clinging round his neck as well.

"Where's your mother?"

It was only when none of them answered and they all went on crying that he realized something was badly wrong.

"Judith?"

He looked at his sister-in-law over Jenny's shaking shoulders, stroking the smooth fair hair mechanically.

Judith Rainsborough was lighting candles with a long wax taper. She paused to blow out the flame before she answered, standing with the taper smoking in her hand, reluctant to speak, shaking her head compassionately.

"She's dead, John. Died above six months ago when the last baby was born. Little Martha."

He couldn't take it in at first, but sat looking bewildered, till Judith signed to the girls to leave their father a moment. Then she led him into the room where the baby was sleeping.

It was their bedroom. His and Rachel's. The bed was their marriage bed where she first lay with him as a bride. The bed in which all their five children had been begotten and born. It was empty.

Dunton stood looking down at the small body in the wooden cradle at the foot of the bed. The baby's face was half-hidden by a soft white wool shawl. He felt no urge to draw it aside.

"She did so want it to be a boy," Judith Rainsborough said regretfully.

"Yes," said Dunton. He had dreaded having to tell Rachel about Richard. Now he would have given anything in the world to be able to do so.

Judith Rainsborough looked at him a little reproachfully. She was a good woman, practical and kind when she could see a way of helping, but not imaginative or sensitive.

"Poor Rachel. She always had such a struggle to give birth. And this time . . ."

"Yes," said Dunton again, sitting down on the bed with his head in his hands, wishing Judith would go away or at least be quiet. She made it seem all his fault and, in a way, it was.

He could only think of one thing. Rachel was dead and he didn't know what he was going to do without her.

Anne Crace, coming to London a few weeks later to seek help from her brother-in-law, found Celia's husband in a very different frame of mind. It was evident to her, after only a short conversation, that Sir Edward Lovell was far from being inconsolable. It was not merely that the carriage of a lady of fashion drove away from his doorstep just as her own drew up at it but his appearance and manner when he greeted her which made Anne suspect he was not mourning her sister's absence.

"My dear Anne."

Edward's welcome was punctilious but not cordial as he offered her his arm and guided her up the steps into his elegant home. It was as cool and tasteful and comfortless as a mausoleum, Anne thought, as he bowed her into a chair and she looked around her at the chillingly austere classical beauty of the room. She began to understand how Celia might have been homesick for the earthy warmth of ramshackle Combe Hall. But Combe was just a blackened shell now, burned by the corsairs.

"You must be exhausted after your journey."

Edward hovered attentively. A poker-faced servant offered her wine on a gleaming silver tray, looking faintly and fleetingly disdainful when she asked for water with which to qualify it.

"This is an appalling business, truly appalling." Edward seated himself opposite her and sipped his wine appreciatively. "Your sufferings must have been - er - terrible."

He glanced away as he spoke and Anne stiffened, recognizing something in his tone which had become painfully familiar to her since her rescue from the *Jacob*. She was disappointed but not altogether surprised to divine that Edward evidently shared the general view, that the Barbary corsairs systematically raped all the women they captured. In fact, the corsairs respected women prisoners, not for altruistic reasons, but because they were valuable merchandise. They had discriminating, wealthy customers who would pay high prices for attractive virgins and it was not good business to damage such a saleable commodity.

Anne, who was modest and chaste, was not yet able to conquer the embarrassment she felt at the prurient stares and whispers she had to encounter in any company where it was known that she had been a prisoner of the Barbary pirates. She had even begun to wonder, ruefully, whether she ought not to get a covey of sober matrons to examine her and sign a certificate to the effect that she was *virgo intacta*. She could not help feeling that Edward, as a man of the world, ought to have known better.

"This is a dreadful thing for your family," he was saying. Anne noted that he did not say "our" family or even "the" family. She inclined her head.

"How is your mother?"

He was solicitous but not concerned, she thought.

"Not well, I'm afraid. Not well at all. She's staying with my aunt at Taunton. All this has been too much for her. The anxiety about father and Roger and, of course, Celia..."

"Yes, yes, indeed." He frowned, saying with more firmness of manner than actual conviction. "Something must be done."

"I wondered," said Anne, looking at him very directly, "exactly what was being done. It's not only our family and," she glanced down for a moment, "Stephen. It's not only our people from Combe even. I never gave it much thought before, I'm ashamed to say, but there are hundreds of English people held captive in the Barbary states and more are being enslaved every year. I'm told there are as many as a thousand in Sallee alone. Some of them have been there for twenty or thirty years. Surely the King..."

"My dear Anne," said Edward hastily, glancing behind him in case they should be overheard by the servants, "what you say is very sad and no doubt quite true as far as it goes, but the situation is a complicated one. Relations with the Barbary states in general and communication with the corsairs in particular is a tricky and uncertain business. Efforts have been made from time to time to redeem captives, but it's difficult and takes a long time."

Anne saw that he was prevaricating, making excuses to cover his own failure to act.

"I have been told," she said coldly, "that there are recognized and time-honoured methods of arranging the ransom of captives. The corsairs encourage the system because it is highly profitable to them. There are middlemen and brokers on the continent, especially in Holland and Spain, who act as intermediaries between prisoners and their families. Surely we can negotiate the release of our family and friends."

"Just so." Edward leaned back. "It is a question of money."

He paused, looking at her face for a moment. It was hard to believe that Anne Crace was Celia's sister, he thought.

They were as different as chalk from cheese. He had no wish to hurt Anne, she had clearly been through enough already, but he didn't want to be bothered with the Crace family troubles either. He'd regretted his marriage to Celia almost as soon as he'd gone through with it. She was not to his taste and he was, quite frankly, glad to be rid of her. She was the sort of woman it was amusing to have for a mistress but who was not at all suitable as a wife.

Sir Edward Lovell shuddered slightly. He had a keen sense of personal dignity and the idea of being made a laughing stock as a result of his wife's amorous indiscretions horrified him. Celia's abduction had come as a blessing in disguise. He would have preferred something less drastic to remove her, such as an accident or death in childbirth, but, as a prisoner in Barbary, she was as good as dead. In any case, he thought with distaste, even if he'd been fond of her, they would never have been able to live together as husband and wife after what had happened.

Of course, he thought, studying Anne's earnest, set face, you couldn't expect her sister to understand that aspect of the affair. It wasn't the sort of thing you could discuss with a woman like her. Or any woman, come to that.

He placed his fingertips together, preparing a careful answer calculated to dispel any unpleasantness, which of all things, he disliked.

"The fact is, my dear Anne, I think any action on our part would be unnecessary, perhaps even positively harmful to the captives' interests. I agree with you that the depredations of the Barbary pirates on our coasts are a national scandal. But my dear girl, you are not the only one who thinks so. Those in high places are not so indifferent to the problem as you suppose. All sorts of people have been pressing for a full-scale naval operation to be conducted against them and I am told that plans for one are actually under way at this moment."

"Against Algiers or against Sallee? If it's against Algiers

it won't help our family. The ship that captured them was from Sallee in Morocco, hundreds of miles from there and . . ."

"Exactly so." Sir Edward frowned. He did not like women who interrupted him. Celia's tendency not to let him finish a sentence was one of the things about her that he had found irritating. "I was speaking to Sir Harry Vane the other day . . ." He stopped, waiting for Anne to look suitably impressed, but she did not comply, so he went on, rather huffily, "He is comptroller of the King's household and also one of the principal lords of the Admiralty and he told me definitely that a naval squadron is being equipped to attack Sallee."

Anne leaned forward. "When, Edward? *When?*"

"Well, as to that, these things take time to organize. There's been a lot of trouble about raising money for provisioning the fleet. Public opinion's been demanding naval action but people don't want to pay for it. There's a tiresome Buckinghamshire squire called Hampton or Hampden or something who's been making a big fuss, saying the King ought to consult parliament first. That's the sort of people we're up against. That's . . ."

"Ship Money. I know," said Anne impatiently. "But when is this expedition to Sallee actually going to sail, Edward?"

"Some time in the new year, I'm told," he said with cold indifference. "I understand your friend, the reformed pirate, Master John Dunton, is to take part in it. Why don't you ask him?"

Anne stood up. Edward had betrayed his feelings openly in the last speech he'd made and she felt he was beneath contempt.

"Ask John Dunton," she said quietly. "You know, Edward, I think I will."

14

When Celia ran out of the wood on to the beach, the old man grunting and complaining as he toiled after her, the first thing she saw was a group of corsairs gathered round a man who was being beaten in a strange and brutal manner.

They had him head downwards with only his neck and shoulders resting on the ground, his ankles secured to a stout wooden pole supported on the shoulders of two of their number while a third belaboured the soles of his bare feet with a thick stick.

Jaffar Rais, who had snatched up a cloak and draped it round himself, stood listening to the excited report of the seaman who had called to him from the wood. They were both staring out to sea where the square topsails of three ships could just be seen in the distance, urgently conferring and totally ignoring the muffled but agonized cries of the victim.

It took Celia a moment or two to realize that it was Sim. As she was impulsively rushing to his aid, Jaffar Rais whirled round, ordering his men into the boats and back to the ship.

They obeyed unquestioningly. The two men holding the pole to which Sim's feet were bound dropped it instantly, releasing his ankles from the rope loops that secured them so that Sim's body fell heavily to the ground.

Celia dropped to her knees beside him. He was soaking wet and she guessed he had been caught trying to escape. He must have slipped overside and tried to swim ashore. He sat up after a moment and gingerly examined his feet with a rueful expression. They were very red and swollen.

"Well, I'm glad they stopped when they did. I wouldn't fancy the idea of crawling everywhere on my hands and knees," Sim said with a wry grimace.

"Oh, your poor feet!"

Celia found herself sobbing out of sympathy.

"Get up."

Jaffar Rais stood over Sim, the hastily assumed cloak hanging loose about him, and Celia saw the blatantly hostile look that passed between the two men.

"Get up," he said again.

"How can he?" she interposed angrily on Sim's behalf. "Didn't you see what they were doing to him?"

"A few strokes of the bastinado." Jaffar Rais' voice was heavy with contempt. "What did you expect?" he went on as Sim got up awkwardly. "Trying to swim for the shore in full view of the whole ship's company! Where did you expect to get?"

"Out of your clutches anyway." Sim sounded defiant, facing Jaffar Rais, planting his bruised feet firmly on the shingle without wincing.

"You're a fool, Greenfield," said Jaffar Rais, turning away. "Some captains would have you crucified as an example to the others not to try to escape. You've been lucky this time. Remember that. Chain him up when you get him aboard," he ordered two of his men who grabbed Sim and dragged him away.

Celia had to watch as Sim hobbled and limped over the sharp stones to the boat.

"It's barbarous," she said to Jaffar Rais, clenching her hands. "Haven't you done enough to him, without that?"

"It's the customary punishment. He got off lightly. Get into the boat. Do you see those sails?"

He took her by the elbow, propelling her forward and pointing at the same time.

"They're Spaniards and this is Spanish territory. If they bottle us up in this inlet we're done for."

He raced on ahead down the beach, shouting orders to his men to make haste, the cloak billowing behind him and Celia ran after him because there was no choice, snatching the bundle of his clothes from the old man and clambering into the stern of the boat in which he sat, her red silk skirts splashed with sea water to the waist and sticking clammily to her thighs.

As before when there was action, Jaffar Rais forgot about her completely. Reaching the ship, he climbed rapidly aboard, going up the ship's side hand over hand, leaving her to manage the best way she could. In the end, with the help of much pushing and pulling and clinging to a rope which burned the palms of her hands, Jaffar Rais' men hauled her aboard.

Celia did not like their rough, familiar handling of her and was glad to flee to the cabin for refuge as soon as she reached the deck.

She saw no sign of Sim, but she supposed he had been taken below. She felt sorry for him and the others and ashamed of her inability to help them. There was not, however, much time to indulge in regrets. Preparations were being made to get the ship under way as soon as possible. Celia was no strategist, but she could see the danger they were in. It was plain enough.

The inlet was a narrow triangular wedge of water and they were anchored at its apex. The Spaniards were approaching its base. If they reached it before the galleasse they could block her way of escape, penning her up in the inlet and pounding her into submission with their heavy guns while she lay trapped and helpless. Celia saw the Spanish ships bearing down on the corsair, square sails billowing white against a blue sky streaked with scudding, ragged clouds. They still looked a long way off but she could not guess how far. The rapidity with which the crew of the galleasse were responding to their orders showed how dangerous the situation really was.

Straining at the capstan bars under the oaths and blows of their officers they hauled the anchor inboard and she heard the now familiar sound of the overseers' whistles coming from the bowels of the ship, signalling the galley slaves to leap to their oars. For they did leap, she knew that now. They didn't sit as they toiled, the shaven-headed naked men manacled below, but leapt continually from the benches to which they were chained, flinging all their weight into the loom of the oars, subsiding after each effort only to be compelled to rise again immediately, obeying the insistent drum-beat that commanded them to use every vestige of strength to drive the ship forward.

The drum-beat was high. Very high, like a fevered pulse. The lashes cracked, urging the slaves to heartbreaking labour.

Celia thought of Roger chained to the oar bench. She thought and tried not to think.

Ought she to pray for a Spanish victory, so that Roger and her father and Sim and the rest would be set free? Yet, if the Spaniards were victorious, would it mean freedom? Celia had heard gruesome tales of English people who had fallen into the hands of the Inquisition. And there was Jaffar Rais. It was certain that if the Spaniards captured him he would be condemned to the galleys or worse.

She clung to the open cabin door, not knowing what to pray for.

Stephen Hillard knew. When the corsair vessel opened fire on the foremost Spanish ship and the ensuing cannonade terrified the captives, penned in the dark hold, his voice could be heard by them, when the thunder of the guns died away, calmly saying the words of the Lord's Prayer. The prisoners, who had been driven nearly frantic by the frightening sound of the gunfire, ceased screaming and joined in. In the intervals of comparative quiet which succeeded the crash of cannon, he recited such psalms as he knew by heart.

"Thou shalt not be afraid," the clear voice of the little parson of Combe went on, as though enunciating a new commandment, "for the terror by night; nor for the arrow that flieth by day; nor for the pestilence that walketh in darkness; nor for the destruction that wasteth at noonday . . ."

"All very well," muttered Tippett Collecock, crouched behind a cask, his hands over his ears, vainly trying to shut out the noise of battle overhead. "It's all very well to tell you not to be afraid. But it's another thing altogether to tell you how to be brave, parson."

"Give her to me, Mistress Derrey," said Charity Lidd to the harassed blacksmith's wife, who was trying to comfort a whimpering toddler while other scared children clamoured for attention from their mother. "There now," Charity scooped the infant into her plump, consoling arms, "I'll see to this one, bless her, and you look after the other poor mites."

Mistress Derrey, who the day before the corsair raid on Combe had been heard to say that no decent woman ought to so much as look at that brazen Charity Lidd, gratefully accepted Charity's help.

Jaffar Rais, indifferent to suffering, heroism and cowardice alike except in so far as they helped or hindered the working of his ship, saw with satisfaction the effect of the galleasse's first broadside on the enemy. They had scored a hit on the largest of the three ships that sought to bar their way. But the Spaniards had the advantage of the weather gauge and her two consorts, smaller yet heavily armed, were now coming into the attack.

Jaffar Rais looked to his chief gunner, a renegade Genoese, ugly and hump-backed but a master of his craft, ordering the forward gun crews to open fire on the two smaller Spanish ships as soon as they came within range. The Genoese passed the word to his men as they stood tensely waiting, sweating and powder-stained, lighted linstocks dangling from their blackened hands.

The galley slaves, prompted by Bastiano's snaking, heavy-thonged whip, roared and rattled their chains, adding their fearsome shouts to the sound of the guns as the galleasse went into action. The wretched captives, hearing the wolfish cries intended to terrify the seamen on the enemy ship, trembled and clung to one another in the dark hold.

"A thousand shall fall at thy side and ten thousand at thy right hand," went on Stephen Hillard's comforting tones, "but it shall not come nigh *thee*."

"Now I just wish," thought Tippett Collecock, his teeth chattering, "that I could believe that. Something tells me that I'm going to be one of the ten thousand!"

Celia, alone in the cabin, was confused by the frenetic activity all around, which she could not understand or take part in, but unlike the prisoners in the hold, she was at least able to see what went on. The gunfire was deafening, yet, strangely, she was too excited to feel afraid. It was terrifying yet exhilarating.

She stood in the cabin doorway, waiting for the smoke to clear after the reverberation of the last broadside died away and saw with surprise and dread how close the nearest enemy ship was. The masts and sails of the Spaniard loomed alongside. She could see men with muskets stationed in the rigging and others, below on the decks, preparing to throw huge cables with curved iron heads over on to the galleasse.

Curiosity overcame caution and she ventured out only to be ordered back by Jaffar Rais who, sweating, sword in hand, shouted to her hastily and wrathfully, "Get down! Get below! Can't you see they're going to grapple?"

He disappeared into the smoke of battle and she was forgotten as the grappling hooks thudded on to the galleasse's decks, drawing the two ships together. The Spaniards swarmed across after them.

Before Celia had time to understand or obey Jaffar Rais'

peremptory warning she heard two sharp cracks, one after the other, and was surprised to see the wooden planking on which she stood suddenly erupt in a cloud of flying splinters as a musket ball struck it. The next moment a man fell from the ratlines overhead, plummeting down to lie spreadeagled at her feet as she remembered seeing a shot bird fall.

There was blood on his face and she saw where the track of a musket ball had grooved the side of his head, ploughing up skin and hair on either side of it. Putting her hands under his armpits, she dragged him into the shelter of the cabin. It was only a few feet away, but he was limp and heavy and hard to move. As she struggled to pull him inside she heard the clash of steel and fierce shouts as the corsairs met the onslaught of the Spaniards hand to hand.

Once inside the cabin she tore strips of cloth to bathe and bandage the shallow scalp wound that bled profusely. She guessed the heavy fall had probably hurt the man more than the glancing bullet wound and wondered if his ribs were broken. She was still tying the ends of the makeshift bandage round his head when she heard the sounds of cheering.

Knowing it meant victory for someone she sprang to her feet, darted to the cabin door and looked out.

The Spaniards were in full flight, running from the corsairs, leaping over the side of the galleasse, back on to the deck of their own vessel or jumping into the sea.

Looking to see the reason for their sudden and precipitate withdrawal, Celia followed the direction of pointing fingers as the corsairs exultantly waved and yelled.

She saw that there were no longer four ships at the mouth of the inlet but six and the two newcomers had at their mastheads great green banners with the sign of the crescent in silver upon them.

As she stood staring the wounded man got to his feet and looked over her shoulder. Holding on by one hand to the bulkhead and pressing the other to his side, he began talking excitedly in a foreign language.

Puzzled, Celia tried to understand. He kept pointing to the two ships with the crescent standards and saying over and over, "Murad Rais! Murad Rais!"

The Spanish captain, who had led his men when they boarded the galleasse, now stood pinioned with Jaffar Rais' sword point at his throat.

"The chance of war, señor," said Jaffar Rais, courteous in triumph. "Your turn today. Mine tomorrow."

"If it please God."

The Spaniard inclined his head, looking disgruntled and unbelieving, but giving up his sword to the corsair with as good a grace and as much dignity as he could muster, seeing there was no help for it. He was calculating ruefully that the dowries of his four daughters would have to be sacrificed to pay his ransom. He wondered if they would ever forgive him for ruining their marriage prospects.

Already those of his men who had surrendered to the Sallee pirates were being stripped for the sake of their clothes, weapons and money.

The two green-bannered ships of Sallee whose opportune arrival had so rapidly deprived the Spaniards of all hope of victory had closed in on their kill.

The largest of the three Spanish ships, damaged in the first stages of the encounter with the galleasse, was already being boarded by the newcomers as was the smaller ship which had grappled on to her, their crews giving way before the furious onslaught of the corsairs.

The third Spaniard was making good her escape. With all sail set she was taking advantage of a favourable wind to put as much distance between her and the formidable pirates as she could.

Jaffar Rais, seeing the Spanish captain led away and the fighting over, settled his sword back in the sheath and wiped his face, turning to welcome his fellow corsair aboard.

The ruffian who now clambered on to the deck from a longboat full of men as ferocious-looking as himself, was a heavily-built, swarthy Dutchman with dark hair and moustachios, twice Jaffar Rais' age. He had a livid vertical scar between his eyebrows like a permanent, sinister frown, the light skin of the cicatrice contrasting hideously with the sunburned colour of the rest. In the broad sash at his thick middle he carried a number of daggers and pistols whose butts and hilts protruded from its folds in menacing array.

The wounded man, who still stood at Celia's elbow in the cabin, where they were both glad to remain for safety while the corsairs bound and plundered the conquered Spaniards, touched her arm and pointed at the old corsair who was greeting his own captain.

"Murad Rais," he said.

"You came in good time." The English renegade grinned exultantly at the Dutch one.

"It's the only time to come and be sure of a welcome, even from a comrade," answered the older man and the two of them gripped each other's arms, just above the elbow, in the ancient fashion of friends when meeting.

"You're slipping, Jaffar," said Murad Rais as they stood together on the deck. "You're on a lee shore here and they had you pretty nigh trapped."

Jaffar Rais grunted. "We had a stormy passage through Biscay and had to put in for water and repairs."

"I know. I guessed as much." The other nodded, watching unmoved as some of the corsairs strung up an unfortunate Spaniard by the heels and beat him with the flats of their cutlasses, demanding to know where there was money hidden on the captured Spanish vessel. "Lost your prize, too, didn't you, after a squall in the channel."

"The *Jacob*?" Jaffar Rais frowned. "How did you know about that? But she's not lost. I've good reason to think that her master is as anxious to see her brought safely into Sallee harbour as I am myself."

"Have you now?" The other darted him a shrewd look from beneath his heavy, scar-bisected brows. "That's not what I heard from the crew of the fishing boat I took off the Lizard five days ago. Their captain said the *Jacob* had been surrendered to the English and the men aboard her taken prisoner. Talk to him yourself if you like."

"I don't believe it." Jaffar Rais glowered.

The Dutch renegade shrugged. "As you will. But it's true, Jaffar. Wasn't the master's name Dunton?"

"It is and if he's done what you say then may God have mercy on him, for, by God, I'll not!"

Celia, seeing him striding towards her across the blood-smeared decks of the galleasse, wondered what had happened to put him in such a towering rage in his moment of victory.

15

"Doing well for yourself as usual, I see!"

Murad Rais leered at Celia as he leaned forward from the cushion where he lolled and dipped his grimy hand in the dish of rice he was sharing with his fellow captain, Jaffar.

The old renegade's look made Celia feel unclothed from head to foot although, in fact, she was more adequately clad than she had been since she was first captured. The Spanish captain's private baggage had contained a selection of women's clothes, mostly of high quality and presumably intended for his wife and daughters. Jaffar Rais who, as leader, had his pick of the plunder, took the best gowns for Celia and she was pleased to find that they fitted and became her.

It was uncomfortable and incongruous, however, to be dressed in bronze satin and flounces over the conventional number of voluminous stiffened petticoats, and yet sit on the cabin floor and eat from a communal dish with the fingers. In particular Celia did not care to be so close to Murad Rais, who reeked of sweat and garlic and kept eyeing her in such a way as to make her wish the bodice of her dress was not cut so low. She drew her taffeta stole round her shoulders with a reproving gesture and he laughed aloud.

"What are you going to do with her?" he asked Jaffar Rais familiarly. "Put her up for sale on the open market or . . . ?" He scratched his nose with a knowing, suggestive expression.

Celia bridled indignantly but Jaffar Rais gave her a hasty,

sidelong look which warned her to be silent.

"Oh, she's a lady of title." Jaffar Rais affected indifference as he reached for a morsel of savoury mutton. "I expect a substantial ransom for her. In the circumstances she can expect protection and preferential treatment. After all, it's good business and customary, as you know. If anything happens to her," he paused significantly, "I stand to lose a lot of money."

"Hm." Murad Rais scrutinized Celia with undisguised interest. "She's a handsome woman, just the sort the Caid would fancy. Is she a virgin or married?"

"Married." Jaffar Rais frowned.

"Oh, well then," Murad Rais laughed. "You might as well sell her. I know these high-born gentlemen. They never want a woman back once she's been captured. All they think about is their honour. They'd sooner she was dead than in our hands. Of course, with virgins it's different. You've got something to go on there." He winked obscenely at Jaffar Rais, to Celia's extreme disgust, and said, "As for this one, if you'll take my advice you'd better by half have the amina look at her as soon as we dock at Sallee."

"And who," asked Celia, unable any longer to endure in silence a conversation which was every minute becoming more insulting to her, "is the amina?"

"She talks as well!" Murad Rais gave a great chuckling belly laugh and leaned back on the green silk cushions, belching as he did so. "The amina, my love, is a woman agent employed by the slave dealers to examine, itemize and estimate the price of female captives. She looks their bodies over in minute detail and assesses the value of their assets. Thus - a pair of fine eyes are worth fifty ducats, a pair of good, firm breasts, say a hundred, while ..."

"That's enough, Murad," interposed Jaffar Rais, noting Celia's rising fury with apprehension and deliberately turning his comrade's talk to the prospects of fair weather for the remainder of their voyage.

For they had left behind them the Isles of Bayonna, lying scattered in the sea off the coast of Galicia like a broken necklace in a woman's lap, Monteagudo, Faro, San Martin, Forcado and some, like the one where they had anchored, too small to name. Celia had watched them fade away into the northern distance as the galleasse sped southward down the coast of Spain, making for Morocco and the corsairs' home port of Sallee.

Leaving the men in the cabin to celebrate their victory, she went out on to the deck, standing with one hand twisted into the rigging to support herself, letting the wind fan her hot cheeks. The talk of Murad Rais had brought home to her for the first time the horrible degradation of slavery. It was not so much that she feared for herself, since she believed Jaffar Rais would be as good as his word and protect her for as long as it suited him, but she thought of the impending sufferings of the other women prisoners with genuine compassion. It was a feeling which, in her superficial life, she had not often experienced and she found it distressing and disturbing.

Jaffar Rais had been furiously angry when he heard of John Dunton's defection but Celia rejoiced that her mother and sister would be spared the humiliation of which Murad Rais had so openly talked. As for the others, she made up her mind to intercede for them although she knew that to do so meant risking the wrath of Jaffar Rais. His temper was frightening, his memory for injuries long. She hoped he cared enough about her for their relationship to withstand some of the strains she would have to put upon it. The trouble was that, being in love with him, she was tempted to forget everything but that.

She heard his step, but not soon enough to turn round before he came up quickly behind her, as he liked to do, sliding his hands under her armpits to caress her breasts, feeling for her nipples and kissing the back of her neck so that she trembled and her knees became weak.

"He's gone," said Jaffar Rais. "Come back to the cabin."

"All that talk of selling," she said, when they were alone and private. "It's degrading. You wouldn't subject me to that?"

He was undressing her and swearing over the complex fastenings of the formal Spanish gown.

"Would I take this much trouble with you if I meant to make you a slave? Don't be a fool, Celia."

She found it difficult to resist him in anything and was strongly tempted to undo the lacings with which he was fumbling so ineptly, but she had made up her mind to speak out.

"What will happen to the other women?"

He gave an exclamation of satisfaction as the bronze satin slid to the floor. Celia's breasts were now effectively bared but there were still the petticoats to contend with. She kept her arms close to her sides and refused to help him.

He gave her a swift glance of exasperation before attacking the petticoats. "Damned furbelows! I'm sorry I gave them to you! Other women? Why should you care about them? I don't. The Greenfields can arrange ransom terms, so they'll be lodged and fed until the money comes through. As for the others they'll be examined in private by the amina and offered for sale to reputable dealers. It'll all be done decently."

"Decently!" The last of the petticoats had slipped down and he stood back to admire her. Celia's body trembled as she demanded furiously, "Do you call selling women decent?"

"You're a fine one to talk of decency!" He took hold of her roughly, one hand placed firmly on her buttocks, pressing her up close to him. "Suppose your fine gentleman of a husband could see you now!"

It was the knowledge that Edward would not really have cared rather than Jaffar Rais' mocking tone that made Celia lose her temper. She pulled away from him, grabbed a jug of wine that came to hand and flung the contents over him. At least, that was what she meant to do. In fact most of it went on the floor and what was left spilt over them both equally.

She stood there with the jug in her hand and the red wine running down over her bare breasts and on to her belly and thighs and trickling between her legs. Jaffar Rais laughed.

"You should just see yourself!"

She slapped his face then, as hard as she could and he pulled her down on the cushions and smacked her rump very soundly indeed as they tumbled together, enjoying the tussle and forgetting, in their mutual pleasure, that there had ever been anything to quarrel about.

When passion had run its course with proper ardour and they lay together, comfortably relaxed, if a little sticky with wine stains, Celia asked him again about the fate of the other women and found him, as might be expected, more sympathetic.

"I'll do my best to see that they're protected," he said, with an air of magnaminity. "We can perhaps arrange for them to go to homes where they'll be well treated." He stretched himself, yawning luxuriously.

"And the men?" Celia stroked his chest, but he only grunted.

"They must take their chance as I had to."

He turned to her again with enthusiasm.

"Is that all you can talk about?" he said.

Physically they were ideally suited and temperamentally, too, they had much in common, sharing a passionately impulsive approach to life, finding danger and insecurity stimulating rather than frightening.

When Jaffar Rais first made love to Celia it was as Tom Chandler from Combe Hollow, the despised, wronged outcast taking his revenge on the sister of Roger Crace, but their relationship had undergone a subtle change in the few days they had spent together on board ship and on the nameless island in Vigo Bay. She excited and satisfied him more than any other woman in his experience. He had an uneasy feeling that he was beginning to need her as a person and not merely as a woman.

"What will you do when we get to Sallee?" she asked, smiling at him drowsily in the warm, companionable peace that succeeds an entirely successful fusion of bodies.

Jaffar Rais put his hands behind his head and looked up at the low deck beams above. He felt in a pleasant state of euphoria unique in his experience, better than when he was drunk or when he fought. Momentarily it coloured the whole of life for him.

"I'll be welcomed into harbour. They'll all turn out to greet us. It's a great time when you return from a successful voyage." He stroked her hair absent-mindedly, visualizing the scene.

"And then?" She looked up at him wonderingly, her hands still on his body, wanting to enter into his thoughts.

"Sell my cargo. Celebrate with my friends. Plan the next voyage." He laughed, thinking of it.

"And I?"

"What do you want?"

She took a deep breath. "Not to return to England."

He turned over on to his side, leaning on his elbow and looking at her.

"You'd stay with me willingly?"

She nodded.

"I wonder," he said, "if you really understand what that would mean. It's another world, it's so utterly unlike England. I thought it was hell at first. But it's different for a man. You don't know what's ahead of you, Leah."

"I know what I've left behind," she answered, thinking of Edward and the empty, lonely days in the empty, lonely house in London.

"I'm a convert to Islam," Jaffar Rais grinned at her. "All of us renegades are. I'm circumcised. For women there's nothing as painful to undergo. You just have to raise your little finger in acknowledgement of Allah and his Prophet. It's purely a formality. That done, I could make you my wife."

"Why, captain," Celia smiled at him, "is this an honourable proposal of marriage?"

"Honourable or not," he grinned back, "it's the best I can do."

Their talk had become unwittingly serious. Celia suddenly realized that she was meditating cutting herself off entirely from family and friends. The thought was daunting.

She said softly, "And my father?"

He paused a moment before answering.

"If you'll do as you've promised I'll release him without ransom."

Celia hardly dared ask the next question.

"And my brother?"

His whole body stiffened and the lines of his face hardened.

"He must take his chance."

She sighed, seeing it would do no good to argue.

"Can I at least look after the health of the other prisoners and do what I can to help them?"

He considered a moment, frowning slightly. Women always took advantage of unguarded moments to prise favours out of you. Was she, he wondered, only like the rest, after all?

Then he looked at her and decided she wasn't.

"As long as you don't interfere with the working and discipline of the ship you can do what you like."

Celia couldn't, of course, but she did all that was in her power to make the lot of the captives more tolerable during the few days that were left before the galleasse docked at her home port of Sallee.

It wasn't easy. With two notable exceptions the prisoners regarded Celia with suspicion and hostility. Her father refused all concessions and comforts offered him because he considered them the price of his daughter's shame. Squire

Crace held stubbornly to the belief that Celia has been the corsair's unwilling victim. Any other view was unthinkable and therefore untenable. Poor Sim Greenfield, more battered and bewildered than he'd ever been before in the course of his comfortable life, would have liked to share the Squire's belief in Celia's innocence. As it was, he tried not to think about it at all. Of the rest, only Stephen Hillard and Charity Lidd were disposed to give Celia the benefit of the doubt.

Celia felt the mistrust of her as she walked among the prisoners on the deck. She had won for them the privilege of more hours of freedom from being penned up in the dark, stinking hold, better food, as much water as they wanted and release from chains, but they thought of her as an enemy, not one of themselves.

"I can't help it, parson," said Mistress Derrey obstinately to Stephen Hillard when he gently remonstrated with her. "I can't take back what I said to that woman. She *is* a harlot. Always was from a little girl, flirting and flaunting herself. And now carrying on like she is . . ."

The woman's tongue rattled on, taking vengeance in words because she had no other means of action and making Celia the object of her denunciations because she was too much in fear of her captors to risk railing against them.

"Never mind, my lady," Charity Lidd smiled comfortably at Celia as they rescued two of the healthier children from a watery grave when they essayed to climb up the ship's side and watch the leaping dolphins following in the wake of the galleasse. "Don't take any notice of those old besoms. They're just jealous because they don't know how to pleasure a man and never will, not if they had twenty children to show for their wedding ring. I've had to put up with their backbiting all my life and it doesn't mean anything. Sheer spite, that's what it is. Look, lovey, see him jump!"

Charity held up the ragged urchin in her arms and let the little boy see how the porpoises leapt joyfully in the sunshine, arched bodies curving as they played in the sparkling blue water. Celia looked at Combe's most disreputable inhabitant with gratitude.

Charity, sharing the child's pleasure in the sight of the playful dolphins, looked sane and sensible and even cheerful, standing there in her stained and torn clothes, leaning against the ship's side. Already her cheeks were beginning to take on a healthy tan from the hot sun.

A flying fish, leaping with more power and abandon than the larger dolphins, came flapping in over the bows to lie feebly pulsating in the scuppers. A grinning seaman, coming down hand over hand through the rigging, picked it up by the tail and made signs to Charity that it was good to eat. She smiled back at him with frank friendliness.

"Well, they're only men, aren't they?" she said to Celia.

But the plight of the children was pitiful. Several were suffering from dysentery in some form or other and were very miserable. Most of the prisoners had never been more than a few miles away from Combe and were filled with dread at the prospect of what awaited them in Sallee.

"What are they going to do with us?" was the question they constantly asked Celia when she went among them and she did not know how to answer truthfully without frightening them still further. "Sold? Going to be sold? You don't sell people. You only sell cows and sheep."

"It'll be like the hiring fair," she answered, desperately trying to think of a parallel for the Moorish slave market.

"But women and children don't go to the hiring fair. Where shall we live? What shall we do?"

Celia gave up trying to say anything in reply. After all, she knew so little herself.

But none of their questions caused her so much distress of mind as the unspoken reproach in Sim Greenfield's eyes.

Greatly daring, she took an opportunity of speaking to him as he exercised on deck with the rest of the prisoners. Seeing Sim stand staring with unseeing eyes at the shores of Africa as they slid by in a shroud of early morning sea mist, a waste of barren white sand beyond the breakers, she placed herself near him.

"I would help you if I could." He was scarcely able to hear her voice it was so quiet, almost drowned by the mere sound of the waves and the soughing of the southerly wind in the shrouds. Neither looked at the other.

Sim said bitterly, "You couldn't help yourself, it seems."

"Can you raise the ransom money? Perhaps I can intercede with..."

"No! No! For God's sake, Celia! Do you think I want help at *that* price?"

He moved away and Celia remembered the words of Murad Rais about gentlemen thinking of nothing but their honour. Even he, she thought, would sooner that she were dead than the mistress of Jaffar Rais. Strangely, the bleak thought straightened her back and lifted her chin, for she was suddenly made aware of the need to keep her pride in the face of so much contempt.

So she stood proudly, dressed in the best of her plundered finery at the side of Jaffar Rais as the galleasse sailed triumphantly into Sallee roads. Crescent banners streamed from the mastheads and the dwarfish Genoese gunner ordered his gun-crews to fire round upon round of shot into the air to proclaim the success of the voyage to the watchers on the ramparts. The two ships of Murad Rais followed the galleasse, one with a Spanish prize in tow, the spoils of the encounter at the Isles of Bayonna.

"Jaffar Rais is returned! Jaffar Rais!"

The word spread through the new town and the old, going from mouth to mouth along the towered battlements that overlooked the harbour, shouted down the narrow streets with their fast-closed doors, echoing through the cool inner halls of the palace of Sidi el Ayachi, tossed along the stalls in the bazaars and bawled through the shipyards and docks where the workmen put down their tools and cheered.

"Jaffar Rais has come back!"

Slaves toiling in the fields or in the stone quarries beyond the town, paused in their labour, if they dared, and, mindful of the overseer with his whip, stole a look out to sea and passed the word along to the next worker.

The Arab slave dealer called to his Negro body-guards to accompany him and, well provided with money concealed about his person, hastened down to the harbour, hoping for first pick of the slaves aboard the galleasse. His fellow dealers, all sharp business-men, Moriscos, Jews and renegades, followed his example, all hoping to buy the best specimens at the lowest possible prices and re-sell at a handsome profit.

Père Gracian, of the Order of the Most Holy Trinity, heard the shouts as he knelt before the altar in the bare stone chapel in the Street of the Mazmorras. The mazmorras were subterranean prisons, hollowed out of the rock on which the casbah of the new town was built, and originally meant to store grain. They were now used to house hundreds of Christian slaves, from captives awaiting ransom to wretches who had been toiling in the quarries for a score or more years. It was the vocation of the Order of Trinitarians to which Père Gracian belonged, to minister to these captives.

Père Gracian had heard the triumphant gunfire of returning corsairs many times during his fifteen years of service in Sallee and knew better than any what misery their human cargoes suffered. He rose stiffly, his joints sore from kneeling on the bare ground, reverently removing his tattered cassock and stole to reveal the worn white habit of his order with the red and blue cross upon it. He looked once more towards the altar and went down to the harbour.

Aboard the galleasse, Jaffar Rais pointed towards the shore.

"The Tower of Hassan," he said to Celia. "The landmark that guides us into harbour."

She saw the great square tower of the ancient but unfinished mosque standing up stark and tall beyond the casbah of New Sallee, along the left bank of the river and gazed with wonder at the city of the corsairs.

Already long narrow galleots manned by swarthy oarsmen were coming out from the town to greet them. One boat, flying a red banner, came alongside as the galleasse rode at anchor outside the harbour bar and Jaffar Rais hurried forward to welcome aboard the portly official who arrived puffing and panting on the deck after an undignified scramble up the ship's side.

Celia heard the words "limam rais" passed along the deck. She knew now that "rais" merely meant "captain" but guessed from the deference accorded the newcomer that he must be the representative of the governor of New Sallee.

He went below to inspect the cargo with Jaffar and Celia watched, fascinated, the array of boats in harbour. The limam rais' barge, she noticed, was handsomely gilded and painted with a device with which she would become familiar – the shoes of the Prophet. Its crimson flag, borne out on the wind, showed an ominous triple device of a winged hour-glass, an arm wielding a scimitar and a death's head with crossed bones. It made clear to all that resistance to the Sallee corsairs brought swift and certain death.

The limam rais departed, returning to his barge with much ceremonious leave-taking, a handsome present from Jaffar Rais for his master, the Caid, governor of New Sallee, and a still handsomer bribe for himself.

Jaffar Rais took the helm, preparing to pilot his ship in over the harbour bar. Seeing his set expression, Celia knew better than to speak to him, but it was the season of deep water after the spring rains so his task was easier than it had been when he left Sallee.

On shore his partners in the venture who had invested money in the voyage waited for him to disembark with eager anticipation as the brothel and tavern keepers did also. Into their hands most of the money allotted in carefully graded shares to the members of the crew would eventually come.

Abdallah, who kept the house with the hand of Fatima above the door, shook Areefa awake. The girl was sleepy after entertaining many customers the night before and cursed him when she felt his hand on her shoulder, rolling over and wrapping herself in her mantle.

"Jaffar Rais has come home!"

"What?"

She was instantly awake and on her feet.

"I thought that would rouse you." Abdallah grinned wickedly at her. "You'd better put some clothes on before you go out on the quayside unless you want to be brought home the way you were last time. Not that it wasn't a good advertisement for the house."

Abdallah watched Areefa as she stooped to pull on her yellow slippers, his eye noting, with professional interest, the firm, full curves of her lithe and sinuous brown body. She'd be good for another three years in the business at least, he thought, unless she got the sickness. That was always a risk, but the physicians seemed to be able to keep it in check. Areefa, decorously clad in a long, shapeless robe of flowing green silk and with a veil over her face, pushed past him, impatient to get down to the harbour and Abdallah smiled at her eagerness, rubbing his hands. A good deal of Jaffar Rais' prize money would come to him through the girl, just as it had before. He was confident of that.

In the slave-quarters belonging to Ali Zuni, the dealer, old William Trevor was doing his best to reassure a thin, fair-haired boy with a remarkable likeness to John Dunton, that all would be well.

"They say Jaffar Rais is back!"

The boy was trembling with excitement and near to tears. "My father will be here, won't he, Will?"

Old William nodded, patting the boy's shoulder.

"He'll be here all right, Dicky boy."

"Poor lad," he thought, "I wish I could be sure. It's a poor look out for him if Dunton's had a chance to escape and taken it. They'll whip him into one of these boys' brothels they're so fond of here before you can say 'knife'. I've known it happen before."

"Can I go down to the harbour with you, Will? Please."

The old man hesitated. He was a privileged slave who had been in Ali Zuni's household so long he was almost like one of the family and enjoyed more liberty than most of his kind. However, he had to tread warily. He knew only too well the arbitrary temper of his employers. One offence, even though slight and unintentional, could wipe out the memory of many years' faithful service and earn him, old as he was, the fiendish punishment of the bastinado or worse torments.

William Trevor looked doubtfully at the boy. Richard Dunton was biting his nails in a fever of anxiety. It was a habit which had much increased since he had been left behind by his father.

"All right," said the old man, adjusting the harness of his rough-haired donkey. "Help me fill the water pots and ask the mistress if you can go with me."

His mistress, Ali Zuni's plump, pale-skinned current favourite, was preparing to go to the public bath house, the bagnio, with *her* current favourite, a muscular Negro, in attendance. With little in mind but the Negro's splendid muscles, Ali Zuni's concubine easily granted William Trevor leave to take the boy with him. She was glad everyone was going down to the docks to welcome Jaffar Rais for it meant that she and her handsome black lover would have a good deal of time to themselves. She wriggled her fleshy hips in their full, filmy trousers in pleasurable anticipation and the Negro smiled at her, a wide, white, beaming smile.

The galleasse drew alongside the wharf at New Sallee. As Jaffar Rais waved, acknowledging the cheers of the crowds lining the quay, the galley slaves, responding to Bastiano's whistle, let go their oars and slipped them overside. Longshoremen in galleots towed them away with ropes and the slaves' chains were loosed. Armed corsairs stood guard over them as new manacles, binding them together in groups of six, were fitted to their wrists and ankles. After the cargo was unloaded they would be taken ashore but these precautions were always necessary, Roger Crace's fellow slaves told him, to prevent escapes or attempted mutiny. Galley slaves, freed of their chains, had seized command of vessels before now, they hinted, looking sideways, wolfish and watchful, at their captors.

Celia's brother, chained to the rowing bench between a gigantic Russian who never spoke but in grunts and a Fleming who swore at him when he didn't react quickly enough to the unfamiliar orders, had no thought but that his life had become hell. His hands and back were raw. He had been compelled to labour beyond the limits of what he had believed physically possible and obliged to live on rock-like biscuit, fighting like an animal over any foul scraps that might fall in the filth at his feet.

When they struck off his chains and his limbs were free for a few minutes before the next set of shackles were riveted on the feeling was strange. The savage Russian bared his teeth like a wild beast and Roger wondered how long it would be before he, too, ceased to be human. He dared not think of what lay ahead.

Stephen Hillard, seeking for words to comfort his flock, found none. The only psalm that came to mind was, "By the waters of Babylon," and the line "How shall we sing the Lord's song in a strange land?" kept running through his head.

Eyeing the captives paraded on the deck of his ship, listening to the clamour of the cheering mob, Jaffar Rais savoured his triumph. He had made good his vow and taken his revenge, bringing back in chains the man who had condemned him to slavery in High Barbary.

He turned purposefully towards the shore and the welcome that awaited him.

16

"I've seen Vane. It's all decided. The expedition to Sallee sails in January."

William Rainsborough knocked out his pipe on the side of the fireplace with an air of satisfaction.

John Dunton shook his head doubtfully.

"The king gave his consent, then. I never thought he would."

"Had to." William Rainsborough leaned forward and grimaced. He was a thin, stoop-shouldered, severe-looking man of forty-eight, one of the most honest and efficient senior officers in King Charles I's dishonestly and inefficiently-run Navy. "Had to," he repeated significantly, scraping out the bowl of his long-stemmed Dutch pipe, then refilling it with good Virginia tobacco which he tamped down carefully with his fingers before lighting it with a live coal deftly gripped in the fire tongs. "The Newfoundland fishing fleet daren't put to sea for fear of being taken by the Sallee Rovers."

"I heard." Dunton looked grim.

"Well," Rainsborough leaned back in his chair, the pipe stem gripped between his teeth, "that's serious, isn't it? English seamen afraid of a handful of lousy renegades operating out of some God-forsaken port in North Africa! Drake would turn in his grave at that. The corsairs are getting bolder every year and petitions are pouring in from all parts of the country demanding that action be taken. The

King's got to show that the Ship Money he's made people pay is being used to good purpose."

"The decision's been taken for political reasons then." Dunton sounded bitter. Expediency, not humanity, would compel the authorities to act now that it was too late to save many who had been prisoners for years or who had died in captivity.

Rainsborough was frowning at him. Dunton's brother-in-law was a harsh, upright Puritan with a strong sense of duty.

"Whatever the reason, the decision to send a squadron to subdue Sallee has been taken. Let's be thankful for that, John. I should have thought you'd have jumped at the chance."

"Chance?"

Dunton raised his head, looking at Rainsborough enquiringly.

"Why, yes." Rainsborough sounded impatient. "I'm to command the squadron and I want you with me, John. I need your skills as a navigator. No one knows those Barbary waters better than you, especially the conditions in Sallee roads. I've already put your name forward as sailing master of my flagship."

Dunton got up and went to the door, looking out into the garden of his home, glimpsing beyond the ragged border of yellow-leaved willows at its end the masts and sails of ships passing on the Thames. In the foreground his daughter Dorcas was pushing her younger sister Deborah on a swing slung from the branch of an old apple tree.

"It's your duty." William Rainsborough's voice sounded uncompromising and inexorable. Dunton sighed. As if that made it any easier!

Emerging from the kitchen, red-faced and flustered, Judith Rainsborough pushed past him, calling shrilly to the two girls at the swing.

"Dorcas, Deborah! Stop idling about and come and get on

with your sewing. Neither of you have done a decent seam today. And I'd be glad, John," Dunton's sister-in-law said, turning to him with an air of indignation as his daughters began dawdling reluctantly towards the house in answer to her summons, "if you'd speak severely to Jane and tell her she must stay in and mind her baby sister instead of hanging over the gate talking to young men to the scandal of the neighbourhood."

Dunton sighed again. He was aware of Jenny standing behind him, tearful and defiant, as she almost always was these days and of the baby, Martha, howling somewhere in the background.

"Do as your aunt tells you," he said with an attempt at severity to Dorcas and Deborah who came sidling in, each as sulky as the other. Apprehensive, he glanced at his eldest daughter who met his gaze with an appealing look. She seemed very unhappy, he thought regretfully, and she and Judith never agreed about anything.

"You too, Jenny." He tried to sound firm. Judith Rainsborough bridled, triumphant, beckoning all three girls after her into the kitchen. They followed with a dejected air but not before the eldest had bestowed a reproachful look on her father.

Rainsborough grunted understandingly. "Judith's a good woman," he said, by way of apology.

"Yes, yes." Dunton bent forward to poke the fire, trying to hide the exasperation he felt. "I don't know what I should have done without her."

Rainsborough cleared his throat. "Of course it's a lot for her. If you'll take my advice you'll give up this house and move in with us. Six months is a long time to leave growing girls but you'd have nothing to fear with Judith in charge of them."

"You assume," said Dunton, "that I shall accept this appointment you're offering me."

"Look here, John," the Puritan sea captain sounded more

ponderous than before, "I've said it's your duty. You know that and it seems to me that should be enough, but it looks as though I need to remind you about Richard and all the other captives who look to us to save them."

Dunton kept his head down and, confident that he had made the desired impression, Rainsborough went on, "I'm getting the *Leopard* for flagship. A sweet craft, John. Six hundred tons, thirty-six guns, one hundred and eighty men . . ."

His voice droned on. Dunton was thinking that Rainsborough had no idea what they would be up against when they reached Sallee. The big ships would have to anchor far out in the bay, beyond range of the shore, unable to venture further in because of the rapid shoaling of the sea bottom towards the harbour bar. It wouldn't be the first time a European punitive expedition had tried to attack Sallee and failed, their ships lying at anchor in thirty fathoms of water whilst the small pirate craft scuttled in and out over the harbour bar under cover of darkness with impudent contempt for their big enemies' unwieldy helplessness.

"Then there's the *Antelope*, same tonnage as the *Leopard*, but you know that, of course." Rainsborough took Dunton's abstraction for absorption and warmed to his theme. "*Hercules*, *Mary Rose* and *Mary*, all four hundred, and two new pinnaces, still on the stocks but nearly finished."

Rainsborough's description of his squadron was interrupted by the sound of Judith's voice shrilling angrily from the kitchen and the sight of Jenny rushing out into the garden in a flood of tears.

"Hm. Needs a firm hand, that girl," he remarked grimly, seeing his wife emerge, prickling and bristling with righteous indignation, in the wake of the weeping Jenny. "At sea you leave all that behind you," he muttered to the downcast Dunton, adding aloud, "I knew I could count on you, John. There'll be a meeting of captains and principal navigating officers in a day or two. I'll send word to you when the time and place are fixed."

Rainsborough rose and turned to Judith, who stood waiting in her hat and shawl.

"Ready, my dear?"

He gave her his arm and they took their leave.

Dunton watched them go, walking stiffly together, William Rainsborough in his sober clothes and shovel hat looking more like a parson than a sailor, his bustling wife as plump and drab as a pigeon in her grey gown. He suddenly found Jenny beside him, pouring out her grievances against her aunt in a torrent of aggrieved complaints, overwhelmed with the untold anguish of being a fifteen-year-old female in a world which did not care and could not understand.

"There now," he said, feeling helpless at the sight of her tear-stained face, not knowing what to say or do. As his eldest daughter started weeping again he heard his youngest break into redoubled yells.

Turning round in desperation he was surprised and very glad to see the slight figure of Mistress Anne Crace coming up the garden path, a tall, robust countrywoman followed her in at the gate.

Jenny fled at the sight of more company approaching. Dunton called a sharp reprimand to his daughter for her rudeness but Anne Crace interposed.

"Please don't disturb yourself or your family on my account, Master Dunton. I was not expected, I know. If it's not convenient I can easily call another time."

"No," he said hastily, surprised to find how important it seemed that she should not go away. "Please come in. My daughter is a little upset, that's all."

"I understand." A smile, modest but candid, accompanied her words as she and her servant followed him into the house.

To Dunton's embarrassment the baby was not only still crying but the maids had started quarrelling noisily in the kitchen. Dorcas and Deborah, having abandoned their sewing now that Judith Rainsborough had departed, hung about in the doorway, scuffling together.

Dunton spread out his hands in an appealing gesture. "I must apologize for all this. It's been very difficult since my wife . . . since she . . ."

He still found it hard to talk about and was not able to finish the sentence but sat down abruptly opposite Anne, who said impulsively and compassionately, "I'm sorry, Master Dunton, so very sorry."

He knew from her tone that she really was and also that she understood something of what the loss meant to him. Yet they hardly knew each other. Out of the corner of his eye he caught sight of Deborah and Dorcas peering at Anne round the kitchen door. She smiled at them and they ventured nearer.

He passed a hand across his face. "Some refreshment?"

"No thank you." Anne raised her hand gently. "It's not really a social call. Perhaps I shouldn't have come."

She looked down at her hands, hesitating about what to say. She wore a lilac-coloured dress, the same shade as the one she had worn on the *Jacob*. It amazed him that he should have remembered. Rachel had always teased him about not noticing what she wore. Anne Crace appeared very appealing and vulnerable sitting there at his fireside, he thought. Deborah came right into the room and stood beside her as the attendant servant said sturdily to Dunton, "The fact is, sir, that Mistress Anne hasn't had a decent night's sleep since this terrible thing happened and she's worried to death about her father and sister and brother, to say nothing of the other poor folk. Them as could and should help," she went on darkly, "won't stir a finger and she doesn't know where to turn, poor lamb. There's her own sister's husband, a fine gentleman and rich," she snapped her fingers dramatically so that Deborah, startled, nestled against Anne for reassurance, "doesn't care that for his wife, nor Master Hillard, nor . . ."

"Hush, Mabyn," Anne Crace interrupted gently and Dunton asked, frowning, "Who's Master Hillard?"

"Why," the stout Mabyn looked shocked at his ignorance, "isn't he the rector of Combe and Mistress Anne's own promised husband that she should have married last month but for all this?"

"I see," said Dunton, looking at Anne's stricken face, adding quietly, "I didn't know."

Dorcas joined Deborah at Anne's side and both little girls looked at her as she asked their father, "Master Dunton, what is to be done to help those who were taken prisoner? I know so little. I did hear that ships were to be sent to Sallee to rescue them. Is it true?"

She sounded so pathetically hopeful that he was relieved to be able to give her the answer she wanted.

"One is planned, yes. I've been asked to sail with it."

"There is? You have?"

Her response contained such eagerness that he regretted admitting so much.

"Tell me, Master Dunton. What will it be like for them?"

Anne Crace was asking him about what would happen to the captives in Sallee. He knew he couldn't possibly tell her the truth. He tried to give a cheerful answer.

"Well, all your family will be decently treated because the corsairs expect to get a good ransom for them. It's just money they want, you know. For the poorer folk, who obviously can't buy their freedom, it's harder. They'll be expected to work to earn their keep. But with a naval squadron being sent against the Moriscos they'll find they've bitten off more than they can chew and will have to give up all their English captives."

"I'm so glad to hear you say it."

Anne Crace smiled at him, pressing her hands together. They were thin and white, he noticed, but there was something firm and capable about them, too, just as there was about Anne herself.

Deborah, who had crept away for a few minutes, now returned carrying a treasured rag doll which Dunton recognized, with a pang, as one which Rachel had made, and laid it in Anne's lap.

Anne lifted the child's offering reverently and Dunton's heart went out to her as she said, "She's beautiful." His child's face lit up with pleasure at the praise of her most beloved possession. Anne Crace's thin, sensitive hands stroked the doll's yellow wool hair but she looked earnestly at Dunton.

"I'm worried about Stephen, about Master Hillard, that is. I've heard the Moors do terrible things to make Christians turn Moslem. Is it true?"

Dunton hesitated over his answer. He was a poor liar and words never came easily to him, even at the best of times. He'd seen men tortured in Sallee in ways that made Fox's *Book of Martyrs* seem like reading fit for the nursery. If they wanted to make a man apostasize the Moriscos might order so many strokes of the bastinado that it could cripple him for life or even kill him. They might torture him for hours, burning him over a slow fire, or crucify him by nailing his hands and feet to a door.

"Master Dunton, Stephen would never renounce his faith. I know it. What will they do to him?"

Not only Anne but his daughters were looking to John Dunton, expecting him to reassure them by his reply. He saw there was nothing for it but to respond.

"Don't you worry, Mistress Crace," he said. "It won't come to that. We'll put the fear of God into those murdering Moriscos. Once they see our topsails at the mouth of the Bou Regreb they'll sue for peace in no time, you mark my words."

The bold speech had the desired effect but he realized with dismay that he had committed himself. For good or ill he was going back again to the coasts of Barbary.

17

Areefa, watching from the quayside as the brown-skinned seamen from the galleasse leapt ashore, saw Celia standing beside Jaffar Rais on the poop deck of the ship and heard the ribald laughter of the crowd.

"He's kept the best of the booty for himself as usual."

"I'll bet she's not for ransom or for sale."

"Who kept the night watches on the voyage home, Jaffar?"

Dirk Janssen, who had followed Areefa from the house with the hand of Fatima over the door, took her by the arms from behind and whispered in her ear, "You've got a rival, Areefa."

Tears of rage welled up into her eyes and jealousy, like the wild hawk it is, buried its beak and talons in her heart.

"I sold my jewels to buy him his first ship," she said, "and now he forgets me. Well, he shall remember."

Dirk Janssen called to her, "Wait!" But she pulled away from him, darting in and out among the crowd with the expertise natural to one who had lived all her life on the dockside and been a barefoot child who lived by stealing what scraps she could find until she was old enough to make her living another way.

Celia, intrigued by the sight of the great bastions of the casbah towering overhead, the distant prospect of endless narrow streets packed with flat-roofed, white-walled houses, the noise and bustle of the colourful cosmopolitan crowd on the quay, was resentful when Jaffar Rais ordered her peremptorily into the cabin.

"But I want to see what's going on."

"You'll see a sight more than you want to if you don't do as you're told," he answered roughly, taking her inside and pulling the door shut. "We're in Sallee now and you must watch your step. From now on you must wear a djellabah - one of those long, shapeless robes here - and veil your face whenever you go out. For the present, dress yourself like that and lie low in here until I tell you it's safe to come out."

"But why?" She was angry and defiant. "If you think you can shut me up behind bars the way Moslems treat women . . ."

He took her by the shoulders. "Now listen. I'm doing my best to protect you. I can't do as I like either. We of Sallee have our ruler and our laws like other men. The Governor of the Casbah, the Caid we call him, is entitled to his pick of all slaves brought into harbour. One in every eight is his. Now, the Caid is a notable womanizer, little Leah. If he sees you he'll want you and there won't be anything I can do about it. Understand?"

She did. He left her and Celia was obliged to watch through a crack in the door which, though it gave her a limited view of what was happening on the deck of the galleasse, prevented her seeing anything ashore.

While she waited nervously, the rest of the prisoners were being lined up, ready for the Caid's inspection, on the wharf. The women and smallest children were led away immediately under guard, to the house of the amina, a formidable Negress known as Lalla. Lalla's house was divided into two parts, the first, consisting of an outer courtyard and rooms opening on to it, was the resort of dealers who specialized in the sale of women and girls. The second, private part, was given over to latticed rooms where women prisoners were kept in more or less respectable seclusion whilst they were examined and priced by the amina and her staff of eunuchs.

The men and all the boys over seven were obliged to stand on the dockside in the blazing sun, having to put up with the jeers of the populace.

"Christ! What a place!"

Tippett Collecock blew out his lips disparagingly as he looked around him. He'd thought the ship's hold was the worst smelling place in the world till he encountered the stench of the docks at Sallee. And all those grinning foreigners babbling away like monkeys! He couldn't understand a word.

"Get off, can't you?"

He aimed a blow of his fettered hands at an enterprising merchant with a forked black beard and yellow turban who had tentatively pinched his arm with a view to assessing his muscle power. The man moved away quickly but one of the corsairs from the ship menaced Tippett with a cudgel, warning him not to strike out again.

"All right, all right," said Tippett pacifically. Already, on the voyage, he'd done his best to get along with the crew. Some of them weren't bad sorts.

One of the Martin boys, hardly four feet high, was standing beside him, unashamedly crying for his mother whom he'd just seen taken away with the other women by a number of fierce-looking black men.

"Cheer up, sonny," said Tippett, pulling a face at him. "Look at that great big bird there!" He pointed to where a stork, red-legged, red-billed, wide ragged wings black-edged, long neck outstretched, flew up to its nest of untidy sticks on top of a pinnacled tower.

The little boy followed the direction of Tippett's pointing finger, sniffing, the tears running down his face. The irons on his wrists were so heavy he could scarcely lift his hands.

"It's a damn shame," muttered Tippett to Sampson Derrey who stood beside him, muscles bulging under his tattered shirt, blue eyes blinking in the white-hot African sun.

"What do they want to put chains on a kid like that for? What do they think he's going to do?"

"It seems to me, Master Collecock," said the smith, who was a God-fearing man and disapproved of Tippett, "that you've discovered your conscience a bit late in life. Didn't I hear something about you being in the slave business yourself, trying to trick young men and women into selling themselves into slavery in Barbados and Virginia?"

"Not as slaves, Master Derrey!" Tippett affected horror at the smith's accusation. "Indentured servants, please!"

"Much the same thing, or so I heard. I could do with a drink of water."

The smith raised a manacled hand to wipe the sweat from his face and the rest grunted agreement. They were all parched, standing bareheaded under the scorching sun.

"Here, drink this, mate."

Old William Trevor, hobbling along with his donkey, laden with water pots and sweating, beaded skin bags also brimming with water, passed the smith a calabash which Derrey took gratefully and drained at a gulp.

"Just come in with Jaffar Rais, have you?" asked the old slave, hastily refilling the calabash which his assistant, a thin fair boy, gave to Stephen Hillard.

"Sir," the boy tugged at the parson's ragged sleeve. "Is my father aboard? John Dunton?"

"Dunton?" Stephen Hillard handed the calabash to Sim Greenfield, looking down earnestly at the boy's anxious face. "Now, we're not just sure where he is . . ."

"Yes, we are though," chipped in another man. "Dunton escaped with some of the others in the Channel. Good for him, I say."

"Why don't you hold your tongue?" snarled Tippett, seeing the look of despair in the boy's face. Then he stared over the child's head. "Well now, who's this?"

A company of blue-veiled Berber horsemen, dressed in

165

indigo robes and mounted on superb Barbary chargers with splendid silver trappings, were clearing the crowd away from before the arched gate of the casbah with their scimitars. Following them came a group of Negroes wearing scarlet turbans and jackets with white trousers, four of their number carrying a litter in which sat a figure clad in robes which had the colour and iridescence of a peacock's breast when the sun catches it.

"The Caid," muttered old William Trevor. "Just pray his eye doesn't light on you. You're better off dead than being a slave to him. Hornachero!"

He turned aside and spat viciously but discreetly on to the dock.

"What's that then?" Tippett could never control his curiosity and he stared at the imposing figure who was approaching through the cowed and bowing mob, flanked by armed guards wielding flashing blades.

"There's two kinds of Spanish Moors rule this town," Trevor hissed in his ear, "Hornacheros and Moriscos. The Hornacheros were here first. There's not many of them, but they've got most of the money. They give the orders and the Moriscos do the work. Them and the slaves and the renegades, that is. But all that may change soon," he hinted darkly. "Well, I'd better make myself scarce. Come on, Dicky boy."

One hand on the child's shoulder, the other looped in the patient donkey's halter, Trevor shuffled away.

The Caid, Tippett Collecock saw, was evidently in a bad temper, striding by the line of downcast, shuffling slaves without so much as a glance in their direction. But for his clothes, Tippett would have taken the Caid for a Spaniard, which he was, in everything but ancestry and religion. Antonio Rodriguez might call himself Malik ibn Khaloud and turn towards Mecca to pray, but he remained, in essence, an arrogant, ruthless and avaricious hidalgo.

Jaffar Rais, who awaited the Caid on the deck of the galleasse, greeted him with the salaam, which his illustrious visitor did not return.

"You have had a prosperous voyage, I believe."

The Caid's restless dark eyes flicked rapidly round, noting the bales of looted merchandise stacked on the deck. "My officials will select the dues owing to me from your cargo."

"Naturally, Excellency."

Jaffar Rais saw that the Caid was displeased and, knowing that this meant trouble, was on his guard. The Caid had brought a larger armed escort with him than was usual, he noted, seeing how the blue-robed Berbers clustered about their master with drawn swords.

"And the slaves?"

"On the dock, awaiting your inspection, Excellency."

Jaffar Rais pointed to the dejected collection, already being looked over by an elderly Negro of the Caid's staff.

Ibn Khaloud snapped his fingers impatiently.

"I saw the men. I mean the women."

Jaffar Rais smiled, opening his hands in a gesture of deferential politeness. "At the house of the amina, as is customary."

"*All* of them?"

Jaffar Rais bit his lip. Somehow his secret had leaked out. He ought to have seen that Celia kept hidden as soon as they sighted land.

"Naturally, Excellency..."

The Caid gave a signal and Jaffar Rais was immediately seized by several of the Caid's guards while others, pushing past him, strode to the cabin and flung open the door. Celia, clad in djellabah and veil, stood there.

The Caid fixed Jaffar Rais with a furious expression.

"All. So I see."

"Excellency!" Jaffar Rais was pinioned by the Caid's guards, those of his own men still aboard were outnumbered by the Berbers who faced them threateningly. "This lady is not a slave or a prisoner, but my guest."

"Who, at your invitation, sailed with you from her home of her own free will, no doubt?" The Caid's black brows drew together in an ominously sarcastic frown.

"Impound the cargo!" His order rang out clearly. Ignoring the cries of protest from the crew and the mutinous mutterings of the crowd, the Caid turned to his nearest guards.

"Take her to the harem and him to the dungeons."

With a swirl of peacock robes he turned on his heel and strode away.

Celia found her ride through the streets in a covered litter to the house of the Caid bumpy but brief. No one spoke to her. No one touched her. Formalized gestures, respectful but cold, indicated what she was to do. The curtains of the litter to which she was shown were drawn as soon as she had seated herself in it and the bearers, muscular Negroes, set off at a brisk trot

There was not time to notice much but she saw that the streets were very narrow and often dark, many of them being shadowed by vines which were trained over them, between the houses on either side.

The door of the Caid's house opened on to a courtyard surrounded by storied galleries which overlooked it. It was crowded and the litter bearers carried her swiftly across it to a doorway on the far side where a number of Berbers and Negroes stood sentinel.

The litter was set down. The door opened and Celia was politely but firmly made to see that she must enter.

A handsome, sulky-looking mulatto woman, richly dressed, ushered Celia behind the lattice screen which shut off the women's apartments from the rest of the house, dropping her veil immediately they were safely inside and motioning to Celia to do the same.

The harem had its own open courtyard and pillared, cloister-like surrounding arches from which doors led off to rooms beyond and it was full of women of all ages in all stages of dress and undress. In a large shallow pool in the centre a number of naked girls were splashing whilst others sat on the brink, dabbling their feet in the water, watched by four tall Negroes of the Caid's guard whose presence at first astounded Celia until it dawned on her that they must be eunuchs and therefore privileged to see what was so sedulously hidden from other men.

The girls disporting themselves round the pool were clearly of all races, like the heterogeneous population of New Sallee itself. There were coal-black Nubian beauties, their crimped hair in multitudes of tiny plaits, and brown, firm-breasted Mediterranean women. Others had the ivory-gold skins and expressive eyes that bespeak a mingling of African and European bloods and there were pink and white Nordic bodies, much more raw-looking in nudity and therefore, to the astonished Celia, much more shocking than the rest.

She stood staring until the mulatto woman jerked impatiently at her sleeve. They picked their way across the courtyard amongst the groups of chattering women, some with small children whom they suckled or dandled, others sewing or preparing vegetables for the pot, others merely lounging or gossiping.

Most of them stared at Celia as she passed, nudging and whispering, looking critically at her face, hair and clothes. One stretched out a hand and tweaked her skirt, shouting something which made those near her laugh. Celia wondered what it was and what would happen to her.

In a room off the courtyard sat a small man with a large ledger and pen and ink before him. He and the mulatto woman exchanged some brief business-like phrases in a strange sounding language and then the woman suddenly thrust her hand into Celia's mouth and began to feel her teeth, one at a time, remarking on them to the small man who proceeded to make entries in the ledger.

"Anyone would think," thought Celia, outraged, "that I

was a horse for sale."

Clearly, she realized, her assets were being catalogued and entered in the records of the Caid's household. She resisted the temptation to bite the woman's probing finger and only bared her teeth instead in what she hoped was a ferocious expression.

She objected, however, to undressing in front of the clerk when the mulatto woman indicated that she should drop the djellabah, and shook her head vigorously. The woman shrugged, clapped her hands and a large Negro, armed with a whip, appeared.

A single stinging stroke of the whip, cutting diagonally across her body from shoulder to thigh, convinced Celia it was no good arguing and she stepped out of her clothes with alacrity, hoping the Negro would not be ordered to continue plying the lash.

He stood by, grinning, as the mulatto woman examined Celia's breasts, prodding them to see if they were firm and reporting, apparently favourably, to the clerk who wrote assiduously, hardly taking any notice of Celia, who stood trying to hide herself with her arms.

Then she was ordered to lie down and the woman thrust her hard ringed hands into the orifices of Celia's body with clinical precision, continuing her professional comments to the clerk in a terse, matter-of-fact tone.

The humiliating business was finally over and Celia was allowed to resume her clothes and left to her own devices for the remainder of what she always remembered as a very long, tedious and unhappy day, full of fears and anxieties for herself and others.

Towards evening her loneliness in the midst of the crowd of strange and mainly hostile women was relieved by the appearance of Charity Lidd, somewhat untidy and dishevelled but otherwise very much her usual self.

"Well, look who's here!" she remarked cheerfully on seeing Celia who was so glad of the sight of a familiar friendly face that she exclaimed with delight as soon as she saw Charity brought in by the sulky mulatto woman.

"They found you, too, did they?" she asked, sitting down next to Celia in the corner of the courtyard where the latter had stayed since being admitted to the harem. "Don't they give you a going over?" she said ruefully. "That old Negress pinched me black and blue and enjoyed it, too, the bitch! I told her, 'You needn't bother searching to see if I'm a virgin, missis, for I haven't been since I was eleven years old. I'll tell you that for nothing.' She still looked, though. Only doing her job, I suppose."

Charity pinned up her torn gown, glancing enviously at the girls sporting in the pool.

"I wouldn't mind doing that myself."

"Were you really only eleven?" Charity's devastating candour had shocked Celia almost more than anything else that had happened on a day full of shocking events.

Charity turned wide, friendly eyes on her. Their common plight as captives in a strange land had done away with all the foolish social barriers which had always divided them until now.

"Who, me? Yes, eleven years old the first time I was tumbled and treated like a public whore ever since. Ask your own brother, if you don't believe me. He was the first. But I forgot," she made a face, "you can't ask him. I saw him taken away. He could hardly walk the chains were so heavy."

"Roger?"

Celia was grappling with two terrible things she had learned about her brother, apart from the accusation of Jaffar Rais, and it was almost too much for her. She hung her head and the tears started.

"Now then," said Charity, putting a plump grimy hand on Celia's arm. "Don't give way. You've got to keep going, you know. Don't let them get you down. It must be difficult, you being a lady and used to being treated respectfully and all that. Look, there's some food coming. I'll get us some."

Food was being brought in on brass trays by some of the eunuchs and the Caid's womenfolk jostled one another to get their share. Celia thought she would have fared badly but for sturdy Charity Lidd who elbowed her way through the press and came back with a couple of bowls of soup made from vegetables with mint leaves floating on the top and a platter with some handfuls of kus-kus.

"The stuff they eat!" remarked Charity, giving Celia her share, "but I dare say we'll be a lot better off than most of the poor souls."

"What happened to the others?" Celia asked Charity as the other drank her soup noisily from the bowl. "My father and the Greenfield girls and the rest of the women?"

"There's a lot of talk about ransom." Charity attacked the kus-kus dubiously, taking a pinch of it between her fingers to taste. "That's all we heard down at the amina's. Mistress Greenfield and her daughters, some old man, very dressy and polite, took them away when he found out they could pay. Surprising how easy these foreigners can understand you when it's anything to do with money! The rest - well, the dealers put them through it. I didn't mind, being used to men, but the young girls were very upset, of course. The older women - well, I don't know," she went on thoughtfully, finishing off the kus-kus, "some of them probably enjoyed being taken notice of by a man for the first time in years. But," she glanced at Celia, "I didn't expect to see you here. I thought you would be with the captain, Chandler or Jaffar or whatever he calls himself."

"I was." Celia found the tears starting to her eyes again. "I thought things would be all right. Not just for me, but for all our people from Combe. But the Caid's men came aboard and just took over. I saw them dragging him away. I don't know what they were going to do with him."

"The biter bit, eh?" Charity shook her head. "You really fancied him, didn't you?" she asked Celia curiously. "You're just the same as me, really, aren't you? Being called a a lady doesn't make any difference to that, it's just how you're treated that's different. Hey, look out! I think someone wants you."

Celia looked up to see the Negro with the whip standing over her and beckoning her to follow him.

18

Celia's sensations of alarm and dismay were a trifle alleviated when her guide led her into an elegant high-ceilinged room, floored and pillared in mottled pink marble and left her there with the stony-faced mulatto woman and two young girls, one black and one white. She had been afraid that the highly personal examination she had suffered was to be repeated or else that she had incurred some punishment, but the eunuch with the whip did not linger and no busy clerk was present to continue the inventory of her physical attributes. She looked around her with interest.

The room was empty except for a sunken bath in the centre of the floor which was half full of steaming water strongly scented with jasmine. The Negro girl, who was dressed only in a short pleated kilt of fine white linen, knelt at the side of the bath pouring the contents of a pottery jar into it.

The mulatto woman, who hardly glanced at Celia, stooped down, her loose purple robe billowing about her, and dabbled her fingertips in the water to test its heat. Apparently satisfied that the temperature was right, she said something to the fair-skinned girl who approached Celia and began to undress her.

The bath looked and smelt inviting and Celia was so glad to be faced with such a pleasant prospect instead of what she had dreaded that she stepped out of her clothes and into the water with feelings of relief and satisfaction. It was deliciously warm and the perfume rising from it was heady and languorous. When she stood upright on the dappled pink floor of the bath the scented ripples reached to her waist. She dipped her hands in the water and poured it over her body. Feeling wonderfully relaxed, she knelt, leaning back, arms outspread and buoyed up. Her hair floated out around her, ray-like on the surface.

The mulatto woman clapped her hands and the two girls seized Celia's arms, pulled her unceremoniously out of the bath and began rubbing her dry. They were hasty and ungentle, especially with her hair, which they towelled vigorously and then combed out till it hung sleek and shining down her back.

Suddenly all three women dropped to their knees with bowed heads and clasped hands. Celia, who had been protesting over the way they tugged her hair, looked up to see a man standing beside one of the pillars at the end of the room. Before she even saw his face she was inexplicably yet positively aware that he had been a silent spectator all the time.

He made a slight but commanding gesture and the other three women withdrew at once, leaving Celia face to face with the Caid who advanced towards her, his sandalled feet making a soft slapping noise on the marble floor.

Celia hung her head and crossed her arms over her breast, afraid and ashamed to look at him until he stood so close to her that the hems of his straight stiff robe brushed against her legs. He put his hand under her chin and lifted her face to his.

He was not much taller than she was, but she guessed him to be at least twice her own age. Seen at close quarters Malik ibn Khaloud was a personable man, aquiline-featured with olive skin and thick dark hair a little silvered. The hand that held her chin was smooth but masculine and his eyes looked deep into hers.

He did not speak but embraced her swiftly with both arms, pressing her body very close to his so that she felt the lean hardness of it through his garment and kissing her mouth firmly and eagerly. She had meant to resist him or, at least, to be passive and unresponsive, but the pressure of his lips made hers open. His tongue touched hers, moist, sensitive, questing and Celia felt herself yielding, as so often she had done before, to a man's urgent desire for her. Then she stiffened and clenched her hands, remembering that he was her enemy, her captor and that surrender without a struggle would be servile and spiritless.

Feeling her try to draw away from him he held her fast, gripping tightly, his thumbs pressing into the sensitive flesh on the inner side of her arms.

"Why do you try to resist?" he asked. "You are not virtuous and you must know it is useless."

"Let me go," she said resentfully, "you insult me."

To her surprise he let go of her, smiling a little.

"So. I insult you. Yet I speak the truth."

Celia held up her head. "I am Lady Lovell. I demand to be treated with the respect due to my rank."

The Caid looked her up and down.

"You are the harlot of Jaffar Rais and the lawful prize of war. Moreover you are a woman whom I desire and intend to take. What have you to say to that?"

Celia realized that her token resistance did her no disservice in his eyes. He was a subtle, worldly man, she saw, no longer young, and sated, perhaps, with easy conquests which failed to stimulate his jaded appetite. She shrugged, affecting disdain.

"If you force me you will be less than a man and I shall despise you for it. You can make me cease to resist you, you cannot make me respond to you."

"I have done so already." He sounded piqued and his dark brows drew together. "You are my prisoner and will obey me. Come."

He held out his hand to Celia, but she hung back, wondering, as she watched him, how far she dared go in opposing him. He was a powerful and dangerous man and she had already seen, in his treatment of Jaffar Rais, how ruthless he could be.

"Shall I send for women slaves to torment you and bring you to a more amenable frame of mind?"

Celia felt terrified at his threat but she answered, "After they have done with me, shall I be fit for your bed, my lord?"

He smiled, a cruel smile, ugly to see.

"Oh, they are expert in such matters. A needle, deftly used, causes agony, but makes no unsightly marks on the body. When their ministrations are over you will be as desirable as you are now, the only difference will be in your extreme desire to please me."

Celia gave him her hand, letting it lie limp in his grasp as he drew her after him, her shining hair cloaking her body, the marble cold to her bare feet.

The room beyond was shadowy and empty except for a large rug made of animal skins in various shades, white and striped and tawny, and cushions scattered on its surface. The walls were patterned with carvings in curving designs endlessly repeated in the warm red sandstone.

"Lie down."

Celia did so, slowly and unwillingly, going down on her side, lying stiffly, knees pressed together, turning her head away. The initial slight attraction she had felt for the Caid had died at the hints of savagery he had revealed. He must be a degenerate tyrant, she decided, beginning to shiver as she lay there, feeling the air of the shady room cool to her naked body after the steamy warmth of the perfumed bath.

Hearing his rapid step behind her she looked up, startled to see him standing over her with a whip.

"But you promised I would not be hurt!"

"I promised you nothing. Do you think you can defy me with your cold insolence? I will have you begging me to take you before I am done."

He raised the whip and Celia cried out, flinging up an arm to defend herself, waiting for the lash to fall.

It never did. She heard a curious choking sound and his body fell forward and across her, pinning her down. She screamed, trying to push him off, finding him roll aside easily and looking down in amazement at his lolling head, staring eyes and wide open mouth.

"Don't worry about him, Leah," said the voice of Jaffar Rais. "He's dead."

She saw that it was so. The whiplash was round his throat, a deep red weal with swelling on either side showing where it had cut into his flesh when it strangled him.

Jaffar Rais gave Celia his hand and his cloak.

"How is it," he said, helping her to her feet, "that I seem always to find you with a man and without clothes, little Leah?"

"I must call it Fate or Destiny since it would be blasphemous to call it Providence," she answered. "But how do you come to be here at all?" She glanced round, seeing armed men at his back and milling about in the courtyard outside. There were sounds of scuffling near at hand and of shouting and cheering in the distance. "I saw you dragged away as the Caid's prisoner."

"And now you see me as his conqueror."

Coolly Jaffar Rais stooped, jerked up the Caid's head by the hair and with his drawn sword sliced it from his body so that the blood gushed out from the severed neck like a fountain, splashing over Celia's feet.

"So perish all tyrants!"

Jaffar Rais raised the streaming head high at arm's length and the men about him yelled triumphantly. Celia saw Bastiano snatch the grisly trophy from his leader and spike it on his own sword point, waving it in the air like a banner and striding out, the other corsairs following him and shouting over and over again certain words in chorus.

Celia, revolted at what she saw, clutched at Jaffar Rais' arm. "What are they saying?"

He smiled down at her as she stood, wrapped in his cloak, in the crook of his arm. " 'The Caid is dead! Long live Jaffar Rais!' If you are to live with me you must learn the lingua franca of the Barbary Coast, Leah."

She went with him into the courtyard where she had spent the day. It was empty of women now and a score of corsairs stood guard. A Negro lay with red blood staining his red jacket to a darker and more sinister shade, beside the pool where the girls had bathed. Beyond, in the larger, main courtyard there was the noisy crowd whose yells she had heard echoing through the Caid's house.

"Morisco! Morisco!"

"Jaffar Rais! Jaffar Rais!"

Over and over again they hailed him. Celia glimpsed the riff-raff of the Sallee docks, some in European clothes and some in Moorish djellabahs, Arabs rubbing shoulders with Dutch and Flemish renegades, Jews, Italian merchants, urchins and proud Hornacheros of the casbah, jostling one another.

"You must tell me what has happened."

"The inevitable." Jaffar Rais pointed to where his old comrade in arms, Murad of the scarred face, came driving the wounded remnants of the Caid's Berber guard before him, urging them on with blows from the flat of his sword. "The town was ripe for revolt. It has been for the last four years. The Moriscos and the corsairs were sick of the domination of the Hornacheros, arrogant devils with money who thought they owned us and took the lion's share of all the loot that came into harbour. I cut the head off the worst of them back there just as he was going to lay into you with the whip, Leah. Well, today was the last straw. A lot of people were waiting for their share in the profits of my voyage, little people most of them, but some influential merchants, too. Then along comes the late Caid and confiscates the ship and the entire cargo, just on the basis of a tale told by some informer. As if he could get away with that!

"His guards had hardly clanged the cell door shut on me before Murad and his crew and mine charged the gaol and got me out again. Then the mob rallied to us and here we are, in command of the casbah and scarcely a hand or a voice raised against us."

As he was speaking Celia saw a girl being dragged through the courtyard, screaming and kicking, between two corsairs who flung her down roughly at Jaffar Rais' feet. The girl lay there panting, her robe torn half off her back which was marked with bleeding weals. Celia instinctively went to her help but as soon as the girl saw her she spat at Celia and made as if to claw her face. The men seized her arms to restrain her and Jaffar Rais said grimly to Celia, "You'd better take care, Leah. You're safer playing with a tigress than with Areefa when she's roused. It was she that betrayed me to the Caid on account of her jealousy of you."

He turned to Murad who stood grinning behind him and to Bastiano, still with the dripping head of the Caid impaled on his sword, and pointed to Areefa.

"What shall be done with her?"

"She should be dragged along the seashore at the heels of a Barbary horse." Murad jeered at the crouching Areefa who looked at him with smouldering hatred. Celia exclaimed in horror.

"You can't do that. I can't believe you would do that to a woman."

"Not even to a woman who betrayed me?" Jaffar Rais scowled.

"But her plans came to nothing. You have the victory and," Celia pointed to the girl's bleeding back, "she has been punished already."

He hesitated a moment. Then his frown lifted.

"You are foolishly merciful. Areefa would have you torn limb from limb if she could. But she is no one and nothing."

Jaffar Rais turned to his men, pointing to Areefa. "Toss her back on to the seafront with the rest of the rubbish washed up by the sea. As for you, little Leah, I suggest you go back into the privacy of the women's quarters and dress yourself as befits the wife of a rais, or, better still, wait for me there as you are. Now that the fighting is over I find I have a great appetite!"

19

It was dark in the mazmorra, dark and damp, but still unbearably hot, with the foetid steamy heat that smells of fever and urine.

The old grain storage pit was fifteen feet deep and its roof rested firmly on a single pillar round which the ropes supporting the prisoners' hammocks were fastened in radial groups of eight or nine, layered one above the other, heads close together at the pillar end, feet further apart near the wall.

The prisoners had entered at sword point and been forced to climb into the hammocks by way of a rope ladder which the gaoler let down and drew up again immediately the last miserable, hesitant captive had crawled into place in his rotting rope sling, poised above the noisome liquid with which the base of the mazmorra was awash.

The gaoler gave a quick glance at his prisoners and slammed the heavy iron grille in place over the round aperture six feet across which provided all the light and ventilation for the dismal dungeon, as well as being the only way in and out of it. Then, ignoring the prisoners' plaintive pleas for water, he ensconced himself in the shade with his pipe. The urchins of the town came, though, to peer and jeer at the despairing upturned faces of the prisoners and throw mud and stones down on them through the bars of the grid.

"Little bastards!" growled Tippett Collecock from the lowest tier of hammocks, swaying perilously above the unspeakable effluent at the bottom of the pit. "I'd give them what for if I could get at them!"

"Cheer up, Tip."

Stephen Hillard spoke from a few feet above him and their voices sounded hollow and resonant, like those heard in a tunnel. The little parson of Combe was doing his best to appear cheerful for the sake of the others, but it was hard work.

The words of the psalmist echoed in his mind, "If I make my bed in hell, behold, Thou are there."

"Run out of comfortable words, parson?" Tippett Collecock mocked, his ramshackle hammock creaking at its moorings. Tippett was frightened to death, but he wasn't going to show it.

"You ought to be ashamed," muttered Henry Lamb, the cobbler, still more shocked by Tippett's flippancy, which he recognized as irreverence, than the bewildering enormities which had overwhelmed his hitherto uneventful life.

There were fifteen men and boys from Combe in the mazmorra which at night was packed with sixty or more slaves from the stone quarries beyond the town. The rest of the captives from the galleasse had been seized by the Caid's guards as his share of the cargo. The prisoners had witnessed the confiscation of the ship and the arrest of Jaffar Rais as they stood helplessly by. Moments later the Caid's guards took away some of their number, seemingly at random, including the smith, Sampson Derrey, Squire Crace and Sim Greenfield's father. The rest had been hailed off to the mazmorra, there to wait until the next day when they would be put up for public auction in the slave market. The prospect was so demoralizing that they didn't care to talk or even think about it.

"If I've run out of comfortable words, Tip," said Stephen Hillard, craning down in the direction of the confidence trickster's voice, "it's because of my lack of faith and not because there aren't any."

Tippett Collecock grunted, "Well you've always got an answer, parson. I'll give you that."

A kind of companionship had grown up between Stephen Hillard and the graceless Collecock which would never have been possible in any other circumstances. They had more courage than the rest and more spirit to bear up under their trials. Tippett had always despised those who allowed themselves to be imposed on and gave way to moaning or apathy as most of his fellow prisoners now did, except for the little parson. And Stephen Hillard found the trickster's irreverent resilience somehow heartening in the midst of so much despair.

"Do you think, now," Tippett was asking, surprisingly, "that if we started singing a psalm together there'd be an earthquake like the one that released Paul and Silas from prison?"

"How did you come to know the scriptures so well?" In the miserable gloom of the subterranean cell Stephen could see that the ropes which bound the hammocks to the pillar and the wall were precariously thin. Too much movement would easily cause them to break, he thought, sending the restive occupant hurtling down into the grisly ooze below.

"I had a pious master once," answered Tippett, who had just been noticing the same thing, "and he beat the King's new Bible into me with the buckle end of a belt till I ran away from him to lead a godless life that I've never regretted. I . . ."

They were not destined to know what Tippett would have said next for the rope securing his hammock finally gave way and he tumbled with a yell into the liquid mud beneath.

Cries went up and all the hammocks swayed crazily in unison. The gaoler, awakened from his comfortable doze, realized what was happening. The breaking of hammock ropes was not such an uncommon occurrence and served to subdue prisoners who might otherwise become too active and troublesome. He did all that was required of him by pulling back the grid and flinging down the rope ladder. That way the man who had fallen would not drown, which was all that concerned him. If the requisite number of slaves was not presented for sale next day the gaoler would be in trouble. Their condition, however, was not his responsibility. He was about to replace the grid when someone shouted his name in the street outside. There were many shouts and the sound of thudding feet running by. He went to see what was the matter.

"Here!" spluttered Tippett, struggling to his feet covered in filthy slime. "Give me a hand up, can't you?"

"Coming, Tip."

Stephen Hillard grasped the rope ladder firmly in both hands before venturing to swing a leg out over the side of his hammock and plant his foot on a sagging and sodden rung. He eased his way down whilst the others nervously urged him to watch his step. Tippett was almost up to his armpits.

"Get hold of me round the middle," ordered Stephen, "and I'll do my best to pull you up. Just pray that the ladder doesn't give way."

"What do you think I'm doing?" said Tippett, spitting mud and taking a firm grip of Stephen. "Now many's the time I've held a girl round the waist but never before a parson."

"Is there no end to your ribaldry?" Stephen was scandalized. "I've a good mind to leave you where you are."

"No offence, parson," said Tippet clinging to him. "Do you see what I see?"

Stephen, looking up as he heaved himself and Tippett up the ladder, saw that the grid had not been replaced. The way out of the mazmorra was open.

"There's a hell of a noise outside," said Sim Greenfield.

"What on earth's going on?"

"I don't know." Stephen went grimly from rung to rung. "But I'm going on up."

"I'm going with you," said Tippett, still hanging on.

There were anxious excited voices all round them.

"Can we get out?"

"For God's sake, let's get out."

Stephen's head emerged through the hole and he briefly surveyed the small courtyard which housed the entrance to the mazmorra. It was empty. The gaoler had joined his cronies in the rebellious mob rushing to storm the casbah, leaving his prisoners unguarded in the excitement of the moment.

"All clear!" Stephen scrambled out, followed by Tippett who gave a cry of alarm when he saw four figures appear out of the shadows of the gateway and come running towards them.

"It's all right."

Stephen had seen the water carrier's donkey in the background and recognized the old man and the boy, Dick Dunton, who had spoken to them on the dockside. Old William Trevor limped up to them.

"You've got a chance to get away now, if you hurry. I thought something like this would happen when I heard the talk in the town. The Father here will help you."

"Father?"

Stephen looked at the figure in the faded habit marked with the red and blue cross of the Redemptionists. Father Gracian said briskly, glancing at the men climbing up out of the dungeon, "How many?"

"Fifteen."

"Sixteen," William Trevor interposed eagerly. "You'll take the boy with you."

"Where?" Events were moving too fast for Stephen to follow. He grasped the priest's arm. "Who are you? What's happening?"

"Père Gracian of the Order of the Most Holy Trinity." The priest touched the bi-coloured cross on his breast. "It is my vocation to assist slaves in regaining their freedom. Now, listen. There has been a revolt. The mobs are rioting and besieging the casbah, demanding the abdication of the Caid. We have been expecting something like this to happen for some time and have laid our plans. You can get away under cover of the disturbance to a place of safety outside the town where you can lie low until you can escape by sea. Are you all here?"

He looked round at the group of men who had gathered in the courtyard. Stephen nodded. Beyond the gateway the noisy crowds were still pouring along the street towards the casbah, yelling for the blood of the Caid.

Stephen said, "We have friends who are captives in the town."

The priest sighed, shaking his head with a mixture of compassion and impatience.

"New Sallee is a town of slaves and prisoners, monsieur. I shall do what I can for them as for all. But you, if you would gain your own freedom, must go at once. The penalties inflicted on those caught attempting to escape are severe. Are you ready to obey my instructions? If not, there are others . . ."

He began to move towards the gateway, tense and hasty, a dedicated, devoted, heavily overburdened man.

"We'll do anything you say, only get us out of here." Tippett voiced the mood of the group, who stood round the priest, not knowing where to turn.

"Very well, then." The Redemptionist's voice was crisp. "Ismail here will guide you."

Ismail, lean and swarthy in a tattered brown djellabah, edged forward out of the shadows when he heard his name.

"You may trust him," said the priest. "He is a Christian and it was he who enticed away your gaoler with the false news that his house in the casbah had been fired by the mob."

"Good for you." Tippett grinned at Ismail and the ragged Moroccan grinned back, recognizing a kindred spirit.

"Go now." Father Gracian touched Stephen on the

shoulder. "*Pax vobiscum.*"

"And with your spirit," Stephen answered, preparing to follow Ismail who was already beckoning and striding off.

"The boy, sir!"

Old William Trevor pushed Dick Dunton forward.

"Jaffar Rais will sell him to Algiers if he gets hold of him. Take care of the boy, sir."

"Come on, Dick."

Stephen pushed Dick Dunton in front of him through the gateway and they ran with the others down the rapidly emptying streets after the long-legged figure of Ismail.

Only a few heavily veiled women, old men and urchins were encountered by the fleeing fugitives. Everyone else, it seemed, was thundering at the gates of the casbah in the opposite direction. Ismail led them through the congested, labyrinthine ways of the poorer parts of the town, loping on swiftly ahead, diving unexpectedly down hidden turnings, disappearing briefly and tantalizingly round corners, only to reappear beckoning impatiently. The Englishmen panted after him, stumbling and sweating, terrified of being left behind, of losing sight of their guide in this strange, hostile place.

"I've got a stitch."

Dick Dunton crumpled up, pale faced, and Stephen scooped him along, feet dragging the dust, surprised to find how light he was.

"Come on. Not far now."

Stephen hoped it wasn't. The boy wasn't strong, he thought worriedly, looking into Dick's face. No wonder, he was as thin as a rake.

Ismail didn't relax his breakneck pace until they emerged on the banks of the Bou Regreb, beyond the town and reached the ancient half-built mosque, called the Tower of Hassan, with its forest of surrounding pillars. Here he let his near exhausted band of escapees pause to take breath a moment, flinging themselves down in the long grass which grew among the pillars and drinking with cupped hands from a stream of brackish water trickling between piles of broken stone left by the builders of long ago.

Even in the urgency of the moment Stephen noticed how a tangle of wiry vetch stems with small purple flowers grew at the brook's edge. He broke off a spray in his hand. The boy Dunton, seeing him do it, smiled as he lay gasping like a newly-landed fish, and said breathlessly, looking at the flowers, "They're just like the ones at home."

"Just." Stephen smiled briefly back at him, hauling Dick to his feet as Ismail, grimacing horribly, motioned to them that they must go on. Pursuit was imminent, his expression suggested, and the tired men hastened to obey him.

"I smell like a fox," grumbled Tippett, on whose body the vile-smelling mud of the mazmorra had dried, making him dark from head to foot.

"Well, you'll frighten off any lions we happen to meet, looking the way you do." Sim Greenfield, almost inebriated by his brief taste of freedom, joked for the first time in weeks, helping Dick Dunton along as they followed their guide down a dusty track through a forest of evergreen oaks. There were clearings here and there and piles of cut logs, no doubt intended for the Sallee shipyards, but no labourers to be seen.

"You don't mean there are lions hereabouts?"

Henry Lamb looked nervously about him as though expecting a ravening beast to leap out at him from behind the next tree he came to.

"Plenty." Dick Dunton spoke up promptly and unexpectedly. "*They* try to frighten you with stories of runaway slaves who get eaten by lions when they hide here. But William says lions won't attack a group of you in broad daylight."

"Let's be thankful for that, then."

Tippett winked at the boy who winked back, brightening up. He was barefoot, his skinny legs spotted with the small sores so common in Africa and wore nothing but a ragged shirt fluttering round his thighs, but he ran along manfully, keeping up with the best.

The mention of lions made all of them quicken their pace, anxious as their hurrying guide to be out of the wood.

"I wonder where he's taking us?" Sim Greenfield looked questioningly at Stephen, nodding in the direction of Ismail. Stephen shrugged. "We can only wait and see. As it is we're lucky to get this far." After four miles of rapid walking they emerged, footsore and breathless, from the shelter of the trees and found themselves on a hillside overlooking the town.

Farms lay scattered over the hillside, a patchwork of small fields planted with maize and vegetables, orderly orchards of almond trees and groves of grey-leaved olives, with here and there a long, low white house, its yard enclosed with a hedge of tall cactus. Far below they saw the river of Sallee, the Bou Regreb, a wedge of shining water between its twin towns.

Stephen Hillard drew a deep breath.

"I will lift up mine eyes," he said, "unto the hills, from whence cometh my help."

"Well, we hope so, anyway," put in Tippett, incurably practical. His eyes narrowed suddenly, flippancy deserting him. "Who are those jokers Ismail's talking to? I hope we haven't jumped out of the frying pan into the fire."

Stephen, turning from his distant glimpse of freedom, saw that a group of armed horsemen, led by a fierce, hook-nosed Arab, swarthy and predatory, had ridden out from the cover of a cluster of trees and was barring their way.

Dick Dunton was clinging to his sleeve, whimpering with terror and pointing to the Arab.

Fear made him slaver as he stammered the name "Ali Zuni" over and over again.

20

"It's a highly improper arrangement, that's all I can say."

Judith Rainsborough was ruffled which made her look more like a pigeon than ever, an indignant one with breast distended and feathers huffed out.

"Improper?"

Stout Mabyn rose slowly from her knees. She was tall as well as broad and Judith Rainsborough was somewhat dismayed to see how long it took her to draw herself up to her full height. Mabyn had been scrubbing the kitchen floor of John Dunton's house and still held the dripping brush in her large red hand. Kneeling she was a substantial figure. Standing, she was positively formidable.

"Did I understand you to say 'improper', Mistress Rainsborough?"

Faced with this Amazonian domestic, Judith Rainsborough wavered. She had come to her brother-in-law's home to state her strong objections to his plan for leaving his house and family in the care of Mistress Anne Crace when he set sail for Sallee. Judith Rainsborough had naturally assumed that she, Judith, and no other, would be in charge of her dead sister's children once John Dunton returned to sea. When William Rainsborough laconically informed her that John had made other arrangements she lost no time in taking a wherry across the river to Rotherhithe, intending to tell her brother-in-law just what she thought of them and him.

"Improper is not at all the word to use, Mistress Rainsborough," Mabyn was saying. "Since Master Dunton will not be in the house but Mistress Anne's mother and I shall, there can be no question of impropriety. Furthermore," she went on, quivering alarmingly, "Mistress Anne is the most devout, well-conducted young lady I ever hope to see and..."

"I'm sure she is," said Judith hastily, observing through the open kitchen door Anne Crace entering the parlour with Dorcas and Deborah in tow.

"Good day to you, Mistress Rainsborough."

Anne's youth and diffidence made Judith feel more assured. She responded with a stiff curtsy while Deborah and Dorcas, discreetly prompted by Anne, came forward to kiss their aunt.

Anne was anxious to please, aware from what John Dunton himself had told her that opposition from his wife's family was to be expected. Looking at Judith Rainsborough, Anne wished that John Dunton were there now.

Jenny came to her rescue, stepping forward, brightly welcoming, to take her aunt's hat and cloak and settle her in the most comfortable chair nearest the fire. Judith glanced suspiciously at her niece, watching as she and the two younger girls settled themselves down to their sewing with an air of conscious virtue. Anne, also watching, had to struggle hard not to laugh and hoped they were not overdoing it. The fact was that, being so near to the three Dunton girls in age, especially to Jenny, and naturally sympathetic, Anne had rapidly made friends with them.

It was because his daughters were so fond of her, that John Dunton had first considered the idea of Anne coming to live at Rotherhithe when he sailed with Rainsborough's squadron. Jenny, Dorcas and Deborah themselves made the original suggestion. Now that Aunt Judith Rainsborough had come with the obvious intention of putting paid to their cherished scheme the Dunton girls were determined that she should have no excuse whatever for doing so, trying their utmost to appear as well-behaved and industrious under Anne's supervision as they had always failed to be under Judith's own. Their heads were bent assiduously over their work and they looked unnaturally good.

Judith was not amused. Characteristically, she went into the attack.

"I wonder," she began, "that you do not find this house too humble for you, after what you've been used to, Mistress Crace."

"My home is now a heap of ruins, Mistress Rainsborough," Anne reminded her gently.

"But your brother-in-law, Sir Edward Lovell. Surely he would provide a home for you and your mother?"

Anne flushed slightly at the other woman's question.

"My brother-in-law is not in a position to do so," she said quietly. She could have added that Sir Edward Lovell had brought an elegant, expensive, cold white mistress to his elegant, expensive, cold white house but she refrained, out of consideration for her sister.

Judith was intrigued.

"May I ask why?"

"No, you may not!"

Stout Mabyn banged the tray with the glasses of elderflower cordial down so hard on the table that she risked shattering them. "Mistress Anne's had no home to go to since those murdering pirates burned Combe, no more has her poor, dear mother, and if Master Dunton likes to offer them one while he's away so that he can keep his own home going for the sake of his motherless children, then it's nobody's business but his, I say."

"Upon my word!" Judith Rainsborough reddened with anger. "You speak your views very freely for a servant!"

"That's enough, Mabyn."

Anne spoke pleadingly rather than commandingly, but Mabyn did hold her tongue, though with an effort.

"I suppose I may be allowed to take an interest in the

welfare of my own dead sister's children?" Tremblingly, the plump little woman smoothed out the folds of her grey dress.

"Indeed! And I am grateful that you do, sister."

Anne was very relieved to see John Dunton enter, shaking a feathering of snow from his hat and cloak. His daughters hurried to embrace him, hanging round him affectionately. It touched Anne to see how tenderly attached they were to one another. Judith, however, only sniffed.

"Yet you do not think me a fit person to care for them."

"Judith!" Dunton was honestly shocked. Drawing up his chair to the fire, he turned to face her. "You know I think no such thing," he said earnestly, "but it meant giving up this house that Rachel was - that we're all so fond of. And it would be a lot for you, Judith, a lot of extra work with four more children besides your own to care for."

"I've never minded hard work."

Anne saw that she was a good deal mollified by the mention of her sister's name. Dunton reached out his hand and squeezed his sister-in-law's work-worn palm.

"You've always been willing to help, Judith, and we're all grateful, truly we are. Aren't we, girls?"

Thus appealed to, Jenny, Dorcas and Deborah nodded earnestly.

"Well," Judith Rainsborough said, smoothing the folds of her pigeon-grey dress, "perhaps it would be an advantage if you kept this house on, John." The relief in the room was almost tangible as Judith turned to Anne.

"I hope you will ask my advice whenever you need assistance of any kind, whether in dealing with my nieces or in running the household, Mistress Crace."

"Indeed, Mistress Rainsborough, I shall be very glad to do so."

It had worked out better than he dared hope, John Dunton thought, when Judith at last rose to go. His sister-in-law had accepted her defeat with dignity, if not altogether graciously, and a family quarrel had been avoided.

"I think it's what Rachel would have wanted," he said, putting Judith's cloak round her shoulders.

"Yes, perhaps you're right, John." She was almost completely melted by the mention of her sister's name. At least, she thought, bidding him and his daughters farewell, he hadn't rushed into a second marriage straight away as a lot of men would have done.

"Mistress Crace was to have married a clergyman who was taken prisoner in the raid, I believe?"

He had walked with her to the garden gate between the dark trees, each separate twig rimmed with hoar frost that glittered in the pale yellow winter sunlight.

"Yes," he answered, smiling faintly, "she has a great interest in the success of our expedition."

His sister-in-law declined his offer to accompany her home, saying she had other business in the village and he watched her plump, trim grey figure disappear down the lane under a scattering shower of thin snowflakes.

The water of London river reflected the leaden sky above it. The masts and spars of the vessels laid up in the docks across the Thames at Wapping were bare and black as the branches of trees along the banks. The only colour he could see was the defiantly bright red shield on the head of a moorhen, picking its way, long-toed and nimble, through the mud and withered sedge at the river's brink, its black and white barred tail jerking briskly up and down.

He heard a laugh behind him and turned to see Anne Crace.

"They always look so fussy and important," she said, pointing to the moorhen, "like a city alderman with a red nose." Suddenly serious, she asked, "Was it all right?" her eyes anxiously searching his face.

"Mm." He made a gruff reassuring sound, brusque and masculine. "Of course. Judith's a good woman."

"Yes." Anne Crace smiled up at him.

"You must go in," Dunton said, taking her arm. "It's snowing and you have no hat."

Her hair was soft and pretty, clustering in curls at the nape of her neck, just as Rachel's had done. It hurt him to think of that. It was the little things he missed. The sight of her sitting sewing at the fireside when he looked up from his book. The quick, confiding touch of her hand on his. The sound of her light, rapid step on the stairs.

"When do you leave?"

Dunton tore himself away from his memories to answer Anne's question.

"The day after tomorrow."

"So soon?"

He smiled at her disappointment.

"I'm afraid so. Rachel always said that I was hardly home before I was off to sea again. I have to see to the victualling of the ship. I'll be able to visit you all a few times before we sail, though."

"You won't sail immediately, then?"

"No, in a fortnight or so, depending when we get a favourable wind."

"When will you return?"

They were walking slowly up the path together, the fallen leaves, made brittle by the frost, crunching under their feet with a crisp, satisfying sound. Dunton considered the question.

"Eight or nine months perhaps. We shall have to return in the autumn. The winter storms make Sallee impregnable. As it is . . ."

He broke off, frowning, hesitating to voice his doubts about the voyage. His feeling was that they must go but they would have to be extremely lucky as well as resourceful if they were to accomplish their mission. He wondered, as always, about Richard.

"I hope you find your son well. I know how much it means to you."

Dunton looked quickly at Anne, surprised at her perception.

"He begged so to go with me," he said. "His mother said he was too young, let him wait a year or two. But I said I was younger than he was when I first went to sea and she'd be saying that when he was . . . O God, Rachel!"

His sudden quick burst of tears startled them both. Dunton wiped his sleeve hastily across his eyes, glancing towards the house, fearful lest his daughters should have seen. Trying to collect his feelings, he stooped, picking up a fallen stick from the path, breaking it and tossing it aside.

"I miss her," he said simply, then he turned to Anne. "I don't think I could have gone away and left the girls again, even for Dick's sake, unless you had been here to look after them. I want you to know that I'm grateful."

"It's I that should be grateful. Mother and I will be happier here than anywhere else that we could go and you will be helping to bring our loved ones home to us."

Suddenly, almost inconsequently, he turned to her once more before they entered the house.

"Mistress Crace, I loved my wife very dearly. In all my days at sea I never wanted . . . That is I never . . ."

He broke off, lost for words, confused that he should have started to make such an intimate and uncalled-for confidence.

Anne Crace looked at him unembarrassed and with steady candour.

"I know that, John," she said.

21

Jaffar Rais had finally fallen asleep on his side, his face against Celia's breast, one hand still between her legs. She lay as she had done all along, on her back, naked in the full surrender of her body to his, but she did not and could not sleep for the thundering of the guns across the river.

It was not only the gunfire that kept her awake. It was close and humid and she was aware of much coming and going in the dark rooms and courtyards beyond.

All day the streets of the casbah had echoed with shouts and trampling feet as the incensed mob of Moriscos from the poorer parts of town, the dockyard workers, seamen, labourers, craftsmen and shopkeepers, had driven the wealthy Hornacheros from their sumptuous houses, proclaiming their own leaders as rulers in place of them.

Jaffar Rais, having led the combined force of corsairs and Moriscos to victory, conferred endlessly - or so it seemed to Celia, waiting for him in the stuffy confines of the women's quarters - with his confederates.

She glimpsed him from time to time as she peered through the lattice that screened the window in the room where she waited. She saw and heard him talking to the dark-skinned men in their robes and turbans whom she took to be citizens of the town, and to his own ragged corsairs, just come home from sea. For hours they talked and caroused and for hours she waited, alone because the other women had fled or hidden. Even Charity Lidd was nowhere to be seen and the warm breeze which occasionally wafted through the inner courtyard and swayed the hanging draperies in the deserted rooms of the harem made it seem a lonely, rather eerie place. Walking through them, Celia had wondered where the other women had taken refuge. Their possessions were lying everywhere - robes, necklaces, bottles of unguent and perfume and many more mundane things such as a loom with an unfinished piece of cloth in it, pots and pans and a bowl of vegetables, some peeled, with the paring knife lying beside it.

She had picked up the knife, listlessly studying it, when Jaffar Rais had suddenly returned, striding through the rooms of the Caid's harem, shouting for her.

"Leah! Leah! Where the hell are you?"

She had run to him gladly, finding him a little tired, very excited and more than slightly drunk, but needing her, needing her very much.

Now he slept, for the noise of gunfire was too commonplace a background to his life for it to penetrate his subconscious mind and wake him, but Celia was restless, afraid of the bombardment and made uncomfortable by the heat. Her hair was clinging damply to the back of her neck and sweat had collected in the hollows of her elbows and knees and where their bodies touched.

Now that it was night the breeze from the sea was cooler. She longed to go and stand by the window, but she did not want to risk waking Jaffar Rais.

She looked at him, slumbering in the crook of her arm, relaxed, bearded cheek a little rounded and oddly childlike in sleep. If she woke him she knew from experience that he would want her again and she was not ready for him. Not yet.

Very gently and gradually she eased herself away from him. He stirred and murmured but his eyes stayed closed. She knelt, watching him, then stood up, gathering her moist hair in her hands and holding it away from the nape of her neck, feeling the refreshing breeze on her body.

She shivered a little, picked up a coverlet and wound it round her under the armpits, standing by the window and looking out, taking deep breaths of fresh air.

It was dark, the line of the ramparts showing black against a midnight sky scattered with tiny brilliant stars, bright as they never are anywhere but in Africa. Then there was a flash like lightning followed by a reverberating boom as all the guns on the far bank of the Bou Regreb spoke together and Celia involuntarily cried out.

There was a swift movement, a light step, and, before she could turn to face him, Jaffar Rais' arms came round her, pressing her body against his. He was silent, rapid and deft as a hunting animal, she thought, feeling him warm, strong and muscular through the thin covering she had draped over herself.

"I put out my hand and found you gone." He sounded aggrieved. "Why did you leave me?"

"The gunfire wakened me," she said. "What's going on, Jaffar?"

The lightning flash came again and she clung to him, glad of the hard arms that held her tightly.

"What did you want to put this thing on for?" He pulled down the coverlet she had round her. "That's better." He gave a sigh of satisfaction as it dropped and he felt her bare flesh against his. "As for the guns, Leah, why that's just our friend the Saint barking his disapproval of what's been done here today. Let him bark!"

"Friend? Saint?"

He kissed the side of her neck before answering her puzzled questioning.

"The ruler of the town across the river is a kind of hereditary holy man called the Saint. There's no English equivalent to his status, but I suppose he's a bit like one of the warrior bishops in the Middle Ages used to be, a temporal as well as a spiritual leader. Anyway," he laughed at her obvious bewilderment, "the so-called Saint is really a warlike fanatic named Sidi el Ayachi who's hand in glove with the Hornacheros that we've just sent packing. Most of the ones who got away will have taken refuge with him. The Saint's had his devout eye on the revenues we make from plunder and slaving and he'd like to rule New Sallee as well as Old. All in the name of the Prophet, of course," he added sarcastically. "When religious men want to justify their lusts they blame their god. Thank God I don't have to hide behind excuses. At least I dare be what I seem."

His hands were busy about her all the time he talked, making it hard for her to concentrate on what he said, though she wanted to understand. He felt her yielding and laughed again, softly.

"Don't worry about the Saint's guns, little Leah. They're just five old cannons that make a lot of noise but can do hardly any damage. Most of the town is beyond their range and all any of the shot can do is send a few stones flying."

"Then it wasn't just a riot. You're at war."

"I'm at war with all the world and so are all the corsairs of Sallee. But it's not war by European standards here in Morocco. The country's never at peace and the Sultan rules it in name only. The Saint's supposed to be his vassal but he's a rebel, really, acknowledging no power but his own. The Saint may think he's waging a holy war against the infidel but what he wants is our money, Leah. The old town's poor, the new town's rich. That's about the size of it. He's been trying to get control of us for years, but he'll not do it. We've got the men, the capital, the armaments. All he's got is a mob of half-starved, half-armed, fanatical Berbers and those old broken-mouthed cannons. Murad and I could hold New Sallee against Sidi el Ayachi till kingdom come, Leah, so forget about him and remember me."

Indeed, he contrived to see that she could do nothing else.

Her head drooped back on his shoulder and his mouth came down, hard and demanding on the vulnerable bend of her throat.

Celia's knees gave way and Jaffar Rais chuckled, savouring his triumph, laying her down on the cushions, preparing to enter her from behind as their initial embrace had suggested. Unexpectedly she pulled away from him, inviting a struggle which ended with a vigorous slapping of her rump, a riotous coupling and ultimate blissful tenderness arising from deep mutual satisfaction.

"Haven't you ever had enough?" she asked him as they lay panting in each other's arms.

"Every time," he said, pushing the tumbled dark hair back from her brow. "Every time. That's why I keep coming back for more. Does that sound foolish?"

She stretched herself luxuriously, enjoying the pleasant tingling sensation in her haunches where his hands had landed.

"No. It sounds wonderful. I think I would love you just for saying that, even if I had no better reasons."

He rolled over on to his belly, resting on his elbows, looking sideways at her.

"You want me, Leah. Yes. But love," he shook his head, giving the word a strange emphasis, "that's another thing altogether. I kidnapped you and your family. Burned Combe. That's the reality. Not this. When you no longer want me you'll remember and hate me."

The poignant regret in his tone, so unlike the triumphant boasting that had preceded their love making and the warm intimacy that had succeeded it, evoked in her an immediate response.

"You need me," she said. "You need me more than anyone has ever done. It's that I shall remember."

"You know," he said, "I believe you will."

* * *

Bastiano woke them, beating on the door with the news that the fugitive slaves from the mazmorra had been recaptured.

"Some of your friends tried to run away."

Jaffar Rais, pulling on his clothes, glowered at Celia as he responded to her sleepy questioning, his night of love forgotten in the harsh light of morning.

Celia sat up, tousled hair round her shoulders, holding up the coverlet before her.

"My friends?"

"The parson and Simon Greenfield and a few others. I'll have to make an example of them."

Bastiano was speaking rapidly to Jaffar Rais in the heterogeneous speech of the Barbary Coast, a kind of pidgin talk mingling Spanish and Italian and many Mediterranean words, with a sprinkling of English and Dutch.

Buckling on his sword, Jaffar smiled grimly.

"Young Dunton, too. Well, I made a promise to his father which must be kept."

Celia called after him, but he left without a word or a look, striding out of the room with Bastiano, very much the corsair leader, vengeful and assertive, bearing no resemblance, now, to the loving, vulnerable human being of a few hours past.

"Lady Lovell!"

It was Charity Lidd, looking incongruous, with her fair hair and light skin, in billowing, filmy trousers and brief, revealing bodice, slipping into the room as soon as the men left it.

"Here, put these on." She handed Celia garments similar to her own, but of richer fabric, helping her into them and talking all the time.

"You'll have to do something for them. They've just brought them in, with ropes round their necks. They've made them run behind their horses all the way here, you can see by the rope galls, even the little boy. Brutes!"

Charity adjusted Celia's sash with a vicious tweak on the last word.

"No, it goes this way." She fastened the scanty bodice which supported Celia's breasts whilst not concealing much more than her nipples and hastily placed a filmy mantle over her head and shoulders.

"Look!"

Charity dragged Celia to the window overlooking the courtyard where the corsairs were assembling, rubbing shoulders with their Morisco allies. Through the gates the miserable train of recaptured fugitives was entering, following in the wake of Ali Zuni and his Arabs.

Celia saw Stephen Hillard, stripped to the waist and with a halter round his neck, stagger a few steps into the courtyard and fall to his knees. A jerk on his halter by the rider who held it brought him up on his feet again with a choking gasp.

Celia exclaimed in dismay as she saw Sim Greenfield similarly haltered and a smallish boy whom she did not recognize.

"Is that the Dunton child?" she asked Charity, who nodded.

"You know what they'll do to them, don't you?" Charity was watching Celia's face closely. "An Irish woman, captured in a raid on Baltimore, told me what was done to some Christians who tried to escape last year. The ringleader was roasted to death in the centre of a circle of slow fires. It took him two days to die. Two others were dragged to death at the heels of horses. The rest were given so many strokes of the bastinado that two died and those that survived will never walk again." She clutched at Celia's arm. "You've got influence with Jaffar Rais. The corsairs have elected him leader. Go down and plead with him to spare them."

Celia bit her lip. The catalogue of tortures was horrifying.

"I don't know that I dare. Women aren't allowed to appear in public here, are they? If I anger him by trying to interfere it may only make things worse."

In answer Charity pointed out of the window. In the square below, under the bright sun, some sort of court was assembling. Jaffar Rais, Murad and a number of men of Spanish appearance but dressed in Moorish robes sat in the shade of the arches. Before them Ali Zuni and his men stood with their prisoners, whilst all around the noisy crowd surged, trying to get a sight of the proceedings.

Celia saw Bastiano standing by, bald head and bulging muscles shining in the sunlight, the long whip in his hand. Ali Zuni had the young boy by the arm and Celia could see from the way Dick Dunton's head hung tensely sideways how much the Arab's grasp was hurting him. But it was the sight of the two men with the foot yoke and cudgel they used to apply the bastinado that decided Celia. She'd seen Sim suffer just a few strokes of it once. She wasn't minded to stand by and see him and the others crippled or dragged away to the worse deaths Charity had spoken of.

"I'll do it."

"This way."

Charity took her arm, leading her through the harem to the courtyard outside. Some of the women had returned, Celia saw, mostly the older ones who had the look of domestics rather than concubines. Their children peered shyly at her from behind pillars whilst their mothers stared suspiciously as she hurried by.

Celia knew she mustn't stop to think or she would lose heart, so at the entrance of the women's quarters she nudged Charity aside and pushed her way out boldly between the guards.

"Who helped you escape?"

Jaffar Rais was on his feet interrogating the line of captives. She could see he was angry and his look frightened her. She elbowed her way through the crowd. A man shouted at her and tore her veil but she pressed on.

Jaffar Rais stopped in front of Stephen Hillard.

"Was it the priest?"

Stephen stared back at him blankly.

Bastiano stroked the thong of his long whip between his fleshy fingers.

"Let me ask him, Jaffar."

"Can't you wait, you old bastard?" Jaffar Rais sounded weary rather than angry. "You'll have plenty to do before long. This one won't tell you. He'd like to be a martyr. Wouldn't you, parson?"

"No. But I won't answer." Stephen looked at Jaffar Rais in his level way.

"Not for some time, anyway," said the corsair grimly. "But everyone does in the end. A bit of a waste of suffering, don't you think, parson? Now, this one," he suddenly grabbed Tippett Collecock by the throat, so that the little trickster choked and doubled up, "will tell me just for the asking. Won't you, little man?"

As soon as Tippett, his eyes bulging, could speak, he stuttered out, "It was the priest."

"Judas!" muttered Sim.

"We knew anyway." Jaffar Rais let Tippett Collecock go with a contemptuous gesture. "The question is what to do with the rest of you," he said, raising his voice and looking at the wretched men and boys before him, tattered, filthy and exhausted, bareheaded in the blazing sun whilst the sweaty crowd, eager for blood-sport, looked on. "We've thousands of slaves here. We depend on their labour to keep our farms and quarries going. Escapes are bad for morale, make for restlessness and disorder. We'll have to . . . What are you doing here?"

The corsair's last words were to Celia, who had finally won her way to his side.

When she saw his expression change from surprise to

rage she knew how terrified she really was. What she had meant to say deserted her and she could only stammer feebly.

"Have mercy!"

And suiting the action to the words, she sank to her knees.

22

"All we want now is for the wind to change," said William Rainsborough.

Standing beside him on the deck of His Majesty's Ship *Leopard*, John Dunton nodded silently, looking up at the grey February sky, thinly streaked with cloud. They needed a south-westerly breeze but the wind was blowing from the north-east and had been for a week. All that time the *Leopard* had lain at anchor off Tilbury Hope with her sister ships of the Sallee squadron berthed alongside, *Antelope*, *Hercules*, *Mary*, *Mary Rose* and *Roebuck*, fully manned and provisioned.

"Nothing worse for ships or men than hanging about in harbour when you're ready to sail," Rainsborough grumbled, blowing on his hands and stamping his feet. The north-east wind was cold as well as contrary and there was nothing to be said in its favour. Rainsborough had received his commission from the King and was impatient to be gone.

"It's the third week in February," said John Dunton in his deliberate way. "If we're not in Sallee roads by the third week in March we might as well not have sailed at all."

Rainsborough grunted. "So you're always telling me. That's why I haven't waited for the two new pinnaces to be completed as my lords of the Admiralty would have liked me to do. I think you make too much of the timing. The main thing is to frighten them with a show of force."

Dunton shook his head. The cold, the adverse wind, all the irritations and delays had combined to put his brother-in-law out of temper. He said carefully but positively, "Come the end of March all those little ships of theirs, and a few bigger ones too, now, will come pouring out of Sallee like hunting dogs on a hot scent. And after the recent success of raids on our coasts most of them will be headed this way. But until the end of next month there's no getting in or out, except for little surf boats. We've got to bottle them up and we've got to be in time to do it."

Rainsborough slapped his arms across his chest, his breath leaving a smoky trail in the frosty air. Overhead two skeins of brent geese, black-necked and rapid of flight, headed south for the reedy shelter of Dartford marshes across the river, making their guttural, croaking cry. Rainsborough followed the track of their flight with a jaundiced eye as his barge drew alongside, her prow cutting a white ripple in the leaden water.

"May as well make our farewells." Grudgingly, Rainsborough prepared for a cold, wet descent of the ship's side. John Dunton felt a curious reluctance to repeat the emotional goodbyes which had already been gone through a few days ago when the departure of the Sallee squadron had seemed imminent. Seating himself in the barge beside Rainsborough he reflected that his return would cause a flutter in his home and perhaps be something of an anti-climax. Nevertheless he had to go.

Rainsborough's eight-oared barge tied up at Rotherhithe's small jetty, its wooden pillars green with water weed, to let Dunton disembark. He climbed awkwardly ashore, stiff from the cold journey in the cramped open boat.

"Pick you up in two hours," Rainsborough called to him as the barge pulled away from the landing stage, northward across the tide to Wapping on the opposite bank. Dunton waved acknowledgement, turning his back on the river and stepping out briskly along the lane to his house.

As was usual in the afternoon, Dunton found the kitchen

door closed but not locked. Lifting the latch, he stepped inside.

"Rachel!"

He spoke the name before he could stop himself, as soon as he saw the woman in the russet gown and white cap, sitting with her back to him near the fire, nursing the baby. She turned towards him, startled at first, then, seeing who it was, smiling and putting her finger to her lips.

"Ssh! She's just gone off to sleep," said Anne Crace.

Dunton stood biting his lip, inching his hat brim round and round between his fingers, cursing himself for his foolish mistake, watching as Anne put the sleeping Martha down carefully into the wooden cradle and began rocking it gently and rhythmically with her foot.

He held his breath, peering over Anne's shoulder, knowing that this was the crucial moment when the child would either wake screaming or settle peacefully. Five minutes passed with Anne keeping the cradle in steady motion before the two of them dared to exchange a glance of relief, so fervently conspiratorial as to be almost guilty, and creep from the room, tiptoeing into the parlour beyond.

"I thought I'd never get her to sleep."

Anne smiled at him, pleased and triumphant, leaning against the door as soon as she had closed it. "She's having such trouble with her teeth."

"I know. They all did."

Dunton looked at her apologetically. He'd fathered five children and the preceding scene had been many times re-enacted by Rachel and himself. He gave a wry smile. "I used to think it was the best reason for being a sailor. Getting away from all the screaming, I mean."

He sat down, putting his hat on the table, looking rather diffidently at Anne Crace. The admission had cost him something and he was not proud of it. Although custom took it for granted that the child's physical needs and all the more tedious aspects of its unbringing were the mother's responsibility, John Dunton had loved his Rachel and never liked to think of leaving her to cope with any situation alone.

He was relieved to see that his confession had done him no harm in Anne Crace's eyes for her quiet laugh had a hint of tenderness in it.

"We didn't expect you. It's good to see you."

She sat down opposite him, smiling with frank pleasure.

He found himself thinking how sweetly at home she looked seated at his fireside and said shortly, "I've only got two hours."

She wrinkled her brow.

"Still waiting for a wind? Two hours isn't long. Stay at least until the girls come home, they've all gone into Greenwich market with Mabyn. They'll never forgive me if I let you go away without seeing them."

He shook his head, smiling at her wheedling tone, watching her swift, deft movements as she fetched him some ale and set it down by him.

"Duty calls, I'm afraid. Is everything all right? The money . . . ?"

"Everything. Don't worry. I get plenty of help and advice." An intimate look of understanding passed between them. Each knew what the other was thinking and they laughed together delightedly, like mischievous children.

Dunton found himself saying, "Judith's a good woman."

"Yes." Anne assumed a grave expression, but her eyes danced. Then she said seriously, "When you come back you'll be bringing my father and brother and sister with you."

Her childlike faith touched him. "I hope so. As many captives as we can. Master Hillard, too."

"Yes, Stephen too."

She was silent, looking into the fire.

"What are you thinking of?"

She turned her candid gaze on him. "Before all this happened I was so worried about so many things. Stephen had just asked me to go to Massachusetts with him. He

211

believed it was God's will that he should go to the New World. My parents were against it. I didn't know what to do. Now all that seems so unreal and far away. I wonder how he feels."

John Dunton studied her face. He was glad she could not really understand what it was like to be a slave in Barbary.

"I expect he's living for the moment when he'll be free and can come back to you."

"I wonder." She bent her head. "For the last few weeks before the raid I was beginning to wonder if I'd ever really known him."

"It takes a long time," Dunton said slowly, "for two people to get to know each other. At least . . ."

She looked up and again they both had the sensation of thinking the same thought at the same time. They were aware that after only a short acquaintance they knew each other very well indeed.

They sat quietly by the fire for a few minutes, neither speaking or feeling the need to speak. They heard the coals settle in the grate.

From upstairs a shrill bell rang. Anne jumped to her feet.

"Mother's bell," she said hastily in explanation and sped out of the room.

Dunton felt curiously lonely when she had gone, impatient for her return and resentful that, seeing he had only these precious few minutes with her, someone else should call her away from him.

Anne returned almost immediately, smiling reassuringly.

"Yes, she's comfortable now," she said in answer to his polite enquiry after her mother's health, "of course she's not able to get about much, but the news of the expedition has given her hope for the future and she's happier than she was. Tell me," she asked in her direct way, "why you called me by your wife's name when you came in just now. You knew I couldn't be Rachel. Why did you?"

He had hoped she wouldn't ask.

"Sitting as you were, nursing my child. I just thought, 'Wife. My wife.' " He paused. "I'm sorry."

"Don't be. I love Martha. I wish she was mine. I love the others too." Her words were all coming in a rush. As though to stem the flood of them, to halt the flow of her feelings, she suddenly said, "When Stephen comes home he'll need me more than ever. I'll have to help him all I can."

"Yes, of course." Dunton spoke slowly and with effort. Their conversation was dealing with deeper things than words allowed for. This unexpected meeting and the still more unexpected opportunity of being alone together had brought them face to face with the truth.

They sat facing one another, the fire between them.

"I must bring him back to her," thought John Dunton. "She's promised to him. What would I have thought of a man who might have tried to steal Rachel from me? It's unthinkable. And yet . . . ?"

Anne Crace thought, "I love this man. I don't love Stephen. I don't think I ever did. If all this hadn't happened I don't believe I would have married him. But now, because it has, I must. If Stephen still wants me, I'll have to marry him."

The church clock was striking the hour. Abruptly John Dunton stood up.

"I must be going. I'm sorry to miss the girls. Give them my love. Tell them . . ."

He was thinking that it was like dying to have to leave her without telling her he loved her, but he must. Being accustomed to hard things did not help him.

Anne was trying to remember the promises she had made to Stephen and praying to be able to keep them.

Dunton picked up his hat.

"You've not drunk your ale."

Anne strove to speak calmly.

"Keep it till I come back," he said with an effort at lightness. "Tell the girls I'll bring them an ivory necklace each." He held out his hand. "Well, God bless you."

"God keep you."

Their fingers just touched. He went out, closing the door firmly behind him.

Half an hour later Deborah ran in, fair curls blown all about her face, calling excitedly.

"Anne! Anne! We met father in the lane. Wasn't it wonderful seeing him again? He's going to bring us all ivory necklaces but I said I'd rather have a monkey. And while we were waiting at the jetty for Uncle's barge do you know what happened? The wind changed so he'll be sailing tomorrow morning. Anne, what's the matter? Mabyn, come quick, Anne's crying!"

23

Celia felt the sun hot on her head. Around her the mass of faces swayed and surged, blurring into one another in a mist of bright light and a noise like the thunder of the sea, rising and falling. Then the face of Jaffar Rais came close, becoming very clear and blotting out all the others as he stooped forward and pulled her to her feet.

"What the hell are you doing here?"

Over his shoulder she glimpsed the watchers grinning at her, Murad Rais mockingly, Bastiano wolfishly, beyond them the Morisco leaders in their flowing robes, some lean, some florid, but all alike disdainfully hostile. Panic prompted her to turn and run. But behind her was that pathetic line of captives. She looked imploringly at Jaffar Rais.

"Don't let them be tortured. Not my friends. Not the child."

"You fool. You're making me the laughing-stock of the town, making a scene in public like this. Get back inside."

Celia had never seen him so angry but just as she was about to obey she caught sight of Dick Dunton, biting his lip so as not to cry, his wrist in the harsh grip of the slave trader, and she clutched impetuously at Jaffar Rais' arm.

"At least spare the child. I won't go without the child."

She thought he would have struck her but the crowd were laughing openly now and Jaffar Rais, judging it best to humour their mood, joined in the laughter.

"I'll make you pay for this," he muttered under his breath

to Celia. Aloud he shouted jovially to the Arab, "Give her the boy, Ali. You owe him to me anyway."

Ali Zuni shrugged, releasing Dick and giving him a push forward that sent him sprawling on his face in the dust of the courtyard, making the onlookers laugh the more. Celia seized his hand and hauled him up.

"Bastiano!"

The shaven-headed overseer, his whip coiled about his neck, came forward instantly at Jaffar Rais' shouted summons.

"Escort this lady back to the women's quarters."

Bastiano nodded, clearing a path through the hooting crowd for Celia and the boy. Celia, hurrying after him, her arm round Dick Dunton, recoiled from the clawing hands and the rank smell of sweat and thought despairingly that she'd done nothing for the rest of the captives. And Jaffar Rais' last look and angrily muttered words boded no good for her either.

At the door to the harem Bastiano halted.

"You are mad, Englishwoman?"

He eyed her with insolent freedom. Celia glared.

"Is it mad to intercede for your friends?"

"As you are placed, yes. You are lucky he is not tired of you yet. If he were you would be sewn into a sack alive and flung into the sea. As it is, he will have you punished. In private, of course." He twitched meaningly at the thong of his whip.

"Go!" Celia stamped her foot at him. "Go!"

Bastiano smiled. "You will see me again."

Beyond the lattice Charity Lidd was waiting.

"You poor things," she said, hugging them both, and to Celia, "Ee, you did well. I was watching. I'd never have had the courage."

Back in the comparative privacy of her room with its window looking out over the ramparts to the sea, Celia set Dick down on some cushions and she and Charity looked at him.

The boy cowered away from them, head hanging, his bleached thatch of long, tangled hair hiding his face. Celia saw how the elbows which showed through the rents in the loose sleeves of his tattered, filthy shirt were sharp and brittle. He was very skinny. Probably half-starved, she thought, remembering vaguely that boys of that age were supposed to be hungry all the time.

She turned rather helplessly to Charity.

"Can you find him something to eat?"

"Surely. And you, too."

Charity bustled away to the kitchens at the back, a place to which she naturally gravitated and where she found herself already at home. The rooms were dingy, bare and smoke-blackened. On charcoal stoves whose embers were kept glowing by constant fanning, pots of vegetable stew and the inevitable kus-kus bubbled at all hours, tended by old crones who seemed to spend their entire life there. It was cosy, though, compared with the cool grandeur of the rest of the house, and Charity made herself useful to the old cooks, who tolerated her presence, and from whom she begged scraps.

Left alone together, Celia and the boy confronted one another.

"What's your name?"

He didn't answer, only raised his head, staring at her. His sunburned cheeks were thin and sunken, making his cheekbones look unnaturally high. His bright blue eyes had dark shadows under them. His steady gaze reminded her of someone. She repeated her question.

"Dick Dunton." He sounded reluctant, mistrustful.

"You're the son of that man Jaffar Rais forced to navigate his ship and then made off with the prize in the Channel, aren't you?"

Celia felt and sounded triumphant. The boy's eyes blazed into life and he leaned forward excitedly.

"You know my father? Tell me about him."

Celia held out her hands and Dick grabbed them, shyness

and suspicion vanished, listening avidly to what she had to say. Celia told him what little she had heard of John Dunton's seizure of the *Jacob*, stressing how his action must have resulted in the rescue of about twenty women and children, among them her own mother and sister.

Dick dwelt hungrily on her words, biting his knuckles. When she finished he took a deep breath.

"I knew," he said. "I knew he must have had a good reason for not coming back." His voice trembled. "I knew he didn't forget me."

He was very near to tears. Celia held his hand tight.

"I'm sure he didn't." The boy was uncannily like his father. Deep feelings, strong affections, determined self-control characterized them both, she thought, remembering her brief encounter with John Dunton. "I'm sure your father never forgets about you for a moment. He doesn't seem to me to be that kind of man at all."

He looked at her with shining eyes.

"No. He's not. He's not at all."

She could see what a relief it was to him to have his faith in his father restored. Charity, coming in with bowls of stew and balls of kus-kus, paused on the threshold. She'd always been inclined to like Celia but had tended to think of her as a high class tart who got away with behaviour for which a common woman like herself was made to suffer because of her rank. Now seeing her comforting the child, Charity's heart warmed with a glow of real friendliness. Their eyes met over Dick's head.

"Here, eat some of this," Charity smiled, setting down the tray.

The boy ate as though famished, as though he feared the food would be snatched away before he had finished, cramming his mouth and wiping it with the back of his hand when there was no more left.

"He'd better not be about when his mightiness comes home," Charity said warningly to Celia.

"They won't make me go back to Ali Zuni, will they?"

Once more Dick was all large, frightened eyes.

"Not if I know it," Celia said stoutly, hoping she could keep the promise. "Charity, is there somewhere . . . ?"

Charity nodded. "Come on, Dickie, or whatever your name is. I'll find you a place to sleep out of harm's way."

Dick glanced questioningly at Celia.

"Yes," she said. "Go with Charity."

But he lingered in the doorway, fingering a space between the curved tiles that framed it, tracing the shape of one and looking down.

"Is a whore a bad thing to be?"

Celia and Charity exchanged astonished looks, dumbfounded by the question. Celia found her tongue first.

"Why do you ask?"

"Because," Dick still looked down, tracing the outline of the tile with his fingertip, "that's what they said you were. Those Englishmen I was with. They said you were Jaffar Rais' whore. Well," he looked up, "if you are I don't see how it could be anything bad."

"Thank you, Dick," said Celia.

Charity came back in a few minutes.

"Sound asleep," she reported. "Worn out, he was, poor child. What a life it is! It's bad enough for the likes of us, but what must it be for a poor infant like that, all alone the way he's been, too!"

"Yes."

Celia sat with her hands in her lap, looking straight ahead of her. Charity said gently, "Frightened, aren't you?"

Celia hugged her arms round her.

"Bastiano said I'd be whipped."

Charity put a hand on her shoulder. "Most likely he'll forget, or think better of it. Jaffar Rais, I mean. He's very taken with you."

Celia said suddenly, "I think I'm going to have his child."

"What?" Charity looked startled. "It's too soon to tell.

How long . . . ?"

"I'm three weeks late. I never have been before."

Charity shook her head.

"You can't tell for certain until you've gone three months. Still, it might help to tell him you are. It might make him soften towards you . . ."

"Get out."

Jaffar Rais' peremptory order sent Charity scuttling as he strode in with Bastiano behind him.

Celia jumped to her feet and backed away, standing pressed against the wall. Bastiano approached, carrying a length of rope, his whip hanging about his neck, the thong loosely twisted round it.

"No!"

Celia clenched her hands, looking past him to Jaffar Rais. He regarded her stonily.

"You'd better submit without a struggle. He's acting by my orders. Did you expect to get off scot free?"

"No." She was frankly terrified now. "No. But I won't have that man touch me."

She darted forward, so suddenly and unexpectedly that her rapid movement took both men by surprise, and snatched the whip from around Bastiano's neck.

"There!" She flung it down so that it lay like a black snake uncoiling at the feet of Jaffar Rais. "Am I a dog?" she demanded. "To be beaten by a slave? If you want it done, do it yourself."

Bastiano looked at his master. Jaffar Rais motioned him to go with a jerk of his head and the overseer swung hastily out of the room. Jaffar Rais stooped and slowly picked up the whip.

"Undress."

Celia did so, hoping the result would distract him, but he did not look at her.

"Now lie down."

She made herself as small as she could, arms folded across

her breasts to protect them, knees pressed close up against her belly.

"Stretch out. Lie on your face."

The cushions felt cold to her body. Waiting for the lash to fall she wished she could have sunk down into them.

When Jaffar Rais touched her she gave a scream, though she felt no hurt.

"You witch," he said, pulling her round to face him and holding her close to his chest. "Did you know this would happen? Did you?"

She could hardly breathe, she was so relieved.

"No. No, I didn't. Will you forgive me?"

"I seem to have done so." He laughed, caressing the bare, tight curve of her buttocks with a firm hand. "I was so angry with you after what happened I thought I wanted to hurt you. Then I saw you lying there and thought of better things to do. Why," he slid his hand between her legs, "I've hardly touched you and yet you're ready for me."

She arched herself in abandon, her body responding to his expert fingering like an instrument to the touch of a skilled musician.

She stroked him and he sighed, a deep, gusty sigh of satisfaction.

"You are a witch," he said. "You must be."

She fetched him wine afterwards, kneeling by him naked with the cup in her hand, her long hair hanging loose about her shoulders. They sipped from the cup together. He touched her nipples with his fingertip, drawing it down between her breasts to her navel.

"I think I'm with child," she said.

"It had better be mine."

"It will be."

She felt that he wanted her again and yielded herself ardently.

Celia didn't learn until later that the recaptured prisoners had got off relatively lightly and when she did Jaffar Rais denied her intercession had made any difference to his decision. It had been, he insisted, merely good business.

In the short term he wanted a good price in the slave market, in the long, a high ransom. A dead prisoner was a dead loss, a crippled one was hardly a better proposition.

He lay beside her, contentedly drawing on his pipe, looking at her with satisfaction. She gave him a lot of pleasure. Made him feel good. Really liked him. Didn't ask much. Lovely body.

The sleeping Celia stirred as though she felt him looking at her and Jaffar Rais chuckled, patting her smooth belly.

He wondered if she was right about the child. He'd like sons by her. He patted her again. She was soft but firm, the way a woman should be.

"Always fancied you, little Leah," he said.

24

"How heavy do you reckon these irons are?"

"I don't know, but it feels like a ton."

Stephen Hillard looked ruefully at the broad, solid metal ring fastened round his left ankle, the four feet of thick chain and the massive weight to which it was anchored. Altogether the fetters probably weighed over fifty pounds. As a punishment for attempted escape they were, by Sallee standards, light, but they certainly prevented any repetition of the offence. All the escapees from the mazmorra had been fitted with them before being herded into the Bedestan and put up for sale. Already the iron cuff had chafed Stephen's skin raw in several places, making movement painful, even at the snail's pace the weight dictated.

"Here, try padding it with a bit o' this."

Tippett Collecock, standing beside him on the crumbling stone block where the slave dealer had displayed them, produced a handful of torn rags and began deftly winding them round the galling fetter on Stephen's leg.

"Thanks. That *is* easier."

Stephen found he could actually move his foot without wincing and smiled at the little man.

"You're a good sort, Tip."

Tippett grinned.

"*Your* sort don't usually think so, parson. They generally put me down as a bad lot. Christ, but it's hot! This place is just like a bloody cattle market."

"Just."

Stephen let the oath and expletive pass. Time was when he would have been shocked by them, but the world in which men watched their language in his presence was now so far away that it seemed to have ceased to exist. And the Bedestan was indeed just like a cattle market.

The bodies for sale in it happened to be human, but there was the same jostling, noisy crowd, the same smells of sweat and ordure and the same sort of dealers with prodding sticks and probing fingers haggling over prices.

It was hotter. There were more flies. Faces were darker and clothes brighter, but the atmosphere was much the same as in any busy English town where animals were bought and sold.

The merchandise was not penned but individually roped or shackled and there were no females exposed to public view. This, even in freebooting Sallee, was forbidden as a breach of the Islamic code. The women's humiliation was profound but at least it was private.

The slaves were all, from the youngest to the oldest, stripped to the waist so that the dealers could judge their physical condition and fitness for labour. At intervals selected ones would be put through their paces, urged on by the dealers' goads, and beaten if they responded slackly or unwillingly. Round their necks they all wore wooden labels on which their names, status and estimated ransom prices were roughly chalked. On the basis of these they had been graded and divided into groups, high ransom prospects and good physique obviously commanding the highest asking prices.

Sim Greenfield, as a propertied gentleman and strongly built into the bargain, aroused the most interest in buyers seeking a good investment, a fact which obviously afforded him no satisfaction.

"Cheer up, Master Greenfield," said Tippett impudently, "I heard Ali Zuni say just now that Jaffar Rais has put a reserve price of six hundred ducats on you. You must be the prize purchase here."

"Hold your tongue, Collecock."

Sim glowered at him, not in the mood for the trickster's raillery, his body sore from the dealers' handling and his heart with humiliation, his own and his family's. There was his father, a landowner and a magistrate, no respect accorded either to his position or his grey hairs, shirt torn from his back, hands roped together, standing amongst a group of labourers. The old man's face was a mask of angry bewilderment at being treated as a common felon would have been in England. His back was rigid with protest.

Tippett followed the direction of Sim's gaze.

"Well, at least your father's not ironed like the rest of us." When Sim did not answer he added, "I don't see her ladyship's father here."

Sim flushed. He hated to hear Celia's name mentioned. That she was known to be living willingly with Jaffar Rais as the corsair's mistress was not the least of his miseries. That Celia's father was being spared the ordeal of the Bedestan as the price of what he would have termed his daughter's "shame" was as little consolation to Sim as it was to Squire Crace himself. His resentment found relief in an explosion of sneering anger against Tippett.

"Since when," Sim demanded, "have you figured among the landed gentry, Collecock?" He flicked a contemptuous hand at the piece of board round Tippett's neck which proclaimed his probable ransom as five hundred pounds. "Who's going to pay that for you? Your employers? My guess is there's not a soul would put up so much as a penny to buy your liberty, Master Trickster."

"Maybe so," said Tippett easily, "but it'll take a few months for anyone who buys me to find out the truth and much may happen in a few months. In the meantime, I'm damned if I'll let these rascals think I'm irredeemable and let myself be sent to the galley bench or the quarry."

Stephen Hillard sighed, wishing they would stop bickering

and raised his hand, sticky with sweat, to brush away the flies buzzing round his eyes. He found himself remembering the look of patient cattle whom he had seen similarly tormented. His own eyes were blue and slightly near-sighted from much study and at present they were fixed on the cluster of little boys, all less than twelve years old, the children of day labourers and poor tradesmen of his parish, who were being looked over by a paunchy, smooth-faced man, remarkably light-skinned for a Moor.

Remembering the pious, monkish tale of St Gregory in the slave market at Rome purchasing the Saxon slaves in order to Christianize them, Stephen sighed again. He was innocent of any direct knowledge of what he would have termed "the sins of Sodom and Gomorrah", but the smooth-faced man appeared even to him as a pederast.

"Looks like a brothel keeper, don't he?" asked Tippett cheerfully, noticing Stephen's look of distress. "Don't take it to heart, parson," he added as the group of children were paid for and led away, "most of them will be well fed for the first time in their lives. There's something to be said for that."

Stephen hung his head. Never before in his sheltered life had he encountered so much wickedness. The words of Augustine came to mind.

"To Carthage then I came, where a tumult of unholy loves sang all about mine ears."

"I said, 'They'll be well fed for the first time in their lives.'"

Tippett regarded Stephen quizzically, his head on one side like an inquisitive sparrow, wanting to know how he really felt.

Stephen rallied himself and answered in his parsonical voice, "Man shall not live by bread alone."

Tippett chuckled, "It keeps you from starving, though, parson. Ever been hungry, Master Hillard? It's bad, especially when you're growing and can't sleep for the gnawing feeling in your guts."

"It must be," said Stephen, ashamed to speak grudgingly, for there was something cheering about Tippett's down-to-earth realism.

"Got to look on the bright side." The trickster shrugged. "Now, what does *she* want?" Tippett's eyes narrowed calculatingly as a group of sweating Negroes, all with splendid shining muscles, set down a curtained litter at the edge of the market square and a plump woman, drawing aside her veil, looked out of it.

The woman was not young and her body seemed bulky and shapeless under her enveloping djellabah, but her large dark eyes were lively and her small, pudgy hand was heavy with jewelled rings that flashed in rainbow colours when the sun caught them.

Tippett, hugging his weighted chain under one arm, moved as near the litter as he dared and directed an admiring, languishing stare at its occupant. Meeting his eye she returned the stare for a moment before replacing her veil. Then she beckoned one of her Negroes who summoned the dealer.

Spirited bargaining followed, with much waving of hands. The woman's sparkling rings glittered as she gesticulated. Finally, the dealer bowed obsequiously, took Tippett's wooden label off and nudged him forward, while the Negro counted out the coins for the purchase price into the dealer's hand with a disdainful expression. Then the litter bearers resumed their burden and Tippett, limping off gamely after his new mistress, waved to his friends left behind in the Bedestan.

Stephen was still looking after him when his arm was seized.

"Your label says 'priest'."

The prospective buyer, a lean European, a Dutchman or a Fleming, Stephen guessed from his looks and accent, pointed at the scrawl on the board round Stephen's neck. Half-contemptuously he said, "Is it true?"

Stephen stiffened. He could endure to be mocked himself but was full of a sense of the dignity of his calling.

"What of it?"

The other laughed. "Do you know Latin, music? Can you cipher? Figure? Do accounts? Teach children? Especially, can you teach my sons? Speak up, man. Surely you'd rather be a tutor than break stones in the Caid's quarries?"

Stumblingly, Stephen expressed his ability to do some of the things asked of him and his willingness to attempt all. The Fleming cut him short.

"Good enough. You're my purchase. Follow that slave there. He'll guide you to my house."

The man Stephen's buyer indicated was old William Trevor, waiting with his donkey.

"You again!"

Stephen smiled, walking slowly beside him because of the heavy weight he was obliged to carry.

"Yes. This way, sir." The old man pulled his forelock. "I'll go first. Some of these urchins are a bit troublesome, shouting and throwing things. You know what boys are," he added apologetically.

He led the way out of the crowded Bedestan into a steep street of the casbah with high walls pierced only by closed, iron-studded doorways on either side, urging his laden donkey on before him.

"Janssen bought you, then," Trevor said to Stephen. "Well you might have done a lot worse. He's a renegade, but he's not a bad sort." He nodded knowingly. Suddenly he put his head close to Stephen's.

"What became of the boy, sir?"

"Boy? Oh, you mean Dunton's son." Stephen recollected Trevor's interest in Dick Dunton. "Lady Lovell's looking after him."

"Jaffar Rais' woman?" The old man chuckled, sounding relieved. "She's a good-hearted whore, by all accounts, if you'll excuse the word, sir. It's a long time since I spoke to a clergyman, barring the Father, and he's dying, poor soul, and grieving that there's no priest near to hear his confession. Of course, 'tis a Romish superstition, that, but . . ."

"The Father dying? You mean the one that tried to help us escape?"

"Why, who would I mean but Father Gracian?" answered Trevor impatiently. "He's the only Christian priest in Sallee, isn't he? What we shall do without him, God only knows . . ."

"Why is he dying?" Stephen would have clutched at Trevor's arm but for the wretched weight he carried.

The old man regarded him with a surprised look.

"Why is he dying? You mean you don't know?"

He sounded incredulous. Stephen halted, leaning against a door, hugging the heavy weight to his chest.

"Tell me."

"Well," said Trevor reluctantly, "it wasn't the first time he'd helped in escapes. They told him what would happen if he was involved again. Never made any difference to the Father though. They nailed him to a door, sir, by his hands and feet, left him to bleed for hours."

"Crucified?"

"In a manner o' speaking, yes."

Trevor sounded faintly scandalized by Stephen's use of the word "crucified".

"Where is he?" This time Stephen contrived to get hold of the old man's arm. "Take me to him."

Trevor hesitated only a moment.

"Well, I suppose it is on our way, in the chapel in the street of the mazmorras. It can't hurt to let you see him."

It was dark in the chapel. There were only two candles on the bare altar and they had burnt very low.

The priest lay on the ground before it, stretched out on a thin palliasse, wearing his faded cassock.

Stephen thought he was alone at first till he saw Ismail

kneeling beside him.

"I've brought another priest to see you, Father," said William Trevor, speaking quietly in the deep Devonshire brogue that thirty years in Barbary had not altered.

"Another priest?"

The dying man stretched out his hand to Stephen, who took it, kneeling down opposite Ismail.

"I'm afraid you come too late. But give me your blessing."

Father Gracian's voice was very faint, the words trailing away into silence almost before they were fully uttered. Bending over him, it seemed to Stephen that his eyes were already glazing.

"Who will look after them?"

Stephen felt the priest's hand close tightly on his, felt blood from the open wound in it trickle into his palm as the other said, "They will be as sheep not having a shepherd. Our Lord laid His command on us, 'Feed My sheep.'"

"Yes," said Stephen, hardly knowing what it was he was saying. "Yes."

"Ah."

The sigh was one of relief rather than pain or exhaustion and Stephen was suddenly aware that the hand he held was limp and lifeless.

Father Gracian was dead.

25

The lazy gecko sunned itself on the wall. It was a young one, its skin almost transparent, its veins showing red in the strong tropic light. The carefree lizard was unaware of its enemy, the sinister, rigid, cadaverous praying mantis, until the mantis struck, pinioning the sleepy lizard in its savage jaws.

"What a brute!"

Dick Dunton tried to prize the contestants apart with a stick but they were too high above his head on the wall of the courtyard and, in any case, the mantis would never have let go, even in death.

"That old praying mantis," said Dick, pushing his mane of bleached fair hair back out of his eyes and turning to grin at Celia, "he reminds me of the Saint, always waiting to pounce. Fancy calling him a *saint*!"

Celia stretched herself, lazy and unsuspecting as the lizard in the sun, but plump now and ripe-looking in the last month of her pregnancy. Her child had been conceived very early in her relationship with Jaffar Rais but neither of them had mentioned the possibility that it might be Sim's. Celia was very well. Pregnancy had brought a new sheen to her hair and glossed her skin. Until only a few weeks ago she had been as sexually active as ever. Now she was waiting for the child to be born, not too impatiently, though she had reached the stage when she felt she should be glad when it was over, when she could hold her baby and enjoy it, have a womanly shape again and once more be able to respond to her lover's advances.

She lounged now, half in and half out of the shade, smiling and content, her rounded body draped in a full, flowing robe of Indian muslin gaily dyed to the colour of corn at harvest and printed in every shade of yellow and gold and orange with a design of myriads of small flowers. The robe had been looted from some merchantman or other beating home round the coast of Africa before it and its cargo fell victim to the corsairs of Sallee, like so many others.

Celia watched Dick Dunton idly, she felt very placid now that the winter and her time of waiting were almost over.

For the winter had been like all winters, not only a season of discontent but a period of mingled fear and hope spent in anticipation of what the spring held in store.

The corsairs' town of New Sallee became introverted in the months between October and March, turning in on itself, preparing for the raiding season when the bar would be passable again. The dockyards were working at full strength, repairing, caulking, careening. The taverns and brothels were full. Internal political disputes flourished and the conflict between the new town and the old continued sporadically, with the Saint biding his time and launching attacks whenever an opportunity presented itself. So far the corsairs had driven off his ill-armed henchmen without difficulty and mocked at his efforts but with their enemy so close at hand, so watchful, they had to be constantly vigilant. Each night the cannon sounded from across the river, thundering a warning.

The Moriscos had elected their own divan, or council, to govern them and nominated one of their own number, Moulay el Caceri, to be Caid in place of the one they had deposed and murdered. They had declared a nominal allegiance to the Sultan of Morocco, against whom the Saint was in rebellion and who, far away, battling with insurgents in a distant province, was powerless to control their activities. They made plans to conduct raids on the coast of Europe on a scale unknown before.

The captives from Combe came to terms with their slavery as best they could, homesick, longing for freedom and worrying about loved ones from whom they were separated. The better off wrote endless letters to relatives in England imploring them to raise money to purchase their ransoms and badgered the few English merchants resident in Sallee to get their letters delivered for them. It took a long time and there were many frustrations and delays. In the vital matter of arranging ransoms Father Gracian had been much engaged and his services were greatly missed. The hard-pressed Order of Redemptionists had not yet been able to replace him and his loss was felt by many, some of whom had been in captivity for twenty or thirty years and who had little hope of ever seeing their homelands again.

Stephen Hillard found himself the only Christian priest in Sallee and though at first he was regarded with suspicion as a newcomer and a Protestant by the large colony of slaves, many of whom were Catholics from France and Spain, numbers of them turned to him, as they had to Father Gracian, for help and consolation.

Stephen was officially the property of Cornelius Janssen, a Fleming renegade and one of the rais of the town. His work was to tutor Janssen's five sons and he spent several hours each day teaching them to read and write in English and Latin, as much history and Euclid as he could remember, the rudiments of music and even - greatly daring - stories from the Scriptures. But his main work was done when his recognized duties were completed. Then he went out wherever he was called to minister to those slaves who were sick or starving, who had been punished by their employers or set upon by other prisoners. He settled quarrels, wrote letters, interceded with the authorities on behalf of those whose ransoms had been paid but whose masters would not release them and did much of the pastoral work that Father Gracian had done. It was the busiest time of Stephen's life. He had no leisure for anything, every minute was filled with service, so, while he would not have described himself as happy, his life was untroubled by doubt and deeply satisfying.

Tippett Collecock, as might have been expected, landed on his feet. He had been bought by a wealthy widow and his main task was to console her loneliness, which he contrived to do very much to their mutual satisfaction. His duties were never onerous and included accompanying his mistress to the bagnio where he was required to entertain her and her friends by playing on his lute while they disported themselves in the water.

"It's a funny thing," he would say, putting his head on one side in his knowing way, "how these Turks are so particular about their women being kept covered up and hidden and yet, in the baths, everything goes. There's quite a few of us slaves there and we can see all there is to see and yet no one cares. I suppose the men think a slave isn't a man, just part of the furniture so to speak. Well, the women don't think so, I can tell you."

And he'd go on his way with a wink, whistling, and the others would envy him. For the life of a slave was bad, very bad for most of them and they ached and chafed to be free.

Sim Greenfield had been bought by an avaricious master who, in hopes of screwing a larger ransom out of the slave's relatives in England, set Sim to long hours of labour on his farm, from time to time even yoking him to a plough and treating him like a beast of burden. Many captives were similarly abused and beaten, starved into the bargain in the hope that their families would be moved to raise larger ransoms sooner. Sim's father was badly treated too, and although his mother and sisters were kept in seclusion and offered no kind of insult, Sim was troubled by a gnawing anxiety that, if money from England were not soon forthcoming, they would be dispatched to various harems in the town and lost sight of for ever.

Roger Crace toiled on at stone breaking in the quarry among men brutalized by years of such labour, living from one coarse meal to the next and almost without hope, for the galley slaves were one class of prisoner for whom the corsairs did not covet ransom, needing them as they did aboard their ships. Besides, Roger knew only too well that Jaffar Rais would take no sum, however high, as the price of *his* freedom.

That was the one thing Jaffar Rais denied Celia and, knowing he had cause to hate Roger, she ceased to importune him about her brother. Her father was treated as his honoured guest and Celia regretted that Squire Crace could hardly bring himself to be civil to Jaffar Rais in return.

Now, idling in the vine-shaded courtyard where Dick Dunton was trying to clamber up the wall to rescue the doomed gecko, she looked up to see her father standing in the doorway and saw, with disappointment, that he seemed as careworn and discontented as ever.

She glanced down again, fingering the printed muslin of her robe, giving the small secret smile a woman gives when she feels her young kick inside her, hoping her father would not complain once more of the food and the weather and the boredom of life in Sallee. She sympathized with his anxiety but thought his fretful carping hard to bear. As her condition became more and more obvious her father found it increasingly difficult to conceal his anger and disgust at her behaviour.

Celia settled a cushion into the small of her back and smiled at him, listening as he poured out his grievances.

"There's no news from England. All these months and still nothing. I've been to Master Willoughby again today to enquire if any letters have been brought in by merchants travelling overland from Spain or Algiers, but there's nothing. Nothing."

Her father paced up and down, twisting his hands together.

Celia bit her lip, watching him, dreading the re-enactment of a scene which had been played many times between them during the past months.

"Got him!"

From the top of the wall Dick Dunton shouted triumphantly. The lizard, finding itself suddenly seized, discarded its tail and scuttled away, sadly attenuated, into a crevice. The mantis, robbed of its prey, leapt out of reach, a sinister, skeletal shape in the sunlight.

Celia laughed.

"Can you reach that ripe bunch of grapes there, just above your head?"

Dick stretched out his hand and twisted the stem sharply between his fingers, letting the dark cluster fall into his palm.

"They're early," he said, sliding down the wall and dropping on to his haunches beside Celia.

"Yes, lovely."

Celia mouthed the sun-warmed fruit, offering some to her father which he refused. She and the boy shared it, spitting the pips into a brass dish between them on the tiled floor.

"Jaffar Rais has promised to send you home to England as soon as a passage can be arranged for you," Celia said gently to her father. "Dick, too." She smiled at the boy and he grinned at her, his mouth full of grape pips.

"Promises!"

Squire Crace turned angrily on his daughter. "I was promised a passage home in March and March is almost over. I don't think that pirate ever means to let any of us go."

"Jaffar Rais keeps his promises." Celia felt her own anger rising to match his. "You should be grateful that you live in his house treated like an honoured guest and are not compelled to toil in the sun with the rest."

"Like your own brother, you mean?" The old man's tone

was bitter. "Have you forgotten him?"

"No," said Celia, standing up awkwardly, leaning on Dick's shoulders for support. She was getting too heavy to move easily now and felt suddenly restless and agitated, as though she wanted to be doing something. "No, and I haven't forgotten that it's because of Roger that all this happened. It's Roger you should blame, Father, not Jaffar Rais."

"You believe that renegade rather than your own flesh and blood." Squire Crace could not conceal his contempt of her. "You're shameless. Utterly shameless. What am I to tell your mother about you when I see her?"

"You had better tell her," said Celia passionately, "that I am dead, since that is clearly what you wish. 'Death rather than dishonour.' Isn't that what you think? Isn't that . . ."

A sudden spasm shook her and she pressed her hand to her side, clutching at a pillar to save herself from falling.

Dick Dunton looked up anxiously into her face.

"Leah, are you all right?"

The contraction passed and Celia relaxed, smiling at him.

"Yes. It's nothing to worry about. Just woman's business, Dick. Fetch Charity, will you?"

He sped away, bare feet scudding and sliding rapidly over the smooth tiles of the courtyard as he ran in search of Charity Lidd.

"Celia."

Squire Crace approached his daughter, looking startled and contrite.

"I was hasty. I didn't mean . . ."

She shook her head, turning from him, feeling another spasm about to assail her.

"No. Perhaps you were hasty, but you meant what you said, Father. Go now, please."

He went, regretful and troubled, passing Charity Lidd as she ran in at the doorway coming to help Celia.

"Have the pains started?"

Celia nodded. Charity took her arm.

"You'll be better walking about until they come on stronger, love," she said. "They'll maybe go on for a few hours yet, seeing it's your first."

Celia took her offered arm and they began to walk together back and forth across the courtyard, Charity frowning threateningly at the women and children of the household who came to stare. But Celia took no notice of them.

"What's that?" she asked suddenly, stopping with her hand pressed against her side, listening.

"What?" Charity stared. "Oh, you mean the guns. Well, it's just them across the river, banging away like they always do. Don't you fret about them, love."

She took Celia's other arm, looking at her with concern. Celia shook her head.

"It's cannon, yes. But not from across the river. I heard guns out to sea. I'm sure I did. Go and look, Charity, please."

Her last words were muffled as another contraction seized her, making her gasp and sway. Charity stayed by her to support and steady her, then, when Celia urgently repeated her request, hurried to a window from which she could see out to sea over the ramparts. Dark against the blue waves and sky Charity saw the masts and hulls of Rainsborough's squadron riding at anchor in Sallee roads and heard what Celia had recognized as cannon-fire from the sea as their guns spoke again.

She turned to Celia in surprise and alarm and they looked at each other, listening to the shouts that reached them.

"English ships! English ships in the bay!"

26

The ships were *Leopard*, *Antelope*, *Mary*, *Mary Rose* and *Roebuck*. The *Hercules* had lost her main mast in a Biscay storm and been left behind at Lisbon for repairs. The two new pinnaces, *Providence* and *Expedition*, had not yet arrived to reinforce them so the squadron was considerably under strength, as John Dunton noted in his meticulously kept journal.

But still, five ships were there, the King of England's warships, fully manned, heavily gunned and with a good number of rowing boats for inshore work, some towed astern of the larger vessels, some carried on their decks and still others brought out in pieces, packed flat and corded together, ready for assembly when needed. The five ships took station at measured intervals, fanwise across the harbour mouth, dropping anchor to guard the entrance to both towns on the Bou Regreb like mastiffs at a gate.

"Let them watch," said Jaffar Rais with contempt. "That's all they can do. We're out of range of their guns and our ships can get in and out under cover of darkness. Let them do their worst."

He snapped his fingers, arrogantly confident, standing on the red sandstone bastions of the casbah whence the cannon of New Sallee had just answered those of the English squadron with a proud defiance. But el Caceri, whom the Moriscos had elected Caid, fingered his pointed dark beard dubiously, eyeing the warships.

"We shall be under blockade," he said. "We are already short of food."

Jaffar Rais shrugged impatiently.

"Commandeer all the grain from the outlying farms and then store it here in the casbah under lock and key. Then we shall be prepared for emergencies."

"It will be difficult."

El Caceri was thinking that the English would demand the release of their imprisoned countrymen and compensation for those captured by the corsairs and sold into slavery elsewhere. An expensive business. However Jaffar Rais might scoff at the squadron's impotence there was no doubt that the presence of the English ships would prevent the corsairs' lucrative slaving expeditions from sailing and gravely hinder all other commerce.

New Sallee was heavily dependent on imported foodstuffs, producing little of its own, and stocks were dangerously low. The rabble which had made him Caid would be howling for his blood once their bellies were empty. He dared not risk a famine in the town. Rather than that he would agree to the Englishmen's terms in order to get rid of them. But English renegades like Jaffar Rais stood to lose too much by any such agreement and would never consent.

El Caceri's eyes narrowed. The English commander might even demand that Jaffar Rais should be handed over to them to be punished according to their laws. El Caceri was inclined to believe that the English warships would not have come to Sallee at all but for Jaffar Rais' last and most audacious raid. He was a zealous pragmatist and a believer, with Caiaphas of old, that it was "expedient that one man should die for the people".

He frowned, troubled and uncertain what course to take.

Sidi el Ayachi was in no such dilemma. He had hoped for and indeed anticipated some such development. On sighting the English warships he immediately dispatched his vizier, in his own barge, flying a flag of truce, with messages of friendship to the squadron's commander. Simultaneously he gave orders for a strong force of Bedouins loyal to him to plunder the farms which supplied New Sallee with provisions and to attack the town from the rear.

Then he waited, shrewd and confident, like a skilled chess player contemplating his opponent's next move.

The foreign slaves were jubilant. The news spread among them as rapidly as a rampant contagion, going from hand to mouth through the households, the bagnios, the mazmorras and through the chain gangs labouring in the forests and quarries.

Roger Crace stood upright in his fetters, drunk with unreasonable hope, oblivious for once to the overseer's lash.

Sim Greenfield spat in his calloused palm, eyes bright above his matted beard. For two pins, he thought, he'd knock the farmer down with a hoe handle, make a run for the shore and swim out to the English ships. But if he did, what would happen to his father, his mother, his two sisters? He couldn't risk reprisals being taken against them. He'd have to bide his time.

About a score of prisoners managed to slip away immediately and reach the squadron, but the distance was too great and the sea too rough for any but the strongest swimmers to attempt it. It happened that most of those who succeeded in doing so were Frenchmen and Spaniards, who made up the majority of prisoners in New Sallee. The only Englishman who was hauled up half-drowned on to the deck of the *Leopard* on the first night that she dropped anchor in Sallee road was, strangely enough, Tippett Collecock.

He stood wrapped in a blanket, teeth chattering, facing Rainsborough and Dunton in the former's cabin.

"Give him another tot of rum," said Rainsborough, frowning, to the steward who stood by, and Tippett, who had pretended to be inarticulate with cold and exhaustion until the second dram was produced, finally found his tongue.

"Tippett Collecock, sir," he said brightly, contriving to make Rainsborough a salute whilst clutching the blanket round him, "agent for the New World Company."

"Ah." Rainsborough frowned again, a more formidable frown than before and Tippett's heart sank as he saw him consulting a written list before him. "Yes. I have details here." Rainsborough regarded Tippett with a reproving eye. "My son is in Massachusetts. One of my daughters is betrothed to Governor Winthrop. I am in possession of certain facts about the activities of the New World Company."

This was dreadful. Tippett shifted from one foot to the other, made uncomfortable by Rainsborough's steady stare. New World Enterprise had certainly been engaged in some questionable practices and Tippett had been involved in some of them himself but he hadn't bargained on being confronted with someone who had inside information on the company's transactions. He began to regret the impulse which had prompted him to seek freedom.

"How did you escape? Were you well treated?"

Tippett listened apprehensively to Rainsborough's questions. He felt like a scapegrace schoolboy before a severe headmaster. He rallied himself.

"Oh, I just slipped off, as you might say, sir. As for being well treated, I could hardly say that, sir. It's a terrible life, sir. Some of the things you wouldn't believe. But I didn't do too bad, not compared with some of the poor dev . . . poor creatures, that is, sir."

The fact was that Tippett had been very well treated indeed until his ageing mistress had caught him *in flagrante delicto* with a nubile female slave, since when she had "led him a life" and had even threatened to have him flung from the battlements to die a lingering death impaled on the spikes driven into the city walls. It was this last threat, which she had seemed bent on carrying out, which had driven the incorrigible Tippett to flight. Now, looking at Rainsborough's stern face, he was wishing he had not been so precipitate. He'd been very comfortable with the plump and indulgent Lalla Fatima and, now he had time to reflect, he began to feel sure that he could have charmed himself back into her good graces.

Rainsborough was asking him all sorts of questions about the strength of the fortifications of New Sallee. How many cannon? How many men under arms? How were they provisioned to withstand a siege? What was their morale like?

Tippett answered as best he could. He was naturally an acute observer, being a cockney foundling, reared in the shadow of Saint Paul's, living on scraps scavenged from the streets till he graduated to picking pockets and thence, being sharper than most, gravitating into the confidence trickery business.

The master of the *Leopard*, a sad-faced man whom Tippett realized he had seen somewhere before, was asking him the names of those English prisoners whom he knew to be in Sallee. Asking him with a peculiarly painful urgency if he knew about a boy called Dick Dunton.

Tippett's sharp cockney face lit up suddenly.

"Why, I know you, sir! You were with Jaffar Rais and stole the *Jacob* out from under his very nose in the Channel. That was . . ."

"Yes, yes. Have you seen my boy?"

Dunton was the opposite of himself in many ways, Tippett thought suddenly. Earnest, serious, sincere, deep-feeling. He hastened to reply.

"Certainly I've seen him, sir. He's a fine boy, sir, and landed on his feet, sir, in a manner of speaking."

Dunton leaned forward.

"Where is he? Where is Dick?"

"The lady that's with Jaffar Rais, Lady Lovell, she took a

fancy to him. He's with her, sir. He's all right, you can be sure of . . ."

He broke off, seeing the glance that passed between Dunton and Rainsborough and wondering why they looked so strangely at him.

Celia was only aware of the gunfire and the sounds of fighting on the outskirts of the town as a background to her labour.

In the early stages her contractions were far apart and there was time to rally and talk light-heartedly to Charity between them. It was Celia's nature to yield rather than to resist and this helped her to relax and give her body freely to the new experience of bringing to birth. In a way, it was like giving her body to a lover and there was something orgasmic, almost voluptuous, about it.

But the second stage was, of course, hard work, something which did not come naturally to Celia. Urged on by Charity she struggled and fought to push the baby out of her.

Charity was no midwife but she was strong, sensible and knew all about the processes of human generation from the initial enjoyable and brief part played by the father through the subsequent long and arduous part played by the mother.

After the baby's head emerged Celia lay back, gasping and sweating.

"Another push'll do it."

Charity sounded excited and exultant. Celia, gripped by pain that refused to let go of her till she responded to its urgent message, pushed again, bearing down with all her might.

"Little boy!" shrieked Charity, red armed, stooping over Celia to cut the cord.

Celia, ears humming, eyes misty, tried to sit up, wanting instinctively to take the baby in her arms.

"Push again," Charity yelled. "There's the afterbirth."

Somehow the now unwanted sack in which the baby had lived inside her was ejected and Charity held the baby close to Celia for her to look at him.

He was still moist with the glutinous fluid from the womb. He was red and raw-looking, like a skinned rabbit, with a wrinkled face emitting hideous yells. Celia had never seen anything so beautiful in her life.

She felt rapturous and utterly content, much as she felt after love-making, only much more tired. She fell asleep even before Charity finished washing her.

Celia woke refreshed, empty and thin. Charity wouldn't bring her the baby till she'd satisfied her hunger. Then Celia nursed and crooned to him, coaxing him to feed a little at her breast, enjoying the experience of feeling his small mouth nuzzle and pull her nipple. Wanting to show him to his father, she asked where Jaffar Rais was.

"Oh, I dare say he'll come when he can."

Charity was cheerful but evasive, holding the child up to her shoulder and patting his back expertly to make him burp.

A shadow crossed Celia's face.

"But where is he?"

She was in the highly emotional state following on childbirth and her lip trembled.

"There's been some fighting," said Charity gently. "The Saint's been up to his tricks again. Knowing your man you don't suppose he'd be left out of any fighting that was going on, do you? He's like an Irishman for that."

"But is he all right?"

"I'm well enough."

Jaffar Rais answered Celia's question himself, striding in with dust and blood of combat still on him. The sight of him made Celia feel warmly mellifluous and she held out her arms to him.

"Be gentle," warned Charity, touching his shoulder as he hurried past her.

"I will be." He laughed, stooping to kiss Celia. "Not that it's easy, when she looks as she does."

The kiss was eager and prolonged.

"Don't you want to see your son?" asked Charity nervously, bringing the baby to the bedside.

Jaffar Rais turned.

"He's like you," said Charity, drawing aside the shawl to show the blond down on the small, red head, where the sensitive area still looked dark.

"Well, damn me," said Jaffar Rais at last. Like all new fathers, he was lost for words on being confronted for the first time with his child. "Well, damn me." He put out a tentative finger and touched the wisp of silvery hair on the baby's head. "I believe he *is* mine."

They all had the sense to laugh with relief at that. Charity took the baby away and left the two together.

Leaning across Celia, Jaffar Rais' sleeve slipped enough to reveal a bandage with a red stain on his forearm.

"You're hurt!"

Alarmed, she tried to pull herself up but found no strength anywhere below her newly restored waist and fell back.

"Easy, easy." Jaffar Rais smiled. "It's nothing. Don't you worry, Leah. We've driven off Sidi el Ayachi's mobs before now and we'll do it again. As for those ships in the bay," he laughed recklessly, almost flippantly, "all they can do is sit out there till their supplies run out, when they'll have to turn tail and go home. And I'll tell you something, Leah." He took her hand. "We're in the clear anyway because I've just found out who the master of the admiral's flag ship is. A letter was smuggled ashore by a fisherman they captured and let go again, addressed to Christopher Willoughby, one of the merchants here in town. It's a very anxious letter asking about young Dick Dunton, signed 'John Dunton, mariner, master of the *Leopard*, lying in Sallee road, this 27th day of March.' So we've got a ready-made hostage, supposing His Majesty's Ships *do* give us any trouble. Of course, the other prisoners will be useful, too. We might threaten to hang one over the battlements every day the fleet stays in our harbour mouth. But the boy's our best bet. I can't see Master Dunton urging the admiral on to any great efforts when he knows we've got his son here. Look after that boy, Leah. I've an idea he's going to be very useful to us."

27

As the rowing boat with muffled oars slid out from the left bank of the Bou Regreb in darkness, nosing its way through the shoals of the broad, ink-black river, Tippett Collecock, crouching in the stern, felt a sudden surge of panic. He'd been a bloody fool to let John Dunton talk him into this!

Tippett stole a sidelong glance at Dunton, sitting close beside him in the boat, noting the white, set face, and shook his head. The man must be crazy.

Yet he'd seemed calm and rational enough when he summoned Tippett to his cabin aboard the *Leopard* the night before.

Tippett had been feeling good. The crew of the *Leopard* had treated him as something of a hero. There'd been a party and he'd regaled them with stories of his amorous adventures in the brothels of New Sallee, some of which were partly true. He'd been the toast of the fo'c'stle. Morale was high in the fleet, Tippett gathered, since emissaries from the ruler of Old Sallee had come out to the *Leopard* under a flag of truce, seeking an alliance against the corsairs. A strong ally on the north bank of the river meant the English could count on getting the corsairs to agree to their terms much sooner than had been expected. The men also had other reasons for rejoicing in the acquisition of a shore base.

Tippett had been having a good laugh with them when the summons came. A greasy-haired seaman put his head round the door.

"The old man wants you," he said laconically, beckoning Tippett.

"Who? The captain?"

Tippett got up a little unsteadily. The man beside him grunted good-humouredly, smiling at the landsman's ignorance.

"No. Dunton, the shipmaster. Rainsborough's captain."

"What's he want, then?"

The seaman sent for Tippett shrugged.

"You'd better ask him. He's waiting."

Coming up on deck had cleared Tippett's head a little.

"What's he like?" he asked his guide, lurching as the anchored ship heaved in the Atlantic swell, putting out a hand to steady himself and clutching at ropes sodden with sea spray.

"The old man? All right. Bit of a sobersides. Puritan, like the captain. They're two of a kind. Don't lie to him."

Thus adjured, Tippett had found himself facing Dunton who lost no time in outlining a scheme he had in mind for entering New Sallee clandestinely to rescue his son. The scheme, it appeared, required Tippett's assistance.

"You know the house where Dick is being held?"

Tippett, watching Dunton's earnest face, agreed that he did.

"You know some of those employed there?"

Tippett wished he hadn't boasted of his friendship with Charity Lidd and other women of Jaffar Rais' household. He assented reluctantly, wondering where the questions were leading. Dunton soon enlightened him.

"You have only just escaped. Many people in Sallee will still not know about it. They may think you're lying low till the trouble with your employer has blown over. If anyone saw you with Dick they wouldn't be suspicious. You could help to get him away without endangering his life."

"Now look here!" Tippett had stood up, appalled. "If you think I'm going back into that place you're mightily mistaken, Master Dunton. I'm sorry about your boy, but I've told you he's all right. He'll just have to take his chance with the rest. Good night to you."

"Come back!"

Dunton's voice was so commanding that Tippett did so at once, turning round to face the master of the *Leopard*, who sat as he had all along, calm and determined, fixing him with a steady gaze.

"Jaffar Rais has been holding my son hostage for ten months. You know my story, Collecock. Once the corsairs know I'm here they'll use Dick to try and force us to agree to their terms. Whatever happens, they won't let him go, even if the rest of the prisoners are released. I won't sacrifice my boy's life for fear of risking my own, Master Collecock."

Tippett leant on the table. "Well, that's up to you, sir, isn't it? But you can't expect me to risk *my* life, now can you?"

"I'll pay you," said Dunton. "I'm not a rich man, but I'll pay you anything you ask within reason. It'll take me time to pay perhaps, but I'll pay."

Tippett hesitated. "I dare say you would, sir, but it's just not worth the risk. You know what they do to escaped prisoners there, don't you? I don't fancy being roasted over a slow fire or nailed to a door to bleed to death. If it's all the same to you, I'd sooner die in my bed."

He turned away again, satisfied now that the interview was at an end.

"Wait!"

Tippett sighed. Did this man Dunton never give up? Then he gaped in dismay as the master flipped open the lid of an iron bound box, drew out a couple of parchments heavy with red wax seals and flung them down on the table between them.

"Warrants for your arrest, Master Collecock," said Dunton grimly, "issued by the magistrates of Exeter and Southampton as a result of your illegal activities there."

Tippett dived for the parchments but Dunton swept them rapidly out of his reach, replaced them in the box, slammed down the lid and kept his hand on it.

"If you don't help me get Dick back, Master Collecock, I swear I'll have you handed over to the authorities the moment this ship docks in home waters. From what I can see of the charges you won't see much but the inside of a gaol for a good many years to come."

Tippett slumped down on the stool in the cabin, feeling suddenly weak. These solid, respectable family men were hard as nails, really. He'd reckoned on having his arm twisted a bit, the sort of thing he did himself in his own line of business, but not outright blackmail.

"And if I do help you?"

He looked at Dunton almost pleadingly. Dunton relaxed somewhat, keeping his hand on the box lid.

"I'll destroy these warrants, pay you an agreed sum and arrange a passage for you wherever you want to go, once we leave here."

"You mean *if* we leave here," said Tippett ruefully. Then he grinned. He knew when he was beaten.

He looked Dunton in the eyes, wryly humorous, all slyness momentarily banished.

"Looks as if I'm between the devil and the deep sea," he said.

He certainly felt that way now as one of the *Leopard*'s longboats carried him and John Dunton nearer and nearer to New Sallee. Desperately he wished he'd made a break for it, but where could he have gone? Anyway, it was too late to turn back now. He'd have to go through with it.

They were half-way across the Bou Regreb, in the wide, treacherous shallows beyond the harbour bar. They could see the lights on the far side clearly. The south bank of the river was well watched and patrolled. Aboard the ships rocking at their moorings sharp-eared guard-dogs, vicious, lean and raucous, prowled about ready to give warning of the approach of strangers. More than one attempt by the English, operating from rowing boats and bent on destroying the corsairs' shipping in the harbour, had been defeated by the vigilant watch-dogs betraying their presence.

Tippett hoped against hope that the same would happen to foil Dunton's mad plan, provided the dogs heard them whilst there was still time to turn the boat round and head back to Old Sallee and safety.

No such luck.

Dunton quietly gave the order to heave to. The creaking of the muffled oars swinging in the rowlocks ceased. The men rested on their oars. The boat moved no more than a cradle on the dark water.

"Ready?" Dunton asked Tippett, who nodded. He was as ready as he'd ever be for anything so crazy. He and Dunton both had their clothes in bundles, fastened round their necks, together with their cutlasses, on lanyards, so that nothing would hamper them in their swim. Tippett, preparing to slide overside as quietly as he could, felt the cold steel of the cutlass against his chest.

"Might as well stick it between my teeth like a bloody corsair," he thought disgustedly.

The coxswain in charge of the longboat was taking his last instructions from Dunton and wishing him luck. They were all fools, in Tippett's view. Dunton was acting without the knowledge of his superior and the boat's crew would all have to face disciplinary charges when the facts came to light.

"Now," said Dunton.

They went together into the black, tepid water, striking out for the shore.

There was just one place where Tippett thought they might stand a chance of getting into the town without being spotted. There was always noise and light and something of a bustle going on near the house with the hand of Fatima over the door. A splash in the river at that point usually meant that a drunken customer was being ejected. If they could once get into the house he was confident Areefa would help them. Anyway, thought Tippett aggressively, deft arms cleaving the water, the girl owed him something. It was all over her that he'd lost his safe, cushy "crib" with old Lalla Fatima. And Areefa hated Jaffar Rais now.

Tippett, treading water, looked about him, getting his bearings, waiting for Dunton, a slower swimmer, to come up with him.

A mess of flotsam and evil-smelling refuse floated by. Tippett wrinkled his nose. Ahead of them a cluster of smallish boats were tied up to the quay. They seemed to be empty. Beyond their black shapes he saw the wide arched doorway, glowing with orange light, which he knew to belong to the house with the hand of Fatima.

A group of figures appeared in it. He heard voices raised. Dunton surfaced beside him, gasping, water pouring from his hair down his face and into his eyes.

"Quiet!" hissed Tippett.

They were so close to the quay he could hear the chink of money passing from hand to hand. The group dispersed suddenly, just as Tippett was about to whisper to Dunton that it was worth making a bid to get ashore under cover of the noise they were making. The doorway showed a blank orange space. A girl laughed high and shrilly. There were muffled sounds of music, but the quay itself was momentarily deserted. The two men waited, beginning to feel chilled as they lingered in the shallows, only their heads above water.

There was a clank of steel and the sound of heavy footsteps as two guards, talking quietly together, came along the quay. They stopped, to Tippett's extreme trepidation and disgust, just a few feet away from where the Englishmen were hiding in the lea of a small boat, hoping the shadows would be sufficient to conceal them.

There was a striking of tinder, grating, sibilant scraping

and a sharp, bright flame pierced the darkness, followed by the whiff of a pleasing, aromatic smell. Tippett cursed inwardly with speechlessly graphic vehemence. The guards were stopping to have a smoke. The minutes that passed whilst he and Dunton waited, their limbs getting colder with every second they stayed motionless in the dark water, seemed to Tippett the longest of his life.

Then, suddenly, a girl shrieked loudly. Struggling figures appeared in the doorway. There were oaths, yells and a clash of blades as knives were drawn. The two guards ran to intervene. The fighters were dragged away down the quay.

"Now!" hissed Tippett between chattering teeth and the two of them stumbled through the shallows, clambering over the edge of the quay, practically naked and dripping wet. All around in the darkness dogs were barking and men were shouting. Under cover of the general confusion they rushed into the open doorway of the house with the hand of Fatima.

A huge Negro confronted them, arms folded across his massive chest.

"Salim," panted Tippett, "where's Areefa?"

The gigantic Negro smiled broadly, eyeing the two shivering men. Dunton pushed something hard into Tippett's hand. It was a gold piece. Tippett held it out.

"Areefa?" he said again.

The Negro took the gold and stood back, grinning and motioning with his thumb. Tippett pushed the curtain aside. He knew where to find her.

It was dim but not dark in Areefa's room, for there was always a lamp burning by the heap of cushions that formed her bed.

She was lying on them now, sleekly sinuous, her smooth golden body wholly naked except for the dark triangle of hair at her crotch. Seeing Tippett standing there she laughed, stretching languorously, like a cat in the sun. Then she raised her knees and parted them, welcoming him in.

Tippett licked his lips. Beside him he felt Dunton grow tense with shame and look away.

"I'll speak to her a minute, sir. You'd better put your clothes on," he added as Areefa impatiently pulled him down beside her, exclaiming at his wetness, running her hands down over his chest, his belly, his loins.

All in all, he'd have liked to stay longer with her. If they had caught him, he thought in a blaze of euphoria, it would have been worth it. A lovely way to go. But there was Dunton, with his white, shocked preacher's face, at his elbow, shaking him, telling him they must go or they'd be caught. Telling him they'd got to find Dick.

Areefa understood at once. She was certainly quick, Tippett thought admiringly. One of the quickest girls he'd ever met. Quick to hear, quick to understand, quick to act, quick to . . . but never mind. Tippett told her what they'd come for while he dressed himself and she nodded, listening eagerly, pulling on her djellabah and veil. A pity, he thought, to cover up all that lovely golden body, but he supposed it was necessary.

"She'll guide us," he said to Dunton, "and do any talking that's necessary."

"Can we trust her?" Dunton's suspicion was evident. "A woman like that?"

Tippett looked at him. "Oh, she's just a woman, like any other." He winked. "Jaffar Rais jilted her. We can trust her all right."

Areefa led them up the stairway, huge steps cut in the living rock that led to the corsairs' fortress on the rock where the house of Jaffar Rais was.

Without her they would never have got past the guardians of the gate. They waited in the shadows whilst she approached the sentries and stood laughing and talking a few minutes, putting them in a good humour with her terse, professional gaiety. Tippett and Dunton watched their chance to slip through the gateway when the sentries' backs were turned.

They stood pressed against the wall, still and rigid, blending with the shadows.

After a brief interval a third shadow joined them, Areefa, laughing softly, adjusting her veil and enveloping djellabah.

"Good girl!" Tippett patted the firm round curve of her hip, feeling the warmth of her nubile flesh through the thin silk of her garment.

They moved through the dark streets to the house of Jaffar Rais. Tippett had a problem now. He could only get into the women's quarters with the help of Charity Lidd and he was afraid of making Areefa jealous. He made a sign to Dunton and dexterously drew Areefa into the angle of a wall.

Dunton watched the two of them in the triangle of shadow, desperately tense and anxious. Somewhere in the dark building outside which they waited Dick was held prisoner and Dunton knew he couldn't live with himself if he failed the boy. He had to get him out somehow, even if he died in the attempt. He wished he could have undertaken the rescue operation alone instead of having to depend on the help of a trickster and a whore whom it was impossible to trust. Even now the two of them might be plotting to betray him.

"Ready now, sir?"

It was Tippett Collecock, motioning him forward urgently. "Areefa's having a few words with the doorman. They're old friends. Follow me." Tippett coughed apologetically. "There's a woman."

"Yes, I rather supposed there would be."

They entered by way of the kitchen, deserted now it was night, except for bright-eyed rats that squealed and scurried away as they entered.

Tippett went to the doorway looking on to the courtyard and whistled softly.

Charity Lidd, who had just settled Celia's baby to sleep,

straightened her back and hurried to the window. The soft whistle, like the note of a blackbird, was repeated.

Charity smiled, wriggling her hips in pleasurable anticipation and loosened her scanty bodice so as to display her full, firm, round breasts to better advantage.

"That Tippett Collecock," she murmured to herself, giggling a little. "I wonder what he wants."

He was waiting in the place where they usually met. Charity sidled across the yard, soft-footed in the dark, and pressed herself against him, putting her arms round his neck.

"Not tonight, Charity," Tippett chuckled softly. "There's somebody with me."

He clapped his hand over her mouth, stifling the cry that rose to her lips when she saw Dunton standing behind him.

"Don't make a sound, girl, for God's sake," Tippett muttered. Charity shook her head, eyes wide with surprise. "We've come for Dick Dunton," Tippett said, taking his hand away.

"Dickie? What do you want him for?"

"I'm his father." Dunton edged forward, his whisper urgent and husky. "Help me get him away from here."

"His father?" Charity stared. "Yes," she said hesitantly, "I remember you."

"Do you know where the boy is?" asked Tippett. "Can you bring him down here to us without anyone seeing you?"

"I might." Charity sounded scared. "I don't know that I dare, Tippett."

"Oh, come on, lass," Tippett coaxed, his hand in her bodice warm against her bare breast, caressing, wheedling, persuading her to do what he wanted. His coaxing was normally directed towards different ends but tonight he was more eager than ever that Charity should comply with his wishes, conscious that the longer he stood there in the courtyard the greater the danger of discovery grew.

"Go back into the kitchen," she murmured at last, swallowing hard. "Stay quiet. I'll try and bring the boy to you."

She sped away and the two men retreated cautiously into the dark doorway of the deserted kitchen.

Inquisitive cockroaches, grown fat on the congealed leavings still adhering to the piles of unwashed platters left lying about, scuttled noiselessly across the floor, long feelers waving. One ran over Dunton's foot, but he took no notice, having grown used to them in his years at sea.

Tippett and Dunton waited, listening, not daring to talk, tense and silent, each minute that passed seeming like ten.

Charity knew where Dick was. Her difficulty was not in finding him but in waking the boy without disturbing those who shared the room with him.

He slept on the floor among three or four other young boys whose mothers formed part of the household. Charity stood in the doorway, trying to see which of the huddled shapes was Dick.

The bundle nearest her stirred and a friendly shaft of moonlight picked out a long tress of bleached fair hair.

"Dick!"

Charity mouthed his name, stooping over him. He looked up at her, blue eyes hazy with sleep. She put her finger over her lips. The haze cleared from his eyes and he began to look fully awake. He sat up. She kept her finger on her lips and held out her hand to him, her expression urgently imploring him to keep silence.

Dick sensed the urgency of the situation and he knew better than to make a noise, having learned, through the bitter experience of his captivity, a certain unchildlike wisdom about the need for secrecy. He glanced round furtively at the figures of his sleeping companions, then he got up slowly and, carrying his shoes in his hand, tiptoed out after Charity.

A sleepy eunuch, on his way to obey a call of nature,

blundered by them in the shadowy passageway outside the room and they flattened themselves against the wall until he had passed.

Charity gasped with relief, pressing her hand to her breast, convinced that the man must have heard the furious beating of her heart. Then she took Dick's hand and they ran together down the steps into the courtyard and across to the kitchen. She opened the door, murmuring, "Your father's there," and pushed Dick inside.

Tippett didn't exactly understand why, but there was a kind of pricking at the back of his eyes when he witnessed the meeting between father and son. There was something about the wide grin of delight that spread all over the boy's face, brightening his eyes and twisting his mouth up into a crescent as he said, "I knew you'd come. I *knew*."

Then they heard the shouting and knew Dick's escape had been discovered.

28

They didn't stop to think or bother to be quiet. All three of them rushed out of the kitchen, pounding through the gateway as fast as they could. Someone tried to block their way and Tippett barged straight into him, charging with his shoulder and knocking the man aside so that he stumbled and fell with a grunt against the wall. He could hear Dunton and Dick running behind him and shouts and echoing feet not far away, but he didn't look back. He ran blindly on, down the dark, narrow street that led to the gateway of the casbah beyond which was the long flight of steps leading down to the river and freedom.

But there were lighted torches flaring in the gateway and armed men guarding it.

"Not that way!"

Dick Dunton plucked at Tippett's sleeve. "Down here."

He darted off down a winding alley, overhung with vines and Tippett and his father ran after him, dodging and stumbling in the boy's wake, too desperate and breathless to ask where he was leading them. It seemed to go on and on. Tippett was nearly winded when he caught his foot on a stone and fell with a groan. He struggled up again almost immediately.

"Are you all right?"

Dunton's voice sounded in his ear.

"Of course I'm . . . God damn!"

He swore helplessly, finding that when he put his right

foot down it wouldn't bear any weight but just crumpled excruciatingly.

"I've sprained my ankle."

In the instant of realization he gave up hope, so certain was he that the Duntons would abandon him. It was what he would have done himself in their position. Amazingly, he felt John Dunton heaving his right arm round his shoulders and hauling him along.

"But," Tippett spluttered, "you can't help me. You'll be caught. You'll . . ."

"Be quiet," said Dunton tersely "Take his other arm, Dick. How far is it now?"

"Just along here."

The boy's voice was as quiet and matter of fact as his father's, Tippett thought wonderingly. They might have been helping an injured traveller down a country lane in peaceful England for all the agitation they showed. He hopped along between them, protesting feebly.

It was pitch dark but the foul stench of overcrowded humanity suddenly assailing his nostrils made Tippett realize where he was.

"It's the street of the mazmorras. It's dangerous. There'll be guards . . ."

"In here."

Dick, who seemed to know his way blindfold, pushed open a low door and shoved Tippett through in front of him.

Tippett staggered, leaning against the wall for support. The room they were in was dark and cold as a tomb. Someone was approaching, carrying a candle whose flickering flame cast weird shadows on the walls.

"Who's there?"

When Tippett recognized the voice he could almost have laughed aloud with relief. Dick Dunton answered, his young voice sounding clear and calm.

"It's me, Dick Dunton, Master Hillard, and my father and . . ." he hesitated and Tippett put in quickly, "Tippett

Collecock, *at* your service, parson."

They were in the chapel which the corsairs had allowed the Redemptionists to use and where, until he died, Father Gracian had said mass. It had once been a store room and was almost bare of furniture, except for the rough stone altar with its tattered covering and a crucifix fashioned from driftwood, which some captive had patiently carved.

Stephen Hillard surveyed them a moment, holding his guttering candle high above his head. A noise of thudding feet and shouting in the street outside signalled the arrival of the pursuers.

"You must hide."

Stephen Hillard set down his candle. Tippett saw that he still wore the heavy irons with the weight attached to his left ankle and they impeded his movements very much.

"Help me tip these bodies out. Quick!"

The parson was pointing to three coffins laid out before the altar, rough shallow boxes with ill-fitting lids. Tippett hastened to obey him, but quailed when he felt the cold, flaccid flesh of a dead man when he removed the cover of the nearest coffin.

"Get him out," said Stephen Hillard briskly. "The poor fellow never did anyone any harm when he was alive and I'm sure he won't now he's dead. In with you, Tip. You others, get into the other two."

Tippett, his injured ankle throbbing, crawled into the coffin. Stephen Hillard hastily replaced the lid. In the confined blackness Tippett's flesh crept as he heard sounds and bumps which suggested that Stephen Hillard was heaving the corpse on top of the coffin.

Then he sweated with terror, hearing the voice of Jaffar Rais near at hand.

"Three prisoners came running this way. Have you seen anything of them?"

Stephen Hillard laughed before he answered. To Tippett,

laid out in the rough wooden coffin, with a dead man pressing him down in it, the parson's laughter sounded not only muffled but exceedingly macabre.

"You can see the only three men I have in here," said Stephen Hillard and Tippett experienced both terror and rage, believing that he and the Duntons were betrayed. He heard footsteps coming nearer.

"You see." He heard Stephen Hillard's voice again, much nearer now. "But there are no prisoners here. Death has set these men free. These foul mazmorras breed disease, Jaffar Rais, as you well know. These three here died of plague. When are you going to house the slaves in decent quarters? And what about food and medicines and . . ."

"Never mind that now," came the swift, brusque answer. "Someone broke into my house tonight and kidnapped the boy Dunton. I want him back, parson. You can tell the rest of your precious flock that if they know who did it they'd better tell all they know or it'll be the worse for them."

There were feet tramping everywhere and Tippett felt sure that any moment the coffin would be overturned. He would be recaptured and die a slow death by torture. He began praying silently and desperately to be delivered from his enemies.

Suddenly he was aware of silence, brief but profound. Then there were vibrations overhead, the body dropped with a soft thud on the ground, the lid slid sideways and he looked up into the face of Stephen Hillard.

"You can come out now, Tip," said the little parson of Combe.

He fed them with the inevitable kus-kus and melon slices and grapes, for fruit was always plentiful in Sallee, though grain was getting scarcer and scarcer. Many were already going hungry, he said sorrowfully as he bound up Tippett's ankle with wet cloths and listened to the story of John Dunton's desperate scheme to save his son.

Tippett and Dick did most of the talking and Dunton, it seemed to Tippett, watched Stephen Hillard with more than ordinary interest.

"You'll have to lie low here tomorrow, till the evening." Stephen Hillard said. "Then I'll smuggle you out in these coffins to the burial ground. I've permission to conduct these poor fellows' funeral then and no one is likely to come very close since I've given out they died of plague."

"They didn't, did they?"

Tippett cast an anguished glance at the three corpses in their coffins. He wouldn't give much for his chances of survival if he'd been that close to a man that had died of the plague.

Stephen shook his head.

"No. They died of hunger and overwork and ill usage, which is what kills most of us captives. But you'll be safe enough here for a few hours. There's a place behind the altar where you can hide. Father Gracian made it and Ismail showed it me since I seem to have inherited the good Father's mantle."

Tippett was nodding, feeling ready to drop from fatigue and Dick Dunton had already fallen asleep, crouched in a corner of the bare chapel, his head on his arms.

John Dunton and Stephen Hillard both looked at him as he slept. Stephen Hillard turned to the boy's father.

"His mother will be glad to see him," he said softly.

"His mother is dead," the other answered. "I still have to tell him that. That will be the hardest thing of all."

"Yes," said Stephen Hillard. He paused and added, "I'm so sorry, Master Dunton. Have you other children?"

"Four. One of them a baby."

Stephen Hillard nodded compassionately. "You have someone to care for them?"

Dunton leaned forward. They were seated on the bare floor, the candle between them.

"Mistress Anne Crace," he said.

Stephen Hillard's hand clenched and unclenched slowly.

"Anne? I did not know you were acquainted with Mistress Anne Crace," he said.

"We became acquainted aboard the *Jacob*." Dunton was choosing his words carefully. "Later she and her mother visited my family in London. My girls are very fond of her."

"Yes. Yes. I'm sure they are."

Stephen Hillard frowned, looking troubled. Tippett Collecock, half asleep, sensed the tension between them and did not understand it.

Dunton said, "You will make your escape with us tomorrow?"

Stephen looked up. "No. I shall stay here."

"But that will be dangerous for you." Now Dunton frowned, perplexed and concerned.

"I have work to do here." Stephen Hillard sounded utterly convinced. "You've been a prisoner, Dunton, you know what misery there is. What utter hopelessness. If I leave there'll be no one to care for the captives here. No one for them to turn to. No one to offer the comforts of religion, of human sympathy, of common sense, even. Who'll write letters for the illiterate, minister to the sick and dying, intercede with the powers that be for those sentenced to torture and death? Who . . . ?"

"I know all this," Dunton interrupted. "But you risk your own life. And what of your responsibilities in England? Your parish?"

Stephen Hillard smiled. "Combe is a good living. Some other clergyman will be glad to accept it. At present most of my parishioners are here in Sallee."

Dunton leaned forward. "They will no doubt soon be released. New Sallee is surrounded and beleaguered. In a little while you'll be set free to return. Why not come now?"

Stephen Hillard shook his head.

"I shall never return," he said. "I have found my life's work, here in Sallee, or, rather, God has found me and called me to His service in this place."

Tippett stirred uneasily. He disliked all this religious talk. It made him feel awkward and embarrassed. Looking at the other two men, however, he saw that Dunton seemed to understand what the parson was getting at. They were rather alike, Dunton and Stephen Hillard, he thought, only Dunton was older, more careworn and earthy looking.

"And your other responsibilities?" Dunton was speaking very earnestly and low. "I understood you planned to go to America, after you . . . married."

"I've thought a lot about that," said Stephen Hillard. "Every day I've been here I've thought and prayed about that and every day the answer's been the same. I've got to stay here, where I'm needed. I was going to leave England, but not for the right reason. Many people were going for the right reasons, but not me. I was just running away. I was trying to escape needful conflict. I was like Jonah, when he went to take ship to Tarshish 'away from the presence of the Lord'. I won't do that again - try to escape. I shall stay and do the work that has been given me to do. Even if the English prisoners are released there will still be thousands of slaves in Sallee needing my help. Your squadron, Master Dunton, is not powerful enough to subdue the corsairs. You know that. You can only inflict a temporary defeat. They'll be out raiding and marauding again as soon as you set sail for England and leave the coast clear. I'm needed here, needed desperately, and I shall stay."

He spoke with such passionate conviction that it was impossible to remonstrate with him. Dunton did not try, only being compelled by conscience to ask.

"And Mistress Crace?"

There was that in his tone and in Stephen Hillard's face when he answered that had the effect of enlightening Tippett as to the cause of the underlying tension he had sensed between them.

"Well who'd ha' thought it?" Tippett grinned sleepily to himself. "Cherchez la femme! A couple of good-living, high-thinking chaps like those two. Just like the rest of us, after all!"

"I shall write to Mistress Crace," said Stephen Hillard soberly. "Will you give her the letter? I think I shall not see her again but I wish her well and happy." He paused, looking at John Dunton. "I think you had better sleep now."

Dunton bowed his head.

Tippett, who had the gift of dropping off to sleep whenever things became insupportable and there was nothing to do but wait until they got better, crawled into the hollowed-out space behind the altar and slept. The boy slept with his head on his arms, close to his father, and John Dunton stayed by him, unwilling to let Dick out of his sight for a moment, leaning with his back against the wall, not sleeping himself at all.

Whenever Tippett woke during the rest of the night, disturbed by the sound of gunfire from across the river or noises in the street outside, it seemed to him that John Dunton and Stephen Hillard were talking together in quiet voices, very earnestly.

The day of waiting that followed was the worst part of the experience. Stephen Hillard had to leave them to go to his pupils. In his absence they were to keep hidden. If anyone came in they were to pretend to be sick with the plague. A rumour to that effect had been spread about on Stephen's orders, by Ismail, and was likely to keep even the most inquisitive away. But still, they knew the risk of discovery was very great.

Left alone, they heard the chain gangs from the mazmorras clattering and shouting down the street, under the oaths and blows of the guards.

"Where are they taking them? They've closed the quarries and no slaves are working in the forests since the warships came," Tippett muttered, half to himself, peering through the crack of the chapel's heavy door into the now sunlit street.

"They've put them to digging earthworks along the river bank," answered Dunton promptly, in a whisper, crawling over beside Tippett and putting his eye to the crack also. "Our men and the Saint's have made gun emplacements on the other side and are keeping up a pretty constant barrage. It's doing a good bit of damage in the poorer parts of the town."

"Yes," said Tippett grimly. "The Moriscos down by the docks have had about enough. They're under bombardment day and night. There's no food or money coming into the town. They're getting desperate."

"Yes," there was cool satisfaction in Dunton's tone, "we counted on that."

He turned back to his son, who was still sleeping, tousled fair head pillowed on thin brown arms, watching over him with a fierce tenderness.

Tippett looked at Dunton, half puzzled, half amused. The master of the *Leopard* had no qualms about inflicting suffering on the poor families of New Sallee, that was all in the line of duty, but he willingly risked his life for Dick. What was his maxim, then? "My family against the world?" Tippett shook his head. Such intense personal feelings were outside the scope of his experience. He rather hoped they'd continue to be.

"I haven't told him about his mother yet," Dunton said in a low voice. "I don't want to tell him here."

"No." Tippett grimaced. His own mother had been a whore of the Southwark stews and he didn't remember much about her except her way of screeching and slapping. He didn't know who his father was. Even his mother hadn't known.

Dick Dunton turned over and began rubbing his eyes. Tippett put his hand inside his shirt and took out his dog-eared pack of cards. He never went anywhere without them. They were a bit wet at the edges but their canvas cover had protected them well enough.

"What about a game?" He grinned at Dunton who frowned with Puritan disapproval. "It'll amuse the boy." Tippett nodded towards Dick who had sat up and was looking round. "We can play for grape pips."

So they passed the time until Stephen Hillard returned crouched behind the altar in the chapel in the street of the mazmorras, playing cards in company with three corpses.

All day the thunder of the guns went on and people came and went in the street outside. Dogs sniffed longingly, lifting their legs in the doorway and once someone hammered at the door, shouting imploringly for "le curé, le pasteur".

All three of them had frozen where they sat, silent and motionless, cards poised in their hands, till the pleading voice ceased in broken sobs and the stumbling footsteps died away.

"My trick," said Tippett, putting his hand down on the pile of cards. The others were so relieved not to be discovered they never noticed he was cheating.

Stephen Hillard came at last, accompanied by Ismail, unlocking the door, limping into the cell rather wearily, encumbered as always by the heavy weight on his leg.

Outside in the street was a narrow, ramshackle cart, half full of straw. As quickly as they could and with a minimum of talk, Stephen and Ismail carried the three coffins with the fugitives hidden in them out on to the cart and covered them with sacking. The three dead bodies, stiff and staring, were stacked behind the altar.

Stephen Hillard climbed into the cart and Ismail took the donkey's head, leading the little funeral procession towards the city gates.

Tippett, jolted along in the closed coffin, felt stifled and terrified, so terrified that he determined to repent and lead a new life in future. He began repeating all the scraps of prayers he knew in order to take his mind off the things that could go wrong.

Stephen Hillard had his Bible out and was reading from it for much the same reason, but also to impress the curious watchers in the streets with the belief that he was really taking the bodies of Christians for burial in the meagre plot of waste ground outside the town, which had lately been allocated for that purpose.

Sometimes the cart blocked the narrow streets, forcing passers by against the walls, and they cursed the Christians and spat at the coffins in the straw, recoiling still further when Ismail warned them that the corpses were infected with plague. But if someone were too curious or too bold or . . .

Stephen read in an undertone from the Book of Daniel, of the heroism of the three Hebrews faced with death by burning.

"Our God whom we serve is able to deliver us from the burning fiery furnace, and he will deliver us out of thine hand, o king.

"But if not . . ."

Stephen paused there. That was the crux of the matter. The crisis of faith. God could deliver you. But what if He didn't choose? What if you had to suffer? Perhaps, after all, there was only one prayer. "Thy will be done," he murmured fervently.

The guard at the gate stood barring the way out, armed men behind him, hostile and bristling with suspicion, shouting questions at Ismail. He peered into Stephen's face. Then he stood back, waving the burial party out through the gates.

He was a Muslim and a true believer, hating all infidels with a passionate hatred, but he knew the face of a holy man when he saw it. Stephen Hillard was clearly no impostor.

The ramshackle cart lurched and swayed through the lofty Moorish portal and the gates swung closed behind it. Ismail jerked the donkey's head, pulling it in the direction of the waste land, hardly able to conceal his jubilation. Stephen, full of heartfelt thanks, dared not meet his eye.

They were not out of the wood yet, however. They must not be careless. Stephen remembered how they had been recaptured before, just when they seemed safe. It would soon be dark. There would be no long twilight such as there was in England. Darkness would come rapidly and under cover of it the three fugitives could run over the fields and swim to safety across the river.

They reached the burial ground, with its dismal array of makeshift crosses, broken, lopsided and pathetic. A solitary dog was scratching at the surface of a shallow, new-dug grave.

Under the shelter of a crumbling wall Stephen and Ismail unloaded the coffins carefully, one at a time, keeping a wary eye open to see that they were not watched. There was no one about. The Saint's Bedouin cavalry had frequently raided the area outside the walls of New Sallee and most of the people who normally lived there had fled to the hills or taken refuge in the town.

"All clear," said Stephen at last when Ismail had signalled from the road that there was no one in sight. Already it was almost dark.

Tippett rolled furtively out of his coffin and lay beside it.

"I never want to be in one of those again till I'm past caring."

"Let's hope that'll be a long time, then." Tippett had never thought John Dunton could sound so light-hearted. "You all right, son?"

"All right. It was dark in there, though." Dick's voice had a certain relish in it. "There were spiders. Wait till I tell the girls. Won't they scream! Won't they *just*!"

"It's only a couple of hundred yards or so to the river,"

said Stephen Hillard, pointing. "You'd better go now."

"Come with us." Tippett put his hand on Stephen's arm. "All that talk about staying here. You couldn't have meant it."

"Ah, but I did though. *Vade retro, Satane!*"

"Eh?" said Tippett vaguely.

"Goodbye, Tip."

When they shook hands Tippett thought Stephen's hand felt firm and warm and steady and he seemed more relaxed than he'd ever known him to be.

Stephen turned to John Dunton.

"You've got the letter?"

"Yes. But if I lose it, I know what to say."

"Good man. God bless you, Dick."

The words were spoken rapidly and in very low tones. Only seconds after the fugitives had climbed out of their coffins they were making off across the fields together towards the river bank, Tippett limping along briskly between the two Duntons.

Panting, they threw themselves down on the bank.

"Can you swim with that ankle, Tip?" John Dunton asked anxiously as they prepared to enter the water.

"Just try me," said Tippett. "I've never looked forward so much to a swim in my whole life." He took a deep breath. "What about Dick here? Can he manage?"

Dunton patted the boy's shoulder.

"Keep close to me, son, and you'll be all right."

"I know I will," said Dick.

29

Celia enjoyed suckling her baby. For her it was a sensuous experience which gave her pleasure akin to that she derived from sexual love. Essentially a tactile being, she expressed her feelings most naturally in a directly physical way.

It was a hot, humid day, the sort of day that makes overactive Europeans in Africa restless and frustrated. Even the nimble geckos dozed, delicate bodies incandescent and splayed out against the pink-veined marble wall under open windows round which vines clung with never a leaf stirring. Across the river gunfire rumbled with a sultry sound like distant thunder. The air pressed down like a suffocating damp blanket.

Celia gave herself up to its ennervating voluptuousness without a struggle. She and her child lay naked, she on cushions and he on her, his small body curved in a crescent round the breast from which he was feeding, the centre of his world. His mouth was fastened to her nipple, his eyes were closed in blissful concentration, his entire being intent on drawing nourishment as he sucked contentedly. His fists were tight, one of them pressed hard into the soft flesh of his mother's breast.

Celia smiled drowsily at him, cradling him in the crook of her arm, caressing his downy head with infinite tenderness. He was a complete man in miniature, full of urgent needs which her body was made to supply.

"Haven't you done feeding that brat yet?"

Jaffar Rais strode in through the doorway leaving the curtain of beaded strands swinging wildly behind him and flung himself down beside Celia. His words were rough, though not his tone. He was sweating heavily and looked weary. Celia glanced at him anxiously.

"In a moment," she said, knowing he wanted her full attention. Evidently things were not going well. Celia's world had contracted since the birth of her child, being limited by the four walls of her room and the courtyard beyond, and Jaffar Rais had been little with her. Being so occupied with the baby, she hadn't minded that, but now she'd recovered from the birth she began to feel lonely sometimes, especially since Dick Dunton's escape, for then she had been deprived of her father's company and Charity Lidd's. By order of el Caceri they and the rest of the English prisoners had been removed from the private households where they had been living and placed in protective custody in the casbah. They received preferential treatment, for it was generally believed that they would soon have to be released in accordance with Rainsborough's demands.

The baby's sucking ceased. His long, fair lashes drooped on his rounded cheek. Aware of his father stirring impatiently beside her, Celia carefully removed her nipple from between the baby's lips.

"What about me?"

Jealously, Jaffar Rais pressed his hand over her other breast. Lactic fluid dribbled out, trickling between his fingers.

Celia laughed. "Wait a minute while I put him down. I get no peace between the two of you."

Kneeling, she lifted the baby to her shoulder, patted his back and laid him down.

Jaffar Rais eyed her, observing how, as she bent over, her smooth shapely buttocks were displayed to advantage. Her breasts, too, heavy with milk, were round and fecund, hanging like ripe fruit from the bough. Childbirth had not spoiled her figure but made it more womanly.

He slapped her rump appreciatively, not hurtingly, but so as to let her feel the firm weight of his hand on her bare flesh as he knew she liked to do. Celia turned to him at once, as eager now for his body as he was for hers.

"You're well at last then," he said teasingly, putting his hand on her belly, tracing with his finger the faint lines of stretch marks that still remained.

"They're like the ridges the sea leaves on the sand after the tide's gone out."

Celia pouted, not caring for his comment on what she thought of only as blemishes, not caring, either, for the simile he used which, for some reason, reminded her of Sim Greenfield, whom she wished to forget. She reached for her garment but Jaffar Rais put a restraining hand on her wrist.

"No. Let me look at you, Leah. I won't be able to for much longer."

There was a kind of despairing recklessness in his voice that frightened her. Petulance forgotten, she leaned over him anxiously.

"Why not?"

He pulled her down on him, muscular forearm hard across her back.

"It's over, Leah," he said dully. "You've got to go home and I've got to get out."

"Go home? Get out? Why? What do you mean?"

He jerked his head in the direction of the insistent gunfire. "Our friends across the river have got a stranglehold on the place."

She shivered, dismayed. "I thought you said they couldn't. That we could hold out."

"I was wrong," he said bitterly. "I didn't reckon on Sidi el Ayachi and the English captains getting together in the way they have. We're under constant combined attack from his forces and theirs. The pressure's on day and night, from both land and sea. They never let up. Not a single cargo ship has slipped through the blockade and not a cart-load or even a camel-load of grain has come in through the gates for weeks. The English are dug in on the Old Sallee side of the river. They've brought guns from the ships ashore, God knows how, and they're doing more damage every day. El Caceri knows he's got to get rid of them. The only way he can do that is to agree to their demands – set free all the English prisoners, pay compensation for those captured and sold elsewhere and promise not to attack English shipping in future. It's only a matter of days now, perhaps hours, before he sends a messenger to Rainsborough under a flag of truce, suing for peace. The poor people down in the town are living on rats and melon rinds and what rubbish they can scrounge. They're starving and starving people get desperate. El Caceri will have to give in to them, and soon.

"So that's why I say it's all over for us, little Leah. You'd better get your things together and go to join your father and your other friends."

"No!" Celia had listened to Jaffar Rais' tale of disaster and imminent defeat with increasing horror, but the last thing he had said frightened her more than all the rest. "What about our child? What about you?"

His arm tightened across her back, but he said, "You can take the child with you. As for me, I must shift for myself, as best I can. They were wanting to make me Caid the last time I came home from sea. Now they blame me for what's happened and want my blood."

"I won't leave you," she said. "You say I can go back to my family and take little Tom with me. I can't do either of those things. My husband had done with me before you even saw me. My father would rather I were dead than known to be the mother of your child. Not one of my family would disagree with him. I think of myself as your wife. That means I'll share your fortunes, good and bad, and take what comes with you. Oh," she laughed a little, her face pressed to his chest, hands gliding down towards his loins, "I know that's not really very noble, seeing I've no choice, but if I had a choice, I wouldn't choose otherwise."

"That's fine talk, Leah," he said, holding her fast. "But that's all it is - talk. What we've had has been good, but it's done. You're Lady Lovell. I'm Tom Chandler from Combe Hollow and that's all I'll ever be."

"Never mind who I am," Celia said. "You're Jaffar Rais and always will be."

She knelt astride of him, leaning forward, arms at full stretch, hands planted one each side of his shoulders, so that her breasts brushed over his face. Reluctantly he kissed at first, then he sucked, his hands exploring and caressing the moist secret places of her body that she offered so freely to his touch. She murmured, moaning softly above him, and his mouth travelled down over her belly to the lips between her thighs.

Now he was more eager than she, putting her on her back, entering her with energy and ardour. In the deep, intimate, ultimate embrace the locking bodies caressed.

When he spoke again it was not of parting.

"Well, if you're game," he said, lying back, his hands behind his head, looking up at the ceiling, temporarily relaxed, "get a few things together. Not too much. There won't be room. The craft I've got is only small. Dress yourself warmly, the baby too. There's no cabin and not much protection from wind and weather, but, with any luck, we'll only be in it a few hours. I mean to slip out of harbour tonight and run up the coast to Mamora. I've got friends there, renegades and privateers like myself. I can throw in my lot with them."

Celia lay with her face against his chest, her cheek pressed into the mass of tightly curled hair that covered it to the throat, hearing the strong, steady thrum of his heart, vibrant as a drum-beat. Her mouth went dry with fear at the thought of the perils he spoke of so casually. She gulped.

"What about the warships?"

Jaffar Rais laughed with something of his old arrogant confidence, rumpled her hair, roughly affectionate, pushed her aside and sat up, stretching.

"If I can't run to safety between those great clumsy King's ships and the shore then I don't deserve to get away. Now, give us a kiss, little Leah, and I'll be on my way. I'll send Bastiano for you as soon it's dark. Be ready."

"I will," she said, "I will," helping him dress and watching him go with his swift, lithe swinging movements so like a hunting animal's.

She told no one what she planned to do and, trying not to think of the dangers ahead, began making her preparations for the flight. Since Charity went she had not seen much of the Moroccan women who made up the household. They left her to herself and seemed to take little notice of her so Celia was surprised when, an hour or two after Jaffar Rais' departure, she found that she had a visitor.

She was kneeling on the floor, cording clothes into a bundle when she looked up and saw Stephen Hillard standing in the doorway of her room. He looked very thin. Thin and brown and the sun had bleached his dark hair with lighter stripes. He was dressed in faded European clothes which did not fit him, probably cast-offs given him by his owner. He looked weary and, unlike the rest of the English captives, still wore the heavy chain and weight attached to his ankle. He carried it, with difficulty, under his arm. The clanking of the chain announced his presence wherever he went. It was that sound which had told Celia he was there.

"Can I help?"

He smiled at her, crossing the room and kneeling opposite her, setting down the iron weight carefully first, with a wry, practised movement.

"It must be awful to have that thing on your leg all the time," said Celia with quick sympathy. She met Stephen Hillard's eyes and was surprised to see how serene they were, not troubled as they had been when she first met him.

"Oh, I don't know. I've got used to it. You should see the weights some poor devils have to wear, and they have to do heavy work in the quarries or felling trees, as well. I'm quite lucky really."

"How did you get in here?" she asked, puzzled and suspicious. The house was well guarded and only the master had access to the women's quarters, other men being strictly barred, according to Moslem custom.

Stephen Hillard smiled again, briefly.

"Oh, I'm a privileged person these days. Father Gracian was allowed to go anywhere and everywhere on his missions of mercy and I seem to be following in his footsteps." He made an amused grimace, settling himself back on his heels. "They think of me as a priest, not as a man."

"I only hope," said Celia, "that you don't follow too closely in the good Father's footsteps." All the Redemptionist priest's saintliness had not saved him from a gruesome death at the hands of the corsairs once they had found him helping unransomed prisoners to escape, she remembered.

"Where are you going?" Stephen Hillard ignored her remark, taking the cords with which she was fastening her bundle of clothes together and drawing them tight.

She didn't answer, but knelt silently, watching him knot the cords securely.

"The English captives will shortly be handed over to the English admiral. You could go with them, Lady Lovell. You ought to go."

"Ought?" His tone and the reproof it conveyed angered her. "I neither ought nor can, Master Hillard. But how do you know that I am not?"

"Many people tell me many things. Even those who think of me as a heretic confess to me for want of anyone better. I see you are making preparations." He pointed at the bundle between them. "And your father has told me . . ."

"My father! Has *he* sent you here?"

He noted her resentment and defiance with regret and

shook his head.

"No. But you should return to your family. You can have no future with the renegade."

Celia shook back her hair. "I can have no future without him. I have my child to think of." She nodded to where little Tom lay on a cushion, toe in mouth, seeming to watch the geckos playing above him on the sunshine-dappled wall. "Would you have me abandon him? And it seems to me, Master Hillard, that you should search your own conscience. What about my sister Anne? You promised her marriage. Now you will stay here in Sallee, to be a saint or a martyr, or what you will. But what about my sister who loves you and is waiting for you?"

When Celia looked into his eyes she was sorry she had spoken. But there was no reproach in them, only deep hurt.

"I think that was over before any of this happened, Lady Lovell. Only a sense of duty would prompt Anne to marry me now."

He paused. He'd talked a long time with the master of the *Leopard* when the Duntons and Tippett Collecock had taken refuge in the chapel, and each of them had spoken the truth from his heart. He liked John Dunton and respected him but still the thought of Anne Crace in another man's arms raised a primitive rage in him. Stephen reflected with mingled amusement and shame that while others might see him as a saint he knew himself to be very much a man.

Celia watched his face. "I have less reason to return to England than you have, Master Hillard."

Stephen sighed. The events of the past months had greatly changed him, bringing him an understanding of himself and others which he would never have gained had he remained parson of Combe, but he felt it his duty to urge Celia to follow the dictates of conventional morality, so often founded upon common sense.

"You are a man's wife," he reminded her gravely.

"I am a child's mother." She looked at him with a fierce

pride and at the child with a passionate tenderness.

Stephen found the words he had read in his bible running through his head. "Her sins, which are many, are forgiven, for she loved much . . ."

He bowed his head and stood up, straightening himself slowly because of the weight he was obliged to carry.

"Have you any message for your father?" he asked with gentle formality. Celia stood up also.

"Tell him to tell my mother whatever will cause her least pain."

"And Anne?"

"No." Celia smiled at him. "Let him tell Anne the truth. The truth will not hurt Anne."

He smiled back, his heart suddenly and inexplicably lightened. "You're right. The truth doesn't hurt the brave and the pure the way it hurts the rest of us. Any other messages?"

"No. Yes!" Celia corrected herself suddenly. There was a brass bowl full of fruit on the low table. Blue-purple grapes with the bloom misty on them. Ripe melons golden yellow. A pomegranate with a rosy, speckled rind. And one apple.

Celia took the apple in her hands, caressingly. It smelt very clean and wholesome.

" 'As the apple trees among the trees of the wood, so is my beloved among the sons. I sat down under his shadow and his fruit was sweet to my taste.' How bawdy the words of the Good Book are sometimes, parson!"

Stephen Hillard looked away. Celia held out the apple.

"Give that to Sim Greenfield for me," she said.

Later, standing on the quayside, she thought she had never seen so dark a night. The stars seemed very far away and a nimbus cloud, heavy and dense, had drifted across a moon as thin as a sliver of lemon rind and obscured it entirely. Wrapped from head to foot in a long djellabah and holding little Tom close she had followed Bastiano down the steep narrow streets of the casbah to the harbour. They had gone stealthily, slinking from doorway to doorway like prowling cats. Bastiano was a heavy man but he moved lightly on the balls of his feet, turning to beckon her forward when the coast was clear.

The harbour seemed almost deserted. Since New Sallee had come under concentrated attack from the guns which the English seamen had placed in position on the northern bank of the Bou Regreb many people had abandoned their homes near the river and retreated for safety into the casbah. Even the house with the hand of Fatima over the door was dark and silent.

When Bastiano left her, with a whispered order to stay where she was, Celia had experienced momentary panic. She felt very much alone, standing there with her child in her arms. The stones of the quay were wet and unyielding beneath her feet and a sultry wind off the sea stirred the hem of her garment, blowing it against her ankles. It was not cold, but she shivered. There was activity all around her. Quiet, purposeful and secret. Bare feet moved rapidly in the darkness, and lowered voices conferred in whispers. There was a boat moored alongside whose shape she could not make out, though now and again a shuttered lantern let out a thin beam of light, cutting a swathe through the blackness in which she glimpsed dark, bearded faces, sweating arms, a pattern of ropes and the stiff angle of a lateen sail. The river water, noisome but unseen, lapped ceaselessly with a soft, casual sound.

Suddenly she jumped. A plank had thudded down on to the quay only a few feet away and Jaffar Rais was beside her. He carried a lantern whose feeble glow he shaded cautiously with his hand. His face was in shadow, his voice quiet but harsh.

"Are you all right? Are you ready?"

She nodded. He guided her forward, shining his lantern on the plank whose roughly splintered ends moved slightly as they rested on the moistly gleaming stones of the jetty. The plank itself was only a few feet long and the lantern light showed muscular hands holding its far end clamped to the side of the boat, but under it the dark water, a long way below, heaved ominously.

Celia clutched little Tom to her.

"Jaffar, I can't."

"You must. Give me the child."

If he had not gone first, with the baby in one arm, the lantern swinging from the other, she would not have been able to set foot on the swaying plank. She followed him, the vibrations of his footsteps making her own yet more tremulous, glad when she stumbled over the side into the waiting vessel and Jaffar Rais thrust the baby into her arms. The lantern was dowsed as soon as she was aboard and she heard him give orders to the unseen, waiting crew.

She heard the creak and dip and splash of oars and felt the boat glide forward as Jaffar Rais, supporting and urging her at the same time, brought her to a heap of canvas, coarse and salt-smelling, in the stern.

"Lie still and keep your head down," he said and left her.

She was so tired and frightened and the movement of the oars in the swelling river current was so regular that Celia, rocking little Tom in her arms, had almost lulled herself to sleep with him, when the strident hail startled her broad awake.

She heard Jaffar Rais, near at hand, swear under his breath and begin cursing his men, who had broken out into a subdued babble, back into silence.

The hail came again, the English voice sounding clear and loud out of the night across the water.

"Ahoy there! What boat's that?"

Celia heard Jaffar Rais answer, cupping his hands round his mouth, she guessed, by the sound of his voice, returning the hail, trying a desperate bluff.

"Longboat of the *Leopard*. What boat are you?"

Then it was quiet for a few moments. Celia heard the shift

and swing of the oars in the rowlocks cease as they hung dripping, clutched in tense hands. The boat rocked on the heaving waves. A wind stirred the limp lateen sail with a soughing, susurrating sound and, far above, sent the heavy cloud packing from across the face of the lemon peel moon. The corsair craft, lean and long, oared and single-sailed like a Viking ship, was lit by an undulating strand of moonlight against the shifting shadows on the face of the midnight sea.

"Damn and blast!" said Jaffar Rais in a fury. "Row, you bastards!" He shouted his orders in another tongue, driving his crew forward with a lash of words as the English patrol boat opened fire with small arms, the barrage of shots cracking sharply and the corsairs rowing for their lives.

Celia crouched over her baby, not now frightened for herself but only for him, fearful lest the boat should be overturned because she knew that though she herself might survive in the sea, he could not. He was crying loudly now, but his howling was drowned by the splashing, the shouting and the sound of shots.

Then the crash came. Just as the corsairs, leaving the patrol boat behind and making for the open sea, were beginning to laugh with triumph because they had outdistanced their enemy, there came the noise of an explosion. There was a muffled roar, a crash, the sound of splintering wood and cries of alarm and pain.

"Row!" yelled Jaffar Rais above the din. "It's well above the waterline and only one man hurt. Bend your backs if you don't want them to give us the same again. There's not enough damage to slow us up if you act like men!"

Celia felt the water that had gushed in over the boat's side swilling about her feet. Holding little Tom fast, she was praying that they might by now be out of range of the small cannon which the English patrol boat evidently had mounted in its bows, for despite Jaffar Rais' confident urgings she knew that another hit on the corsair craft could well cause enough damage to let the patrol boat overtake it. By now, too, the other boats belonging to the English warships blockading the harbour would be alerted and they might have more than one foe to deal with.

But their luck held. The cruel crescent moon, sharp as a scimitar, the symbol of Islam, that had seemed to betray the corsairs by revealing their presence, now hid itself again behind a bank of cloud and the swinging oars clove through the darkness with desperate speed, leaving pursuit behind them.

Celia was not sure how many hours it was before the rowing ceased as, one by one, the exhausted men ceased pulling and the damaged boat floated aimlessly on the open sea.

30

"You'll ruin that boy, Master Dunton."

Tippett cocked an impudent eyebrow as he caught the master of the *Leopard* watching with fond pride as Dick swarmed up the ship's ratlines, nimble as a monkey.

"You think so, do you?" John Dunton made a wry face. "I suppose I do make a bit too much of him. It comes of thinking I wouldn't see him again. I'll knock it out of him later," he added with a hint of apology.

"You won't, you know," said Tippett familiarly, leaning his forearms on the taffrail beside Dunton. "Kids are like women – give 'em an inch and they'll take a mile. Next thing you know, they're running you."

Dunton smiled. Far above their heads Dick swung a leg over the mizzen yard and sat there, poised aloft, his back against the mast.

"Turned philosopher, have you, Tip?" said Dunton lightly, drawing on his pipe. The observant Tippett thought he'd never seen him look so well. He was relaxed, bronzed, fit. The careworn expression erased from his face, he looked years younger.

"Have you told him about his mother yet?" Having come to like both father and son, Tippett felt really concerned to know.

John Dunton's cheerful expression was only momentarily clouded before he answered.

"Not yet. He still has nightmares. I'd like to see him put

on a bit of weight and get his strength back first."

Tippett eyed young Dick, still perched on the yard, legs dangling, whistling untunefully.

"He's all right. Lads his age never have any flesh on them. Green wounds heal fast. The sooner you tell him the sooner he'll get over it."

Dunton grunted. "Some time on the way back I'll break it to him."

Tippett shrugged. After all, it was really none of his business.

"When do we sail?"

Dunton glanced at the pennon streaming from the *Leopard*'s masthead.

"As soon as our business with the shore is finished. We've got a following wind. All we're waiting for is to see the last of our people taken aboard the *Antelope*."

Tippett looked out over the water to the towering red bastions of New Sallee and the beaches and wharves below them.

"There's a boat just putting out now."

"That'll be the *Antelope*'s longboat bringing the last lot of released prisoners," said Dunton with satisfaction. "That's a sight for sore eyes." He laughed. "El Caceri didn't hold out long after Jaffar Rais slipped away That's my only regret - that I didn't settle with him personally. I'd have liked to bring that renegade to justice."

"Someone else will, soon enough," said Tippett. "His sort never last long. Jaffar Rais has lost everything but his life."

"I thought I had, once." Dunton's eyes narrowed. "I wonder how long it'll be before he's back in Sallee and up to his tricks again?"

"We have made a treaty with the Sultan of Morocco himself and he promises that no more English shipping shall be molested by ships sailing from Moroccan ports," pointed out Tippett.

"The Sultan's promises are not worth the paper they're written on," said Dunton contemptuously. "Oh, I dare say the Sultan would keep his word if he could. He's grateful to us for pulling his chestnuts out of the fire for him. We've beaten the corsairs for the time being by starving them into submission and that's made it possible for the Sultan to assert his authority over them and the Saint. Up till now both Old and New Sallee have openly defied him. Once we're gone they'll do it again. No, we've got our prisoners back and some compensation, but that's all we'll get."

"What now then?" Tippett was somewhat disillusioned about the extent of what had seemed a resounding victory.

"The plan is for the squadron to split up," Dunton said. "Captain Rainsborough's ordered *Antelope*, *Hercules*, *Providence* and *Expedition* to make for the coast of Spain and try to capture a few Barbary corsairs on their way home to Tunis or Algeria."

Tippett stared. "That's bad luck for the prisoners! Some of them have been captives for more than thirty years and they're all dying to get home."

"I know." Dunton shook his head. "It's the demands of the service, Tip. But if you'd been in the Navy you'd know that no matter what you accomplish all the high-ups at home are interested in is the value of the prizes you take that goes to line their pockets or, what's left of it, into the Treasury. We've successfully blockaded Sallee and destroyed above a score of pirate ships that might have done untold damage to our shipping, let alone the depredations they were planning to make on our coasts this year if we hadn't stopped them. But all that won't mean much to His Majesty if we don't make a profit on the expedition. A lot of money's been spent on this big new ship they've got on the stocks at Deptford, the *Sovereign of the Seas*, and everyone at home's groaning about having to pay Ship Money. His Majesty would be better pleased to see a solid financial return than the return of some hundreds of his subjects be they never so loyal."

"Mm," said Tippett. "That's what you might call a business-like way of looking at things. But," he added hastily as an alarming thought occurred to him, "what about the *Leopard*? Are we going a-roving too?"

"Ah!" Dunton laughed. "I thought the idea of that might shake you, Tip. No. We're going up the coast with the *Roebuck* and *Mary Rose* to pay a personal call on the Sultan at Saffee. There's a few more prisoners there and we have some money to collect which he's agreed to pay in lieu of ransom for some of the poor devils who were captured by Salleemen and sold to dealers in Algiers." He paused a minute, glancing upwards to where Dick still sat, sunning himself amongst the rigging, remembering how easily that could have been his son's fate. Then he went on, more cheerfully, "We're also picking up a distinguished passenger - the Moroccan ambassador who's coming to London to pay his respects to the Court of Saint James. He's bringing King Charles a present from the Sultan too. One His Majesty will appreciate. Four Barbary horses. Barbary horses!"

Dunton let fall an expletive which, though sailorly, was distinctly unpuritanical and Tippett smiled mischievously as the indignant shipmaster added, "I've hardly got breathing space aboard for Christians, let alone horses."

"Ah, but a good Barbary steed is valued at fifteen hundred pounds, which is more than even the best Christian is." Tippett gave a sly grin. "And they're the gift of one king to another, remember."

"You ought know better, Master Collecock, than to talk like that about kings to anyone in the Navy. None of us, from captains to deckhands, have any time for them. I signed on in a King's ship as master for this voyage only, just to get my boy back, but I'll be in my own ship when I go to sea again. They do say service in a King's ship can be worse than the galleys and there's some truth in it. In the galleys they feed you better."

There was silence between them for a time, with Dunton drawing on his pipe and Tippett watching as the captives were embarked on the *Antelope* which was anchored at some distance from them in the roadstead.

Among them Tippett recognized the Greenfields, father and son, and their three womenfolk, a handsome old lady and two plain young ones. Not normally reflective, he couldn't help wondering how they and the rest of the prisoners who'd been uprooted from Combe would settle down there again. None of them would ever be the same after the familiar pattern of their daily existence had been so violently disrupted. For better or worse their lives would have a new dimension now. From what he'd heard, the Craces wouldn't return to Combe. The old man hadn't the heart, after hearing his ancestral home had been burned down and Roger Crace, lucky to escape from Sallee with his life, wouldn't dare show his face there again. No one really knew what had become of Lady Celia Lovell but he was rather curious about the future of her younger sister. He glanced sideways at John Dunton.

"The little parson didn't change his mind, then?"

"Stephen Hillard?" Dunton knocked his pipe out, looking a trifle self-conscious. "No. You heard him yourself. He's set on staying. As you know, the English prisoners only made up a small proportion of all the slaves in Sallee. Even when Father Gracian's order send out a replacement Hillard will still be the only Protestant minister in Morocco. Just now, he's the only Christian one. He feels he's needed. Well, that's true enough."

"It's beyond me," said Tippett bluntly. "Who'd want to stay in a hell-hole like New Sallee if he could get out of it?"

"Not you or I, Tip." Dunton was busy tamping down the tobacco in the bowl of his pipe. "We're just ordinary sinners. But a saint might."

"Saint?" Tippett wrinkled his brow in perplexity at the turn their conversation was taking. "I don't think I know what a saint is. I used to think they were figures in stained-glass windows with round yellow things stuck behind their heads that look like cheeses. You know, the sort of thing you Puritans are always going on about. Since I've been in Morocco all the talk has been about 'The Saint of Old Sallee', who's some kind of fighting holy man. How can Stephen Hillard be a saint?"

"Well," Dunton paused. He was a religious man, like many sailors, but talk of deep things embarrassed him. "You might say Stephen Hillard is a fighting holy man."

Tippett's puzzled face brightened. "The Saint of New Sallee, eh? He certainly threw the book at Jaffar Rais. I saw him do it. And I think he was the only one of us who was never really afraid of him. But what about the young lady he was going to marry, Mistress Crace?"

John Dunton's pipe was taking him a long time to relight and his face was still hidden in his cupped hands when he answered.

"He knows he couldn't have made her happy."

"But you could?" said Tippett, greatly daring. If he knew nothing about saints he knew a good deal about women. "Saints don't hanker after . . . marriage, then?"

"I didn't say that." Dunton seemed to be having a good deal of trouble getting his pipe to draw properly. "He just thinks she should be able to make her own choice."

"And she has, eh?" Tippett grinned knowingly. "Women usually do, whatever we like to think. Give you joy, Master Dunton."

"What about you, Tip?" John Dunton blew a cloud of tobacco smoke into the impudent Tippett's face by way of acknowledging his congratulations. "What plans have you got for the future?"

"Well." Tippett looked almost shy as he answered. "I'm thinking of emigrating. I fancy the idea of settling in

America. I thought I might try my hand at farming and ..."

"You, Tip?" Dunton's incredulous laughter interrupted him. "Go to the New World, after all the people you've hoodwinked into going out there on false pretences?"

"Some of them aren't doing so badly, after all, from what I hear," countered Tip. "It's like everywhere else - depends what you make of it once you're there. Anyway, it looks to me as though there's going to be war in England between King and parliament before long, things are getting to such a pitch, and I've no taste for soldiering. Besides, England's a bit too hot for me. By the way," he glanced sideways at Dunton, "what happened to those warrants for my arrest you showed me the night before we broke young Dick out?"

John Dunton, though clearly much embarrassed, looked at Tippett frankly as he answered, rather hesitantly, "Oh yes, Tip, I was meaning to speak to you about those warrants."

"Why?" Tippett was anxiously on edge. "You promised to destroy them. Haven't you? Aren't you going to?"

"The fact is," said Dunton, "that I haven't and it wouldn't make any difference to you if I did."

Tippett gaped. "You mean they weren't real warrants at all?"

"Oh, they were real all right," said John Dunton slowly, "they just weren't for you. They were a couple of old ones made against a seaman who'd signed on after escaping from prison. I'm sorry, Tip."

"Well ... I'm ... damned," said Tippett Collecock.

"I did it for the boy's sake." Dunton clearly had some difficulty in justifying his action to himself. "I needed your help and there didn't seem any other way to get you to give it."

Suddenly Tippett laughed out loud.

"And they call *me* a confidence trickster! That's a case of the biter bit and no mistake."

He put his hand on John Dunton's shoulder. "You're a

deep one, Master Dunton. When good, honest family men like you start getting the better of me it's a sure sign I ought to start going straight. But you'd better keep an eye on that boy of yours. If he's anything like you he'll stand some watching."

"Don't you worry," said John Dunton. "I will."

His time for talking was over. He knocked out his pipe, preparing to report for orders to Rainsborough, while Tippett, with no such responsibilities to burden him, strolled across the deck of the *Leopard* to where Charity Lidd stood waiting, rosy and robust and smiling.

"Now, Charity," he said coaxingly, "I hope you've had second thoughts about what I asked you."

She put her head on one side and spoke with suppressed excitement. "Are you sure you're not making a mock of me, Tippett Collecock?"

Tippett put his arm round her.

"Now, would I do a thing like that?" he asked in aggrieved tones and then added hastily, "I bet that's the first time in your life you ever said 'No' to a man, Charity Lidd. Now, ask yourself, does it make sense to refuse the first honourable proposal you get after having agreed to so many dishonourable ones?"

Charity's eyes were very bright.

"Most men wouldn't so much as think of marrying a woman like me."

"More fool them, then," said Tippett, kissing her.

31

They had drifted for three days and the sun was hot above them.

Jaffar Rais woke Celia, his hand hard on her shoulder, and she sat up with a start, feeling instinctively and anxiously for little Tom who lay beside her, sheltered from the burning heat by a canvas rigged across the thwarts. He was asleep and breathing naturally, though his fine, downy hair was wet with perspiration and the pale, sensitive baby skin was blotched with heat rash.

"He can't go on long in these conditions," she said, glancing round her at the crowded open boat where weary men toiled at the oars and others lay collapsed over their feet.

"He won't have to." Jaffar Rais' voice came gruffly from his dry throat. He held out a pannikin of water to her. "You'd better drink this while you can. There's not much left."

Feeling the envious eyes of the sailors on her, Celia drank thankfully. With a baby wholly dependent on her milk she was always thirsty, even in the ordinary way, but in the boat, exposed to the merciless tropical sun, she was parched and suffering more than any of them. She drained the cup.

"When will we reach land?"

She knew they'd been driven off course by the pursuing patrol boats, slowed by the damage they had sustained from the ball which had struck them and further delayed by unseasonable squalls during the night. The journey of hours she had expected had become one of days and she dreaded its continuance.

For answer, Jaffar Rais raised her in his arms and pointed out over the boat's high gunwale, across the ceaselessly moving, seemingly endless expanse of viridescent sea, bluer in the distance, glinting harshly in the sunlight. Celia shaded her eyes with her hand. Far off, almost on the horizon she saw a line of white-maned breakers and, beyond them, the sweeping curve of the African coast, a silver-grey swathe of sand dunes between shore and sky.

"Mamora," said Jaffar Rais briefly. "We're almost there."

Celia sighed with relief. "I'm glad. I was afraid."

He gave her a wry grin, his tired, grim face looking younger suddenly. "So was I, Leah."

Then, as he was smiling at Celia's incredulous expression, Bastiano, who was at the tiller, hailed him suddenly.

"Sail on the port bow!"

Jaffar Rais turned instantly, knocking the empty pannikin from Celia's hand. It fell into the bottom of the boat and lay clattering to and fro, unheeded, while everyone aboard stared at the square sails of the distant ship which had just come into view and then at their leader.

Jaffar Rais peered intently at the newcomer, face set, blue eyes narrowed.

"Well, what is she, for God's sake?" The voice of the man who asked the question was cracking with nervous impatience. "Is she one of the English warships?"

Bastiano muttered something and Jaffar Rais shook his head.

"No," he said with finality. "She's a Spaniard."

"Friend or foe?"

"Allah knows!" Jaffar Rais seized an oar. "We're not going to stop to find out. She's bearing down on us. You've seen Mamora straight ahead. Now row for it Get there before she gets to us."

Even if the boat's crew had not been weary and they had had more way on the Spanish ship, it would have been a tall order, Celia realized despairingly. The galleon had evidently not only sighted them but was holding course to intercept them, which, since they were still far out to sea, with many fathoms of deep water beneath them, she could easily do. Seeing the Spanish vessel had all sail set and a following wind, the corsairs' small, Viking-type craft with its single lateen sail and score or so of tired rowers could not hope to evade her by reaching the shore first.

"Do you see what ship she is?" shouted Bastiano to Jaffar Rais as the Spanish captain's hail sounded over the water and a warning shot from one of the galleon's many wicked-looking cannon plummeted into the water a few yards from them, sending up a cloud of spray.

"Yes." Jaffar Rais gave the order to his crew to cease rowing and rested on his own oar, panting and sweating from the almost superhuman efforts he had made. "She's the *Santa Catharina*." He glanced up at the bows of the great floating castle which seemed almost near enough to overshadow them. The figurehead showed a crowned woman in a purple mantle leaning on a golden wheel. "It's our old friend, de Ortiz," he said, watching as a boat, gay with gilding like most of the woodwork of the galleon above the waterline, was lowered slowly over the Spanish ship's side.

"Listen," Jaffar Rais spoke swiftly and harshly to Celia who had snatched up her baby and was looking on in alarm and dismay. "It's the end for us."

"No," Celia said. "No." But he put his hand over her mouth with an insistent gesture of rough tenderness.

"This ship is commanded by Hernan de Ortiz, the Spanish captain we captured at the Isles of Bayonna. Do you remember? We are old rivals and enemies. He has been ransomed since but he will want revenge. For me and my men it means being chained to the oar bench of a galley if we're lucky, torture in the dungeons of the Inquisition if we're not. But de Ortiz is a gentleman, a Spanish hidalgo, an aristocrat. As a lady of rank you will be respected by him. Tell him you're my prisoner, brought along by force. Not a word about being my mistress."

All the time he was talking the Spanish ship's boat was approaching them, more like a state barge than a boat, with a scarlet awning and brown-faced seamen in red shirts at the oars, and soldiers whose weapons and armour glittered, shouting insults at the defeated corsairs.

"I don't want to live without you," said Celia to Jaffar Rais, and meant every word.

"Oh yes, you do," he answered fiercely. "You do and you must. What about the child?"

The Spaniards' barge was almost alongside. The corsairs glowered sullenly as grapples were cast to bring their boat in tow behind their captors', who grinned triumphantly at them. Celia hung her head, tears on her face. Jaffar Rais pressed her arm, quickly, surreptitiously, turning from her to face the Spanish officer who shouted his name, calling on him to surrender.

"Always fancied you, little Leah," he said, preparing to give up his sword.

Don Hernan de Ortiz had the face of an austere voluptuary, like a self-portrait of el Greco. It was twenty-three years since they had laid the great painter to rest in Santo Domingo el Antiguo and no other now lived who could have done justice to Don Hernan's long, cadaverous face, with its lofty forehead, arching brows, high cheekbones and expressive eyes. The well-cut beard and moustache did not quite conceal the sensuous fullness of the lips. He had a look which was melancholy, haughty and full of smouldering fire, resembling those which may be seen in the background of pictures like "The Burial of Count Orgaz" and "The Martyrdom of Saint Maurice". Even his clothes, the white collar opened on the black velvet doublet and the handsome steel breastplate with its intricate inlay, were in keeping with his el Greco image of pious patrician dignity tinged with subtle sensuality. Only one aspect of Don Hernan's appearance would not have appealed to el Greco and that was the expression of undisguised triumph he wore when he saw Jaffar Rais being brought aboard the *Santa Catharina* as his prisoner.

Jaffar Rais stood before Don Hernan with lifted head, his mouth firm, his back straight, returning Don Hernan's look unfalteringly.

Don Hernan bowed.

"It is the custom of war, señor Morisco," he said mockingly, making a deprecating gesture as he spoke the formula used by the corsairs when they had captured him.

"And change of fortune," returned Jaffar Rais, smiling defiance. "My turn today, yours tomorrow, señor," he added with a hint of menace in his voice even as one of Don Hernan's men knelt to shackle his feet.

It was when she cried out, seeing the corsair shackled, that Don Hernan noticed the woman who had just been brought up on deck with the rest of the prisoners. She wore a long blue robe and carried a child in her arms. Seeing her face for the first time he thought she looked like a fallen Madonna. But at the second look he changed his mind. She was Magdalene and unrepentant Magdalene at that. And she was no el Greco subject. Her figure might be shrouded but the wind blew the damp folds of her garment tellingly against her body revealing its generously beautiful shape. She was pure Rubens, thought Don Hernan approvingly, the tip of his tongue beginning to work round the inside of his lips with a piquant savour, if you could call anything painted by such an ardent, unashamed sensualist as Rubens, pure.

"Lady Celia Lovell," said Jaffar Rais in a loud voice, "is my prisoner and of high rank. I leave her to your protection, Don Hernan."

He would not look at Celia as they led him away with the rest of the captives, but she looked at him and Don Hernan, seeing the look, smiled.

The polished table in his cabin reflected the light from the heavy silver candlesticks in clear, deep mirror images. The burnished platters and goblets engraved with his coat of arms were rich and heavy, like all the rest of the furnishings. Don Hernan's obsequious personal servants waited on him and on Celia as they dined. Celia remembered with a pang that she had not had a meal in such surroundings for a year. Not since she was last at home in burned and plundered Combe Hall.

She ate in silence, thinking of Jaffar Rais in chains being fed with coarse scraps if he was lucky and wondering what would become of him. Near by, wrapped in soft cloths and lying in a shallow basket to duty for a cradle, little Tom slept. As she sat at the table Celia glanced towards him from time to time.

"You will take some more wine, Lady Lovell? Or some fruit, perhaps?" The Spaniard was a courteous host.

Celia shook her head.

"Thank you, no."

She felt weary, distrait, desolate. Her presence caused constraint among the Spanish officers at their captain's table and one by one they made their excuses and withdrew, bowing themselves out, darkly moustachioed, wary, reserved.

A discreet signal from Don Hernan dismissed the servants so that he and Celia were left alone except for the sleeping child at whom the captain glanced thoughtfully.

"Your child is very young, Lady Lovell." His tone was soft, carefully modulated, enquiring. "Was it born during your captivity?"

He studied Celia's face as he waited for her reply. Her beauty attracted him and he was impressed by the courage she showed after the hardships she had suffered, but he was puzzled and intrigued by her attitude. She was not grateful as a woman in such circumstances should be. And he had seen the way she looked at the corsair when he was led away. Was it possible she had been a willing captive?

"I was taken prisoner by the corsairs a year ago," Celia said. "My child is three months old."

Don Hernan thought with some impatience that she had answered his query without satisfying his curiosity. Then she asked a question of her own which gave him a clue to what her feelings really were.

"What will become of Jaffar Rais?" she said.

Don Hernan leaned back in his chair, his long el Greco fingers, smooth, hard and deft, stripped plump dark fruit from a bunch of grapes.

"He will go to the galleys most likely, until he is ransomed."

He saw how Celia's hands clasped each other and his eyes narrowed as she asked with painful anxiety, "And if he is not ransomed?"

Don Hernan shrugged his shoulders, taking the grape pips from between his lips, wiping his hands and mouth on a damask napkin.

"He will toil at the oar until he dies. He is a strong young man. That might be as much as twenty years."

"Twenty years!"

Don Hernan observed Celia's look of horror with cold disapproval.

"Corsairs, who are, after all, only common criminals of the lowest order, frequently end their days as galley slaves, Lady Lovell. May I ask why you should concern yourself so much over the fate of such a scoundrel? Surely all your thoughts are of re-joining your family in England?"

Celia raised her eyes to his.

"I can never re-join them," she said.

"Ah. Now we have it."

Don Hernan dropped his ceremonious manner and spoke in a familiar tone, coming round the table to stand close beside Celia. Despite her title she had, he considered, forfeited all right to being treated as a lady. She had admitted voluntarily leaving her family to live with a criminal. She was a wanton woman, a whore, deserving neither his protection nor his respect.

"The child is the corsair's, I take it," he remarked, casually placing his hand on Celia's shoulder. "Or are you not sure?"

"It is his," she said, shaking off his hand.

"You have some shame left, then?"

"Not where he is concerned."

She returned his contemptuous gaze proudly and Don Hernan smiled. Celia stood up.

"I'm your prisoner," she said. "You have just told me that the man I love will be condemned to the galleys for the rest of his life. Isn't that enough for you, señor, without making a mock of me?"

"Señora," said the Spaniard, with renewed respect, "I am not making a mock of you. Upon my honour, I am not. When I smiled it was with self contempt. I had not thought I would live to see the day when I would envy a condemned felon. Sit down, I beg you."

"Envy?"

Puzzled, Celia sat down. The Spaniard was a strange man, she thought, so aloof and yet so human. She waited to hear what he would say.

"I am lonely, señora," he said, still standing close beside her. "But do not pity me. I cannot endure pity."

"I would not presume so far."

She looked up at him. He must be almost as old as her father, she thought. His dark hair, receding at the temples, was tinged with grey though his lean, hard body was as supple as a young man's still, judging by the swift smoothness of his movements.

"Your corsair was lucky to have won your love," he said. "You have much to give a man, I think."

"I told you I loved him. I gave him not less than all. Is there any other way to love?"

"By God, yes! A thousand, as I know to my cost." Celia's

passionate rejoinder produced in him a vigorous, bitter response. "My lady wife is a devout woman and denies me her bed on saints' days. In recent years I have discovered that every day is dedicated to some saint or other. My mistress never refuses me but if ever I went to her empty-handed she would shut her door against me. Yet both claim they love me. There are many ways of loving."

"I know only one." Celia rested her head in her hands. A curious mood of apathy had settled upon her. "If it weren't for my child I wouldn't care what became of me."

"The mood will pass." The Spaniard's cynicism was not untouched by compassion. He watched her with a worldly-wise expression, calculating but oddly tender. Three of his daughters were older than Celia and he had known many women. "You are young," he said, "and may live long."

She made no answer, keeping her head bowed. After a moment Don Hernan put his hand lightly on the nape of her neck. This time Celia did not shake it off.

Taking her silence for acquiescence, he slowly slid his long fingers into the opening of her robe and down over her bare breast. Although she wished to give him no encouragement, her flesh responded to his touch and when he stooped to kiss her, her mouth opened under his.

Then, suddenly, as he grew more ardent, she pulled away from him.

"Why resist *now*?" His dark face was flushed and angry.

"Oh, for God's sake, señor!" Celia looked appealingly at him. "Do you think I could willingly give myself to the man who is sending Jaffar Rais to the galleys?"

The Spaniard turned away from her, offended by the rebuff. He reseated himself and said coldly, "You will never see the renegade again. Take my advice and forget him." He poured himself a glass of wine. "You are unwise to be stubborn. You need my protection."

"What you say is true." Celia was forcing herself to face facts. "But for a man like Jaffar Rais to be condemned to the galleys for life is worse than death. Be merciful, Don Hernan. Give him his freedom. I know I shall not see him again. If you will only let him go I will . . . I will . . ."

Under his searching gaze her own faltered, her voice died away and she sat with bowed head.

"So," he said, "you will make a bargain with me. Is that it? Your body for his." He leaned forward. "Has it not occurred to you that I do not need to make bargains. I can take you as and when I choose."

"I know." Her voice was so quiet he could hardly hear her. "But you spoke of many ways of loving as though none had ever satisfied you. You can take me but you cannot make me give myself. If you are merciful to Jaffar Rais I will give you all that a woman can give."

"And afterwards, when you regret it, you will be bitter with me, no doubt." The Spaniard was watching her keenly. He had set down his glass of wine and the candlelight shone through it, casting a reddened glow on the shining table between them. His hands rested on the arms of his chair, one hanging loosely from the wrist, the other tensely gripping the carved wood, an attitude in which el Greco once painted a cardinal.

"No." Celia made the denial with great earnestness. "Having made my bargain I will keep it. I will . . ."

"Like most women," Don Hernan interrupted her coolly, "you talk too much. All my life I have been a man of action, preferring deeds to words. Let me see the merchandise you offer and I will judge for myself whether it is worth what you ask."

He made an expressive gesture at the long robe which covered her from neck to ankle and sat back, contemptuously smiling, expecting an indignant refusal.

Celia stood up, unfastening the loose djellabah which opened to the waist and slipping it down over her shoulders. The smooth silk glided to the floor and she stepped out of it. Her brief bodice supported her bosom without covering it and below her full breasts, heavy with milk, she was bare to the hips, showing her soft white skin and slim, supple waist. Under the harem trousers of light gauze which she wore, Don Hernan could see the shape of her thighs and the pubic hair between them. This garment too she removed, her flimsy bodice also and, obediently naked, knelt between his knees, putting her arms round his neck and pressing her body against his.

So much eager passion aroused in him the vigorous physical response of a young man, such as he had not felt for years. He lifted her in his arms, carrying her to his bed where he laid her down, hastily pulling off his own clothes, impatient to possess her, looking at Celia's white body on the red velvet coverlet.

He embraced her with enthusiasm, surprised and delighted at the warmth and evident pleasure with which she returned his caresses, and at the desire he was able to arouse in her.

He felt her moan and cling to him in desperate need and his climax came in a moment of supreme mutual satisfaction.

Afterwards she lay limp in the crook of his arm and neither of them spoke for a long time.

Then the Spaniard flung back his head on the pillow and laughed with sheer lightness of heart.

"It's a bargain," he said. "Any man's life is cheap at the price. I'll set Jaffar Rais ashore tomorrow with a musket and twenty ducats, free to go where he will. I'm in the rascal's debt."

He turned to her again, as Celia had known he would and she gave herself as ardently as before, stimulating them both to new heights of passion.

He slept before she did and she cradled him in her arms, comforting him like the child he was and that all men are, soothing him into peace and quiet slumber.

She did not sleep herself for many hours, but lay with his head on her breast and tears on her face.

When it was not far off daylight she looked down at him wonderingly, touching his dark hair lightly with her hand and smiling.

After all, she thought, he was a handsome man. And there might be others.

32

"I can't think," said Judith Rainsborough to Anne, "why you won't come."

She was dressed in her best. Puritan disapproval of finery lacked the power to quench her feminine interest in clothes altogether and though Judith's gown was a sober dark blue, it was of the very best quality broadcloth and fitted her extremely well. Her fine linen collar and cuffs and the little frilled cap she wore under her broad brimmed hat were of the whitest, too, and gave her much secret satisfaction.

"The Moorish ambassador is due to disembark at Tower Wharf at five o'clock," she went on importantly, looking round at her nieces who, assembled in the living-room of John Dunton's house at Rotherhithe, were listening with an unusual and most welcome interest to all she had to say. "He's bringing quite a few of the returned prisoners with him. They're to be met by the mayor and aldermen and most of the principal merchants, all in their red robes and gold chains. There's to be a torchlight procession through the streets to Whitehall. Oh, it'll be a fine sight, I can tell you."

"Will Father and Uncle Rainsborough be there?" asked Deborah, who was so excited she couldn't keep still and kept jigging up and down and running to the door to see if John Dunton was coming up the path.

News of the squadron's safe return had reached the family three days ago. The *Leopard*, with *Mary Rose* and *Roebuck*, had touched at Deal just long enough to set her passengers ashore before sailing further up the coast to the naval dockyard at Chatham. John Dunton wrote that they had had an uneventful homeward voyage of only fifteen days. The Moorish ambassador, who had suffered much from sea sickness, would complete his journey to London by road. Dunton himself would join his family as soon as his duties allowed.

The two younger Dunton girls were wild with impatience to see their father and brother. Jenny, just as excited, remembered that there were always heart-rending delays whenever her father returned to port after a long voyage, and tried to calm her sisters.

"Now, don't be silly, Debbie," she said, with the immeasurable superiority of wisdom which sixteen has over twelve. "You know Father can't get home till after the crew's been paid off."

"But the other ships were back ages ago." Deborah pouted. "Patience Harrison's father's been home for three weeks. And I do want to see Father and Dickie and . . ."

"You will, dear, very soon."

Anne put a comforting arm round each twin, hugging them to her. She knew just how they felt and after all, her own father and brother, returning with the four ships which had sailed from Sallee directly after the corsairs surrendered, had also been back in England for a whole three weeks. The need to care for and comfort the children was a relief to her feelings. If she had not been constantly occupied she herself would have found it intolerable to have to wait so long for John Dunton's return.

She smiled at Judith Rainsborough over the twins' heads.

"The girls would love to go with you to see the procession. It's so kind of you to offer to take them."

Judith beamed. "And you'll come as well?"

Anne shook her head. "I can't. Someone has to stay with Martha."

"Oh." Judith made a little moue of disappointment. She glanced rather dubiously over her shoulder towards the kitchen. "But surely Mabyn . . ."

"With my father only just returned, he and my mother take up nearly all her time and attention," said Anne gently. "She's been with them for years, you know, and is like one of the family. I don't want to burden her too much."

Momentarily, Judith looked as though she thought this would be impossible, but she refrained from comment and only said, "Your poor dear mother must be so happy to have your father back. I dare say she thought she'd never see him again."

Anne smiled. To see her parents re-united was a continuing joy. It had brought them both a new lease of life. She could scarcely remember having seen her mother so animated and cheerful. Even the loss of Celia was insufficient to dampen her spirits.

"I think there may have been times," Anne said, "when my mother was nearly despairing, but she never actually gave up hope. She and my father are planning to return to Combe after all, you know. My father talks of re-building already."

"Does he indeed?" Judith Rainsborough was bursting with inquisitiveness to know more. "And will your brother go back with them?"

Anne lowered her eyes. The subject of Roger's conduct was not one she cared to discuss. Neither was that of Celia. What they had done and what had been discovered about them during the past year had made her brother and sister strangers to her. The same was true, for very different reasons, of Stephen Hillard, whose letter, together with one from John Dunton, had been brought to her by her father immediately on his return to England.

"My brother is, I believe, with Sir Edward Lovell. I can't say what his future plans might be."

Anne had chosen her words carefully. "I can't say" rather

than "I don't know". In fact, she shrewdly guessed that Roger, finding himself shunned by his acquaintances and even by most of his relations, intended sponging on his brother-in-law for as long as he could. His health had been badly affected by his brief but rigorous spell of slavery and he was drinking heavily. Roger Crace's future did not seem to promise much except brevity.

"Oh. Staying with your sister's husband, is he?" Judith's eyes were bright with curiosity. There was a mysterious conspiracy of silence about Lady Lovell that she would get to the bottom of, one of these days. In the meantime, however, there was much to occupy her. She collected her nieces, pleased that, for once, they really wanted her company, and prepared to escort them across the river to witness the spectacle of the Moorish ambassador's official reception.

"I'm sorry I can't persuade you to come as well," she said, as Anne came to the doorway with Martha to wave goodbye.

Judith found herself regretting that Anne would miss the fun as much as she regretted not getting her own way. She had at first resented Anne, thinking of her as an intruder who was trying to take her dead sister's place, but during the past months she had come to like her more and more. Judith was still a little jealous of Anne's influence with her nieces, but she liked to give credit where it was due and the girl certainly had done wonders with those harum-scarum children. She made up her mind to tell John so as soon as he came home.

"You know," she confided to Anne, as they stood together on the doorstep, "the King has offered William a knighthood as a reward for the success of the expedition, but William's going to refuse it. I know it's only a worldly honour and William doesn't approve of the King and all that, but it would have been nice . . ."

"To have been Lady Rainsborough?" Anne nodded sympathetically, interpreting Judith's slightly wistful expression aright. It was impossible, she thought, not to be fond of Judith, she was so profoundly human, and gave her hand an affectionate squeeze at parting.

"Well," said Judith, Anne's spontaneous gesture bringing a glow of pleasure to her face, "you know what men are!"

Anne nodded again. "It's a good thing we love them."

She watched Judith go down the garden path with Dorcas and Deborah on either side of her, looking very neat and trim in their brown serge gowns, and Jenny following, fair curls blowing, carrying Judith's basket.

A little later in the day, walking with Martha along the windy stretch of marshy strand by the river, she wondered about what she'd said.

"It's a good thing we love them."

To Anne, as to most unselfish people, any consideration of her own feelings seemed like self-indulgence, but the letters she had received from Stephen Hillard and from John Dunton himself had given her much food for thought. A year ago she had believed the pattern of her life to be decided and clear cut. Now it was entirely changed.

Stephen Hillard's letter was long, serious, devout, tender, resolute and final. John Dunton's was brief, manly, direct and contained a proposal of marriage. Anne had read and re-read both letters time and again, alternately saddened and delighted by their contents.

She had believed herself to be in love with Stephen Hillard and thinking about his chosen life of lonely dedication moved her to tears. Yet she realized now that even in a lifetime of love she would never have come to understand him.

She was overjoyed by John Dunton's proposal, but she was troubled by self-doubt, wondering if she had made the same mistake again. They had seemed so close to one another when he went away, but he had been gone almost a year. Would it be the same now that he was returning with his son?

Martha, toddling along purposefully beside her, a handful of moist, compressed breadcrumbs grasped in her small, grubby fist, tugged at Anne's hand, looking up into the adult's preoccupied face with an expression as much as to say, "I'm here."

"Yes, darling."

Anne stopped thinking about the letters, remembering that they had come to feed the swans.

They stopped at the water's edge, where the sandy bank sloped steeply for a few feet above a clear space with a tangle of sedge and rushes on either side. The October sun, low in the sky, had made a path of gold across the river that shifted and shimmered with the lifting of the ripples. The mute swans sailed over it, coming for the fragments of bread Martha threw to them with flailing gestures of her short plump arms, while Anne held her, wary, watchful and protective.

Westward, over London, where the city dignitaries were waiting to welcome the Moorish ambassador, the sky was reddening, to become a blaze of colour like fire and rubies and roses, against which the turrets of the Tower and the sharply tapering spires of the City churches stood out as starkly as though they had been cut from black paper.

"'wans," said Martha firmly, with the wise singlemindedness of a happy child, entirely absorbed in the experience of the moment. She stared fascinated at the handsome waterfowl stooping their proud necks to scoop up the bread with their bright orange bills. She held out her hand to Anne for more bread to throw to them, confident that it would be provided.

They lingered till it was all gone and then turned back along the strand.

In the distance Anne saw two figures approaching. After a minute she made them out to be a man and a boy. It was too far away to distinguish their features but she knew who the man was. At the same moment she recognized him he began running towards her, the boy alongside him, their boot heels sending the shingly sand flying. She picked up Martha, hurrying to meet them, laughing and crying by turns, because John Dunton had come home to her and the shadows were all behind him.

33

Celia yawned. Seated on the balcony of the narrow yellow stone house in Seville to which Don Hernan had brought her she looked longingly towards the busy harbour and the open sea. An elaborate iron grille, distorted rather than decorated with rigid formalized flower shapes, protected her from the stares of the vulgar and prevented her enjoying a good view of the outside world.

It was late afternoon, the time of siesta was over and the dusty streets were thronging with people, but the small private house in which Don Hernan had installed Celia with an elderly duenna to watch over her was as silent and sequestered as a convent. It was a dull, shadowy place whose high narrow windows seemed reluctant to admit any sight or sound of gaiety into its sober interior. The grim duenna sat upright on her hard chair in the room beyond the balcony, snow-white needlework arranged on severe black lap. The very flies which buzzed over the tired-looking fruit on the dark table buzzed in a subdued fashion as though apologizing for their noisy intrusion. Only a few red geraniums in earthenware pots showed a defiant splash of lusty vulgar colour fit to lift the heart.

Celia stooped from her uncomfortable stool to break a leaf from one of them, deriving a transient comfort from the pungent, earthy smell. She wore a gown of black taffeta shot with gold, heavy and cumbersome, over stiff corsets and bulky petticoats which impeded her movements. Her shining hair was hidden by a black lace mantilla held in place by a tortoiseshell comb. She did not like the clothes and they did not suit her, but she had to dress, as the duenna frequently pointed out, not to please herself but her generous protector. Celia reflected with regret that when she became the Spanish captain's mistress she had never imagined that she would be required to live a life far more circumspect and restricted than his lawful wife did, more, in fact, like that of a nun. He had honoured her with the status of "barragana" or concubine, a position recognized and sanctioned by every part of Spanish society except the Church. But it was not an enviable one, or, at least, Celia did not find it so. Society tolerated her existence so long as Don Hernan should please to maintain her, but she was ostracized from it. The Spanish women she passed in the street drew their skirts aside when she went by as though they feared her touch would contaminate them. Urchins shouted obscenities at her. The duenna watched her every action with the suspicious vigilance of a gaoler.

Even Don Hernan's visits to Celia were becoming rarer. During the six months they had spent in Seville, she in her lonely house, he in his family home, he had slept with her at intervals, indulging what he began increasingly to think of as "sins of the flesh". But she guessed from the way he talked that his father confessor was urging him to give her up. Whipping figured in their relations now, not as an erotic stimulant but more as a sadistic form of punishment. Celia, whose enjoyment of sex was natural and healthy, found this distressing not to say disgusting. The last time Don Hernan had been with her he had even spoken of the possibility of his entering a monastery to expiate his sins. Celia had suggested, not without a certain bitter amusement, that he might consider joining an order of flagellants and had been horrified to find herself taken seriously.

She wondered how long it would be before he thought of consigning her to a similar fate. The prospect of mortifying her flesh by submitting to rigorous penances under the eye of a stern superior filled Celia with dread and it was by no means an idle fear. She was a foreign woman and a heretic. How long would it be before the Inquisition began to take an active interest in her?

Celia stifled a sigh, stooping down again to stroke little Tom's hair. He was just beginning to crawl, creeping purposefully after a golden orange which she rolled across the polished tiles for him to play with. But for him she might have been tempted to break out of her captivity. Whilst the duenna was sleeping Celia often longed to slip down to the quayside where the tall ships of all nations rode at anchor and mingle with the seamen who lounged in the taverns there. She wanted news of Jaffar Rais. She knew enough of Don Hernan to be certain that he had kept his promise to set the corsair free but since he had been marooned on the west coast of Africa six months ago there had been no word of Jaffar Rais and she did not know whether he was alive or dead.

Without him she herself merely existed. The smell of the sea and the sound of the seamen's voices, rough and sailorly, vibrant with life, that the wind wafted to her window from the street below, filled her with yearning for him. She thought of the days she had spent with him on the galleasse and in Sallee with a passionate nostalgia. Sometimes, during those days, she had been afraid, sometimes sick, sometimes in pain, but always always, she had been alive. Now, she felt that her life had come full circle. As the kept woman of Don Hernan de Ortiz she felt much as she had done as the wife of Edward Lovell - bored, frustrated and emotionally starved.

"Señora!"

A rich voice, ingratiating, conspiratorial, sounded in Celia's ears. She jumped up and leaning as far over the balcony as the restrictive grille allowed, peered down into the street.

"Señora!"

A man stood there, smiling up at her. He was an old man, with very bright dark eyes and curly grey hair and beard. He wore a curious square cap and long robes with full sleeves, elaborately embroidered. Beside him a small boy with a smooth olive skin, soulful black eyes and brown matted locks like sheep's wool carried a chattering monkey who crouched on his shoulder and a large bundle wrapped in a striped cloth.

The old man pointed to the bundle, "I have fine merchandise here, señora. Combs, jewels, fine Morisco work..."

"Come up."

Celia beckoned him eagerly. Behind her, the duenna, with a rustle of stiff skirts, got up and hurried forward to protest.

"Surely," she said with haughty disapproval, "you will not wish to buy anything from that Jew?"

"No Jew, señora," called the Hebrew merchant from the street, "but as good a Christian as yourself. If the lady wants to buy a trifle or two from me, why not?"

The duenna turned indignantly to Celia, muttering something about "Marranos". "The impertinence!" she said with acid fury. "You will not admit him."

"I will!" Celia stamped her foot. The word Morisco had claimed her attention as she knew the man had meant it should. "I want to see what he has to sell. Am I mistress here or are you?"

For a moment it looked as though the duenna might contest the point but she gave way before Celia's obvious determination and went, grumbling under her breath about Don Hernan's displeasure when he heard of it, to let the merchant in.

She returned to stand behind Celia, stony faced, while the merchant, doffing his cap and bowing, followed her, gesturing impatiently to his attendant boy to open the striped bundle and spread out its contents on the floor. The monkey, jerking his chain free of the boy's restraining hand, leapt on to the table and began to eat a banana.

The duenna snorted with disgust but Celia laughed and little Tom, hearing her, sat up with the orange in his hands and crowed delightedly.

The Jew sat down on the floor at Celia's feet, crossing his legs and disposing his robes about him, pointing to the glittering array of trinkets the boy had placed on display.

"A necklace of moonstones, señora?" He held up a rope of milky gems that glowed with a strange hidden fire when they caught the light. "Ivory fans, figures? Ebony carving from the forests of Africa? Silver filigree work from Morocco . . . ?"

"Let me see some filigree work," said Celia quickly, very conscious of the duenna's presence, of the woman's sharp eyes and ears observing all she did.

The bright-eyed merchant laid silver brooches and bracelets before her.

"Beautiful jewellery," he said, in a professional sing-song. "Look at this exquisite ring - the fineness of the stone. 'It was my turquoise,' " he quoted, not varying his tone, " 'I had it of Leah when I was a bachelor. I would not have given it for a wilderness of monkeys.' I know your English poet, you see, señora."

He knew much more, she was sure of that now. The reference to Morisco had alerted her to the possibility that he came from Jaffar Rais. The mention of the name "Leah" confirmed her belief. What had he to tell her of Jaffar Rais? She looked at him with an urgent appeal in her eyes. If only that dragon of a duenna were not jealously observing her every word and gesture!

Suddenly, as though by a pre-arranged signal, the boy exclaimed, made a dive to recover the end of the monkey's chain and in so doing overturned not only the fruit bowl but a carafe of wine beside it. The duenna, momentarily distracted, left her post behind Celia's stool, calling out angrily, stooping to retrieve the scattered fruit and upset decanter while the startled monkey, leaping out of the boy's reach,

317

sprang on to a high shelf, swinging his chain and scolding back at her.

"Tell me what news you have of Jaffar Rais!" Celia leaned close to the merchant under the cover of the confusion, pretending to admire the turquoise ring.

"Meet him tonight at nightfall," the Jew muttered, "in the church porch of Our Lady, Star of the Sea, on the waterfront. Ah, a unique piece, that, señora, and a gift at ten ducats. If all the ladies bargained as astutely as you do I should be ruined in a month, but, seeing it's you..."

Celia paid for the brooch under the watchful, disapproving stare of the duenna who was bristling with rage at the mess made by the mischievous monkey who had now abandoned his high perch and resumed his place on the boy's shoulder. Both he and the boy wore expressions of preternatural innocence.

Celia had to quell an impulse to break out into a fit of giggling she was so excited and relieved. Every minute of every hour until nightfall would seem like ten, but she would see Jaffar Rais again and the thought made her heart sing within her.

The church porch was shadowy and filled with the heavy scent of incense filtering through from the sanctuary beyond which blazed with gold and the brilliant light of a myriad votive candles. The faces of saints, long and solemn and stiffly gilded, looked down on Celia from their niches in the carved portico.

Holding little Tom, neither so little nor so light as he had been the last time she fled with him, Celia stood in the darkest corner, looking about anxiously for Jaffar Rais.

It had not been easy to leave the house. She had been obliged to invent a pretext for sending the duenna to Don Hernan with a message before she could escape. Even so, the woman went grudgingly, appearing suspicious, and Celia was afraid that she might have been followed when, a few minutes after, she herself slipped out to make her way to the church.

Now she waited, increasingly fearful, as the minutes dragged by. People were entering and leaving the church, talking together and casting glances in her direction. If she lingered too long she risked attracting notice.

An old woman, bent and shawled, gnarled hands clasped, an aroma of garlic heavy about her, shuffled by. She saw Celia and muttered something under her breath. A masculine tread sounded and Celia's heart leapt. She moved forward, hoping to see Jaffar Rais, but two seamen pushed past her, rough and heavy shouldered. One of them said, "Not tonight, sweetheart," and the other laughed.

Celia shrank back into her corner, grateful that she was so near the church, knowing that otherwise she might have been assaulted. But surely in this holy place...

"What are you doing here, my daughter?"

She turned to see a tall figure in the black and white robes of a Dominican friar, the heavy cowl hiding the face from sight. Strange, she had not heard him approach. He must have come from inside the church. The voice was harsh as though from fasting, harsh and reproving.

Celia was dismayed. It was as she had feared. One of the church dignitaries had noticed her presence as she lingered in the church porch and come to find out the reason for it.

"Forgive me, Father," she said humbly, "I am waiting here for my husband, a sailor just come home from sea."

The tall figure took a step nearer.

"His name?"

Celia was searching desperately in her mind for an answer which would allay the suspicion of this most unwelcome stranger when she saw his hand. It was no bookish clerical hand, but the hard, strong brown hand of a seaman and she knew every finger, for it had many times intimately caressed her body, bringing it to an exquisite pitch of desire. She stretched out her own and touched it.

"His name," she said, "is Jaffar Rais."

"Come on, Leah," said the erstwhile Dominican, as though they had been parted only minutes instead of months and there was no need of explanations. "The ship's waiting. If we don't look sharp we'll miss the tide."

So she put her hand in his and they went down together to the waiting ship and the wide, wide sea.